Kimberley Freeman was born in London in 1970. She worked as a musician for a number of years, both as a classical singer and in pop bands, before turning her hand to writing. She lives in Brisbane with her husband and two young children.

GW00480988

DUET

Kimberley Freeman

HACHETTE AUSTRALIA

HACHETTE AUSTRALIA

Published in Australia and New Zealand in 2007
by Hachette Australia
(An imprint of Hachette Livre Australia Pty Limited)
Level 17, 207 Kent Street, Sydney NSW 2000
Website: www.hachette.com.au

Copyright © Kimberley Freeman 2007

This book is copyright. Apart from any fair dealing
for the purposes of private study, research, criticism
or review permitted under the *Copyright Act 1968*,
no part may be stored or reproduced by any process
without prior written permission. Enquiries should
be made to the publisher.

National Library of Australia
Cataloguing-in-Publication data

Freeman, Kimberley.
  Duet.

  ISBN 978 0 7336 2177 2 (pbk.).

  I. Title.

A823.4

Cover by Christabella Designs
Cover images courtesy of Getty Images
Text design by Bookhouse, Sydney
Typeset in 12.4/16.2 pt Adobe Garamond
Printed in Australia by Griffin Press, Adelaide

Hachette Livre Australia's policy is to use papers
that are natural, renewable and recyclable products
and made from wood grown in sustainable forests.
The logging and manufacturing processes are expected
to conform to the environmental regulations
of the country of origin.

For Selwa, who started it all

ACT I

Weeping? And why? And why?
Ah, 'tis faith you are lacking.

Un bel di, FROM *Madama Butterfly*, GIACOMO PUCCINI

PROLOGUE
Western Queensland, Australia: 1997

*S*he liked the mornings best. Mornings promised something that evenings never could: freshness, a new start. She tried to get any outdoor chores completed in the mornings, before the burnished sunlight hazed the sky and bit her skin. Afternoons were for dozing under the fan, or drinking chilled chardonnay on the patio. Mornings were for gardening, and the walk to collect the mail.

If it was very hot, or on the rare occasions it rained, she drove: the mailbox was one kilometre from the homestead. But today she had walked, because she was vain about her figure; not that there was anyone around to see it. Out here, the mail only came three times a week, and her box was usually very full. Yet there was only one letter, a plain white envelope with no return address on the back. The front was addressed in close, spidery writing: *Penelope Bright, Mununja, Queensland, Australia, 4940.* She absently slit the side of the envelope with her fingernail. A single sheet, folded twice, dropped out.

A pair of cockatoos flew overhead, screeching to the morning sun. She unfolded the paper, and read the single line inscribed upon it.

I know all about Angie Smith. Now you'll get what you deserve.

Ice touched her heart.

Dropping the letter, she reached out to support herself on the mailbox. The envelope landed in a puddle from last night's storm, the muddy water making her address bleed. A flood of memories came back to her, snatches of things disconnected by time and distance. The smell of a fur coat she'd once worn, the blaze of the spotlight, the caress of a lover long since lost. She lowered herself to the muddy ground and rested her head on her knees. Her history lurked close like shadows, brimming with secrets and lies. People had written about her over the years, but none of them could know the truth.

For it was not just a story about how a girl with nothing had become a woman with everything – wealth, fame, power – then turned her back on it all.

It was also a story about how she had stolen another woman's life.

ONE
Kokondorf, Northern Germany: 1969

The day that Ellie Frankel's mother died was clear, blue and silent, with sun sparkling on the snow. Ellie, only fourteen years old and having difficulty coming to terms with the dark moment, had not felt the loss at first. It hardly seemed real: Mama couldn't be dead. By the day they buried her, however, the elements realised what a terrible emptiness Mama's death had left behind; and so had Ellie. Rain had been threatening over the village of Kokondorf since she awoke, huge sweeps of dark cloud hanging low and cold over the thatched roofs. Drizzle overnight had started the snow melting, and dirty slush had been cleared from around the grave to make room for the cheap wooden coffin. Ellie's eyes and nose streamed with the cold and the grief as the coffin was lowered into the ground. Only eight mourners waited at the graveside, including Ellie and her father. It was too cold and wet to come out, and Ellie's mother had no relatives in Germany. Ellie scanned the mourners' faces: the butcher and his wife, Frau Pottsmann who had given Mama work sewing and ironing, and Frau and Herr Neumann from the neighbouring farm, with their eighteen-year-old son Dieter. Papa nudged her, nodding emphatically.

'I can't, Papa,' she said, struggling with her tears. 'I can't.'

'You must. Despite your tears, you must.'

Ellie took a deep breath to ease the shuddering sobs. Then, in a clear, pure voice, she began to sing the first sublime notes of Schubert's *Ave Maria*. Never mind that her throat was raw from crying, never mind that the sky chose that moment to open up and pour freezing rain on the scene, Papa had trained her since she was eleven years old to sing like an angel. And so, as the gravediggers scooped the sod into her mother's grave, she did.

As she sang, she conjured her mother's face in her mind. Not the pale, thin invalid that stomach cancer had reduced her to, but the full-cheeked, soft-voiced woman who had sat beside her father at the fire every night, embroidering cushions and humming gently to herself. It was impossible that she wouldn't hear that humming again, take comfort in that warm embrace. Her voice almost cracked, but she wouldn't allow it to, wouldn't let Papa down.

Papa fell to his knees in the muddy snow and Frau Neumann went to him and squeezed his shoulder. The last notes of the song rang out and the rain intensified. Ellie didn't know what to do so she stood, watching Papa's back shudder with the effort of holding back tears. Dieter approached her, positioning his umbrella over both of them.

'You're wet,' he said. 'You must be cold.'

She looked up at his dark hazel eyes, but didn't draw the same pleasure she usually did from looking at him. All her life, she had adored Dieter. She had followed him around as soon as she could walk, drawn his name in love hearts on her schoolbooks and, before her mother's long illness had taken hold, other strange and addictive new feelings had made her tongue-tied and restless around him. Today, she had a heart too full of other emotions.

'I don't feel the cold,' she said.

Dieter's eyes went to the grave. 'I'll miss her,' he said. 'I'll miss her English lessons...'

Ellie smiled in spite of herself. 'You weren't a very good student.' She adopted her mother's crisp English accent and said, 'If I can teach you, I can teach anyone, Dieter Neumann.'

Dieter laughed and shook his head, but his expression soon grew serious again. 'Ellie,' he said, 'I'm so sorry.'

'Ellie!' This was Papa, climbing to his feet and reaching his big hands for her. His knees were muddy and his hair was dripping wet.

Ellie turned away from Dieter and put her arms around Papa. 'Shh, Papa, it will be all right. I'll take care of you.' The rain eased as she led her father back down the slope to their dented Volkswagen.

He sat behind the wheel sobbing for a few moments, then gathered himself and started the car.

'You sang beautifully, my girl,' he said as they pulled onto the narrow road. 'Your mother would have been so proud.'

Ellie's gaze returned up the hill. 'I hope Mama heard,' she said, her breath fogging the window. 'Wherever she is.'

Winter was long that year, but the spring thaw came as it always did. With the melting snow and shoots of green, Ellie decided that she hadn't the luxury of languishing in her grief for much longer. Papa had allowed his sorrow to drown him. Some days, Ellie couldn't get him out of bed before eleven o'clock. Papa taught music and languages in schools at the neighbouring villages. They had always got by on his small income and Mama's part-time work, but one by one his employers grew impatient with him turning up late, or not at all. Ellie returned from school too many times, to see the Volkswagen parked on the side of the road exactly as it had been in the morning: a sign that her father hadn't been anywhere. Hadn't earned any money.

Two or three times a week she managed to coax him out of bed. She laid out his clothes for him and fixed him breakfast, practically pushing him out the door before getting ready for school herself. It exhausted her, and she began to feel as though she was his parent, rather than the other way around. The responsibility was heavy; she didn't relish it. But all she could do was keep going.

What little income they did make was disappearing rapidly too. The only thing that brought Papa a measure of relief was a glass or two of whisky every afternoon. He had always liked a drink, and

Ellie knew it was a source of tension for her mother, who was too meek to complain. But now one or two glasses weren't enough, and three or four became normal. By July, he was trading cabbages and beets for homemade whisky with a snaggle-toothed man named Thorsten who came by every Thursday. Ellie couldn't bear the way Thorsten looked at her, as though he were hungry and angry at the same time, so she had started appearing on the Neumanns' doorstep every Thursday after school, and staying until nightfall.

Frau Neumann was a woman made up of warm colours and textures. Ellie loved her soft skin, her dark auburn hair, and her laughing dark eyes. She also loved Frau Neumann's feisty temper, a contrast to her mother's cool patience. They spoke very little, but Frau Neumann sensed that Ellie needed to be kept busy, and gave her little jobs to do to pass the time.

'How are things at home, Ellie?' she asked one Thursday, just as she asked every week.

'Fine,' Ellie replied, just as she replied every week.

Frau Neumann's mouth turned down a little at the corners, indicating she didn't believe Ellie. They were sitting at the long wooden table in the Neumanns' kitchen, while the appetising smells of spicy cabbage and roasting meat filled the room. 'Your father is well?'

'Yes.' Ellie put down the silver fork she was polishing, and said in a quiet voice, 'He still misses Mama.'

Frau Neumann touched her hair gently. 'Of course he does. He probably always will.' She stood and went to the wooden sideboard, where she began pulling down plates for dinner. 'Will you stay to eat, Ellie?'

'No, I'd better get home to make Papa some dinner.' Ellie never stayed, as much as she would have liked to. She understood that it was too much of an imposition, and Papa's ugly friend was usually gone by the time the sun went down. She pushed back her chair, and it scraped loudly against the stone tiles. 'Thank you for letting me visit.'

'It's always a pleasure, Ellie.'

Dieter appeared then, poking his fair head around the door. 'Are you heading home, Ellie?'

Ellie smiled in spite of herself. Dieter became more attractive as he grew older, but she had convinced herself that he never noticed her. 'Yes,' she said.

'I'll walk with you. Let me grab my coat.'

Prickling with expectation, Ellie left the Neumanns' house with Dieter by her side. He wore a light coat, his hands thrust deeply in its pockets and his dark eyes fixed on the road ahead. They wound down the hill, the linden trees bowing above them. Ellie could see the lights of the village in the distance, and the dark spire of the church against the horizon. Dieter didn't say anything for a long time, then he casually remarked, 'I'm going away after Christmas.'

Ellie's heart sank. 'Oh?'

'National Service.'

Of course, Dieter was eighteen and was expected to undertake military training as were all young men of his age. 'Where are you going?' she asked, trying to sound bright.

'Bremen, for training.'

'That's not so far,' she said, thinking how far away it was. Her father's old Volkswagen would never make it. 'And it's only eighteen months.'

'No, Ellie. I've enlisted. What else can a man like me do? I didn't finish school, and I can't get that kind of money staying in the village.' All the time he spoke, his eyes were on the road in front of him.

A night breeze gusted past, rattling the leaves in the trees and whipping Ellie's long, dark hair into her face.

'So,' she said softly, 'when will you come back?'

He shook his head. 'I don't know. Perhaps I won't come back.'

They walked on in silence and Ellie's house came into view.

'I wanted to tell you myself,' Dieter said as they stopped outside her front door. 'You've been a good friend to me, Ellie.'

'Dieter, I –'

Just then the door flew open, and her father was there. His greying hair stood up crazily on his head and he stank of whisky. 'Ellie, you're home! Good. I have exciting news.'

Dieter was already turning away, raising his hand in farewell. 'I'll see you next week, Ellie.'

'Yes, I'll see you then.' Christmas was still three months away. There would be time to see him, to memorise the adored contours of his face. But she knew that after he had gone, that was the end. He would meet somebody in Bremen, somebody more mature and beautiful, and marry her and *never come back*. Her instincts told her to get into her bed, pull the covers over her head, and nurse her sad imaginings until she fell asleep. But Papa had an idea in his head and wouldn't let it go.

'Come inside, come inside,' he was saying, leading her gently by the wrist. 'Thorsten brought me a newspaper, I've seen something wonderful.'

Curious, she followed him into their messy lounge room. Dust and music scores were piled on every surface. He found the newspaper and opened it for her, indicating a little square in the bottom right-hand corner of the second-to-last page. She read, *Regional Aria Singing Competition*. It listed several locations, and Papa had circled, *Wiesenbach-Kokondorf area. Kokondorf Village Hall, 1 February 1970. Prize 50DM.* Below the announcement was an entry form, which her father had already filled out in his sloping left-handed scrawl. He had even filled out the three songs she would sing; one of them was murderously difficult.

'You want me to sing?' she asked.

'I want you to win. Imagine what we could do with fifty marks!'

'Papa, I will sing for you, but I can't guarantee I'll win.'

'I *know* you will win. Nobody sings as beautifully as my Ellie.' Infused with new excitement, he moved to the old upright piano in the corner and began to fiddle with the stained yellow keys. 'We'll start with the Giordani and the Handel to warm up, then go straight to the Mozart –'

'Not that song, Papa! I'm only fourteen.'

'You'll be fifteen by the time of the competition.' Here he puffed his chest out proudly. 'And you have the best teacher around.'

Ellie had to smile. Her father had once been an opera singer of great promise. He had been the star pupil of the famed German tenor, Franz Auerbach, who had called Papa the most promising voice of the decade; he had studied languages with Honours at the University of Hamburg. But a bout of pneumonia at the age of thirty-five had scarred his lungs and put an end to his career. His disappointment over this turn of events had been alleviated by meeting her mother, who was a nurse in the hospital. She was an English girl, looking for adventures in travel. He was keen to provide her with some and they had lived and worked all over Europe and the Isles. Papa had many stories of their travels, and Mama had always smiled and nodded along when he grew passionate and excited telling his tales. Soon enough, Ellie had come along and Papa had poured all of his ambitions into his young, talented daughter. She had learned to read music at the same time she had learned to read words, her first trembling notes as a six-year-old had been coaxed into tunefulness, and the techniques of an operatic soprano had been trained into her body and her throat since she was eleven. Her ability far exceeded her age, but the only places she had yet sung were local weddings and at her own mother's funeral.

'Come, let's try it now,' he said, searching on top of the piano for the score.

Ellie waited patiently. Since her mother's illness, Papa had barely touched the piano. Her singing lessons, which had once been offered daily, had dwindled to weekly or less. To see him so full of purpose, riffling so assiduously through the layers of mess, made her heart glad.

'Here it is,' he said, pulling out the piano and vocal score of Mozart's *Così fan tutte*. He found the page, and played the introduction to *Come scoglio*. Ellie scanned the music with her eyes and winced. It was a fiendishly difficult aria, certainly too hard for her.

'Papa, are you sure?'

'Here, here,' he said, banging her first note hard on the piano, then began to sing in falsetto, '*Come scoglio…immoto resta…*'

She sang, and of course the first few notes weren't hard. But soon they were flying up over the top line of the stave, and as her father flipped the page she saw the long lines of florid runs and caught her breath.

'Papa, Papa, wait. Let me study the score a few days,' she said, placing her hands over his on the piano. 'I need to get the Italian right. I need to learn those runs…those runs…'

Papa turned to her with serious eyes. 'My girl, I know you can do this, and you will do it beautifully.' His gaze went to the empty bottles on the table. 'I will do everything I can to help you. I'm sorry if I have let you down lately.'

Moved by his sad eyes, Ellie climbed into his lap and threw her arms around his neck. 'Papa, I love you. You never let me down. Let's learn this song then. Let's not wait.'

At first he was true to his word. He stopped drinking or, at least, he limited himself to one whisky every evening. He went back to work, and in the afternoons when she came home from school the house was almost tidy. Lessons began the moment she came in the door. Sitting at the piano, he would warm her up with long rows of scales. Then he would strike up the opening notes of her first song, Handel's *Care Selve*. That one she could sing, and the other pretty Giordani piece. But his smile, his nods of approval did not carry over to the Mozart piece. And so *Come scoglio* became a five-minute nightmare, repeated over and over, as she sang and he shouted at her sternly.

'Don't sing from the throat… Use your diaphragm… Neutral vowels, neutral vowels… Open the vowel there or you'll kill yourself… Open, open, open above the *passagio*, foolish girl, open!… Stop croaking, start the note clearly… No, no, no, terrible onset, no *portamento*… I said no *portamento*…' And when the long runs came up, he would start his chant, 'Faster, faster, faster…' as his fingers flew over the keys and she tried to manage her breath.

12

One evening, on the eighth rehearsal of the song, she was singing one of those diabolical runs, when her brain refused to continue any longer without breath. She fainted.

When she came to, her father was leaning over her, smiling.

'Now we are getting somewhere,' he said.

But after the first month, the level in the whisky bottle began to creep down too quickly, and Ellie had a horrible realisation. On the evenings that she sang well, he stayed sober afterwards, bustling about cooking dinner and making merry chatter. On the evenings she sang poorly, he would sag in his armchair in front of the fire and drink everything in the house. The pressure was almost unbearable: sing, and sing well. Some days she could do it, but some days she couldn't, and her father's drinking worsened.

Ellie never told Frau Neumann how bad things had become at home, and being at the Neumanns' house once a week certainly relieved the anxiety. She saw Dieter from time to time, but never alone. He would come in from the cowshed, blond hair falling in his eyes, and his mother would say, 'What will I do without you, my boy?' and Dieter would smile weakly.

Christmas came and went, and Papa was so consumed with training Ellie for the competition that he didn't seem to notice it was his first Christmas without Mama. Ellie noticed, of course. Mama had always insisted presents were opened on Christmas morning, not Christmas Eve as they were in Germany. This year, there wasn't money for presents so Ellie didn't have to carry on the tradition. Papa didn't offer to go and cut down a tree, so Ellie pulled out their tired decorations and hung them around the fireplace, saving for her bedroom a little glass angel that Mama had loved.

Then, in the cold of January, the day came for Dieter to go away. Frau Neumann organised a little farewell party, and Ellie sat with Papa by the fire in Frau Neumann's cosy kitchen letting the voices of the Neumanns' family and friends wash over her. Her gaze kept returning to Dieter, who was talking animatedly to another young man of his own age, and who had barely looked her way all afternoon.

'Ellie, could you get me another drink of wine?' Papa said, handing her his empty glass.

Ellie cringed. Papa had already drunk seven glasses. 'Papa, can you wait a little while?' she whispered. 'I don't think Herr Neumann has much more wine.'

'Nonsense,' he slurred. 'I know he has a cellar full.'

So Ellie stood up and, embarrassed, returned again to the table set up with Herr Neumann's wine bottles.

'Another for your father, Ellie?' Frau Neumann said, eyebrows shooting up in concern.

'Um...yes,' she replied.

Herr Neumann frowned, casting his glance over to Papa. 'He's nearly unconscious in his chair.'

Ellie turned to look back at her father. His head drooped to his chest, then jerked up again. 'He's tired, he hasn't been well,' Ellie lied.

Herr Neumann poured the wine and handed it to her grudgingly, and she returned to Papa.

'Here, Papa. Would you like to go home after this one? Perhaps you need a rest.'

'I'm fine,' he said, sipping the drink. 'Stop fussing so much.'

'The Neumanns must think –'

'What do I care what the Neumanns think?' he snapped, in a harsh whisper. 'They're ignorant farmers, they've never even been out of the pigsty.'

A gentle tap on her shoulder turned her around. It was Dieter, his deep, liquid eyes fixed on hers.

'Ellie?' he said. 'Can I have a word?'

'Yes.'

Dieter's gaze went to Papa, then back to Ellie. 'In private.'

Ellie was sure that Dieter wanted to talk to her about Papa's behaviour, and died a little with shame. 'I...'

'It will only take a minute,' he said.

'Go on, go on,' Papa said gruffly. 'I'll be all right.'

Ellie followed Dieter out of the kitchen and down the corridor to the storeroom. From here, they crossed into an enclosed sunroom.

Dieter led her in and then shut the door behind him. Ellie sat on an old armchair, glancing at the snow outside. The sky was grey, and the sunless windowpanes were chilly.

Dieter pulled a chair up beside hers, and leaned forward so his elbows were resting on his knees. She dared not meet his eyes.

'Ellie, it's not your fault.'

She pressed her lips together, then said, 'What do you mean?'

'I've known you since you were a little girl, Ellie. You always take too much responsibility on yourself. When your mother was ill, you worked so hard. And now I see it with your father –'

'There's nothing wrong with my father,' she said sharply.

Dieter just smiled. 'Oh, Ellie. Anyone can see what's happening. You run about after him, looking guilty if he asks for another drink, acting as though it's your fault that he is the way he is.'

Ellie shook her head. 'It *is* my fault. If only I could sing better…'

Dieter laughed softly, kindly. 'No matter what you do, he will still drink. He's a grown man. What can a girl as young as you do?'

That stung. She had hoped that he might have seen the glimmer of womanhood in her.

'Mama is worried about you,' Dieter continued. 'You can come to her if you need help.'

'Thank you. I mean… I know that.'

He stood, and reached out a hand to help her to her feet. 'Goodbye, little Ellie,' he said, leaning in to kiss her cheek gently. 'I know you'll bloom in years to come. I'm sorry I won't be here to see you.'

'You'll come back, won't you? To visit?'

He shrugged. 'Who knows? After training, I'm heading to Munich. Mama and Papa will come to visit when they can, but I expect to get posted somewhere. Perhaps I will get home from time to time. I hope to find you happy if I do.'

Dieter turned away and Ellie lingered a few moments in the sunroom. The cold outside seeped quietly into her heart.

On the evening of the competition the snow was piled up high outside the Kokondorf village hall, an echoing brick construction adjoining the church. Inside, two rusting radiators tried vainly to heat the dank space. Ellie sat in the front row along with the other contestants, trying to warm her hands under her jacket. Papa sat next to her, sober, smoothed and shaven, smelling of soap and hair cream. On the low stage, a woman no younger than eighty was running through scales on a slightly out-of-tune piano. Ellie felt the first flutter of stage fright, but took a deep breath and wouldn't allow it to take her over. She glanced up to where the adjudicator sat, at the side of the stage, dressed in his elegant suit and wearing an expression of bemusement at the small provincial event. He was from Hamburg, a voice coach with an opera company there. Ellie could see his gaze judging the limp left-over Christmas decorations, the mismatched chairs, and the contestants' clothes. Ellie wore her best pinafore and a clean white blouse, but her tights were spotted with darning, and her shoes were scuffed.

Five minutes before the competition was due to start, the door of the hall flew open and a young woman in a red taffeta gown and a fur stole strode in. She walked tall and held her head high, and her lips were turned up slightly at the corners in a smug smile. As Ellie feared, she came down to sit in the front row with the other contestants. Ellie squirmed, feeling like a dull moth next to her. The other contestants all seemed to sense that they were outclassed already, exchanging glances and tight smiles with their parents or spouses or friends.

Thirteen singers sang that night, and Ellie was sixth. She tried to clear her mind as she watched women and men of all shapes and ages climb the three steps and wait with frightened eyes for the accompanist to play them in. Ellie was easily the youngest there. Among the other singers, Ellie saw a lot of earnest interest, but no real spark of talent, and her mood began to lift. By the time it came to her turn to climb the stage, she had convinced herself she might win.

She paused a moment on the stage as Papa had told her to, offered the audience a smile, announced herself and her first song, then nodded to the accompanist. The music started, and she began

16

to sing. The Handel piece went smoothly, the Giordani piece even better. Papa beamed at her, eyes alight with pride and relief. But when she announced the final piece – the Mozart, the nightmare – the woman in the red dress let slip a snigger of derision. Ellie lost her nerve.

Her breathing went first. Rather than the deep supportive breathing she needed to undertake such an ambitious song, she started shallow breathing in her chest. She tried to correct it, but was already in mid-phrase and her first high note came out sounding forced and thin. Papa had tensed forward; he made a fist and slammed himself under the ribs, signalling to get her breath under control. But the harder she tried, the more she lost her focus. The long, fast runs were approaching too quickly, and her vision brightened at the edges with fear. The unthinkable happened: halfway through the first run, she had to take a breath. It was all over, she had failed.

Ellie made her way despondently and perfunctorily to the end of the song, then took her seat next to Papa. He put his arm around her and squeezed her tight against his side, kissing the top of her head. But she knew how disappointed he was.

'Don't you worry,' he said quietly to her. 'The first two songs were brilliant, and much better than anybody else who has sung here tonight.'

Then the red-dress woman took to the stage. She announced herself as Christa Busch, the smug half-smile never leaving her lips. As the introduction to her first song started, her eyebrows began to emote madly, and a Schubert love song oozed from her mouth. Everything about her was polished, shining, radiating self-belief and painfully faked emotion; no matter that her voice was a touch hooty, she had all of the confidence that the other contestants lacked.

It was no surprise, an hour later when the adjudicator took to the stage, that Christa Busch won the fifty marks. Papa, who had been trying to convince himself that Ellie's performance wasn't a train wreck, finally had to acknowledge that the last four months of work had not brought him the result he'd dreamed of. Shoulders sagging forward, he led Ellie from the hall.

He opened the door to the Volkswagen, then his eyes caught on something across the road.

'Ellie,' he said, 'wait here in the car for a minute.'

Ellie turned to see where his gaze was leading. The local pub, of course. She watched him walk away, off to buy a bottle of whisky to douse his disappointment. A sense of desolation washed over her, as though she were in a boat drifting further and further from shore, with no hope of making her way back. She had lost more than the competition: she had lost her father. Rather than getting into the car, she waited in the cold, clear air, watching the other contestants leave, watching Christa Busch climb triumphantly into a shining new BMW, watching the adjudicator emerge with his long overcoat on and move towards his own vehicle.

He saw Ellie, and raised his hand in a wave. She gave him a cautious wave in return, and he approached her purposefully.

'Ellie?' he said, a fog of breath emerging from his mouth. 'That's your name, isn't it?'

She nodded. 'Ellie Frankel, sir.'

'The Mozart piece was too big for you,' he said plainly.

'I know.'

'Then why did you sing it?'

She shrugged, feeling young and foolish. 'My father…'

'How old are you, Ellie?'

'I'm fifteen.'

He broke into a grin. 'Really? Fifteen?'

Ellie couldn't help smiling back.

'Fifteen… God in heaven, only fifteen.' He touched her shoulder lightly. 'The West German Opera runs a program for promising young performers. You have to be at least twenty, but no older than twenty-five. Remember that. In five years, Ellie Frankel, if you keep practising and don't take on any more stupidly ambitious songs…' Here he smiled again '… I can't imagine them turning you down.'

'Do you think so?' Five years seemed a long time.

'I make no promises, but you are a very talented young woman. I wish you the best of luck.' He nodded and turned to go.

Ellie called back to him. 'Excuse me? Can you tell me, does the West German Opera pay its young performers?'

'Why, of course. A real wage, as all professional singers are due.'

'Thank you,' she said.

He moved away, letting himself into his car and reversing it into the road. As he drove past, Papa emerged from the pub clutching a brown paper bag. Ellie wouldn't let her heart sink. This was temporary, only temporary. In five years, everything would be different. She considered telling Papa about the West German Opera, but decided against it. No more of this awful dance of expectation and disappointment. No more competitions. Just practise and practise every day, single-mindedly, with unwavering focus.

Perhaps five years was not such a long time after all.

TWO
London, England: 1975

*T*he limo was late and Penny Bright wasn't happy about it.

She sat on the corner of a leather armchair in her manager's Lambeth townhouse while he frantically made phone calls. Live interviews always made her nervous.

'I hate being late, George,' she muttered to him as he waited on hold. 'You know how tense it makes me.'

'You're a pop star,' he replied good-naturedly, drumming his fingers on the coffee table. 'Everybody expects you to be late.'

She worried a fingernail with her teeth and rolled her eyes at him, an expression masked by the large sunglasses she wore despite the fact that it was evening. Dressed in a satin mini, lace-up knee-length boots, and a fur coat, with her dark hair artfully dipping over one eyebrow, she was ready for her live interview at Radio One to promote the release of her new single, the album that was recorded and soon to follow, and announce plans for a concert tour in the new year.

Only the interview was in twenty minutes and the limo was late.

Finally, George got hold of somebody who could help. He was talking in hushed, urgent tones, and Penny's ears pricked up. She watched him closely.

'What is it?' she asked, when he had hung up the receiver.

'It seems the DJ announced that you were coming in for a live interview. There's a crowd gathering outside Broadcasting House. We can't go in the limo, they'll know it's you. They'll mob the car.'

'What are we going to do?'

He snatched up a set of keys from near the front door. 'We're going to take my wife's car. Come on.'

She rose and followed him out to the street, where a neat, white MG stood waiting for them. She forced a smiled as he unlocked her door, brushing a strand of dark hair out of her eyes. 'I suppose this means I'm really famous now?'

George gave her his customary disapproving frown as they climbed in. 'Two top ten singles usually does count as fame.'

'The first single doesn't count, though,' she replied as he started the car. 'You bought most of those.'

'It worked,' he replied, pulling into the street.

She patted his wrist as he changed gear. 'Where would I be without you?'

'Where I found you, I expect,' he said.

'Maybe you're right,' she murmured. She fell silent, watching the night-time London streets flash past. Over the Thames and up past St James Park, then into Soho; the place where George had discovered her two years ago, just after her eighteenth birthday. She loved the grimy, bohemian streets for their variety and texture, as much as she hated them for knowing things about her that nobody else knew. Back then, she had longed to play music, had hustled for gigs, had sat for hours in her bedsit tooling around on her guitar with song ideas. She'd thought being Penny Bright, pop star, could lift her out of her grim reality. It had been alarming to realise that her problems had followed her.

The car sped on. She was going to be late. Her stomach itched. Soon they were turning into Portland Place. Penny caught her breath.

'My God,' George gasped, slowing the car.

People everywhere. They crowded the footpath, spilled out onto the road. As the car rounded the corner, the imposing 1930s façade of Broadcasting House came into view, lit up warm against the chill London evening. Two policemen were trying to disperse the crowd.

George frowned at her. 'Duck down. I'll go round and see if there's a back entrance.'

Penny loosened her seatbelt, slid down into the footwell and tried to pretend it was all a game. People were here because they loved her, not because they hated her or wanted to hurt her. George accelerated, then slowed again.

'The police are getting me to pull over,' he muttered harshly. 'Damn it, I could have got past.'

Penny got back into her seat. Eager eyes spotted her, the crowd surged towards the car. One of the police officers, realising what was happening, hastened to her door. George climbed out and fought his way through the bodies to let her out. With George on one side, a police officer on the other, while the second police officer attempted to separate the crowd in front of her, Penny made her way towards the Broadcasting House entrance.

'Penny! Penny!' Her name echoed all around her.

The cool caught her cheeks. Everything moved in slow motion. Dutifully, she smiled and waved, flash cameras went off all around her. She let George and the policemen protect her while the sea of adoration rolled and pitched around her.

'Penny! Over here!'

'Smile for me!'

'I love you!'

Their progress slowed. Hands tried to shove autograph books in her face. George was shouting at people to move back. She tried not to let it bother her. This was what she wanted, wasn't it?

Then, one brutal voice from the edge of the crowd chilled her heart.

'Angie!' He spat it. Like a curse.

Despite herself, she whipped her head around to see who had called that name – that name that nobody here should know – but she couldn't see who had said it. Only glistening eyes in smiling heads, like grinning marionettes in the reflected light of the building. Too many people. She couldn't breathe.

George must have felt her body tense. He pulled her hard against him and barrelled forward. A security guard opened the door to the foyer, and finally they were inside, safe. People hammered on the door behind her, but she was already being hurried to the studio, the echo of that harsh male voice refusing to fade.

Back in her own little flat, far away from the attention and adoration, Penny found she couldn't sleep. She tried for a long time – her right side, her left side, flopped over pillows on her front – but eventually even the trying was keeping her awake, so she got up.

Switching on her light, she checked the watch lying on her dresser. Midnight. That was the problem with this crazy business. Most nights she was up at this time anyway, working. Rehearsing late, or fiddling around with a new song in the studio. During the down times, George insisted she rest, catch up on sleep. But how could she? Her body clock had been rewired now.

It hadn't helped that somebody had called her name – her old name, her real name – outside the Radio One interview. *Angie.* Who could know her? She supposed it was crazy to assume that nobody would remember her from before: before George, before two top ten singles, before *Top of the Pops* and the cover of *Jackie* magazine. But who from that unformed part of her life would bother to queue with hundreds of fans, just to call her name and disappear? Not her family. Her ageing mother had made it clear long ago she wanted nothing to do with her wayward daughter; her cousins and other extended family – who, to be frank, had never been particularly interested in her anyway – were dotted around Wiltshire and rarely ventured into London. There were others from her past, but she hoped she had left them behind forever.

She pulled open her top drawer and rummaged around inside. Her fingers closed on a small clear container, half-filled with white tablets. She shook one of the tablets into her hand. That would help her sleep.

Penny went to the bathroom and filled a glass with water. As she swallowed the tablet, she studied herself in the mirror. She hated herself without make-up. Her skin was sallow, dark shadows under her eyes, irises so black that they looked like two drops of murky oil. Without thinking, she reached for her make-up bag. As the tranquilliser worked to slow her movements and her mind, she lined her eyes in electric blue, swept mascara onto her lashes, dabbed foundation on her skin… It didn't matter that nobody would see her. Penny could see herself.

Finally, she felt tired enough to return to bed. With the light out, her thoughts turned once again to the voice in the crowd. What was she so afraid of anyway? So what if somebody knew about her slightly shady past? She had done nothing unforgivable, she had done only what she had to in order to survive. Whoever he was, he couldn't hurt her.

Penny drifted off to sleep, vague impressions of years-old shadows working their way into her dreams.

Angie Smith had run away from home at sixteen. If it could be called running away when nobody bothered to come after her.

She'd always wanted a normal family. Her friends at school had normal families, with two parents and siblings. They went on holidays to the seaside, they attended school fetes and sports carnivals, they lived in houses busy with noise and cooking smells and friendly dogs who got underfoot.

Instead of a normal family, Angie had a mother: forty-five years older than her daughter. Her mother had been made hard by her abusive Greek husband, Angie's father, who left for a much younger woman on the morning of Angie's seventh birthday. After his departure, all traces of him had been erased: not a word of Greek was uttered in the house again; his surname had been carefully replaced on all official documents; wedding photos and sports trophies had been consigned to the rubbish bin. Angie's mother became strictly religious, tyranically harsh, and obsessively clean. Of all the things Angie felt for her – sometimes embarrassment, sometimes pity, often anger – love was not one of them. Love needed warm light and gentle tending to grow. Love had been beaten out of Angie in the cold, hospital-scented bathroom with her father's wide leather belt, one of the only things he had left behind.

Like most mistreated children, Angie had put up with this harsh life for a long time. She never questioned it; it was all she'd ever known. Twice a week she stayed an afternoon with her neighbour, Mrs Archer, while her mother was at work. Mrs Archer ran a bed and breakfast hotel, and Angie loved to help her fold towels and arrange the little breakfast jam jars. Mrs Archer was kind, and asked a lot of questions about her home situation. Angie knew there was something shameful about her relationship with her mother, so confessed nothing. Nevertheless, one day Mrs Archer came around to talk to her mother, voices had been raised, and after that Angie wasn't allowed to visit her again.

Adolescence, however, had woken Angie. Her natural drive for independence had brought about clash after clash, and now that she was taller than her mother she couldn't see why she should put up with the physical bullying anymore.

A kiss behind the school shed had brought the situation to a head. Angie didn't particulary like Jamie Green, but kissing was new and interesting to her so she'd given it a try. Precisely as her mother was pulling up in their old Vauxhall to pick her up from school.

The beating had been particularly savage, and Angie was by now old enough to figure out that there was jealousy in her mother's actions. After the long prayer that they always had to recite together after a beating, her mother had taken Angie by the shoulders, met her eyes evenly and said, 'Don't you dare touch a boy again. I'll put you out on your ear and never take you back.'

To Angie, this didn't sound like a bad option at all. A month later, she lied to her mother, told her that she had missed a period. She had to endure another belting, but she almost smiled through it, knowing it would be the last one. That night her mother packed her a bag and told her never to come back. With five quid in her pocket, Angie headed out with her thumb pointing towards the main road.

It was a clear night, with a frosted quarter moon tipping the shadowy trees with blue light. An ineffable smell of earth and rotting leaves washed over her as she left civilisation behind and tracked towards the A363. The only sounds for a long time were her footfalls and the occasional hoot of an owl. Then a lorry had come rattling out of the dark, headlights blazing, diesel fumes spewing. She turned to wave it down, and at first it didn't slow. Then the brakes squeaked. It stopped a few hundred feet ahead.

Angie ran towards it, the door opened. A burly man in a musty pullover smiled down at her.

'Where you goin', luv?'

'London.'

'What a coincidence.'

She began to climb in, when he said, 'You'll have to pay.'

'I've no money,' she lied. She was saving what she did have for when she arrived in London.

'Don't need money, just need your right hand.' He winked. 'Reckon a lass like you might know what to do, eh?'

Angie hesitated, confused.

'Hop in, luv. I'll show you.'

She slid warily into the seat next to him, and closed the door against the cold. He gently grasped her hand and pressed it into his groin, fumbling with his zipper.

'It's just like shaking hands,' he said, 'only faster and firmer.'

It was over in moments, and he gave her a hanky to wipe her fingers clean. Then he put the lorry back in gear and offered her a gap-toothed smile.

'Ever been to London before?' he asked.

She shook her head.

'What's your name?'

'Angie Smith.'

'Well, Angie Smith. I reckon you'll get along just fine,' he said. And the lorry roared off into the dark.

George unlocked his front door at one a.m. As always Aila, his wife, had left the outdoor light on for him: a sign of her endless thoughtfulness as much as a welcome back to the cheery brightness of domesticity, after the shadowy excesses of the pop music world. Usually, on a night with a late rehearsal, she would be fast asleep by the time he got home, and one of his chief pleasures in life was to watch her sleep unknowing, as she curled on her side with her fair hair trailing on the pillow, eyelashes half-moons on her still-soft cheeks.

He was surprised, then, to find lights on inside the house. He slipped out of his shoes and left them in the entranceway, moving into the lounge room in his socks. The house had been shut up against the March cool, and trapped the mineral smell of Aila's oil paints inside. Aila loved to paint, still lifes mostly. Despite years of devotion to her hobby, she confessed (and George reluctantly agreed) to no real talent for it. He had organised for her most recent attempt, a bowl of flowers against a black background, to be framed in gilt and glass, the expensive trappings lending it the aura of real art. She sat under the painting now, on the leather couch, wearing a button-up, long-sleeved nightdress in pale blue, her silky hair loose about her shoulders. He could tell immediately something troubled her: her fingers fidgeted with the piping on a cushion, her blue eyes were anxious saucers.

'Aila?' he said, pocketing his keys. 'Is everything all right?'

She leapt to her feet. She was always pale, but looked even more so tonight. 'I don't know. I've been... I had an odd phone call.'

'Odd?' He took her shoulders gently. 'When?'

'At around seven. A man with a strange voice. It sounded muffled or strangled, like he was trying to disguise it. It frightened me, it...'

'What did he say?'

'He asked for Penny. Only he didn't call her Penny. He called her by her real name. He said, "I need to speak to Angie." At first I thought it might be a relative, somebody important. I told him she didn't live here but I could take a message for her, and then...' She took a deep breath and slowed her words. 'He threatened her. He said he knew what kind of person she was, and he was going to make her suffer.'

George's heart went cold.

'He said such awful things, George. Awful, violent things. I hung up on him and I was so afraid he'd call back that I left the phone off the hook.'

George pulled her close. 'Don't worry. Don't worry. You know what fans can be like.'

'But how did he get our phone number?'

'I don't know.' He kissed the top of her head. 'Aila, it's very important you don't tell Penny about this.'

Aila stood back, perfectly curved eyebrows shooting up in surprise. 'We have to tell her. If there's somebody out there who wants to –'

But George was already shaking his head. 'We don't know who it was, we don't know if he has any intention other than to frighten us. Penny and I are leaving tomorrow for a promotional tour. We have forty-six interviews lined up over five days. I need her to be calm and focused.' George knew that Penny was vulnerable. Any little trigger could start her obsessing, turn her mind in on itself. She already relied too much on her pills: sedatives to calm her and help her sleep, uppers the next day to give her her spark back and help her be the perfect pop star. 'Let me take care of it. Are you worried about being home alone? I can call the security company and have somebody come by tomorrow.'

'I'll go to my sister's until you come back. If that man, whoever he is, can get our phone number, he might be able to get our address too.'

Already, George was explaining the phone call away. He'd been in the business for more than twenty years, and had encountered plenty of odd people. Fans liked to declare their love in weird ways, or their anger: over time he had collected packages full of imported chocolates and packages full of bloody nails from the post office. But, in the end, none of these odd people had tried to touch one of his artists. Usually, an incoherent poem or a veiled threat in a letter were as close as they got. People who did such things were strange and furtive by nature; they didn't want to come out of their holes for a confrontation.

Aila was snuggled against his chest again, and he stroked her soft hair, heart-weak for her: home alone, worrying about the stranger on the phone. She was small and birdlike and his arms closed around her ribs. The instinct to protect her, always strong, was keener than ever tonight.

'There's nothing to worry about,' he murmured against her hair. 'Trust me, nothing will come of this.'

Penny was sick to death of talking about herself. Forty-one interviews down, five to go. For five days she had been in and out of radio stations, some shiny and grand, others grimy and cramped; in and out of newspaper offices, record stores and pubs. Smiling, shaking hands, pretending to flirt, all over England, Scotland and Wales. George said that top ten singles weren't enough. If she wanted to cement her place in the pop pantheon, she needed a number one. She needed big attendances at the concert tour in the new year. This meant she had to work harder. She didn't complain; she was just glad that George had enough ambition for both of them.

On the road back south, due for an interview in Sheffield, George took an unexpected exit off the M1 just past Darton. Penny, who had been idly gazing out the window at the early morning mist, turned to him sharply.

'Where are we going?'

'A little side trip. Won't take long.'

Shortly, they were turning into a winding country lane, under trees and past lichen-dotted stone walls. The mist gathered in hollows, lit gold by the morning sun. George indicated, then turned the Mercedes into a dirt side road that wound up to a cemetery. He pulled over, leaving the engine running.

'I'll leave the heater on for you,' he said, opening his door. He pulled his woollen scarf snugly about his neck. 'Wait here.'

Then the door had closed behind him and she was left alone to watch him trudge over uneven ground, down a slope and out of sight. The car idled quietly, the dry heat stinging her eyes.

She sighed, leaning back in her seat. She didn't feel like talking. In fact, she was tired from a late night and an early wake-up. Instinctively, she felt in the pocket of her fur jacket and pulled out a bottle of uppers. She dry-swallowed a couple then flipped down the visor to check her reflection in the mirror. Hating what she saw, she flipped it back up and closed her eyes.

She didn't like having to rely on the pills, but reassured herself that if doctors prescribed them, they must be safe. As always, she did what she had to in order to survive: her schedule was punishing and her flesh too weak to get through it without assistance. Other drugs, the illicit ones that the musicians in her backing band took so casually, were not for her. Penny liked to stay in control, know what she was saying and doing. Her only experimentation with cocaine, a few months before she'd met George, had scared her to death. It was in an overheated nightclub, surrounded by cigarette smoke and loud music. At first, she had loved the rush of shadowy excitement. But when the inevitable sag came, it was accompanied by a horrible paranoia. The delicious shadows had got inside her mind and twisted themselves into nightmares.

An awful, grey dread had crept over her. She'd rushed out onto the street, where the moist cool was soothing on her hot face. The conviction that she had to get home, away from the night and the lights and these horrible feelings, became so compelling that it threatened to unhinge her completely. No cabs anywhere. She decided to make her way out to Wardour Street, but her sense of direction was shot to pieces by the cocaine and she wandered into a dead end instead. The smell of rotting food and old beer bottles confronted her; flashing neons outside a dingy club; a prostitute wearing a cat mask, idly twirling a velvet tail. She backed up, thought she'd found the right street but realised too late she hadn't, found herself in a narrow alley. Dirty bookshops brazenly displayed their wares in the flickering streetlight. Smoky strip clubs spewed music and laughter. Two men and a woman kissed and groped each other behind a stinking drainpipe. And everywhere, people. Tall people, short people, fat and thin people, staring at her with glassy eyes and smiling grotesque smiles, shouting comments and catcalls. Her legs were freezing, and tears chilled on her cheeks. She ran and ran, finally arriving at the quiet green space of Soho Square. Here, on a bench, she sat.

'It's all right, it's all right,' she had said, hugging herself against the cold and the dread. Quiet began to creep back in. It was just the cocaine, that was all. Poison in her blood, whispering lies to her brain. She vowed she would never touch drugs again.

Penny opened her eyes, blinking away the distressing memory. Where was George?

She reached across and pulled the car keys out, then went to follow him.

Her breath fogged the air in front of her as she made her way down the overgrown path. The morning's dewfall had left the grass glittering in the sunlight. George, all in black with his black hair untidily flopping in his eyes, stood by a simple cross-shaped headstone. Curious, she joined him, peering at the inscription on the weather-eaten cross.

'Dorothy Fellowes?' she asked.

'My mother.' He indicated the headstone. 'You know, I've often thought about replacing this with something more beautiful: a weeping angel, perhaps, or something fancy with lines from Shelley.'

'Why don't you?'

He shrugged. 'It doesn't seem authentic somehow. A grown man, wealthy now, trying to revise the past. My sisters and I chose this cross because we liked it. To change it now...it would be almost dishonest.'

Penny peered closer, reading the dates. She wasn't certain how old George was, but suspected he was approaching his mid-forties. If that were so, his mother had died while he was still a child. She felt a stab of pity for him, imagining him as a solemn dark-haired boy coping with such a loss.

'And your father,' she said, 'is he...?'

'Dead too, yes. I don't know where he's buried. I don't care to know.' He smiled grimly.

She was curious but didn't want to pry so she said nothing. Her fingers were twitchy as the uppers began their work on her nervous system; she was keen to get back in the car and on their way.

George sensed this, and turned away from the grave, moving back towards the path.

'So you come from around here originally?' she asked, falling into step beside him.

'I was born two miles up the road.'

'But you don't have a Yorkshire accent.'

'Not anymore. It's a long story.' He put his hand out for the car keys. 'We'd best get going, I know you hate to be late.'

THREE
South Yorkshire: 1939

*G*eorge Fellowes made his first quid in the entertainment industry when he was seven. He'd just discovered that his friend Arthur Patterson was able to belch *God Save the Queen* on cue. Charging a ha'penny admission, he set up a makeshift stage in the back of the janitor's shed and packed in fourteen school friends. Later, he and Arthur split the proceeds, and he bought a paper bag full of red licorice after school. He knew he'd have to share it with his four sisters if he went straight home, so he took the long route past the canal. As he sat on the marshy edge of Oakenshaw Beck, watching the way the saplings dappled the sunlight, he savoured the sticky treats. Even though his father later gave him a walloping for tardiness, it couldn't take the sweet taste out of his mouth.

George loved music. He loved music almost as much as he loved breathing, but as the fifth child of a Methodist family in a mining village just outside Barnsley, the times he actually heard music were very few and very infrequent. The wireless was only for news about the war, they certainly had no gramophone, and his father was highly suspicious of local concerts and performances, even the brass bands so beloved of other coalminers. So music was a stolen pleasure, to be listened to on random gusts from the bandstand, drifting quietly from other people's homes, or in the passing whistle of Tom the milkman, whom everybody said had once been in a real choir. His own forays into performance, trying to sing or pick out a tune on the school piano, had proven to him only that he had no innate ability, and this conclusion was reinforced by his mother, who pronounced his humming 'tone-deaf'. He was accepting of this, and decided that even if it wasn't a language he could speak, it was still a language he understood every nuance of just by listening.

Many years later, he would reflect on why his parents had so many children. After all, they weren't Catholics. But one conversation from his early childhood did replay itself over and over in his mind. His mother, pregnant again, was frying sausages in the dim kitchen while his father, smelling of soap but never really able to get the coal grit out of his pores and fingernails, berated her.

'It had better be a boy this time. Girls are a bloody curse. You've already given me five daughters.'

At the time, George had explained this comment away as a slip of the tongue. Of course he meant to say: four daughters and a son. But later, after the storm of violence and confusion that engulfed them all and scattered them to the four winds, he thought he understood better. To his father, he was weak, effeminate, interested in all the wrong things. His one trip down the pit – his father had invited him with the jocular challenge that he was never interested in what the old man was up to – had been a disaster. The further he receded from light and air, the more panicked his heart and lungs had become, until his father had shamefully been forced to make a special trip up to the surface to bring the boy back to his mother.

But he was a son, not a daughter, not even in an honorary sense. His sisters were an exclusive club into which he was never invited. Their games made no sense to him; in fact he suspected they changed the rules regularly to confound him. They were a wild, giggling mob of tangled fair hair and darned stockings, switching to immediate saucer-eyed sobriety the instant their father walked in the front door. They were as one; sharing secrets until late in the night in private code, holding hands on the way to school, wiping each other's tear-stained faces. Belle, Violet, Rosie and Annie. For a long time he wished fervently that he could be part of their world. But he soon learned not to envy them. He discovered that they hadn't bonded so closely simply because they were sisters, but because they were survivors.

George's nightmares as a child were often the same: a male figure, hulking and black and smelling of coaldust, creeping into his room and watching with glittering eyes. He and his sisters all slept in the same room. Belle and Violet, the eldest two, shared a bed with him; while the younger girls slept on a mattress on the floor. Belle and Violet were both teenagers by this time, and he liked to pretend Belle's warm, womanly body belonged to his mother. He usually slept well, and his abrupt awakenings after the nightmares were easily soothed by Belle's sleepy fingers on his brow.

But knowledge came, as it does, with age. The black figure in his dreams was not always in his dreams, it was sometimes in his room. He'd crack open tired eyes to see his father stealing in, silently, silently, rousing one of the younger girls and taking her gently by the hand... somewhere. She would return within half an hour, wordlessly climb back in with her sister, and sleep would claim them all again. It wasn't his curiosity that was aroused, but his jealousy. What special indulgence were Rosie and Annie being afforded? Just before his eighth birthday, he found out.

He had to be careful climbing out of bed. Belle slept lightly, and would hear him. He got his feet free of the covers and wriggled on his stomach to the end of the bed, dropping lightly to the floor and padding across the peg rugs to the door. He cracked it open a fraction, peering into the living room. He couldn't make sense of the firelit scene. Rosie, shivering on the couch in her nightgown, arms tight across her chest, eyes fixed firmly on the ceiling. His father's muscular, shirtless back was turned, he was fiddling with the buckle of his belt.

A hand closed over George's mouth. He struggled for air, as Belle pulled him back into the bedroom and closed the door quietly. Her eyebrows were drawn down sternly.

'Get back to bed,' she hissed, releasing him and propelling him towards the bed.

'What's Rosie doing?'

'Bed!' she ordered. 'Now.'

George scrambled into bed, where Violet sat up watching them. 'It's not his fault, Belle,' she said.

'He shouldn't be such a peeping Tom.'

'He's just curious. We should tell him.'

'He doesn't need to know.'

George was bewildered. 'What? What's happening?'

Belle slid into bed beside him. 'He did it to all of us,' she said. 'He did it to me, and to Violet, and then it was Annie's turn, and Rosie's.'

'Did what?'

Belle refused to answer, but Violet picked up the thread. 'You're not to worry, George, he won't do it to you. And he'll stop as soon as Rosie and Annie are old enough. He doesn't want them to make babies, not slow ones or ones with fingers missing.'

'I don't understand.'

'Enough!' Belle hissed in the dark. 'It doesn't do to talk about this. Go to sleep.'

Make babies? George's understanding of the process of making babies was incomplete, but he had grasped the basics from what Loose Lizzie Hawkins had whispered to him while pressing her skinny chest against his down at the canals one afternoon. Even though nobody had told him so, he knew with instinctive certainty that what his father was doing to his sisters was horribly, horribly wrong.

Over the coming months, as his hatred for his father grew, he plotted elaborate and violent revenge. It was a man's job. Mother was too scared to stop his father, his sisters too weak. He counted the days until he would be ten, the magical age that he believed would bring him enough strength and courage to take the villain on. Something dark and primitive had awoken within him, and his secret drawings of knives and guns and fabled German war tortures became more frequent. Perhaps these violent imaginings would have eventually warped him, transformed him forever from a clever, music-loving boy into a twisted bully. But something soon happened to put an end to it. His father left the mines to join the army. On the day that his father was despatched to Italy, George hid down at the canals and refused to say goodbye.

The rest of the war was an idyllic dream. The closest the German bombers came was a chemical factory on the road to Sheffield. The sounds of the buzzing planes and the bombs exploding were muffled by distance, as though under a thick blanket. It had been exciting, not frightening, a reminder somehow that he was connected to a larger world beyond the narrow window of village life. The new baby was born, a girl named Carol, and Violet took care of her while Belle and his mother went to work pegging rugs at the rug mill. His mother didn't seem to miss his father at all, and Carol grew into a beloved toddling sister, full of sunny smiles and giggles. She was as mute as a little woodland creature, though. Perhaps she didn't speak because she didn't need to, with five siblings to speak for her and to answer all her whims even before she knew she had them. His sisters' wild humour went unchecked, and it was as though light and air had been allowed into their dark, stuffy home for the first time. George thrived in the new environment and he began to return to his old love of music.

His school teacher, Mrs Fogg, also played piano for the local dance studio. George attached himself to her very closely, spending most Saturday mornings at the dance studio, turning pages for her and learning the mysteries of rhythm and melody. She invited him back to her house for lunch every week, where she had a gramophone and records, and a wireless permanently set to the American Forces Network. Swing and jazz poured through her house, and her husband played the guitar and sang in a shaky baritone voice. Mrs Fogg was so impressed with George's commitment that she arranged a treat for him. A real swing band from London were putting on a concert in Sheffield, and Mrs Fogg and her husband were going. Would he like to come with them?

George's mother agreed happily, and they took the late afternoon train to town. As dusk closed in, George's excitement grew. The band were playing at the Lyceum. He had never seen so many well-dressed ladies, with their tidy hairstyles and clicking high heels. Inside the richly decorated theatre, in a seat that squeaked every time he moved, he watched with awe as the lights dimmed and the curtain swung back. Magic! The hot lights and loud music intoxicated him. When Mr and Mrs Fogg dropped him off outside his house later that evening, his blood was still dancing.

Spare keys were an expense beyond the family budget, so he knocked at the door while the Foggs waited. The door creaked open, leaking light and warmth from inside. Violet peered out.

'Come in quickly, George,' she said, hurrying him in.

He turned to thank his hosts. 'I had a lovely time and –'

Violet yanked his arm. 'I said quickly.'

Bewildered, he allowed himself to be led inside, and the door was shut firmly behind him.

'What's wrong?' he asked, but he spotted the figure before the question was out of his mouth. A man, his bearing and profile horribly familiar, hunched by the fire. His father.

'Well? Are you going to say welcome home, or are you going to stand there swallowing air?'

Still George couldn't bring himself to speak. His father rose and spat in the fire. It hissed momentarily. 'Just as I thought,' he grumbled. 'You would have all been happier if I'd taken an Italian bullet.' With that, he loped off to the bedroom. He slammed the door so hard that the house shook.

George's family didn't celebrate VE Day like most folk.

Tension had been growing since his father's return, and the tension centred around little Carol who was four years old, now, and had still never uttered a word. Until one afternoon when she spoke up loud and clear.

'Don't!'

George and his mother rushed from the kitchen, and the girls from the bedroom, to see what had jolted her out of her muteness. Carol was outside on the patchy grass, her little tear-stained face indignant. His father stood a short distance away by the chicken coop, looking angry and guilty all at once. Everybody suspected what had happened, but nobody said anything.

'Come on, inside,' his mother said, leading Carol firmly by her shoulder.

George and his sisters shuffled inside too, and it felt like being woken up from a long sweet dream.

At midnight, George was roused from sleep by the sound of raised voices. Rosie and Annie were already awake, climbing onto the bed that George now shared with Belle, Violet and Carol. They huddled together, listening as their parents shouted at one another. George's blood chilled. He'd never heard his mother fight back. Ever.

'You're not going to touch her.'

'She's my daughter too. A man's allowed to spend time with his children.'

Back and forth the shouts went, growing more and more intense. There was a thump and a yelp. Violet clutched Carol, silent, against her chest and wept. George's heart began to pound. The noises grew more animalistic, grunts of struggle, pants of attempted escape. George knew he should go out there, tell his father to leave his mother alone. But he was terrified; he had never felt more like a little skinny boy.

Then his mother started to scream, 'No, no, no!'

Rosie clapped her hands over her ears. With a loud flat bang, the screaming suddenly stopped. Then another bang, and a thud. The children waited in the dark. The clock on top of the wardrobe ticked loudly. Violet choked on little sobs. George's heart shivered with searing ice, the moment too real, too hot, to comprehend.

Finally, Belle said, 'I'm going out there.'

'No, Belle,' Rosie said. 'You shouldn't, you –'

'Mum might need our help.'

'I'm coming,' George said, leaping off the bed. Together they advanced towards the door.

The living room was lit up brightly. Belle saw the still, pale arm and the oozing river of blood from behind the sofa and backed away, stifling a scream. George, unable to fathom what had happened, began to cry softly. 'Mummy? Mummy?' he said.

But she was silent and cold as the grave.

The unfamiliar smells of George's new home seemed more acute now that it was night-time, now that objects were obscured by shadows and he couldn't imagine accurately the dimensions of the large bedroom he'd been given. Despite the fact that there were radiators under every window, the house seemed chill, and he felt very small under the high empty ceilings. He curled on his side and tried not to cry.

The war had made many orphans, and nobody wanted six of them at once. Belle and Violet were old enough to fend for themselves, and now rented a tiny room above the mending shop on Barnsley's high street. They worked hard, too hard to look after anyone but little Carol. Rosie had been taken in by the local preacher's family and Annie had been despatched to her godmother in Wales. George, by dint of the fact that he was a boy, had been singled out for special treatment. The headmaster of his school knew of a couple in Brighton, childless since their three-year-old daughter had drowned, who were willing to foster him. The Lewinses were very wealthy, in their fifties, and kindly enough in their way. But for a thirteen-year-old boy missing his mother, reeling from the shock of his father's violence, their weak smiles and handshake greetings provided little comfort.

Deep in the dusty room, a clock ticked its methodical rhythm. He was used to warm bodies around him, light under the door. Not this quiet darkness, where his edges blurred as though he could disappear into the night.

The door cracked open. A slow footstep: Mr Lewins. He approached the bed, smoothed the cover in a gentle, paternal gesture. It was so different from his own father's actions that it stunned George into wide-eyed surprise. After a moment, Mr Lewins realised George was still awake.

'Boy?' he said. 'Can't you sleep?'

George shook his head vigorously.

'Why not?'

'I... Everything feels different.' George's voice trembled. *Don't cry, don't cry, don't cry.*

'Everything *is* different,' Mr Lewins said. He hesitated, as though he was thinking about sitting on the edge of the bed but then decided against it. Instead he stood awkwardly. His voice was gentle. 'Everything *should be* different. You came from a bad home. Your father was a bad man. You can leave that behind you now. Forget it. Be a new boy...a new man.' Here he placed his hand over his heart, almost as though he was taking a vow. 'There's great shame in having a murderer for a father, and a self-murderer too. Let everything be different, and guard yourself against repeating his mistakes.'

George grappled with his feelings. He *was* ashamed of his father, but he still loved his mother, his sisters...he didn't want to forget them.

'I know, boy, that life can deal you a savage blow. Your character is measured by your ability to put it behind you, embrace the future and forget the past.'

A long silence ensued. Finally, George said, 'Thank you, Mr Lewins.'

'You're welcome, boy.' He turned and left the room, closing the door quietly behind him.

Embrace the future, forget the past. It became George Fellowes's new mantra.

FOUR
Kokondorf: 1975

'*P*apa, come on. We don't have much time.'

Papa lifted his head from his chest, fixing bleary eyes on her. 'Practise, Ellie? Today? It's your birthday. The Neumanns will be here soon.'

'Exactly. Which is why we have to practise now. Before they come.'

Papa heaved himself out of the chair by the fire. He had grown swollen and ruddy from the years of alcohol, and now even the mornings weren't safe from his drunkenness. Sometimes at dawn, as she left for the dairy – she had a poorly paid job there that barely covered the rent – she would find him sipping whisky and gazing out at their overgrown garden as though the meaning of life was hidden somewhere out among the rocks and fallen leaves.

The sickness was affecting his coordination, too. He could barely play the piano anymore, his fingers slurring and tripping over the keys. But he still had a good ear for teaching, and found the threads of the man he once was when she began to sing.

'No, no...here, again. Curve your tongue or that "ee" will come out too thin... Not so lazy, Ellie. Open your throat. Find your support.' And so on. His extreme perfectionism had transformed Ellie, over her teenage years, into a singing machine. On her twentieth birthday, she possessed a sound beyond her years. Not even Mozart's

Come scoglio was beyond her capabilities now. Along with technical skill, the years of anxiety about Papa and the creeping poverty they suffered had caused a rapid emotional maturity. Every disappointment over selling some cherished item to pay the debt collectors, every misery over finding Papa sprawled unconscious on the kitchen floor, every ache in her bones from the long days washing bottles at the dairy, now went towards her art. She surrendered everything to the music, developing a haunting, aching tone that made her voice utterly unique.

In the middle of a high note, a knock sounded at the door.

'That will be our guests,' Papa hurrumphed, struggling to his feet and shuffling to the front door.

Ellie folded away her music and when she turned to greet Frau and Herr Neumann, she realised there was somebody else with them. A tall man, with wheat-blond hair and deep hazel eyes.

'Dieter,' she yelped, suddenly wishing she had bothered to put on a pretty dress and brush her dark hair.

'Surprise,' he said, moving forward to take her hands warmly. 'Ellie, you look wonderful. Last time I saw you, you were just a little girl.'

'I was fourteen,' she protested, but Dieter had already moved on to shake Papa's hand.

'And Herr Frankel, I am pleased to find you well.'

'Well? Well? You are surprised to find me alive, I should imagine,' Papa replied gruffly, heading towards the kitchen. 'I suppose some birthday cake is in order.'

Frau and Herr Neumann hugged Ellie in turn, and Frau Neumann handed her a wrapped package. 'Go on,' she said, 'open it.'

Papa hadn't been able to afford a birthday present for her, so Ellie was touched by the gift. She picked off the ribbon and found inside a little silver music box. When she opened it, it played *Un bel di* from Puccini's *Madama Butterfly*.

'Oh, it's beautiful!' she exclaimed.

Frau Neumann leaned close, whispering directly into her ear. 'No matter how bad things get, Ellie, promise you won't sell it. It's yours to keep, not his to drink.'

Ellie's face flushed with embarrassment, and she was glad that Dieter hadn't heard. 'I promise,' she said.

As they ate cake and drank hot coffee, Ellie couldn't help seeing the house as Dieter must see it. They had sold so many possessions, that now it seemed bare and blank: a tablecloth washed clean of colour, two glass candle holders, three mismatched chairs, a threadbare armchair. There wasn't a piece of good china left in the sideboard, a photo frame left on the mantel, a single one of Mama's English books on the shelf. Even the drapes Mama had sewn so carefully had been sold, and folded calico had been hung in their place. Nor could she take her eyes off Dieter. She hadn't seen him for such a long time, but still she felt the familiar pull on her heart. The honey-coloured skin on the back of his neck looked so warm and inviting, his long square hands moved so gently and so precisely as he explained something to Papa.

When the birthday cake was finished and Papa was inviting Frau and Herr Neumann to sit with him by the fire and have a glass of port, Ellie moved to clear away the dishes.

'Let me help,' Dieter said.

'There's only a little,' she replied, not wanting him to see the kitchen.

'I insist.' He followed her to the kitchen. Empty bottles lined the windowsills; Papa saved them so Thorsten could refill them, but they were never rinsed well enough and the room stank like an old pub.

Ellie filled the sink with water while Dieter told her that he was home for good now. He had served his time in the army and hadn't enjoyed it.

'I want to grow my hair,' he laughed. 'I want to think about life, not death. So I've come back to help Mama and Papa with the farm.'

Ellie was overjoyed, but trying not to show it. He carefully dried the dishes and stacked them on the bench as he told her about Munich, about the things he had seen and done in his time away. Munich sounded wonderful, a big city where all manner of marvellous things were available at any time. Their rural life seemed positively backwards by comparison, and she wondered that Dieter could bear to return to a town that only offered one bus service a day, and where the shops still closed at midday for lunch.

Dieter explained that he had bought the music box for her birthday.

'Mama asked me to get you something nice, and I remembered you loved to sing.'

The music box was twice as precious now.

'Do you still sing?' he continued.

'I do little else. I've finished school, I've looked after Papa, I've worked at the dairy...but mostly I've spent the last five years just singing.' She dropped her voice to a whisper as she explained to him about the West German Opera's program for young performers, and how she had already signed up for an audition in March. 'Papa doesn't know,' she said. 'I haven't told anybody, not even your mother.'

'How will you get to Bremen for the audition?'

'I've put a little money aside. I'll have to catch the train.'

'Save your money, Ellie. I'll drive you.'

'You have a car?'

'It's an old heap. I bought it in Munich. But it will get us to Bremen and back without any trouble.'

Ellie beamed. Dieter smiled back and something passed between them. She couldn't describe it; it was like electricity, like a sudden knowingness blooming out of the dark. Their eyes connected, there was a spark, and then she found herself looking away, confused and flushed.

Frau Neumann was there a moment later, standing at the door to the kitchen. 'I think it's time we go, Ellie,' she said. 'Your father isn't well.'

The familiar anxiety needled through her. She saw them off, then turned to Papa, who breathed heavily and could barely lift his head. He wasn't sick, just drunk.

'Papa?' she said, kneeling next to him and rousing him with a gentle shake.

'I'm so tired, Ellie,' he said. 'So very tired.'

'Let's get you to bed, then.' She helped him stand, and supported some of his weight as he stumbled towards the bedroom. She tucked him in, and sat on the edge of the bed. 'Would you like me to sing a song, Papa?'

He mumbled something, it may have been a yes or a no. In any case, her heart felt happier than it had for a long time and she wanted to sing. So she sang a lullaby while Papa drifted off and the snow fell silent and soft outside the grey windows.

On the first Monday in February, after two days of rain that had washed the snow into muddy rivulets, Ellie returned home from the dairy to find the front door of her house open. It wasn't unusual for Papa to go out to the pub in the afternoon, and he was certainly forgetful enough to leave the door unlocked, but she was wary all the same. A large white van was parked out the front. As she drew closer, she could hear men's voices inside the house.

She hesitated on the threshold, listening hard.

'You take that end.'

'It's too heavy.'

And then the clunk of a piano key.

Her heart started. She raced inside to find two men, burly and clothed in overalls, trying to manhandle the piano out of its corner.

'Stop!' she shouted. 'Don't move it. You'll throw it out of tune.'

'What does it matter to you if it's out of tune?' one of them said, angrily. 'You won't be playing it.' He pulled a sheet of paper out of his pocket and held it up for her to read. They were from a debt collection company, and Papa's debt was much higher than she had thought. They had orders to remove anything of value from the home.

'I said stop,' she said again with more force, as they made to heave the piano.

'Just get out of the way, little miss,' the other man said. 'There's nothing you can do.'

Ellie laid a firm hand on the top of the piano, lying to buy time. 'You'll never move it like that without breaking your backs. It has an iron frame, it's too heavy. You need four men.'

'Well, I'll come back tomorrow with four men,' the first man replied, quite happy to give up his end of the instrument.

She thought quickly. 'There will be no need. I'll discharge my father's debt immediately. Wait here.' She dashed into her bedroom. The little silver music box was the only shiny thing in a room full of washed-out colours. A white bedspread now faded to grey, rose cushions stained and darned into incoherent colourless patterns. She flipped open the music box, and the theme of Puccini's great aria tinkled and plinked on a loop. But it wasn't the music box itself she intended to give away. It was worth nowhere near enough for such a large debt. She intended to give away what was inside.

Ellie pulled out her mother's wedding ring. When Mama died, Papa wore it on his pinky finger for two years, until he lost it in the snow one January. They had found it, and he had given it to Ellie for safekeeping. Ellie rested it on her palm now, hesitant and guilty. Mama's words returned to her memory. She always took the ring off before doing laundry, perching it high on a ledge above the tub. 'A ring is a circle, it stays together and never ends. Like a family. Like our family,' she used to say. 'I can't let it wash down the drain.'

Ellie's fist closed over the ring. She couldn't let them take the piano. How would she practise? The piano was her future, this ring was her past. With searing clarity, she knew that she should never endanger her future by clinging to the past.

'I'm sorry, Mama,' she said in English, Mama's native language. She kissed her fist once then returned to the living room. 'Here,' she said, holding out the ring on her palm. 'Take this instead.'

The second man, the kinder one, plucked the ring off her palm. 'Is it gold?'

'Yes. It was my mother's wedding ring.'

The other man narrowed his eyes. 'We'll have this valued, and if it's not gold, we'll be back to take that piano.'

'You won't be back.'

He laughed bitterly. 'The way your father runs up debts, I think we will.'

47

They left, and Ellie slammed the door on them and on the cold. She ran her fingers over the keys, checking the intonation. It was still fine. She sang the first lines of her audition song. Only five weeks to go. If she didn't pass the audition, there would not be another chance for her. The debt collectors were right: eventually they would be back, they would take the piano.

Now she had given away Mama's ring, there was no room for failure.

Ellie stood under the ash tree at the bottom of the hill, stamping her feet in the melted snow and fogging the air with her breath. She refused to put her heavy coat back on though. It was moth-eaten and ugly, and how she looked was important today. Not just for the audition, but for the drive down there. Dieter was taking her. She checked her watch. He was supposed to pick her up five minutes ago, and now she was getting anxious. The whole operation had to be secret. She had left the house that morning as usual, telling Papa she was going to work, her best blue dress hidden under the ugly coat. Then she had sheltered behind the church to put a little lipstick and mascara on, crouching out of the cold morning breeze and peering into a tiny plastic mirror. She hoped now, as she waited under the ash tree, that she had put it on straight. Ellie had never spent much time thinking about her appearance. She knew she was a little too generous in her curves, like her mother. She had much darker eyes than Papa and good, clear olive skin. How Dieter saw her or what his taste preferred was a mystery. Maybe he still saw her as a little girl, nobody to take seriously. Today's act of kindness was probably brotherly, and perhaps he would be embarrassed to see her made up with lipstick. She thought about wiping it off, when the distant beep of a car horn drew her out of her reverie.

She turned to see Dieter's old Opel rattling down the hill towards her. She smiled and waved, and a few moments later was mercifully inside the heated car and out of the cold. Just in time, too, as it started to rain.

'Sorry I'm late,' he said. 'The car wouldn't start. Did you slip away from your father easily enough?'

'Yes, he thinks I'm at work.' There was something almost delicious about sharing this deception with Dieter, though Ellie reminded herself that she was sneaking out for an audition, not for a date.

Dieter told her that he still didn't understand completely why she hadn't told Papa about the audition, it seemed to him that her father might need things to look forward to, to keep him going. It wasn't easy to answer him. Many times over the past few years she had thought of telling him, precisely for that reason. But she always stopped herself, imagining the worst: if she failed, it could plunge him into a decline that he wouldn't come back from. Dieter was silent, and she knew he was thinking that Papa seemed already to be on such a decline. Perhaps that was right. Perhaps even the news that Ellie had passed the audition, had found paid employment singing opera, would not get through to him.

No, she wouldn't allow herself to think that. If she passed the audition, she would save him, simple as that. The pressure that these thoughts created was immense, but Ellie had learned to thrive on it. The harder she was squeezed, the better she sang.

The drive down was wonderful. Yes, the car rattled and smoked, a spring in the seat poked her thigh, and at one stage the rain grew so heavy that it spat in through the heating vents which then all had to be turned off. But she was in Dieter's company. Just the two of them, his firm hands on the steering wheel, speeding through the grey morning on the way to the city.

The audition was in a small theatre four streets back from the Marktplatz. She wished that Dieter would take her hand on the short walk there, but he didn't. She felt all elbows next to him. Bremen was so different from the village: bustling with people and rattling with trams. Despite all this noise, the people here were much more relaxed than back home. A young couple slouched against the sill of a music shop, kissing lazily, their hands in each other's back pockets. Nobody even looked twice at them.

A sign for the auditions was taped to the stage door. Dieter left her there with a smile and a 'Good luck' and she went in. In a well-lit backstage room, an attractive young woman with long pale hair in plaits took her name and her sheet music to give the accompanist. The young woman wore a long, lacy dress with a vest and knee-high boots, and Ellie felt hopelessly old-fashioned in her button-up blue floral. Ellie lined up against the wall to be photographed with an instant camera. The young woman wound the handle until the picture popped out, and clipped it to the top of a form. As Ellie filled it out, she listened to a tenor singing inside the auditorium. Her years of training made her able to pick everything that was wrong with his voice. His tone was too covered, he sounded like a cow mooing. The form asked questions like, 'Why do you want to sing with the West German Opera?' and 'Are you willing to relocate to Munich?' Of course she had considered all these questions before, especially the one about moving. She knew that opera singers didn't live in Kokondorf, and knew that a change of scenery would do Papa the world of good. She answered the questions as best she could, then closed her eyes and gathered herself, imagining in her head what she would do. Go in, make eye contact and smile, choose the member of the audition panel with the friendliest face to focus on if she felt nervous, remember her breath, remember her support, sing like an angel...

'Fräulein Frankel?'

She looked up. The tenor had stopped singing and was slipping through the door and out into the street. The young woman was smiling at her. 'It's your turn.'

Ellie leapt to her feet, the young woman directed her through the wings and onto a cross made of tape marked out on the stage. A bright light shone directly into her face, she could vaguely make out rows and rows of empty seats, and three silhouetted figures about a quarter of the way back. As for making eye contact or finding the friendliest face, she would have to suffice with smiling somewhere near the three black figures and hoping they were smiling back.

'Ellie Frankel?' one of them said.

She resisted the urge to shield her eyes with her hand. 'That's correct.'

The accompanist began to play the introduction to her song, *Se una pudica vergine* from *La traviata*. Ellie pushed aside the many thoughts that crowded her mind, focusing on the music, on the production of her voice. When she began to sing the first few notes, she knew it would all be fine. She slipped into the music with ease, opening up the highest notes so that they shivered with silvery overtones, calling up the troubled emotions of her heart to give Violetta's last aria emotional depth. Every phrase brought her more confidence for the next; she sang, enjoying the pure act of singing. When the aria drew to a close, she waited in the quiet that followed, secretly elated that the performance had gone so well. She could hear whispering, the shuffling of papers.

'Ellie,' said a voice from the dark at last, 'how long have you been singing that song?'

'I've been practising for this audition for five years now,' she said.

There was good-natured laughter. 'That's rather a long time,' said another voice, this time a woman's. She hadn't realised there was a woman there.

She shielded her eyes, trying to peer into the dark. Only the shadows of faces. 'I heard about this program when I was only fifteen. I had to wait a long time.'

'You're very lucky, then. This is the last year we're running auditions for it,' she said. 'We have a new director, and he's keen on cutting costs.'

Another voice piped up, this time with a strong English accent. 'What other languages do you speak, Fräulein Frankel?'

With a grin she switched to English. 'I speak English, actually. My mother was English.' Here she switched back into German. 'But also a little Italian and French.'

The first voice cut in again. 'Thank you very much, Ellie. We'll be in touch.'

Ellie turned to leave, but then the Englishman spoke again. 'Fräulein Frankel, you haven't left a phone number on your form. How can we contact you?'

It had been a long time since Papa's phone had been cut off. 'By mail?'

'We'll be making a shortlist for the entry interviews tonight, and conducting them the day after tomorrow. Mail is too slow.'

Ellie's mind raced. She had to come back to Bremen? How was she going to get another day off work? But then, what did it matter if she was in trouble at the dairy? She was going to be an opera singer, she knew it. She gave them the Neumanns' phone number and Dieter's name as a contact, then made her way backstage.

The young woman greeted her with her music, then let her back outside into the street. A clock chimed ten somewhere in the distance. She was supposed to meet Dieter at the statue of Roland at quarter past ten, so she ambled back through the streets to the cobbled Marktplatz, a sense of destiny pulsing warm and sweet in her veins.

Papa wasn't well the next afternoon, complaining about nausea and aches in his back. Deep grey clouds crowded out the sky, bringing twilight early. Ellie cooked him some stewed cabbage and mashed potatoes – they could only afford meat three times a week – but he hardly ate any. She settled him with a blanket over his lap. Cleaning up the kitchen seemed almost fatally mundane. Her heart sped. She couldn't keep her mind on the simplest tasks. Every noise outside had her wondering if it was Dieter, coming with the good news… or the bad news. Papa was dozing in a chair by the fire when there was a purposeful rap on the door.

'Who could that be?' Papa mumbled.

'I'll go and see,' she said, throwing down her dish towel and bustling to the front door.

Dieter stood there, smiling cautiously. She held a finger to her lips, then called behind her, 'Papa, it's Dieter Neumann. I'm going for a little walk.'

He made a gruff noise of assent, and Ellie reached for her coat before closing the door behind her. She wanted to savour the moment, but she also wanted to know *immediately*.

'Well?' she asked, when they were out of earshot of the house.

'They called ten minutes ago,' he said. 'They want you to come back for an entry interview tomorrow.'

She shrieked with joy, spontaneously wrapping her arms around his neck and pressing her body against his. She realised what she was doing, and pulled back shyly. His face was flushed too. That brief moment, his warm hard body, threatened to push all other thoughts out of her mind. She gathered her composure, and they kept walking. 'What time is the interview?'

'Nine. I'll take you. Are you going to tell your father?'

'Not yet,' she said. 'Not until it's one hundred per cent certain that I'm in.'

He smiled. 'You know you're in. Don't you?'

'I sang so well,' she said. 'I have to tell somebody. What about Mama?'

His eyes lit up. 'Come on,' he said, pulling her hand.

Laughing, she followed him down the hill and along the back path around the village. The sky grew darker, and Ellie realised she should have brought an umbrella. But she wasn't going to be so practical as to suggest they return home, not with Dieter's warm fingers around hers.

The snow had melted off the cemetery, and Ellie even thought she saw the first brave shoots on the linden trees in the grove. They found her mother's grave, and Ellie said a silent prayer. *Everything is going to be all right, Mama. I'm going to take care of Papa. I've been given the most wonderful opportunity, a magical opportunity. I'm going to be a singer.* When she looked up, she saw that Dieter was considering her in the twilight. His hair had started to grow out of the strict military style, and curled untidily around his ears. Her fingers longed to smooth the errant strands, trace the strong lines of his jaw.

'You've been so helpful. I can't thank you enough, Dieter,' she said, bravely meeting his deep, dark eyes.

Everything switched to slow motion. He raised his hand, grazing her cheek with the backs of his fingers. Her breath caught in her lungs. He twined her dark hair and smiled slowly. 'You can thank me by promising not to forget me when you're an opera star,' he said.

She was too tongue-tied and flustered to reply.

'I never forgot you while I was away, Ellie,' he continued, his voice dropping to a soft whisper. 'I never told you this before, but you were one of the reasons I came back.'

A quick spattering of rain fell then moved on; Ellie was trapped in his gaze. His hands went to her waist, grasping her firmly and pulling her towards him. A delicious heat fluttered through her, her spine had become liquid. He pressed her against him, and his hot lips touched hers firmly, passionately. The rain came again, heavier this time. She slid her hands around the back of his warm neck, as he parted her lips with his tongue, sighing deep in the back of his throat, the kiss transforming from gentle to intense. She had not known a kiss could trigger such an astonishing bodily reaction. Her blood sang, her flesh ran with hot shivers, her legs trembled, and still he held her against him.

Finally, the rain's descent broke them apart.

'You're going to get soaked,' he said. 'Your voice... I don't want you to catch a cold.'

All Ellie could do was smile.

'Come on, I'll walk you home.'

They briskly returned home, making plans for the drive to Bremen tomorrow. Dieter left her at her front door with a gentle stroke of her hair. She closed the door and returned to Papa.

But Papa was not in his chair.

'Papa?' she called, checking the bedroom. Not there either. Could he have gone out in the rain? Surely not.

'Papa?'

A groan, from the bathroom. A jolt to her heart. She ran, found him in an enormous pool of sticky blood. There was so much it confused her. Why was he bleeding? Had he cut himself? Then she realised. It was dribbling over his chin and onto his shirt. He had vomited this blood.

'Papa! God in heaven. Papa!' She leaned over him, her knees in the sticky mess.

His eyes fluttered open, the panicked whites rolling into view, and he uttered that horrible groan again. Ellie was reminded of an old bull she'd seen led to slaughter once. The fear galvanised her; she ran to the front door from where she could see Dieter. She filled her lungs and shouted for him.

He turned with a puzzled expression.

'Call the doctor! Papa's very ill!'

Dieter turned and began running towards the village. Ellie returned to Papa, whose shuddering breaths echoed around the tiles of the bathroom. She pulled his upper body into her lap, nursing his head. He was unconscious again, but she spoke to him anyway.

'Hang on, Papa, help will be here soon,' she said, all the time knowing that the magical opportunity was slipping through her bloodstained fingers.

FIVE

'Aila?' George dropped his keys and closed the front door behind him. He could sense immediately that she hadn't yet returned from her sister's. The house was locked up tight, stuffy. Her fragrance, gentle and floral, was nowhere in evidence. He scooped up the mail and flipped through it on his way downstairs to his basement studio.

George flicked on the light, illuminating the honey-coloured floorboards, the gleaming glass that separated the mixing desk from the recording booth. It smelled warm and woody. His was the only independently owned sixteen-track studio in London. For this luxury of independence, he and his wife had been through a lot, and he still felt the shine of pride every time he came down here. Empty, stained teacups gathered in the corner of his writing desk. He dropped the mail and, gathering the cups, was about to take them upstairs when the phone rang. He stacked the cups again and picked up the receiver.

'Hello?'

'I want to talk to Angie.'

George's skin prickled, and he knew instantly that this was the same caller that Aila had encountered. 'There's nobody here by that name,' he said coolly. 'I think you must have the wrong number.'

His fingers were already reaching for his leather-bound diary, flicking through to find the number for the security company.

'Don't give me that rubbish.' A faint accent, barely perceptible. 'You know who I mean. Whatever she calls herself now, I know who she really is. I know what she is really like.'

George knew better than to engage the caller. 'Goodbye,' he said.

'Don't hang up yet. I have a message for her.'

George waited, silent.

'Tell her I have not forgotten what she did, and I intend to make her pay for it. Tell her –'

George hung up, his stomach knotted with indecision. On the one hand, he wanted to tell Penny, to see if she had any idea who this caller was and whether he was any real threat to her. On the other hand, the rehearsals for the tour were about to go into full swing. Penny was a train always threatening to derail. He cringed, remembering how she had nearly quit the day before her first single had been released. He'd had to sit outside the door of her apartment, talking her through her fears under the door until finally, tear-stained and shaking, she had let him in. Or her first performance on *Top of the Pops* when she had simply refused to get out of the car for fifteen minutes, while a bemused security guard had looked on. George had sunk a significant sum of money into the tour so far and had no desire to see it endangered. Especially if the caller, like most other fans, was content only to talk and not to act.

He always wondered later whether, had Aila been home, he might have talked it over with her, made the right decision. Instead, concerned as much for Penny's fragile nerves as for his investment, he made the wrong decision.

Somebody dangerous was determined to hurt Penny, and she didn't know.

Instead of the flea-pit rehearsal room at Cricklewood in which Penny had prepared for her album, George had organised an empty theatre at Leytonstone for the concert tour rehearsals. Penny was first to arrive, with George nowhere in sight. She waited out on the street for a little while alone, watching the morning traffic as it stuttered and flowed past. Smells of frying bacon and coffee periodically emerged from the café next to the theatre, and Penny wished she'd had more for breakfast than toast and jam. The door to the theatre opened, and a young Spanish woman with a mop and bucket clattered out. She struggled with shouldering the door, dropped the bucket, tripped backwards and started to fall. Penny rushed forward to catch her.

'Are you all right?' Penny asked, helping the young woman to stand.

'Yes, yes, I –' Here the young woman stopped, staring. 'Penny Bright?' she said in a heavy accent.

'Yes,' Penny replied.

The young woman gaped, open-mouthed at her, tears beginning to well in her eyes. 'I love you. I love all your songs.' Then she lapsed into speechlessness.

Penny smiled kindly. 'What's your name?'

'Gloria,' she managed.

'I'm glad you were here. My manager's late and the door was locked. Do you mind if I go in?'

Gloria shook her head mutely, huge eyes fixed on Penny. Penny felt uncomfortable around such intimate adoration. She found it impossible to relate to people when they wore that expression. Somehow, becoming a pop star had cursed her to an awful solitariness. She couldn't become close to ordinary people – like Gloria, with whom she might have much in common and under other circumstances befriend – because they were always in awe of her fame. She had left her past so thoroughly behind her, there weren't friends from then who she could turn to either. Others in the industry she couldn't trust, as she was never sure of their motives. If it wasn't for George and Aila (and sometimes she suspected that Aila didn't like her at all), she would go days without talking to another human.

'Look,' Penny said kindly. 'If you're finished work...we're about to practise. Do you want to come and watch?'

Gloria became flustered. 'I...oh, I... Do you think?... Would that be all right?'

'Of course, come in.' Penny led the way through the foyer and into the theatre. Her heart twitched; too many uppers too early in the morning, but she'd need them to get through the day's rehearsal.

It took a few moments for her eyes to adjust to the dim room. On stage, their equipment had already been set up. She showed Gloria a seat halfway back where she could sit, then climbed onto the stage. The stage floor squeaked, the wings were dusty. Remnants of the last production still lingered: a painted backdrop of snowy mountain peaks, the remains of an archway, a table set with a chequered cloth and fake flowers in the back corner. Penny gazed out towards the seats. It was a small theatre, mostly used for pantomimes and low-budget theatrical productions. The venues on her concert tour would be easily five times as large. George had promised an extravagant show, with a two-level stage and huge banks of lights. Up until now, she had played mostly in pubs and small theatres, apart from a charity performance with ten other artists at the Royal Albert Hall. While part of her relished the chance to take her music to a larger audience, to spread her wings and own a huge stage, another part wanted to stay in bed with the covers over her head. George said this was normal, that most creative people were so divided. She wasn't sure whether she believed him.

The door to the foyer opened, letting in a shaft of white daylight. The two guitarists. She had only met them once before, in the record company offices the day George had hired them. She strained her memory for their names... Tony and Paul? She sat on the edge of the stage while they set up and checked their sound. The sound technician arrived... was his name Jeff? Other musicians came, she confirmed their names by listening to them talk to each other... everybody was there except George.

'Perhaps somebody should call him,' Paul suggested when ten o'clock came and went and still there was no sign of him.

'Does anybody have the new number?' Jeff asked. 'I used to know the old one, but he changed it last week.'

Much head-scratching and hum-hahing ensued. Nobody had George's new number committed to memory, and Penny had left at home the little book with addresses and phone numbers in it. The clock was ticking, and already Tony and Paul were talking about slipping out to the café next door for morning tea. Penny's nerves were prickling: she had prepared herself to work *now*, and pretty soon the drugs would wear off and the tiredness would seep into her bones again and everything would become too hard.

'Let's just rehearse,' she said, aware that her voice sounded thin and breathy. 'So he's late, it doesn't matter. We can still rehearse.'

This suggestion was greeted by more head-scratching, more idle chatter. Bryan, the drummer had already gone outside for a cigarette; they were ignoring her completely. Penny's irritation was made worse by knowing that Gloria, with her big adoring eyes, was watching the whole exchange. Finally, Penny walked up to her microphone and indicated to Jeff that he should turn up her volume.

'Come on, guys, please,' she boomed, and her voice echoed off every surface in the theatre.

A sudden quiet fell as they all turned to look at her. She felt young, vulnerable. They were all seasoned musos, in their thirties and beyond. Their eyes judged her: silly little upstart, trying to tell them what to do. Her heart thudded in her throat, but at least they were moving now, strapping on instruments, tuning up. She waited, her fingers still locked hard around the microphone. Anger towards George boiled up inside her. Why had he put her in this situation? Why couldn't he just be here on time?

Once the music started, Penny began to relax. They ran through the new single, she made no eye contact with the others. But in the third chorus, she noticed that Paul and Tony were playing something different from the recording.

She stopped the band.

'What are you playing?' she asked.

They exchanged glances, stifling amused expressions. 'We're just playing the song.'

'It sounds different.'

'No, it's not. That's how it goes. Right, Pat?'

The bass player averted his eyes and nodded, hiding his smile in his collar.

She damned herself for not knowing more about music, not knowing the names of the notes so she could accuse them specifically of playing a joke on her. She had learned music by ear, by feel.

'From the second verse,' she muttered, and the music started again. Once more, they played the wrong chord, all of them now, including the bass and the keyboards.

White-hot anger steamed up behind her eyes. She turned, microphone in hand and ordered them to stop, hating that she sounded petulant, babyish. They were laughing openly now, and her instinct was to flee, to find a corner to cry in until George came.

Precisely then, the door opened and George blustered in, apologies tumbling from his lips. 'Sorry, so sorry, I got held up. Something unexpected. I…' He paused midway down the aisle, taking in the scene in front of him. Penny versus the assembled musicians, hostility palpable in the air. 'Is everything all right?' he asked.

Penny jumped off the stage and ran down to him, fighting tears.

'What's wrong?' he asked, holding her at arm's-length, an expression of concern on his face.

'I…' She glanced back over her shoulder at the band. Tony was glaring at her openly, as if to say, *Don't say a word.*

'It's okay,' Penny said, forcing a smile. 'I was just worried about you. That's all.'

He smiled, clearly touched. 'Don't worry about me, just look after yourself. Come on, back on stage, please.'

Under George's guidance, the rehearsal continued. Penny resolutely faced the auditorium, refusing to look at any of the band members. She couldn't let them see how they had got to her. She couldn't let them think she was weak, or foolish.

She hadn't endured what she had endured to be taken for a fool.

The first weekend break, George steeled himself to give Penny the news he had received before the first rehearsal; the news that had made him late, causing her to worry about him. Her sweet neediness had impressed itself upon him distinctly that day, making it even harder to perform this task. He'd waited, until she had some time and space to breathe.

He arrived at her apartment block midmorning, stopping out front to assess it. Penny's flat, looking over the road to the square, was three storeys up: too high for anyone to climb. The security doors were solid wood, double-locked. The road was busy, probably seeing enough traffic at night to make any break-in attempt impossible. He was satisfied that she was safe here. He hadn't heard from the anonymous caller again, but occasionally the doubt would flash across his mind and he'd have to reassure himself that he was doing the right thing. The anxiety would make Penny's life a misery; he would stay quiet. Besides, after she heard what he had to say, she'd have enough on her mind.

He pressed the buzzer, and a moment later a voice floated down from above.

'George!'

He looked up. She was leaning out her window, waving madly, happy. Trepidation touched his heart.

'I'll come down,' she said, then disappeared inside. A few minutes later – the lift was very slow – she was unlocking the front door for him.

'What a nice surprise,' she said. 'I was just watching the telly. Bored.' She was immaculately made-up as always, with sweeps of blue glitter on both eyelids. Her hair, newly streaked with strands of auburn, fell over one eye and curled back in an expert flick.

He followed her inside. 'You complain about all the work I make you do, then you complain of boredom when I give you a few days off.'

'I think I need a hobby,' she said, leading him into the lift. 'What do you think? Knitting? Macrame?'

'Don't you have friends you can spend time with?'

She shook her head as the lift rattled to life and began to grind its way upwards. 'You're my only friend, George,' she said, and he couldn't tell if she was serious or not. 'So whatever business you're here on, you'll have to stay for a cup of tea.'

A short time later, they were sipping tea on her sofa, under the bright window. Her flat always smelled of hairspray and toast. She had redecorated it herself, with patterned wallpaper and thick shag carpet. It was a strangely impersonal space, free of books and knick-knacks, as though its occupant was wary, ready to run at any moment. A framed copy of her *Jackie* magazine cover hung above the television.

'So, why have you come to see me?' she said at last.

He put aside his teacup and turned to meet her gaze.

'Oh dear, now you're scaring me,' she said with a nervous laugh. 'Has something bad happened?'

'Penny, your mother has died.'

He watched her face as she fought for comprehension. He wasn't sure what her next question would be, but wasn't surprised when she asked, 'How on earth did you find out?'

George drew a deep breath, knowing he had to reveal a long deception to her. 'I'm sorry I haven't told you before, but I was in touch with your mother from time to time. When you first started working with me... I let her know you were all right.'

She hung her head so that her hair covered her face. He wondered if she was crying.

'I know that this was against your wishes, Penny. I know you wanted nothing to do with her –'

'I told you what she did to me.'

'– but she was your mother. I did what I thought was right. I gave her my address, in case she ever needed to contact you.'

'But she didn't, did she?' Penny looked up, tossing her hair back. She shrugged, a nonchalance that George suspected was feigned. 'So. How did she die?'

'I'm not certain. An illness. She died six weeks ago. The solicitor's letter was vague. But I had no idea that she was sick. I would have told you if I'd known, in case you wanted to see her.'

'What makes you think I'd've wanted to see her?' She rose and began to pace, worrying the edge of a fingernail with her teeth. 'Funny, isn't it, that she could have died six weeks ago and I didn't know? You'd think I'd've felt something.'

George fell silent a few moments, letting her pace. Then he drew an envelope out of his inside pocket. 'There's a letter for you.'

Penny stopped, a mixed expression of hope and alarm crossing her face. 'From her?'

'From the solicitor.'

She reached for it. 'I expect I've inherited something.'

'I expect so.'

She propped the letter up on top of the television, against the aerial.

'Penny,' he said slowly, 'are you sure you don't want to see any of them? Your family, I mean. Presumably you have cousins, aunts, uncles...'

She shook her head vehemently. 'No. There's nothing back there for me.'

'Back in Silkfield?'

'In the past. I've left it behind, I've a new life now. There is no Angie Smith anymore, you know that.'

George rose and gave her shoulder a squeeze. 'It's your decision. I'm sorry I didn't tell you I'd been in touch with her.'

She forced a smile. 'Very naughty, George. No other secrets, I hope?'

George felt a twinge of guilt, thinking about the phone calls. 'No, no other secrets.' He indicated the letter. 'I'll let you be. Call me if you need me.'

'I will.'

Living on the streets was not for Angie, and it had only taken her a week to realise this. Sheltering under a sagging cardboard box against miserable London rain, being abused by passers-by who thought she was a beggar (and sometimes more insulted by the passers-by who doled out money and righteous pity in equal measure), eating stale leftovers from the bins of a bakery on Compton Street. No, not for her. She cleaned herself up as best she could and went looking for a job. That's when she found the photographer.

His name was Alan and he worked part-time in a photographics shop on Camden High Street, selling cameras and sending prints away to be developed. But in his heart, he told her, he was an artist. And he wanted to photograph her. Her face, he said, was structured as though God Himself had carved it by hand. She could come over after work, he had a studio at his place. He'd pick her up from her home. Angie assessed him: late thirties, thin sandy hair combed hopefully over shiny pink scalp, new clothes, but unironed and with a gravy stain on the shirt cuff. A lonely single man with money but little judgment.

She turned down her eyes sadly. 'I've got no home, Alan. My mum kicked me out.'

Within minutes, his spare room was offered in exchange for her willingness to be photographed. She was off the streets.

Alan's flat was at Greenwich, and could not have been more different to Angie's mother's home. Instead of white surfaces and the smell of bleach, the flat was dimly lit and grimy. He had more record albums than she had ever seen in her life, stacked haphazardly and horizontally beside a stereo record player with huge speakers. He bragged that he had inherited money from his parents, both dead before their fortieth birthdays. The flat was his, he paid no rent. Artists shouldn't have to pay rent, he said as he showed her around. Angie had to admit that his photographs were good. They hung in not-quite-even lines along the walls of every room. Portraits in starkly lit black and white, close-ups of body parts at unusual angles, distant shots of naked white figures in empty rooms. There was something almost sinister about them, depersonalised.

Alan showed her into her room. 'There's not much here at the moment,' he said. 'I've been thinking about getting a lodger, but I like my own company too much. Too set in my ways.' He grinned, revealing two rows of uneven teeth.

'I won't trouble you,' she said. 'I'm just grateful to have a place to stay. And as soon as I get a job and can stand on my own two feet, I'll be out of your hair.'

'Well, we'll see...' He smoothed his thinning hair self-consciously.

She dropped her bag on the sagging metal bed, eyeing the half-peeled wallpaper, the bare dusty floorboards. Yes, it was different from her mother's house, and that suited her perfectly.

Over the coming months, Angie thought about sin a lot. She had rejected religion along with rejecting her mother, but growing up steeped in her mother's fire-and-brimstone ideas had worked its way under her skin. As Alan let down his guard, became loving with her, and confessed his innermost thoughts, the frisson of guilt became colder and more compact, until it sat like a stone in her stomach.

On one occasion they were out at the fruit shop together. He was making a show of feeding her grapes, she was letting him. A tall woman, with heavy-lidded eyes approached, laughing derisively.

'Robbing the cradle, then, Alan?' she said in a clipped accent. 'I suppose it's the only way you'll ever get a girl.'

Alan froze, said nothing. The woman turned and left. He waited until she was out of earshot before responding. 'Mind your own business, you fucking bitch,' he shouted, spittle flying from his lips. An elderly man choosing a cantaloupe turned to eye him with disdain. Alan kicked a wire rack of honey jars. They rattled ominously.

'Alan?' she asked.

He grabbed her hand and pulled her out of the shop, so violently that her skin burned. Finally, he stopped, slumping against a brick wall.

'Who was she?'

'I used to work with her. Uppity cow. Asked her out once. She said no, of course. Too good for me.' Then his scowl turned to sadness. He grasped her hands, softly this time. 'You're too good for me, too, Angie. I know that. I can't believe you're real, sometimes. And if you can like me... Well, you do like me, don't you, Angie?'

'Of course,' she said, reassuringly stroking his hair. 'Of course I do.'

'A lot? As much as I like you?'

'More.'

He smiled, placated for the moment. He was needy, she became adept at reassuring him. She felt certain that she would be punished somehow, not necessarily by God, whom she had long since decided did not exist. But at some distant point in her future a price would have to be paid for this deception.

She took a part-time job waitressing drinks at a nightclub at Piccadilly Circus, after lying extravagantly about her age. It made her a little money, but she didn't need much; Alan bought her everything. She spent her days listening to every album in his collection. Her mother had never allowed her to have records, so it was a whole new world to her eager ears. As she fell more deeply in love with music, Alan fell more deeply in love with her. Hardly a day went by when he didn't come home with a little gift of some sort: usually clothes, or make-up, or something that he would insist he wanted to photograph her in. She, desperate to survive, encouraged his growing feelings and pretended they were reciprocated, allowing him kisses and hugs at first, then finally agreeing to share a bed, if not their bodies, every night. Late at night, after making her way home from the club on the last bus, he liked her to rouse him and sing to him. He would gaze at her face as though memorising it for recall in less happy times. To save herself from his sexual advances though, she pled her virginity, her desire to wait a little longer. She promised him that, on her seventeenth birthday, he could possess her body as he already possessed her heart. But not before then.

As the promised day slowly approached, his demands on her as a photographer's model became more and more intimate. The clothes he brought home for her to pose in were soon ordered removed, as though he wanted to chart every inch of her body through the lens, to compensate for his inability to see it and touch it outside his studio. Angie went along with it. What choice did she have? She had a roof over her head, clothes and food, a warm place to sleep. She found she could dissociate her mind from her body while he took the pictures, play music in her head and disown her arms, breasts, legs

67

and all the places in between; just as Alan disconnected them from each other for his photographs. Perhaps this was the worst it would ever get, perhaps her day of reckoning, the punishment for her sins, could be bargained away by suffering through this humiliation.

The morning of her seventeenth birthday was bitterly cold. He always rose before her to get to work by ten. She feigned sleep until he left the house, shuffled to the kitchen to find a rose lying on the table for her with a note.

Tonight, my love.

Angie finally understood the expression 'cold feet'. The nerves in her soles and toes prickled with ice. She knew for certain that she couldn't go through with it. Her bag was packed within twenty minutes, and she was cracking open the door to his photographic studio. Behind the dropsheet was a metal filing cabinet, all of the photographs of her crammed untidily into the bottom drawer. She found the negatives in there, too, inside a plastic sleeve. One or two prints were still pinned to the line to dry. She gathered it all together, took it to the fireplace and sat cross-legged on the floor. Slowly, carefully, she fed the photos and all the negatives to the flames. Then she headed out into the cold, clear morning without a backwards glance.

It took Penny three hours and two tranquillisers to prepare herself for opening the letter. She was annoyed with herself for being so affected by the news of her mother's death, by the incursion of a long-abandoned part of her life. What if she'd inherited the house? Would she have to go back there and see it again? The idea filled her with dread. Would it still smell the same? Would the religious samplers still be hung on the walls above the gleaming dining table?

She needn't have worried. The solicitor's letter was to the point. Her mother's estate was to be liquidated and donated to her church. Penny had inherited nothing. Good: she didn't need the money and she certainly didn't need the bother. But the final clause of the letter captured her attention.

Please be advised that a safe-deposit box is held at Bayley Financial and Security Society, 14A Hay Street, Silkfield, Wiltshire, in the name of Angela Annette Smith. This box contains documents pertinent to you, including important information that your mother wished you to know upon your twenty-first birthday. Therefore, you should make arrangements to collect these documents on or soon after 21 January 1976.

Through the fog of the pills a vague unease stirred in her. What documents? What important information? It was too mysterious, it itched her stomach. What if the documents contained something awful? Vague, half-formed fears flashed through her mind: A horrible curse in the family, murder or madness? An illness passed down? The photographic secrets of her past with Alan somehow in her mother's hands? She didn't want to wait until next year, she wanted to know *now*.

Under other circumstances, she might have laughed. Her mother had been dead six weeks – prior to that, Penny hadn't seen her in four years – and somehow, the old woman had still found a way to make her daughter suffer.

SIX

*I*t was her father's hands that Ellie remembered most clearly from that awful night. Big, square hands, with long fingers and round nails. Calloused by time, but not physical labour. The hands of a musician, a teacher, a thinker. Their image was pressed into her memory forever. They lay still, but warm, by his side as she waited for the doctor to arrive. A thousand thoughts plagued her mind: snatches of memory, feelings of regret, hopes that she knew would be dashed but couldn't help hoping anyway. Doctor Freiburg arrived, Dieter dripping wet at his side, just as the rain deepened and started sheeting against the bathroom window. Between them, the men managed to clean off the worst of the blood and carry her father to his bed. Ellie waited outside the bedroom while the doctor examined him.

Ellie paced. Dieter tried to capture her in his arms but she shrugged him off.

'He'll be well, won't he?' she murmured. 'Perhaps it isn't so bad.'

'Ellie –'

'The doctor would have said by now if he thought it was terribly bad. He would have called an ambulance, had him taken to Bremen.' She turned pleading eyes to Dieter. 'Don't you think so?'

'I don't know. We have to wait and see. It's only been a few minutes.'

She looked towards the bedroom door, puzzled. 'Surely he's been there more than an hour?'

Finally, Dieter managed to seize her and press her against him. 'Be patient, Ellie. And have courage.'

She struggled away from him again, afraid that inertia would crush her. 'Courage? Why are you talking about courage?'

The door opened, she spun around. Doctor Freiburg looked grave.

'Oh,' she said, and it was all she could say. A tiny sound that echoed in the sparse room.

'I'll clean up the bathroom,' Dieter said, leaving Ellie alone with the doctor.

'He's still alive, isn't he?' she asked, terrified.

'Yes, yes,' the doctor said, 'but I'm afraid it won't be long.'

'Won't be long? Until...?'

'You have a choice to make, Ellie. Your father is dying. We could transfer him to the nearest hospital, pin our hopes on a blood transfusion...but I'm certain that either the shock of moving him or treating him will kill him. If we leave him be, he can be peaceful, at home with you.'

Ellie's mind whirled, unable to grasp what was happening. Her imagination filled with images: the panicked scramble of getting him in an ambulance, cold hospital sheets, glinting sharp instruments. She turned to watch her father through the bedroom door, in the dim pool of lamplight. He was very still, his breath rattled loudly. Hot tears coursed down her cheeks, and she palmed them away.

'How long?' she said, and it came out in a whisper.

'A matter of hours.'

'Leave him here with me.'

Doctor Freiburg touched her hand. 'You've made the right decision. Would you like me to stay?'

'I don't... I don't know. Will it be awful? When he...dies?'

'It's hard to say. It will probably be quiet. Peaceful.'

'Then go home. Tell Dieter to go too.' She glanced back into the bedroom. 'I want it to be just the two of us.'

'As you wish.'

Once the house was empty, Ellie took a bath to wash the blood off herself. Dieter had cleaned up the bathroom; the only sign of the evening's horrors was the blood-soaked towel that he had rolled up in the top of the laundry basket. She put on her nightgown, and climbed into the bed next to her father.

Ellie picked up one of his hands and pressed it against her cheek.

'I'm here, Papa,' she said, and began the long wait.

As the hours passed, his breathing became more ragged, but he didn't come to consciousness. She kept hoping he would, that he would pass on to her some deathbed wisdom or comfort. But there was nothing, and she knew she should be glad. No struggle, no moans. Just his laboured breathing, just his warm fingers in her own. Somewhere in the early hours, Ellie drifted off to sleep.

When she woke, weak sunlight was in the room. It took her a moment to remember where she was. A coldness had woken her...

Papa. She was in Papa's bed. She sat up startled, and checked on him. The realisation was immediate: there was no need to feel for a pulse or listen for breath. It was clear in his limp profile, his bluish lips, that his soul had escaped his body. She laid herself across him and wept, sobbing until her chest ached. Minutes and hours melted into one another, meaning failed. Papa was gone, and all the light had fled the world. Finally, her sobs slowed. Wiping her eyes with her palms, she glanced at the clock next to the bed. After nine o'clock – the time allotted for her entry interview – and dimly she grasped that along with her father, her dreams had died without her even being aware of it.

She didn't leave the house. She didn't go out to get Doctor Freiburg, because she knew that Dieter would come eventually. The clouds had cleared, leaving the village exposed under a cold clear sky. Ellie lit the fire and wandered the house like a ghost. She started in the kitchen, packing all the empty bottles away. He had no need for them now. Then in the living room, she folded up his glasses and the rug he wore over his knees on cool nights. The glasses were bent, ill-mended with tape and crossed fingers. She was careful not to break them; but she didn't know why.

Then to the piano. The stained ivory keys stared up at her. She imagined she could see grooves worn by Papa's fingers, and her own fingertips sought warmth in them. There was none. She folded up all the music spread about, and stacked it neatly in the piano stool. Old newspapers she packed up with the empty bottles, then put the lot outside the back door. Tidied, the house looked empty, and she wished she had left the clutter for a little longer.

A knock at the door. She glanced down at herself, still in her nightgown. Did it matter?

'Ellie? Ellie?' It was Dieter.

'Just a moment.' She quickly went to her room and threw on a dress. Still in her slippers, she opened the door.

He waited on the other side, face expectant. She shook her head, mouthed the word, 'Gone,' but was unable to make any sound come out. Dieter folded her in his arms, but there were no tears left. Just great soundless sobs that contorted her face and rattled her ribs.

Dieter was practical where Ellie simply couldn't be. He fetched Doctor Freiburg to organise Papa's body to be taken away, went to the village to see the undertaker, went to the dairy to let them know she couldn't come in, and promised Ellie he would phone the West German Opera and tell them what had happened. She was numb, but knew that there was one other thing he had to do.

'Papa had debts, Dieter,' she said. 'You have to find out how much. The butcher, the general store, and the pub. Can you see them for me? I'll have to pay them out.' The idea made her blood uneasy: she hoped it wouldn't be more than she could afford.

The day after somebody's death is such an empty, unmeasured time. Minutes bend and hours melt, and grief paralyses those left behind. So it was for Ellie, who sat in her father's favourite chair watching the procession of people in and out: doctors and ambulance officers and undertakers and well-wishers. She didn't move from her chair to eat or drink, her fingers worried the frayed edge of Papa's rug over and over, searching for something that had been lost forever. At last, the sky dimmed and blessed evening appeared to be on its way, and Dieter returned from the village for the last time. He wore a serious expression.

'It's bad, isn't it?' she said, as he stoked the fire and pulled up a chair next to her.

He fished a piece of paper out of his pocket. In his untidy writing she could see figures added up. 'I've been to see everybody whom your father might have owed money, and I've spoken to Herr Glauber about the price of the coffin and the rest of the funeral. He's very kindly cut his rates.' He hesitated before handing the paper over. 'Ellie, he had a lot of debts.'

'Let me see it,' she said, steeling herself. Still, reading the total at the bottom of the column of figures sent cold electricity to her heart. She pressed her fingers into her forehead. 'Oh, my.'

'You're not to worry. I'll talk to Papa and we'll help you if we can, we'll –'

'Then I'll owe *you* the money. No, I have to find it somehow.' She tried to smile. 'Is there any good news? Did you speak to the West German Opera?'

There was no return smile. 'You probably have other things on your mind... You don't want to think about all that now.'

'I wish I didn't. Then I wouldn't feel so guilty, like I'm only mourning him with nine-tenths of my heart.' She shook her head wearily. 'But I see in your eyes it's more bad news.'

'They had their interviews today, the six places have been offered and accepted. There's no room for one more. They were disappointed that you didn't come, but nothing can be done now.'

Ellie swallowed hard. The disappointment was like a rock in her throat. 'I see.' For the first time in her life, she didn't want to be accepting of her lot. She wanted to cry and shake her fists with anger and frustration; why should she be poor and facing a bleak future, when somebody else blithely scooped up her dropped opportunity?

'I'm so sorry, Ellie,' Dieter said, taking her hand.

She shook him off. 'Please don't pity me. If all I have is my dignity, then let me have it.'

'I don't pity you. I'm grieving with you,' he said, a little too sharply. Then his voice softened. 'What can I do to help you?'

'The funeral must be paid for, his debts must be cleared,' she said. 'And I have one thing left of value to sell. Tomorrow, you can take me to the village, to Frau Schinkler's secondhand shop. Perhaps she'll give me a good price for the piano.'

Dieter's eyes rounded. 'Ellie, no. You should keep the piano.'

'Why? Papa is dead, Dieter. The music must be buried with him.'

Ellie hid in the kitchen on the afternoon they took the piano away. They left a bundle of notes on the floor in its place, and she pocketed the money to take to the village. One by one, she paid Papa's debts, and the rest she used to pay Herr Glauber after the mercifully short funeral service. The long wandering hours between death and farewell were over, and Ellie knew she had to pick up the threads of her life. She knew that the poor didn't have the luxury of time for grieving.

The morning after the funeral, she turned up at the dairy dressed for work as usual. Her supervisor, Franny, gave her a puzzled look. 'Ellie? What are you doing here?'

Ellie almost laughed. She knew what was coming, with the bitter certainty that only those who have suffered through great hardship know.

'I'm back at work,' Ellie said.

'We filled your job.'

'But Dieter Neumann came, didn't he? He told you my father died?'

'I can give you some hours next week. Eight or ten. Will that do?'

Ellie scribbled down her new roster, calculating in her head how much she would be paid and immediately seeing it wouldn't be enough to cover the rent. Then she left, determined to go to the village and find some other work. In and out of shops and businesses she went, acquiring pity in handfuls but not paid work.

She ran into Frau Neumann, on the street outside the bakery. An icy wind was whistling through the bare branches above them, and Ellie tucked her hands into her pockets and stamped her feet. A bus roared past, sour fumes in its wake.

'Ellie, how are you?' Frau Neumann asked, removing a mitten and resting a soft hand on Ellie's wrist.

Something about the generosity and gentleness of the gesture broke through the stiff wall of Ellie's bitterness. She began to cry, to pour out the whole story, of how she had no money, no work, and would soon have nowhere to live unless somebody had a job for her. But what she couldn't put into words was how it felt to be standing on the edge of this abyss of uncertainty, with the ground crumbling away from her feet little by little. Frau Neumann pulled her close and smoothed her hair.

'Sh, sh,' she said. 'You aren't to worry. You will come to live with us. There's room for you, and you can earn your keep helping with the animals and helping me in the house.'

'I can't, I can't,' Ellie said. 'You offer too much. More than I can accept.'

'Oh, hush. What nonsense. You are dear to us, Ellie, all of us. Herr Neumann always regretted not having a daughter, and Dieter has been your friend since you were children. Let us take you in. One day soon, you will find your feet. I know it. I know *you*. You're made of stronger stuff than most of us, little sparrow.'

As Ellie allowed herself to be held, breathing in the warm floral scent of Frau Neumann's perfume, she realised she would have to accept the offer. Without it, there was no way of getting from this terrible moment to the future. She would be swallowed alive.

'Thank you, then, I will,' said Ellie. 'But only for a few months, and no more.'

'You can stay as long as you like.'

'No, it won't be forever. It can't be.' She disentangled herself from Frau Neumann's embrace and stood back, wiping her nose with the back of her mitten. 'I'm on my own now. I must learn to look after myself.'

The Neumanns were gentle with her, letting her find her own rhythm in the days. Knowing that she wanted no charity, Frau and Herr Neumann made sure she had plenty of tasks to fill the hours. She was up early to milk the cows, then back to cook breakfast and clean the kitchen after. Then she had some time to herself, to sit in her little room – she shared it with a fold-out bed, a thick rug, a deep freeze and a wall of storage shelving – and think, or read. Sometimes, if the snow wasn't too thick on the ground, she would walk for hours, until her nose was running and her cheeks were chafed from the cold. After lunch there were other little jobs, animals to be fed, sheets and socks to be mended, and she was grateful for the distraction. By the time the new shoots had matured on the linden trees that lined the road to the village, she had begun to feel settled. She had even begun to imagine that one day – in the distant future but certainly one day – she might not feel sad all the time.

Her relationship with the Neumanns was a loving one. But one aspect of her new situation troubled her: Dieter. The day he had kissed her at her mother's graveside – it seemed a million years ago – she had thought he might be falling in love with her. But since Papa's death, he had become brotherly. At first this had barely registered, she had so much on her mind. But gradually, it began to bother her. The problem was, they were never alone together. And it sometimes seemed to her that Dieter arranged it that way. If Frau and Herr Neumann were heading out to the village, Dieter would volunteer to go with them. If Frau Neumann asked him to hose out the cowshed at milking time, he would make an excuse and do it after Ellie had left for the morning. Ellie couldn't help but feel rejected, as though her sorrow had tainted her and he couldn't find her attractive anymore. Perhaps she would have believed this wholly, and never said a word about it, but sometimes she saw him stealing glances at her and she thought... maybe, maybe... that she saw the flicker of desire in his eyes. With so little left to lose, Ellie decided she might as well confront him. As hardened as her heart was to disappointment, a rejection by Dieter would be painful but bearable.

But first she had to get around his defences. She waited until Frau and Herr Neumann were planning a trip to the village. Dieter, as always, volunteered to accompany them.

'You might need a hand carrying the shopping,' he said, reaching for his coat on the hook near the door.

'Wait, Dieter,' Ellie said, leaping to her feet, hiding her shaking hands. 'I need your help. The hinge on the cowshed door is making a terrible noise.'

Dieter stopped, frozen. Ellie was still, too. Only Frau and Herr Neumann kept moving, winding scarves around their necks and pulling on coats, the two of them excluded from the subtle moment of drama that was playing itself out.

'I could look at it when I come back,' Dieter offered.

'I've already forgotten to tell you about it for two days. Another day and it could break. Then the door would hang out of the jamb and it would be much harder to fix.' Her pulse was thudding hard in her throat. 'Please?'

Herr Neumann frowned. 'Dieter, your mother and I will be fine with the shopping. Ellie's right. You should fix it before it gets worse.' He jammed his hat on his head firmly. 'We'll be back in a couple of hours.'

They left, closing the door firmly behind them.

Ellie, nervous now, offered Dieter a smile. He smiled back, warily. She sat down at the kitchen table.

'I'll get my tool kit and head out to the cowshed,' he said.

'There's nothing wrong with the cowshed.'

Puzzled, he sat down opposite her. 'Then why...?'

'I just wanted to talk to you, Dieter.' Her fingers traced anxious arabesques on the table, and she couldn't bring herself to meet his eyes.

'You can talk to me any time.'

'No, I can't.' She lifted her head. 'Not alone. You avoid me. Your parents are always around and I think you like it that way. It's as though you're afraid of me. Afraid of what I'm going to say to you.'

'Ellie...'

'I thought, once... I thought you might be falling in love with me, Dieter.' She hung her head again, her heart thundering and her face flushed.

A long silence followed her words, and she began to fear the worst. She wondered how long this moment could draw out. Was Dieter embarrassed? Angry? She heard him rise, scraping his chair back on the tiles. Was he just going to leave, run after his parents and continue avoiding her forever?

But then he was there, crouching in front of her, reaching for her hands. His eyes were dark and soulful, and looking into them was as calming as watching deep, still water.

He pressed her hands to his lips. Then he rested his head on her lap and his hands slid up to encircle her hips. A bolt of warm desire speared her. Her fingers went to his hair. It was growing too long now, and tangled over his collar in lazy curls.

'Ellie,' he mumbled against her skirt. 'You are so brave. I wasn't brave enough to speak to you.'

'Speak to me now. What's going on?'

He lifted his head. 'You were broken. Your father's death, the piano, the opera interview. I would have felt like I was preying on you, to force my feelings on you at such a time. So I made sure that we were never alone together, so that I'd never be tempted to.'

'Didn't you think that I might want you to? Need you to?'

He smiled ruefully. 'Ellie, you didn't see yourself from the outside. You had the weight of the ocean on you. But now, I can see...' He lifted his hand and brushed her hair behind her ear. 'I can see that weight is starting to lift.'

'Make me a promise, Dieter,' she said, her voice catching on its intensity. 'Promise that you will never hide your feelings from me again, no matter what the circumstances.'

'I promise.'

She caught his hand and kissed it fervently. He rose and drew her into his arms. She tilted her head and for an electric moment they were poised like that, gaze to gaze. She dropped her eyes to his mouth and then he was kissing her; deep, burning kisses that inflamed her skin and made her thighs weak with desire. He pressed her back against the wall and kissed her again, warm hands sliding around her ribs.

'Ellie, Ellie,' he murmured against her ears, her eyelashes, her cheeks, her mouth. His breath was hot, his hands were strong and firm. Ellie's spine ran with liquid electricity. She caught his kisses on her hungry lips, pressed her hips against his. His fingers were picking at the buttons on her blouse now, and she found her own hands wandering under his shirt, scalding her fingertips on his hot velvety skin.

'I've never done this before,' she said to him, close against his stubbly cheek, as he pushed her blouse off her shoulders and his hands closed over her breasts.

'I'll be so gentle,' he whispered.

A rattle at the front door had them jumping apart, guiltily. Ellie quickly buttoned her blouse back up.

Frau Neumann bustled in muttering, 'Your father forgot his wallet.' She searched around on the kitchen bench. 'Ah, here it is.'

She turned, seemed to notice them for the first time. 'Ellie? Are you all right? You look flushed.'

'I'm fine.'

Frau Neumann frowned. 'I hope you aren't coming down with something. Dieter, if you're going to fix the door of the cowshed, you'd best get on with it. There's more rain on the way.' Then she was gone, and Dieter and Ellie broke into relieved laughter.

Dieter pulled Ellie towards him again, but now his voice was serious. 'We must be careful. Mama and Papa are old-fashioned, stuck in the fifties. If they thought we were together, they'd think twice about letting you stay under the same roof as me. Mama worries terribly about other people's opinions.'

Ellie nodded, soberly. She hated to be reminded of how she was only ever one step away from penury, but he was right. 'It can be our secret,' she said.

He smiled at her, and the melting feeling started again. He took her hand and tugged it gently. 'Will you come with me, Ellie? To my bed? Will you let me love you?'

Ellie took a moment to savour the delicious feelings of promise. 'I will,' she breathed. 'I will.'

SEVEN

The record company party was already swinging when Penny arrived. One of the conference rooms of the Grand Chancellor Hotel at Islington had been decorated in a tropical island theme. Cardboard and crepe palm trees inclined towards each other on every wall, bright tropical-coloured streamers crisscrossed the ceiling, and a table in the middle of the room was heaped up with sand, while a tower of champagne glasses was prepared in the centre to become a waterfall. A small stage had been set up: Penny was to perform her new single. Instruments and equipment were at the ready. Alice, the normally buttoned-down receptionist at TRG Records, was dressed in a grass skirt and bikini top at the double wooden doors.

'Hello, darling!' she exclaimed, hanging a necklace of plastic frangipanis around Penny's neck where it sat on her silver-sequinned vest. 'You look beautiful.'

Penny smiled. She liked Alice, who was impatient with nonsense and generous with praise. 'You've certainly been hiding your light under a bushel. Or at least, under a business suit,' she said, indicating Alice's bare midriff.

Alice leaned close. 'Let's just say a bikini in autumn is a little chilly.'

'Come on,' George said gruffly.

'Try one of the tropical cocktails,' Alice said, hooking a second flower-necklace on George. 'Bar's that way.'

Penny, already buzzing from uppers, decided to stick to pineapple juice.

'How long before we go on?' she asked George.

'An hour and a half. I could only convince them to let you play one song. Somebody complained that you can't mingle and talk while there's a pop band playing live.'

The room was crowded and the air felt close. Paunchy men in safari suits, elegant women with their hair pulled back under scarves, pretty long-legged starlets and dancers, real pop stars and wannabes dressed alike in leather jackets and jeans. Everyone looked her over as she approached, trying to determine if she was important or not. Their eyes were greedy, hopeful. Most recognised her and produced broad smiles that were almost sincere. Some ignored her, not yet sure who she was. After her performance they would know, then they wouldn't dare to ignore her. Two weeks at number one already, and selling well enough for at least a third. The album was being mixed in a hurry to release early, in the hope of capitalising on the single's success. Penny Bright was a pop star, a big pop star now. She held her head high, brushing her hair out of her eyes, but staying close to George all the same.

The band arrived, and soon it was time to perform. On stage, the music pulsing through her, its insistent rhythm jumping in her blood, she found herself. Whoever she was – past, present or future – was possessed entirely by Penny Bright, pop star, gleaming in silver and glitter. She was dimly aware of the audience, the smiling faces, the jealous glances, the lustful expressions. Then the song finished. The audience cheered and hooted their appreciation, and George was there holding out a hand to help her down. She reluctantly returned to her job of chatting and charming. Music was sacred, but the vast creaking machinery that fed off it was profane.

She met a million people afterwards, and barely remembered two of their names. They all wanted a piece of her, asking her questions they thought were original or interesting, but which she had heard a dozen times before. Some were genuine – sales reps and typists who had loved her performance and were suitably awe-struck – while others wore the hungry expression of envy. She was pleasant to them all the same, signing autographs and making small talk.

'Would you like me to get you a drink?' George asked, in a break between people.

Penny realised just how dry her throat felt. 'Yes,' she said. 'Yes, I'll have one of those cocktails after all.'

George disappeared towards the drinks table, leaving Penny alone, gazing around the room. A tall man in a crisp white shirt appeared at her elbow.

'Hello,' he said.

She turned to him. 'Hi.'

'So you decided to change to pop music? I must say you've done well for yourself.' He wore neat sideburns, spoke in a clipped accent, and his blue eyes were very clear.

Not completely sure of his meaning, she replied slowly, 'Yes, I'm very pleased.'

'What made you change?'

Penny's heart rate picked up a few beats. Was this somebody from her past, somebody she had failed to recognise who knew things about her? 'I'm… I'm sorry, I don't quite understand. Change from what?'

'Last time I saw you…' He laughed, a little self-consciously. 'You didn't sing like that.'

George was back then, no drinks. He must have seen her discomfort and returned. 'Penny, this is Ivan Hamblyn from our classical music division.'

'We've met,' Ivan said. 'Earlier this year.'

Penny was shaking her head, now, relieved. 'No, no we haven't met before. I think you have me mixed up with somebody else.'

He assessed her carefully with his clear gaze. 'I'm very sorry,' he said. 'I just assumed… now I look closely I can see I have mistaken you for somebody else. A girl I heard sing back in March. Not here in London.' He smiled sheepishly. 'Forgive me, the resemblance led me astray.'

Penny wasn't sure what to say, so she looked past Ivan Hamblyn and over towards the champagne waterfall, which was now flowing. A group of squealing women were gathered around it.

'It was a pleasure to meet you in any case,' he said with a brilliant smile and moved off.

George squeezed her hand. 'I'll get you that drink.'

'I'll come with you.'

'No, you stay here. I won't be a moment.'

Again, she was abandoned. One by one, it seemed every person in the room came up to introduce themselves. It was as though the centre of gravity at the party had shifted, and Penny was now the point around which they had gathered. She smiled, she charmed, she put up with the flirtations of businessmen more than twice her age, always with one eye on George. He had stopped and was deep in conversation with Ivan Hamblyn. He hadn't even been to the drinks table yet. What was taking him so long?

The evening wore on, and Penny began to run out of steam. George offered to take her home, but she could see he was enjoying himself and volunteered to get into a taxi. David Preston, an unctuous sales rep with small white hands, was in conversation with them at the time, and he offered to drive her. He lived not far from her apartment complex, and he was getting ready to leave. She had to wait another twenty minutes while he said his goodbyes, but finally she was on her way. The big double doors slammed shut behind them, muffling the sounds of the party.

'You were the star of the evening,' he said to her as they waited for the lift.

She produced her charming smile one more time, but the muscles in her face were tiring. 'Thank you.'

The lift doors slid open and they moved in. Once alone in the small, quiet space, he said, 'You know there's a wager on in the office. Perhaps you can clear it up for me. Are you and George…?' He winked at her.

It took a moment for his meaning to sink in. She recoiled. 'Why would anybody think such a thing?'

He loosened his wide, striped tie, oblivious to the fact that he'd offended her. 'Darlin', you two are joined at the hip. You're pretty, he's powerful…' He shrugged, finished with the topic.

The lift opened again and she followed him across the foyer and out into the cool street. She was too preoccupied to realise she wasn't wearing a jacket. Penny turned David's comment over in her mind. Were she and George really such a cliché? Pretty young thing and powerful – good-looking, too, she admitted – manager. Such loose talk was dangerous; what would Aila think? Did George know people were talking about them?

'I'm just parked around the back,' David said, jingling his car keys in his pocket.

'Mm-hm,' Penny said, distracted by these thoughts. She felt insulted, but too much time had elapsed between the comment and the feeling to say anything. George was always telling her she had to grow a thicker skin. They passed an elderly couple rugged up for an evening walk. The man tipped his hat, but she barely noticed.

They moved out of the bright lights of the street and down a damp alleyway that led to the car park. Penny heard footsteps behind them, but her mind was elsewhere. The elderly couple returning, or a hotel guest, perhaps. The sudden rush upon them was startling, but incomprehensible. Why was there a man in a black shirt knocking her down? As she struggled to stand, she glimpsed David Preston lying on the ground clutching his chest and groaning. A glistening black stain was spreading across his pale shirt. What the hell was happening? She opened her mouth to scream, only to have a rough piece of material shoved in it. The man's violence was shocking, impossible to believe. He yanked her head back and held something cold and metallic to her throat as he pulled her to her feet. Penny's heart thundered, and she thought she might die from fright. Surely somebody would come, somebody would rescue her.

'Stay quiet or I'll cut your throat,' the man said, half-marching her, half-dragging her to a white van.

She struggled, the point of the blade was pressed into the soft flesh of her neck.

'Just do what I say, Angie,' he muttered, close to her ear.

Angie?

Penny froze, a scream trapped in her mind and echoing like a nightmare, as the man bundled her into the back of the van.

Angie Smith lost her virginity on her seventeenth birthday after all.

From Alan's flat, she went straight to work to see her boss. The Windmill was a revue bar, featuring a floor show with scantily dressed women in cowboy hats and holsters, or feathery fans that they danced with cleverly to hide their bare breasts. Angie waitressed drinks, but only eight hours a week. She'd need more than that to get her by now she didn't have a place to live.

The bar was closed, the cleaner was mopping the floor, but her boss was in his back office shuffling paperwork. He told her he couldn't help her with more hours, but he had a friend who ran a bar in Soho who was looking for staff. They didn't open until seven. He scribbled down the name and gave it to her. *Sebastian Marten.*

Angie filled the day dropping into bakeries and dress shops, asking for work. Nothing was forthcoming. At seven p.m., she found herself approaching the Heat Club. It was situated above a Chinese restaurant in the southern corner of grimy, bohemian Soho. The smell of frying fat and spices was strong as she clattered up the inside staircase, reminding her that all she'd eaten that day was a cream bun at Leicester Square. The painted green walls were peeling, and smoky beery smells wafted down the stairs towards her. Inside, the club was long, dark and narrow, with pool tables at the back, a stage at the front, and the circular bar right in the middle. A band was tuning up, but only half-a-dozen patrons milled about, buying drinks and finding places to sit. Angie approached the bar.

'I'm looking for Sebastian Marten,' she said to a young, blonde woman who was emptying glasses from a dishwasher.

The woman indicated a painted blue door at the far end of the room with the jab of a thumb. 'Just knock. He's in there.'

Angie did as she was told, trying not to hope too hard that Sebastian could help her. She could get by for one or two nights camping at a bus shelter, but she really needed to get some money together for a place to stay.

She knocked, the door opened. A man stood there, tall, lithe. He was much older than her, perhaps in his late thirties, with close-cropped fair hair and scythe-like cheekbones. His skin was pockmarked, his eyes pale and icy.

'Sebastian?' she asked.

'Yes,' he said, in an imperious tone that intimidated her.

'I'm Angie Smith,' she managed. 'I'm looking for a job.'

He looked her up and down, and a smile tugged the corners of his mouth. The relaxed expression transformed his face. Now he looked boyish, almost naughty. Angela couldn't help but smile in return. He stepped back and invited her into his office.

'Sit down,' he said, moving to his side of an immaculately tidy desk. 'You have come at a good time. I am in need of staff.'

She detected an accent, Dutch or Scandinavian, but didn't ask. She dropped her bag on the floor beside her feet. 'I've a little experience,' she said, 'and I'm willing to work very hard. John Roberts over at the Windmill suggested that you –'

'You have been working for John? He is an old friend.' He stood and came to crouch next to her. 'Show me your hands.'

Angie was startled by his closeness. 'I...'

He clicked his fingers impatiently, the imperious tone returning. 'Your hands,' he said, holding out his own to receive them.

Angie offered him her hands, palms down. He grasped them firmly, turned them palms up and scrutinised them.

'Are you trying to tell my future?' she said with a nervous laugh.

The joke failed. He fixed her in his pale eyes, and his disapproval made her shrink inside herself. Then he returned his gaze to her hands. He dropped the left one, and closed his fingers over her right. 'They are warm, which tells me you have a cold heart. Is that true, Angie?'

'I...don't think so.'

He spread out her palm again and, with one hot fingertip, traced the length of her middle finger. Slowly. Angie caught her breath, too inflamed with sudden desire to be puzzled by his behaviour. His fingers left her skin at her wrist, and she tingled in the absence of his touch.

'You say you will work hard,' he said, 'but these are not the hands of a hard worker.'

Jolted back to reality, desperate for a job, she spoke too quickly. 'I can work very hard, I promise you. I won't let you down, I'll do whatever it takes.'

Sebastian nodded slowly. 'You know, I believe you. I'm sure you'll fit in well here.' He stood and began riffling in a drawer for papers. 'Can you start tonight?'

Angie was confused, but relieved. 'Yes, I can.'

He pushed the papers and a pen across to her. 'Fill these out. I'll be back in a few minutes.'

She watched him go. His movements were graceful, almost sinuous. He closed the door behind him and she turned to the paperwork. She shook her head to clear it. Filled in her name and fake age, but hesitated over her address. What was she to do? Tell the truth and let him know she was desperate? She heard the music start, the thumping of a bass, the clatter of drums. She put down the pen, chewing her lip. Not her mother's address, not Alan's...

The door opened again, and Sebastian returned with a plate of food and a glass of lemonade. He dropped them at her elbow.

'What's this?' she asked.

He indicated her bulging bag. 'Is that everything you own?'

'I...yes.'

'I thought so. Are you running from somebody? Should I be worried?'

She shook her head.

He glanced at the unfilled form. 'There is a room upstairs. You will have to share it with a few cartons and some furniture that needs repair. But there is a bed and it is warm. I'll deduct the rent from your wages.'

He sat on the desk in front of her, and she became acutely aware of his proximity, his woody fragrance, the heat of his body. He fixed her in his gaze and electricity snapped through her senses. She had a sudden conviction that he was going to kiss her, but he didn't. Instead, he smiled that naughty-boy smile again, and told her that her shift started as soon as she'd eaten. Eager to please, she wolfed the food down like the starving young woman she was.

Angie enjoyed the work. She loved listening to the band, the bar was busy, the other staff were friendly. But she found she couldn't take her eyes off Sebastian. Every time he walked past, her gaze was drawn to him. If he was behind the bar with her, she found herself becoming too aware of her body, so that she felt clumsy and vulnerable. It puzzled her. He wasn't good-looking; in fact, he was almost ugly. But his cat-like grace and his arrogant self-possession attracted her like a magnet.

And he knew. Of course.

After her shift, he led her upstairs and into a tiny room. Smoke from the bar had risen through the floorboards and grown stale in the curtains and rugs. Despite the cold, Sebastian opened the window a crack to let fresh winter air in. Angie dropped her bag and looked around. Stacked against one corner were three broken chairs and a dozen unopened cartons of wine. There was a sink, an old bedstead with a yellow bedspread, and a bench with a cooking hob.

'Will this do?' he said, leaning languidly in the threshold as she looked around.

'Yes.' She could barely meet his eyes, she was so intimidated by his presence.

'Goodnight then.'

He made to leave, but she called out, 'Wait.'

He turned, eyed her coolly.

'Thank you,' she said, finally meeting his gaze. 'I'm very grateful.'

His eyes locked with hers, and she felt a warm uprush of desire. The desire must have been written in her eyes, her lips, her stance. He made a sighing noise: the kind of patronising expression of half-exasperation parents might make, right before they give in to the

90

whims of an indulged child. He pulled the door closed behind him and moved towards her.

Angie was struck dumb. Her experience of men was limited. A kiss with Jamie Green behind the school shed, her sordid experience with the lorry driver, Alan's fumbling caresses. Sebastian stood in front of her, carefully unbuttoned her shirt and pushed it off her. With strong fingers, he caressed her arms – shoulders to wrists – bringing her skin out in goosebumps. Then he grasped her waist firmly, his thumbs pressing into the soft flesh around her ribs. Her senses flared with heat.

'Do you want this?' he said. 'Are you sure?'

She almost couldn't make her mouth work. Her skin prickled. 'Yes,' she said. 'Oh, yes.'

He leaned forward to kiss her. His tongue tasted like rum and cigarettes. She dissolved into his embrace.

From that moment on, she was his.

Penny's assailant forced her onto the floor of the van. The carpet was gritty and smelled like oil and old food scraps. He tied her hands tightly, and she grunted into the gag. Then the door slammed and the van was moving. She struggled vainly. The gag was working loose so she spat it out and screamed, but could hear too clearly that her screams were confined to the van. She tried to sit up, but her arms were tied behind her at such an uncomfortable angle that to move hurt. She craned her neck, could see only one person in the van. His face was obscured by the dark.

Penny's terror felt surreal; her blood grew spikes. 'Who are you?' she shouted at him. 'What do you want?'

'You know who I am,' he said. 'And if you know who I am, you can certainly guess what I want.'

Penny dropped her head to the floor. Now the voice was familiar, now she knew which piece of the past had caught up with her.

'No,' she said, heart thundering in her throat. 'Oh, God, no.'

∞

Angie's relationship with Sebastian was never a relationship of equal loving partners. Right from the start, they were owner and possession. She thought she loved him, so she never questioned this. Every night after work, he took her upstairs and used her body however he pleased. Then he went home to his luxury flat in Islington, and left her in the grimy digs for which he was charging her exorbitant rent. He never flattered her, nor told her he loved her, nor spoke any words of tenderness to her. On the contrary, soon after they became involved he started dropping snide little comments. Her eyes were too small to go without mascara. Her breasts were the wrong shape. Her thighs were too heavy. She wore her hair all wrong. Angie tried harder and harder to please him, and one little scrap of praise from him, no matter how oblique – 'That colour suits you,' or, 'My business associate Walter thinks you are very pretty,' – would send her spirits soaring.

Any indulgence on his behalf she would interpret as a sign of his love for her, brewing deep inside him but unable to be expressed. When she confessed to him that she loved music and wanted to sing, he showed his heartfelt encouragement by allowing her to sing unpaid with the band two nights a week. When he loaned her out to Walter as an escort to an important business function, she knew it was because he was proud of her and wanted to show her off. And when he occasionally hid a stash of money or drugs in her bedroom and told her not to give it to anybody, no matter what they threatened her with, she read this as a sign of his faith in her. In fact, she almost hoped somebody would turn up and ask for it, threaten her so that she had to stand firm, prove her loyalty to him. If he ever seemed displeased with her, she tried not to blame him. He was busy, he had a lot on his mind; sometimes she forgot that and demanded too much of him.

One night, when summer's promise had kissed the air outside the window of her room and Sebastian's naked, exhausted body was twined next to hers in the little bed, she asked him when she would get to see where he lived.

'It's too sad to say goodbye to you every night,' she said, kissing his warm shoulder. 'I'd love to wake up next to you in the morning.'

He didn't answer, and for a few minutes she thought he'd fallen asleep. Then he said, 'This is where you belong. You do not belong in my home.'

Angie sat up, her long hair falling over her breasts. 'Couldn't I, though? One day?'

He flung back the covers, stood up and reached for his clothes.

The familiar fear. 'Sebastian? Are you angry with me?'

'You want too much. Look at what I have already given you. A job, a place to sleep, a chance to follow your dreams of being a singer.'

'I'm sorry,' she said, not entirely certain why she was apologising. 'I'm sorry, Sebastian. Don't go yet.'

He sat down again and sighed. 'Angie, I have a lot on my mind. I do not mean to be cruel to you.' He took her hand and pressed it to his lips.

This was the closest she had ever had to an apology. It took her by surprise and she didn't know what to say.

'I have problems,' he said. 'Big problems.'

'Tell me, maybe I can help,' she replied.

He smiled ruefully. 'You can help, but it's too much to ask.'

'Nothing's too much to ask,' she said. Foolishly. Meaning it.

He spoke plainly, without hesitating. 'Walter has enjoyed his dates with you. He would like to know you better.'

Angie was confused. 'What do you mean?'

'He's a very close business associate and I... I have some debts to him. Debts that are very hard for me to discharge. I might lose the club. You would have no place to sleep or sing. But he has made me an offer. He will cancel those debts. All you have to do is let him share your bed.'

A speechless instant followed, then he said, 'Just once.'

Of course she did it. And not just once.

Over the coming months, she slept with Walter three times, with a friend of Sebastian's visiting from the Netherlands, and with another man whose name she never asked. On each occasion, she learned to hate herself a little more, so the next time it was a little easier. On each occasion, Sebastian claimed another terrible financial debt hanging over him, but Angie wasn't a fool. She knew he was probably receiving money for her services. But by the time it had happened on half-a-dozen occasions, she cared very little. For a week or so afterwards, he would be very pleased with her, come and see her sing, tell her that one day he would make her a star. His kindness was almost enough.

Almost.

It may have continued for years. After all, she had endured her mother's treatment for sixteen. But the catalyst was waiting downstairs one evening when Angie arrived for work. A young man, roughly the same age as Angie, was behind the bar, barking orders. He was tall, meaty, with tattoos covering both arms, and eyes like cold pebbles. Sebastian introduced him.

'Angie, this is my son. Benedict.'

Angie was at first so taken aback that this large, doughy man could be the offspring of lithe, graceful Sebastian, that she didn't think to ask if this meant Sebastian also had a wife somewhere, as yet unmentioned. But there was no wife. Benedict was the product of a failed union in Sebastian's youth. Now Sebastian was trying to make up for the lost years, teaching Benedict the ropes of the business so he could take over one day. Benedict was off to a good start showing the employees who was boss: roaring at Angie when she dropped a glass, threatening to fire another waitress over a mixed-up order. His cruelty was made more acute by the pleasure he took in deploying it. Angie felt she had never met such a thoroughly unpleasant person in her life, and was depressed that Sebastian did nothing to intervene.

Later that night, up in her room, the familiar knock on the door came. She opened it, the smile dying on her lips. It was Sebastian. With Benedict.

'You know what to do,' Sebastian said to her.

Benedict smiled. Angie thought of his big meaty hands, his violent temper, his bullying and shouting. Her spine stiffened. 'No.'

Sebastian frowned. 'No?'

Angie's heart thudded hard under her ribs. 'No,' she repeated, more firmly.

Benedict turned to him. 'Papa? Isn't she your little whore?'

'If the girl says no, Benedict, we have to listen to her,' Sebastian said with a shrug of feigned indifference.

The girl. Somehow, she had lost her name. She almost relented, but couldn't bear the thought of Benedict touching her. At least with the others Sebastian had given her reasons, spurious though they might have been. But she wasn't a whore; at least, she didn't think she was…

'I'm… I'm sorry, Sebastian. It's just…'

'Goodbye,' Sebastian said, yanking Benedict out of the threshold and closing the door behind him.

From then on, Sebastian no longer came to her room. He avoided her at work, refused to use her name or treat her any differently from the other waitresses. Benedict's reign of terror continued, his hair-trigger temper became a regular feature of her evenings, and Angie slowly came to understand that Benedict was not just an ordinary nasty individual: there was something wrong with him, deep down. Some switch that malfunctioned, some wires that were misaligned. Angie's misery was complete. She died inside, sick for love. When Sebastian finally came to her, three weeks later, with a desperate gleam in his eyes, she almost cried for joy.

'Sebastian, I'm so sorry. I didn't mean to upset you, I –'

'Hush,' he said tersely. 'There isn't much time.' He held a black briefcase in his right hand. 'Put this under your bed.'

Angie took the briefcase, puzzled.

'Quick now,' he said, checking over his shoulder. 'I have to get going. It won't do for me to be here if they come.'

'Who?'

He mustered a smile for her, a caress for her cheek. 'Just keep it under your bed, and whatever happens, don't tell anybody you've got it.'

Angie nodded, pleased to be back in his favour. But the threads of her devotion had been frayed in the last few weeks, and in her heart she doubted him. She doubted him terribly.

Then he was gone. She slid the briefcase under her bed, covering it carefully with folded towels. Downstairs, the club grew quiet. She slipped into bed and dozed off into a troubled sleep.

In the deep of night, she was woken by the sound of breaking glass. She jerked upright, her heart hammering. She listened. Men's voices shouting, furniture being tipped over. They were trashing the club. Whoever *they* were. And it wouldn't be long before they were up here, looking for the briefcase.

As though waking from a long dream, clarity suddenly pressed upon Angie. She jumped from her bed and started slinging items into her bag. Clothes, make-up, a packet of biscuits. Already footsteps were thundering up the stairs. She pulled on a pair of jeans, a warm top, scraped back her hair. The door banged open, its lock cracking and flying to the floor. The light from the hallway silhouetted two men in black pullovers and pants.

'It's under the bed,' she said. 'Just don't hurt me.'

They let her pass. She ran for her life.

The van came to a halt. Penny was paralysed with fear, wondering what was going to happen next. Would he kill her straightaway? Or would he amuse himself with her first? The van door slid open, and she could see that she was inside a brick garage. Wooden shelves on metal brackets lined the walls, stacked with cartons, tools, spare car parts. He reached in and turned on the interior light of the van, and she saw him for the first time in three years. He'd hardly changed.

'Hello, Angie,' he said.

She gathered her courage, determined not to let him see how afraid she was. 'Hello, Benedict,' she spat.

EIGHT

Six months after Ellie's father had died, Herr Neumann brought home an old record player he found cheaply in the village. The Neumanns were wealthy on paper, they owned the farm and all the animals. But they didn't have a lot of spare cash for luxuries, so a new record player was beyond them. Their television, another cheap cast-off, only worked on windy days; and usually they spent the evening reading books, or playing cards for matchsticks.

This new piece of furniture took up four feet of space behind the couch. It had a radio tuner with a huge tuning knob, an empty stalk where the volume knob used to be, and one big speaker built into the cabinet at either end. The turntable didn't turn, and the right front leg was wobbly.

'I don't understand why you bought it,' Frau Neumann said with a frown. She and Ellie sat with a basket of mending between them on the opposite side of the room.

Dieter crouched behind the couch, fiddling with the tuner. Static burst from the left speaker.

'Because it was so cheap. We'd never get a record player for that price.'

'But if you can't use it –'

'Dieter and I are going to fix it.'

Frau Neumann rolled her eyes at Ellie, who stifled a giggle. Herr Neumann had only a month ago pulled apart the deep freeze to fix it. It had lain in pieces on the floor of Ellie's room until Frau Neumann had lost her temper and organised a repairman to come while Herr Neumann was away.

Suddenly, from the static, a man's voice jumped out. A radio announcer talking about the weather.

Herr Neumann gave Frau Neumann a triumphant look.

'If you get the record player working; that would be a surprise,' she hurrumphed.

'Do you even have any records?' Ellie said, trying to keep the amused smirk off her face.

Dieter nodded. 'Papa bought a box of them for two marks. They're still in the car.'

The announcer finished and music came on, English pop music. Herr Neumann instructed Dieter to find another station, but in trying to tune it he lost the signal altogether. More static.

For the next two weeks, the record player became the focus of regular good-natured family arguments, and the occasional ill-natured family argument. Dieter, who had learned a little about electronics during his National Service, pulled the device apart and put it back together piece by piece. Ellie loved to watch him, his smooth hands were so dexterous, and a little muscle in his jaw tensed with concentration, begging her fingers to touch it. She was careful, though, not to arouse the Neumanns' suspicions about her and their son. Ellie and Dieter spent many hours sitting next to each other – he working on the record player, she on the polishing or sewing – without ever exchanging a glance. The sun spent longer and longer in the sky, and still the record player was in pieces on the floor. Frau Neumann was at her wit's end, threatening on a daily basis to sweep up the collection of screws and rolled-up wires, and throw them in the rubbish. She never did.

Ellie was in the pig shed one fine October morning, when she noticed a shadow at the door. She turned. It was Dieter, outlined in yellow sunshine. She smiled.

'Have you come to help?' she asked, turning back to the bucket of scraps.

'I have a surprise.'

'For me?'

'Yes.'

Ellie put her bucket down and wiped her hands on her apron, puzzled. 'What is it?'

'If I told you, it wouldn't be a surprise.' He took her hand. 'Come on. Mama and Papa are out.'

A little thrill licked through her. What did he have in mind? She untied her apron and left it on a post, allowing herself to be led inside.

He left her standing in the middle of the living room, and went to the record player.

'Don't tell me it's fixed at last?' she asked, incredulous.

'Close your eyes and listen.'

She did as she was told. A hiss started out of one of the speakers, and then Dieter was there, his arms encircling her waist. Music began; slow, rich violins. Ellie recognised the song straightaway, and her body stiffened.

A voice joined in, the sublime soprano of Maria Callas. Ellie would have known her anywhere. It was Puccini's *O mio babbino caro*. Dieter wasn't to know, he had no knowledge of Italian, or of famous opera arias. To him it was just a song, a singer, a record that he had dug out thinking it would make her happy. But it had not made her happy, it had brought only the old sadness.

'Ellie?' Dieter asked, sensing the stiffness in her body.

'Oh, Dieter, it's not your fault...' she said, wiping away tears.

'What's wrong?'

Ellie hurried to the record player and turned it off. A burst of static filled its place, then died away to nothing.

Dieter looked embarrassed. 'I thought you'd like it. It's opera and...'

How was she to explain to him? That opera was poison to her ears now, that it only reminded her of how much she had lost? It was as though he'd opened up a window to another world that she was in love with, but absolutely excluded from. Her fascination for it could only ever be mingled with painful longing, with memories of loss and sorrow.

'I don't like it, I'm sorry. I can't listen to it anymore,' she said, all the while feeling guilty and ungrateful. 'Not after everything that's happened.'

Dieter took her hand and led her to the couch, sitting down next to her. 'But it was everything to you. And I assumed that eventually you would come back to it, and you would sing again.'

'Sing? Where?'

'At weddings, maybe. Like you used to when you were younger.'

'Weddings? You think all my voice is good for is weddings?'

Dieter was taken aback. 'Or competitions. You could even audition again. We could make phone calls, find out about –'

'Stop, Dieter. Stop. I haven't sung in months. My teacher is gone. I have no music to practise with. Those dreams...the stage...they aren't for me.'

'Why not?'

She wanted to scream, 'Because I am poor; because I am alone.' But she didn't. Instead she stood and shook him off, hating herself for hurting him but unable to do anything else.

'Because I want to forget it,' she said. 'Can you not understand that? I don't want to hear that music again.'

Before he could call her back, she had hurried outside, away from the music that both tempted her and tortured her.

Four days late.

Ellie counted the days in her little paper diary again, came up with the same figure. Her period was four days late, and a primal terror gripped her heart. She and Dieter had been careful; she couldn't be pregnant. Once more, she flicked through the pages, counting carefully. Once more, four extra days accrued.

A soft knock, and Frau Neumann was pushing the door open. Ellie shoved her diary under her pillow, feeling hot-faced and guilty.

'Ellie, could you come and help me with the laundry?'

'Of course,' Ellie said, springing to her feet, forcing a smile.

Ellie helped Frau Neumann manage the wet laundry from the tubs to the mangler, then took the clothes out to hang. Long laundry lines hung over the yellow grass in the autumn sunshine. Wildflowers were blooming all over the farm, and insects buzzed around low to the ground, the sunlight glinting off their wings. It was a beautiful day, but Ellie's mind was elsewhere. She needed to speak to Dieter, only they had so little time alone. Another week could pass before she had a chance to tell him of the weight on her mind, and by then she felt she would go mad with anxiety.

Later that day, she saw her chance. Frau and Herr Neumann were set up with their creaking adding machine on the kitchen table, and Dieter was down in the vegetable garden pulling weeds. Ellie excused herself and went to find him.

The vegetable garden was at the side of the property, obscured from the house's view when the stable door was open. Ellie carefully opened the stable door and ducked around it. Dieter looked up.

'Mice have been into the pumpkins again,' he said ruefully. Then he saw her expression and rose to his feet. 'Ellie? What's the matter?'

'I think I'm pregnant.'

Dieter's face transformed. His hazel eyes crinkled at the corners, and a grin formed. 'Really?'

Ellie was baffled by this reaction. 'How can you be pleased about it?'

'Is it not even a little exciting to you, Ellie?'

'No. I'm not excited, I'm horrified.'

Dieter hid his smile, pulling her into his arms. 'How certain are you?'

'Almost certain. I'm four days late, and I'm never late.'

He stood back to look at her. The smile broke through again. 'Do you not see? We may have created a life. Is there anything more miraculous and wonderful than that?'

'But we're so young. We're not married, we have no place to go. When your parents find out they'll throw me out...'

He was shaking his head. His index finger reached out to calm her lips. 'I'm twenty-four, you're twenty. We're adults, Ellie. We can get married, Mama and Papa would get used to the idea. They may be offended that we've been sneaking around behind their backs, but they love you. And they'd love their first grandchild.' His hands moved to her waist, caressing her stomach gently. 'We'd love him too, Ellie.'

An autumn breeze moved over the fields, sending the grass waving and causing a rush of gentle sound in the trees. Ellie's eyes were drawn into the distance, the wide flat fields, the blue of the hills rolling away behind them. She tried to let Dieter's words calm her.

'I didn't think my life would be like this,' she whispered.

At first she thought he hadn't heard her; he was silent a few moments. But then he said, 'The worst thing you can do is imagine life a certain way. Things never go to plan. You'll always be disappointed.' He kissed her cheek.

She leaned into him, tears pricking her eyes. Perhaps Dieter was right. Perhaps that was her problem. Papa had raised her with one function: to sing. Now that was gone, she felt purposeless, adrift, as though she had lost some thread of herself that was vital. But what was she to do with her life now if not to be with Dieter, raise a family, tend the farm?

Could she, though? Would she ever stop gazing towards that distant blue horizon, wondering about what might have been?

'I'd better go inside,' she said, pulling away.

He grasped her hand, squeezing it tightly. 'You'd better go to the village and see Doctor Freiburg.'

She nodded, tight-lipped.

'Make an appointment for Tuesday. Mama and Papa will be out. I can come with you.'

On Monday night, before the dreaded appointment with Doctor Freiburg could eventuate, Ellie was dressing after her bath when she realised the bad dream was over. She had never been so glad to see blood.

She pulled on her nightgown, then, in her room, added an overcoat and a pair of gum boots. Quietly, she slipped out of the house and ran down behind the barns to shout with joy and relief. The stars twinkled softly above, and she sagged into the side of the barn and gazed at them. The season had turned, the leaves were falling, the breezes growing brisker. Ellie closed her eyes and leaned her head back against the barn. The afternoon sun's warmth was still trapped in the wooden boards. She relished the soft solitude. Music came unbidden into her head, Richard Strauss's *Im Abendrot*; she could feel how the vowel sounds would form in her mouth, hear the sweet violins vibrating in the bones just behind her ears. A fantasy formed in her mind. She was on stage, singing, her voice soaring out of her like a bird of prey over treetops: precise, elegant, dangerously beautiful. Lights were focused on her, the audience waited beyond in the gloom...

She snapped her eyes open, and saw only dewy fields under the velvet sky. She was a farmgirl, not a singer. Back at the house, warm lights glowed in the kitchen windows. Frau Neumann would expect her to help with the washing-up.

Ellie realised then, that it mattered little she wasn't pregnant. The same path still waited for her: marriage, family, the farm. The sooner she reconciled herself to that fate, the sooner the pain of longing would stop.

Dismissing the song from her head, she trudged back to the house.

NINE

*G*eorge hurried out of the lift and into the cool street, holding Penny's coat in the crook of his right elbow. She'd left it behind the stage, and he hoped to catch her before she was whisked away by David Preston. If he were honest with himself, he'd admit too that he was checking up on her. He didn't like to see her go off into the dark with Preston, who was a pond-dweller of the slimiest variety. Outside the hotel, the street was empty. In the distance, sirens wailed. He rounded the corner to the car park, and discovered a sight that at first didn't make sense. David Preston lying on his back, very still. An elderly woman dressed in a cream jacket that was stained with blood, kneeled over him.

'What the – ?'

'I think he's dead,' the woman said, looking up with a teary face. 'I tried to help him but...'

'What happened?' George looked around. 'Where's Penny?'

'The man, he came out of nowhere. My husband and I saw the whole thing. He took the young woman in a white van. My husband's gone to call the ambulance and the police.' She searched around with frantic eyes. 'You haven't seen my husband, have you? I'm worried. The man who did this was... Who would do something like this?'

George's mind reeled. *He took the young woman in a white van.* His own shock and panic overwhelmed him to the degree that he couldn't comfort the elderly woman, who was clearly distressed.

At that moment, the woman's husband came jogging up, panting. 'They're on their way,' he said to his wife.

She stood and folded herself into his embrace, sobbing. Sirens wailed in the distance.

'Don't worry,' he said, 'I gave them the licence plate. They'll find him.'

George watched this exchange with surreal detachment. This couldn't be happening. Penny couldn't be in danger... The icy dread was matched only by the sickening guilt. It had been months since the threatening phone calls, and he had almost forgotten them. But the caller hadn't forgotten Penny. If only George had warned her. If only he'd called the police...

This was all his fault.

George would never forget the night he found Angie Smith, singing in a dingy theatre-restaurant in Soho. An old friend had seen her first, when she was fronting a barely tuned top forty band at a seedy club called Heat. But before he'd had an opportunity to go and see this talented beauty for himself, she had vanished unexpectedly. It was only by chance that he happened on her, four months later, singing in a duo with another young woman who played guitar. Angie's voice had drifted out onto the street as he was walking past, and attracted to it, he had gone in. While he sipped a martini at the bar, he had listened. By this time, she had taken to calling herself Penny Bright, but George knew it was the same girl he had heard of. Her looks were unmistakable: almond-shaped, liquid brown eyes; the cheekbones of a classical sculpture; a full, sensitive mouth with a beguiling, hesitant smile. He saw every ounce of potential in her. But it was more than that. Her voice aroused feelings in him he hadn't expected, a connection. It had made him almost angry to see her so low: with drunken fools leering at her, and gossiping women ignoring her. He wanted to take her and put her on top of the world, he wanted to make her rich.

Between sets, he approached her.

'I'm George Fellowes,' he said, handing her a business card. 'Is your name Angie Smith?'

At the mention of her name she flinched, handing him back his card as though it were boiling hot. 'Who wants to know?'

He saw that she was frightened, and decided to proceed more gently. 'I'm very impressed with your voice, Miss Bright. May I call you Penny?'

She smiled tentatively. 'Just so long as you don't call me Angie.'

He pressed the card back into her hands. 'I'm in the record business.'

Her expression was dubious. 'No offence, Mr Fellowes, but I've heard that loads of times and it's never true.'

So he rattled off the list of his top ten artists, and she hesitantly began to warm to him. He stayed to see her second set, then asked for a phone number he could call her on to arrange a trial recording session.

She waved the card. 'Why don't I call you?'

'Will you?'

'I'll think about it.'

He had been surprised: she was not immediately trusting; sometimes he wondered what hardship she had been through to make her so wary at such a young age, to make her adopt another name and be so frightened to hear the old one. A week later – she had taken some time to do some 'research' about him, she told him – Penny Bright finally called. She abandoned her old life and embraced the new. They recorded a single, and it had been signed promptly. A faltering start to sales had been fixed by George investing some money in chart padding: he hired two dozen people all across England to go to every store in a twenty-mile radius and buy the single in huge quantities. It worked, Penny got her spot on *Top of the Pops*, and they hadn't looked back. Everything looked rosy.

He could never have predicted then that such a dark shadow was waiting for them in the future.

Benedict marched Penny into the house, a knife held against the soft flesh at the side of her throat to keep her from struggling or screaming. Through a smelly kitchen whose benches were overloaded with old newspapers, filthy dishes, and pots caked with food. He kicked open a door that led to a dark staircase, and Penny hesitated. The point of the knife was pressed inwards; she gasped and kept moving. Trapped, terrified, unable to believe her body could still work. Down two flights of stairs, he flicked on a light and she saw she was in a basement room stacked with damp boxes and old furniture. On the floor was a hessian sack. He made her sit on it while he tied her to a drainage pipe.

'What's all this about, Benedict?' she asked, trying to keep the fear from her voice.

'You know.'

'Look, if this is about that briefcase under my bed all those years ago –'

'My father is dead.'

This made her pause. 'Sebastian's dead?'

He finished tightening the last knot and came to squat in front of her. She got a good look at him, and was appalled by what she saw. His skin was pallid, sweating. His pupils were pinpoints. He stank like a farm animal.

Benedict drilled a finger into her shoulder. 'You killed him. You killed my father.'

The accusation was absurd, but Penny realised that Benedict was not in control of his faculties. How could she reason with a crazy person? 'I haven't seen him for three years. That doesn't make any sense.'

Here he smiled, and the expression was so abnormal that it made Penny's heart cold. 'The men came for the stash that night, but you took it and ran.'

'I didn't take it. They took it.'

'They told a different story, I'm afraid, Angie, and I know what I'm more likely to believe. So while you were selling my father's gear so you could live comfortably –'

'I didn't!'

'– he was having his head kicked in. By the time he was brought to a hospital, he was brain damaged. I've sold nearly everything we owned to pay for his therapy, and he was getting better. Slowly. But he could barely speak, he hated being incapacitated, and in March he took a gun and blew his brains out.' He stood, stretching to his full imposing height. 'You see? You may be a pop star now, you may be on the telly, but I know what you did. And I'm going to make you pay for it.'

'I did nothing. I didn't take the damn briefcase, I didn't even know what was in it!'

But he was walking away now, flicking off the light and moving up the stairs.

'What are you going to do to me?' she gasped at last, unable to keep her horror out of her voice. When he didn't answer, she called, 'I have money! My manager has money. He'll give you whatever you want, just don't hurt me.'

He said bluntly, 'I'd rather hurt you.' And the door at the top of the stairs closed.

Penny struggled against the ropes around her arms. Already her fingers were growing numb from lack of circulation. Her mind was a scrambled mess of terror and disbelief. Surely this was all a horrible nightmare and she'd wake soon in her own bed, safe. But the sensations were too vivid for it to be dreamt. The rough rope biting her skin, the smell of rising damp and rat urine, the cold of the cement seeping through the hessian, her heart beating so fast that she feared it might explode. He had tied her cruelly tight. The ropes wouldn't budge.

She was caught like a butterfly in a spider's web.

Hours passed, perhaps they were minutes. Time had bent, she lost all sense of everything in the bright cold light of her fear. She struggled a while, then stopped to weep, then struggled some more. She called out into the empty dark until she was hoarse. At first, she cried for help. Then she began to swear and scream at Benedict. Dimly, she knew that she would have to keep her head, have to focus if she was to escape this situation. But her dread was unbearable, blocking her thought processes, tearing up her mind and memory until all that was left was cold, animal fear. Every creak, every drip, every whisper of sound set her heart alight, wondering if it was Benedict returning. She tried to breathe softly, to still her pulse so she could hear properly. Her ears rang faintly.

Then, when the silence stretched out for too long, she began to worry that he wasn't going to return at all, that she had been left for dead, buried alive in the middle of suburban London.

A thump. A voice – was it Benedict calling something? Her skin prickled as she listened hard into the dark. Would he torture her before he killed her? She had to get away. She struggled against the ropes again, but the knots grew even tighter, her blood more frantic.

Then footsteps. Hurried footsteps on the stairs. Her heart pounded hard enough to burst out of her chest. Dizzy shadows gathered on the edges of her vision. This was it, this was the end. With a groan, Penny passed out.

George paced on the street beside his car, outside the house at Islington to which the police had led him. He thanked God that the elderly couple had taken the van's licence plate; and cursed the devil for the way the police had kept him too distant to see anything. Lights flashed, emergency vehicles were parked at uneven angles. Neighbours in their dressing-gowns and slippers were gathering. The press couldn't be far away. He hoped the police worked quickly. He was determined that this would not make the papers; that Penny would not become a sideshow exhibit.

The anxiety that gripped him was primal, and he remembered the times that Aila, embarrassed to ask for reassurance, had questioned him on how he felt about his young star. 'It's just a business relationship,' he always said. The desperate fear of losing her that overwhelmed him now proved otherwise, too eloquently for comfort.

So far he had heard the police break their way into the little, dark house. He had heard the shouting and struggle inside. But he had no idea if Penny was here, if she was still alive...

Then noises outside. Shouting. George hurried over, as close as he could to the action. Four police officers were manhandling a large man out of the house. He was struggling and swearing.

'Where's Penny?' George called. Nobody answered him. The large man was shoved into the back of a police van. Its headlights bloomed in the dark, and more police officers divided the crowd so the van could get out. Then all was quiet. Some of the neighbours started to move away, shaking their heads and clicking their tongues.

George hurried over to an elderly woman in a pink robe. 'Who was that man?' he asked her.

'Always thought he was trouble. Him and his dad. Always up to something.'

'What's his name?'

'Benedict Marten.'

The name meant nothing to George. Who was this Benedict Marten and why would he want to hurt Penny? He realised he was still wearing the ridiculous frangipani chain around his neck, and cast it to the ground with violence.

A relieved shout and a scattered round of applause from the house drew his attention. Emerging, propped up by a young woman constable, was a stooped and trembling girl. A blanket over her hair threw her face into shadow, but he knew it was Penny.

'Oh, thank God, thank God, thank God,' George exclaimed. 'Penny! Penny!'

She heard him and broke away from the constable, running to the edge of the police cordon. She fell into his arms, sobbing like a tiny child. His heart thundered as he pressed her close.

'Sir, we need to get her to a hospital,' the constable was saying.

'George has to come with me,' Penny said.

'Very well.' The constable lifted the tape for George to duck under. An ambulance was roaring around the corner.

George squeezed Penny gently and said, 'It's over.'

Penny shook her head, sobbing into him. 'It'll never be over.'

George was nervous. The shirt that Aila had freshly pressed for him that morning was damp and clinging to his armpits, his tie was too tight, his palms clammy. The Monday morning traffic was slow and he had to wind down the window of the Mercedes to let in some cool fresh air. As he parked and walked to his meeting, he reminded himself to mask his anxiety. He wiped his palms on his trousers, rolled his shoulders, put a spring in his step. Tried not to look like a man who had spent the last month splitting himself in three: comforting Penny, who had fallen into a heap; placating Aila, who knew nothing about the incident but sensed that George was distracted by something; and somehow managing the juggernaut of administration that accompanied preparations for the tour. When he arrived at the office of Packenham and Powell Entertainment Finance, he applied a broad smile to his face and offered a firm handshake.

'George, glad you could come by,' said Harry Packenham, leading him beyond the overdecorated foyer and into a boardroom. James Powell, the other partner in the firm, waited for them at the end of a long table. The size of the room, its expectant quiet, added to George's apprehension. He sat, carefully propping his briefcase against the leg of his chair.

They made small talk. Weather, wives and football scores. But then Harry, a sharp-eyed man in his sixties with a mind like a razor, leaned forward, steepling his hands and resting his chin on them.

'I'm hearing things that are making me nervous, George,' he said, fixing George with his gaze.

'Nervous?' George replied disingenuously. 'What kinds of things?'

James Powell was still in a relaxed position in his chair, fingers entwined behind his head. 'That Penny Bright's album has been shelved, that she's out of her head on drugs and can't get to rehearsals, that the tour is on shaky ground.'

'I can assure you that none of that is true,' George said. 'Penny has been ill and that has meant we've held off the album release so that she doesn't have to do any promotion until she's well again. But we are still absolutely on track for the tour to kick off in four months.'

Harry smiled, but it was a cold smile. 'Are you certain?'

'I'll remind you that half of the money for the tour is out of my own pocket. I have to be certain. I have as much to lose as you.'

James slid a folder of papers across the desk. Figures in rows. 'We've been looking closely at what might happen if the tour doesn't go exactly as planned. As you can see, with eighty-four per cent of the tickets sold, and a significant investment already made into the building of stage sets, the employment of musicians and crew, the promotional costs…we don't want to be refunding tickets to the punters, George. We'd suffer a significant loss.'

'And we don't want a postponement either,' Harry added. 'Rumours of downscaling are poison. We're legally bound to refund under those circumstances too, and if punters think they're getting a half-arsed show with a floppy pop star who can't keep her nose clean –'

'Penny is not taking any illicit substances,' George said firmly. 'She's had a viral infection that affected her voice, but she's well again now. In fact, after I leave here I'm meeting her at rehearsal.' He tapped his watch for emphasis. 'The girl's a hard worker. She won't let us down.' George had precisely the same set of concerns as his co-financiers: if they pulled out now, he would lose a lot of money. More money than he could readily access. If they decided to take legal action, maybe even more money than he had. He offered the smile again, faking a confidence that he didn't feel. 'Don't worry.'

Penny is in a dark room. She can't make out shapes and she knows somewhere around here there is a hole in the floor. If she steps through it, she will fall forever and forever. She moves hesitantly, toes stretched ahead of her. But then she hears him behind her. His hot breath. She must move quicker, he mustn't catch her. She must get back up the stairs and out the door. The room swells and grows, she can't find her way. He draws closer, terror crushes her ribs, she begins to run. Her foot sails into a void, the ground disappears beneath her and she pitches forward, falling and falling into nothingness…

Heart thudding, Penny woke up. Sweat gathered at her hairline and under her breasts. She clutched the sheets in stiff fists, in her own bed, her own flat. The blue-grey of the quiet sky before dawn pressed through the curtains. Distant and muffled, the sound of traffic moved beyond the double glazing. She lay still for long minutes, slowly releasing her hands, listening to the sound of her own ragged breathing. That was the eighth time she'd had the dream in the month since it had happened, but she would never get used to it. It was as though the terror of that night had opened up a fissure in reality, and that was where she now resided all the time. The slightest anxiety bathed her heart in cold electricity.

Penny rolled over, reaching for the tranquillisers on the bedside table. She had long since given up worrying about how many she was taking: she did whatever she had to do to make these feelings shrink down inside her. Doctor after doctor agreed she needed them. After she swallowed two, she lay on her back and watched the ceiling, waiting for the relaxation to work on her bunched muscles and overworked mind. Dawn light was glimmering under the curtains when she finally drifted back to sleep.

An insistent buzzing noise woke her, many hours later. At first she couldn't make sense of it, it became tied up in a dream about a bee in a box of ribbons that needed to be sorted. But then, as she rose towards wakefulness, she realised it was her doorbell. She sat woozily, head in hands, on the edge of her bed.

The doorbell buzzed again. Who could it be? It must be George, it was always George. Only George knew where she lived, only George cared to come and see her. But until she looked and saw his familiar dark silhouette on the street, the icy fear gathered around her heart again. What if it was somebody else, a stranger, somebody who had found her address, somebody who wanted to hurt her? She knew that it wasn't just Benedict Marten she had crossed in the past. Any of those people could come back to her now, wanting revenge. Alan, the photographer. Or any of the men who Sebastian had made her sleep with. Or somebody from her mother's church . . . the possibilities were endless. The chains of consequence stretched back

113

far into the past: she could have done something that she didn't even remember, that had triggered somebody's sick hatred and *she wouldn't even know* until they came looking for her. Sometimes she tried to sit down with a piece of paper and write out all the possibilities – people, events – but it made her so anxious, as the lines crisscrossed the page, that she had to take sedatives and lie down.

Penny went to the window and lifted the sash. Of course, it was George.

'George!' she called.

He looked up. 'Penny, I've been trying to rouse you for ten minutes. Are you all right?'

What a question. She hadn't been all right since the night Benedict abducted her. Her life had been turned on its axis. Fear ruled her, everything else she experienced dimly.

Penny grabbed the keys off the dresser and dropped them over the window ledge. 'Let yourself in,' she said, and stumbled back to bed. She caught sight of herself in the mirror: hair unwashed, face puffy, dark shadows smudged under her eyes. She looked terrible, but what did it matter? Sitting cross-legged on her bed, she waited for George.

The door opened. She heard him close it behind him, then footsteps approaching. Then he was in her bedroom, offering her the keys.

'Keep them,' she said. 'I've another set.'

'Penny, it's nearly noon,' he said.

'I was sleeping.'

'You were supposed to be at rehearsal at ten. You promised me.'

The conversation of the night before came back to her. Rehearsals. She had skipped them for a month, but had given a solemn undertaking to turn up today. She tried to imagine herself back into the mindset that had made that promise, and couldn't. It confused her. But then she remembered that when she had spoken to George last night, she had been up on Dexedrine.

'I forgot,' she said.

He sat on the bed next to her. 'That's not like you.'

'I don't even know what I'm like anymore, George.'

'You know that Benedict can't hurt you now.' He gave his usual long speech. Benedict was in prison, bail had been refused. The prosecution was gathering a case to try him on David Preston's murder. At significant cost, George had engaged lawyers to make the prosecution drop the abduction charges. He didn't want Penny traumatised by a trial or the media circus that would ensue, and they didn't need her evidence: two witnesses had seen David Preston stabbed to death. A murder conviction would put Benedict away for a long time, especially given his frighteningly impressive criminal history. As far as George was concerned it was over; it had never happened.

But it *had* happened, and Penny wasn't afraid of Benedict especially. She was afraid of everyone.

'I can't rehearse today,' she said.

She could tell George was forcing his voice to be gentle. 'When do you think you'll be able to rehearse?'

'Tomorrow?' she replied, but knew tomorrow wasn't a possibility either.

'How about we try to start again next Monday? I'll pick you up myself and take you down to the theatre. Between now and then, you could try to prepare yourself mentally.'

She nodded, grateful. 'Yes, that sounds like a good idea. I'm sure I'll be feeling better by then.'

Aila sat on the couch, bare feet tucked up under her neatly, reading a long letter. George touched her hair.

'I'm off,' he said. 'I'll be back around three.'

She looked up, smiled tightly. 'Are you picking her up again?'

'It's not that far out of my way.' He'd told her nothing about Penny's ordeal. Guilty, knowing she would blame him for not warning her. 'She hasn't been well.'

'A taxi ride wouldn't tire her unduly.'

'She's too famous for taxis.'

'Perhaps she should use that driving licence you insisted she sit for.' Then Aila shook her head, held up the letter. 'I'm sorry, I'm grumpy. It's nothing to do with you.'

'What is it?'

She sighed. 'This letter from my sister. Julia's pregnant.'

Julia was Aila's niece. 'That's good news, isn't it?' he said, careful.

'Oh, of course. It's lovely news. Only she's due in March. They've known for months and they haven't told me. Pussy-footing around me... Pity can be such an insult.'

He leaned over and kissed her cool forehead, trying very hard not to pity her. 'You're reading too much into it. They probably just forgot to tell you.'

'Maybe you're right.' She smiled weakly. 'You'd better go. You'll be late.'

The traffic was very light, and he was actually early when he let himself into Penny's flat. She was pacing the living room. His heart leapt with hope. She was dressed: bell-bottomed jeans, loose white shirt, a choker of beads wound around her neck. She was made-up, all dark eyes and dark lipstick. She looked like the old Penny. But her pacing troubled him.

'Are you ready, Penny?' he asked.

'Yes, yes absolutely,' she said, wearing a path in the shag carpet. 'I've been ready for a while. Are you late, or was I just early? I must have been early, I've been up since the crack of dawn. I haven't eaten yet, though. Do you think I should eat first? I suppose I could take an apple or something. There's a café next to the theatre, do you think? – '

George caught her around the shoulders, holding her still. Her eyes were pinpoints. 'Have you taken something?'

'I couldn't get going,' she said. 'Not without the uppers.'

'How many pills are you taking?'

'The doctor gave them to me. I need them. Don't make me feel bad, it's not fair.' She shrugged him off. 'I'll fetch my jacket and we can go.'

She slipped away, into her bedroom. George waited anxiously, helplessly. The clock next to the television ticked loudly. Penny didn't return. He moved to her bedroom door, peered in.

She lay collapsed on her bed, sobbing silently. George sat next to her, stroking her back.

'I can't,' she whispered. 'I can't. Maybe tomorrow, George? Can I go tomorrow instead?'

George listened to her crying quietly for long moments. His mind was in turmoil. His golden goose was refusing to behave and that was exasperating, but he was not a man without compassion, especially where Penny was concerned. She needed a proper break, she needed to get out of London and see some sunshine, get off the pills which were shredding her nerves. There were still four months until the concert. The band could practise without her...though if Packenham and Powell got wind of that, they would pull their money.

The glimmer of an idea leapt into his head. Perhaps it was possible to give Penny the break she needed, and still not arouse suspicion. The idea did not come without trepidation, but it had a kind of tidy justice; almost as though fate had aligned it this way. If he could pull it off.

'Penny,' he said, helping her to sit up. 'I don't want you to rehearse tomorrow. I want you to have a holiday instead.'

The tension drained from her shoulders. 'Really? A holiday?'

'I know a little place in Spain. A friend owns it. There's sunshine, a fat cat, a housekeeper to look after you for as long as you need. But you'd have to promise me you'll try to get off these pills.'

She gazed up at him with huge, teary eyes. Her mascara had run to halfway down her cheeks, her nose was moist. She looked about twelve years old, and he felt a pang of conscience.

'I will. I promise,' she said.

'I'll arrange everything, then,' he said.

'Will you come too?'

He shook his head. 'No, I can't come to Spain. I have some urgent business to take care of.' He smiled. 'In Germany.'

TEN

Ellie tried not to be dismayed by how raw and red her hands were becoming from farm labour. As she twisted Herr Neumann's overalls through the mangler, she watched her cracked knuckles bend over the handle and remembered a time, long in the past, when she had been vain about her hands. Strong and well-shaped like her mother's. The smooth whiteness of them, the pink half-moons in her fingernails. But then, her father had got sick, she'd had to work and she'd been working ever since. Now they were a farmgirl's hands. Not a soprano's hands, she told herself bitterly, then vowed for the millionth time to stop comparing her real life to a life that was only ever a fantasy.

Deep in the house, she heard a knock at the door. She reached into the tub for the next set of overalls. A few moments later, Dieter's voice. 'Ellie?'

She turned. Dieter stood at the threshold to the laundry, a strange man standing beside him. He was in his forties, dark-haired with thick sideburns and large, unblinking eyes. He was dressed all in black, from his shirt to his wide tie to his jacket and pants.

'This man is here to see you,' Dieter said.

'To see *me*?'

'It was difficult to find you,' the man said, in such painfully accented German that Ellie almost laughed.

She switched immediately to English. 'Then how did you find me?' she asked.

'You're well-known in the village,' he replied, relieved. 'I'm George Fellowes and I need to talk to you.'

Warily, she wiped her damp hands on her skirt and offered him one to shake. 'Talk to me about what?' She could see Dieter, with his loose grip on English, trying to follow the conversation.

'Could we go inside? Sit down for a few minutes?'

Ellie nodded, beckoning Dieter to follow. Herr and Frau Neumann had gone to the village. The kitchen was crowded with breakfast things, her next job. The smell of bacon still hung in the air. She offered George Fellowes a seat and sat opposite, inviting Dieter to stay.

'I'll get straight to the point.' George snapped open a briefcase and removed a large, glossy photograph, which he pushed over the table to Ellie. 'Look at this woman.'

Dieter peered over her shoulder and gasped.

Ellie, too, was taken aback. 'Who is she?' she asked.

'Penny Bright. She's a London pop star.'

'Ellie, she looks exactly like you,' Dieter said in German.

'I wouldn't say *exactly*,' Ellie replied, but couldn't put her finger on precisely why *exactly* seemed too strong a word. It wasn't just the clothes, the hair, the make-up. Perhaps it was the odd feeling of displacement that crept over her, the sheer puzzlement that somebody somewhere in the world could look so similar and she could have been ignorant of it until now. She returned her attention to George. Switching between English and German was taxing her mind. 'You'd better explain what you want from me.'

'I'm Penny's manager. She's ill. I need somebody to replace her in the short term.'

Ellie processed this information, feeling puzzled and a little overwhelmed. 'What makes you think I can sing pop music, Mr Fellowes?'

'I heard about you from Ivan Hamblyn, who manages TRG's classical music division. He was on an audition panel back in March. He said you sing like an angel. He also said your English was superb.'

'I'm an operatic soprano,' she replied quickly, wondering if this man knew anything at all about music. 'The techniques I've learned are for –'

'I'll pay you five thousand marks.'

Dieter understood this line. His eyes rounded like saucers. Ellie was shocked into silence, while her brain galloped ahead of her tongue. *Five thousand marks.* What she could do with five thousand marks! She heard the sound of a hundred doors opening all around her, doors that she had believed shut forever. A move to the city, a brilliant singing tutor, auditioning for companies...

George moved to fill the silence. 'It would only be for a few months, three at most, only for rehearsals with a band. You may have to do the occasional interview, but I would coach you in what to say and do. Obviously you'll need a haircut, some new clothes, you might have to...er...lose a little weight.' Here, he had the decency to blush. 'But it would be fairly straightforward, then you could come home and pretend it never happened. I'd pay you half the money up front, the other half at the end of the three months.'

'Ellie?' Dieter said, unable to keep up.

She quickly translated for him, unsure how he would respond.

To her surprise, he laughed. 'Ellie, you must do it,' he said. 'Where else could you get money like that?'

'I'd have to go to London,' she replied with a pang of realisation. 'I'd miss you.'

'It's not so far. Nor so long.'

'I'll give you the night to sleep on it,' George Fellowes was saying, pushing a business card across the table. 'But I need to move quickly on this. I hope I can rely on your utmost confidentiality. I'm staying above the pub, I've written the number on the back of this card.'

Ellie pushed the card back. 'I don't need to sleep on it, Mr Fellowes,' she said. She had a sense of mingled fear and excitement, her heart raced but she couldn't keep the smile off her face. 'I'll do it.'

Aila was painting on the enclosed terrace when George arrived home.

'How did it go?' she called, as he tried to slip away into the bedroom to unpack.

He knew, of course, that he couldn't get away with telling her nothing. But how much to tell her was the question. He rested his suitcase on the creamy carpet, and joined her on the terrace. Muted sun caught silvery highlights in her hair. She stabbed at the canvas with a thoughtful blob of violet, then muttered, 'Darn,' softly: the closest she ever came to swearing.

'That's very nice,' he said, studying her painting.

'What is it?' she shot back quickly.

'I... don't know.'

She sighed, wiping paint from her hands on a rag. 'It's supposed to be a bluebell. Up very close. The ladies in my art group say I need to think more like an artist, see things differently.' She smiled, leaning up to kiss him. 'You didn't answer. How was Germany?'

'Fine. I closed the deal.' The satisfaction of saying it was sweet. Ellie Frankel had said yes. He was relieved, of course. A little frightened about whether it would work. And, he had to admit, excited about the possibilities.

'Which deal was that?'

This was his chance to tell her. But he couldn't. Too difficult to explain, it would arouse suspicions, mistrusts. So he lied. 'Foreign contracts... very boring, Aila. You know I prefer not to talk about business at home.' His pulse quickened with guilt, but she didn't notice.

She never noticed.

Thirteen-year-old George had taken Mr Lewins's philosophy to heart. On the first day at his new, posh school – full of rich boys with plummy voices – he decided to be a new person. Afraid of them hearing his rough, northern accent, George didn't speak for a week. At home, he mastered their clipped, overbred tones. By the end of the first term, he spoke like a native of the south.

Life with the Lewinses wasn't bad. They were good people, affectionate in their awkward way. They knew the right thing to do and they always did it. George wrote only half-a-dozen letters to his sisters. Their infrequent, cursory replies reminded him of what he had always known: he wasn't one of them, he never had been. Instead, he pursued arbitrary friendships at school: choosing the right boy to know at the right time to get ahead. As he approached manhood, he realised that his heart was becoming cold, that a brittle shell was forming around it. But he had no way of knowing how to stop the process, so he carried on. He excelled at study, he chose the right path, he found himself invited up to Christ Church College, Oxford, accepted in a program of study that the Lewinses were immensely proud of: medicine. He was going to be a doctor; it was the right thing for a man of his education to do. He hoped to specialise in psychiatry eventually, vainly seeking answers to the twisted feelings in his heart.

Perhaps he would have stayed on that path; perhaps he would have forgotten about music and warmth and laughter; perhaps he would have become a cold man, even a cruel one. But at the end of his first term, he met Aila.

The Lewinses had been planning their New Year's Eve party for months. It was the end of 1949, time to usher in a new era. War was behind them, the future seemed filled with promise. Many hopes were hung on the five and the zero of the new decade. The parlour, usually locked up and draped with dustcovers, was decorated with gold and silver streamers, wait staff had been hired, and the well-heeled guests began to arrive shortly after six o'clock. George was little moved by the preparations, unaccountably irritated with his foster-parents for their silly sentimentality. Every time Mrs Lewins said something like, 'Just think, George, this is the last time I'll take a bath in the forties,' or, 'The last time I'll water my plants in the war decade,' he felt an uncomfortable mix of embarrassment and impatience with her. He found himself experiencing such feelings more and more lately, and not just with his foster-parents. People's little foibles got under his skin, making him exasperated, averse to associating with the human race. But he had been brought up well, and so put on a smiling face to greet the guests with the Lewinses.

At six-thirty the doorbell chimed, and George dutifully rose from the tapestry chair and made his way to the entrance hall. He opened the door to a mismatched trio of people. A tall, elderly man with dark hair, his small, fair-haired and full-lipped wife, and the lucky product of their union: a tall, pale-haired, alabaster-skinned daughter.

'Pleased to meet you,' George said perfunctorily. 'I'm George Fellowes.'

With a strong accent that George couldn't place, the man said, 'I'm Esko Kiveli. This is my wife Vanska, and my daughter Aila.'

George shook all their hands in turn, but still nothing about Aila had struck him particularly.

'Is there somewhere we could hang our coats?' she said.

'Allow me,' he replied, and leaned in to help her shrug out of her bulky coat. It was then that he caught sight of himself in the tall mirror next to the hatstand; more precisely, he caught sight of himself next to her. He was dark – almost gypsy-dark with his black eyes and his thick hair – and clothed all in dark shades. She was the opposite. She wore a cream dress, beaded with pearls; her hair was impossibly fine and fair, catching the light; her skin was as flawless as a marble statue, but as his fingers brushed her arm he could feel that she was warm, not cold. She resembled nothing so much as a fallen angel, and the contrast of their appearances stirred something deep inside him. *He needed her.* The thought was as sudden as it was certain.

As the night wore on, he watched her, fascinated, from a distance. He had no experience of women, so no way of knowing how to approach her. From Mrs Lewins he managed to glean some basic information. The family was Finnish, but Aila had grown up in London. Her father was an investment banker and – Mrs Lewins dropped her voice here – 'They have more money than you could count.' George drank too much champagne, despite Mr Lewins's assertions that sobriety was more becoming in a young man of his age. The parlour grew hot and stuffy, too full of electric heating, polite laughter and expensive perfumes. He lost sight of Aila, then finally found her with his gaze. Out on the terrace in the cold. He thought about her coat, and before he could convince himself to stay away, had hurried to the entrance hall to find it and bring it to her.

The cold air hit him like a blow. His head immediately began to throb.

'Miss Kiveli?'

She turned. It was then that he realised a man stood with her, in the shadows. George couldn't remember his name. Robert? Rodney? He was the son of one of Mrs Lewins's oldest friends. A barb went to George's heart, thinking about Aila out here with him; and then embarrassment took over his tongue.

'Your coat,' he managed, holding it out to her. 'I... I thought you might be cold.'

Robert-Rodney grinned patronisingly. 'I could've managed to get the lady's coat, had she wanted it,' he said. 'But she insisted she wasn't cold.'

Aila gave George a weak smile. 'I insisted that I'd like to go inside soon, actually,' she replied to her companion. 'I think you might have misheard me.'

'Now, you promised to listen to my story. Where was I? Oh, yes. So, the mechanic told me the car would cost one hundred pounds to fix. "One hundred," I said, "I didn't become a success by paying grease monkeys sums like that."'

George tried to take stock of the situation. The man... Roderick, that was his name... Roderick tapped a cigarette on the railing of the terrace, then perched it in the corner of his lips. Aila looked at George and inclined her head slightly, her eyes pleading with him. It slowly dawned that she was not out here with Roderick willingly.

He cleared his throat. 'Miss Kiveli?' he said. 'I brought you your coat because...your mother has asked me to tell you...um...it's time to go.'

'Oh? So soon?' She turned mock-regretful eyes on Roderick. 'I'm sorry, we'll have to resume this conversation another time.'

Roderick narrowed his eyes, unsure whether she was genuine. 'But it's not midnight yet.'

'We have another party to go to. George,' Aila said to him, 'could you show me around to the driveway?'

George nodded. She shrugged into her coat.

'Goodbye, Roderick.'

Roderick made a hm-mm noise, dragging heavily on his cigarette and turning to gaze out into the garden. George led Aila down the stairs and around the side of the house to the gravelled driveway, where she stopped and let out a huge sigh.

'Thanks, George, you rescued me. He was boring me to death.'

'How will you...? I mean, he'll notice you haven't gone.'

She shook her head. 'It doesn't matter. He'll have found another victim soon enough. Perhaps a more willing one.' She smiled at him. 'Why do you keep calling me Miss Kiveli? Have you forgotten my name?'

George's cheeks flushed. 'No, it's Aila.'

'Then just call me Aila. Miss Kiveli is so nineteenth century, like Jane Austen or some such.' She turned her face to the stiffening breeze. 'How far is the sea from here?'

'Just down at the bottom of the street.'

'I love that smell, the sea air. You're very lucky to live here.'

'I know,' he said. Then, gripped by a sudden burst of drunken confidence, he said, 'Would you like to walk down to the pier?'

'Won't it be freezing?'

'Probably,' George said, a doubtful expression crossing his face.

'Well, I have my coat. What about you?'

He wanted to say, *I won't feel the cold with you next to me.* Instead, he said, 'We won't be long. Just a quick stroll, eh?'

It was a heady combination – champagne, Aila's soft beauty, the brisk sea cold – and the quick stroll became a long evening tucked in a bus shelter, hiding from the cold, sharing stories of each other's lives and thoughts. As the evening deepened towards midnight, she wove her spell on him. In some moments, he would glimpse something familiar in her smile or the way she inclined her head, and he was reminded of his sisters and their easy laughter. Somehow, she found the boy he used to be inside him. He told her about his love of music, his dream of working with musicians, of organising performances and recapturing that delight he'd felt at the swing concert all those years ago. She asked him one simple question: 'Why on earth are you studying medicine then?' It was a question so profound that he could not bring himself to answer. Fireworks in the distance alerted them to the turning of the decade. He watched their bright colours reflect on her face. Earlier that evening, she had joked that he'd rescued her; but it was she who had rescued him.

One thing he didn't tell her, though, was the truth about his parents. It was easier to say that his father hadn't come back from the war, that his mother died of illness, that his sisters were now strangers to him. Perhaps he should have trusted her not to judge him for his father's crimes, but he couldn't trust her: not if it meant the possibility of losing her. On their wedding day, just over a year later, he wondered about the untruth lying beneath their marriage, wondered if one day it would come back to haunt him. But it never did.

And in the meantime he drew other, more dangerous untruths towards himself.

Ellie paced near the front door of the Neumanns' house, waiting for her taxi. Herr and Frau Neumann knew nothing about her plans. She had told them that George was an old friend of her mother's, and that he had arranged a trip to England to meet her mother's estranged family. Dieter knew everything, but she was unable to hold him, to steal that last desperate kiss from his lips before their long separation. His parents still didn't know about their relationship.

'Stop pacing, you're making me anxious,' Herr Neumann said good-naturedly.

'You were sick with nerves the first time you had to fly in an aeroplane,' Frau Neumann countered with a wry smile.

126

She couldn't tell them she wasn't frightened of the flight. There were far greater things to feel trepidation about, and pacing held them all at bay. So she kept moving.

The taxi came into view, winding up the hill.

'Let me hug you,' Frau Neumann said, enfolding her in her arms. 'I'll miss you, little sparrow.'

'I'll miss you, too,' Ellie replied. She felt an extraordinary sense of satisfaction in knowing that, on her return, she could repay the Neumanns for their kindness and generosity. Whoever said that money couldn't buy happiness had obviously never been poor.

Herr Neumann gave her a diffident squeeze, and then she was in Dieter's arms, trying not to press her body too hard against him.

'I'll write every day,' she whispered into his ear.

'I'll love you forever,' he whispered back, his hot breath tickling her.

The taxi pulled up, she gathered herself and her suitcase and moved down the front path.

A new life beckoned.

ACT II

The pleasures of love last only a moment,
The pains of love last a lifetime.

Plaisir d'Amour, JEAN PAUL MARTINI

Western Queensland, Australia: 1997

*S*he parked the LandCruiser on the grass verge in front of
Sergeant Osbourne's house. It had been a ninety-kilometre
journey, and this twenty-resident town was the nearest civilisation.
The blue burnished sky hung like a blanket over the red dust, the
sun was hard on the yellow-green grass. The landscape was breathtaking
in its cruel way. For a long time she had relished the barrenness, the
isolation out here. But as the letters began to arrive regularly, at least
one a week, the distance aroused feelings of vulnerability, not
independence.

Sergeant Osbourne was sitting on his front step, eating a sandwich
off a chipped enamel plate. He saw her, and gave her a grin.

'Well, if it isn't our local canary,' he said good-naturedly, his eyes
crinkling at the corners. He was a large man, as red-faced and moist
as a side of beef. 'We don't see you out on the town much.'

She tried to smile in return, but faltered. 'Sergeant, I really need
to speak to you. Police business.'

He stood languidly, wiping his hands one by one on his blue
pants. 'Police business, eh? Sounds serious. You'd better come in to
my office.'

He led her into his house and through to a sun-drenched side
room, the town's official police station. A fly trapped in the window

buzzed and tapped itself against the glass: a vain bid for freedom. She sat opposite him at a large, rickety desk, while he booted up a creaking old computer. A faded map hung over his desk, the boundaries of his jurisdiction marked in red felt pen. She noted with amused interest that only about half of her twenty-thousand-hectare property was included: she would have to be careful not to have a police emergency in any of the far northern paddocks. Sergeant Osbourne spent a few moments swearing at the computer, then he pulled out a paper and pen.

'Sometimes I just like to do it the old-fashioned way,' he said. 'Tell me how I can help.'

'I've been receiving threatening letters.'

He started taking notes. 'In the mail?'

'Yes.'

'How many?'

'Five, now. They've been arriving regularly for the last four weeks.'

'What do they say?'

'Here,' she said, pulling the letters out of her bag and dropping them on his desk. He read them one by one, out loud in a deadpan voice, and as he did the chill passed over her again.

> *I know all about Angie Smith. Now you'll get what you deserve.*
> *You can't hide. I've seen the other side of the Penny.*
> *Are you frightened yet? You should be.*
> *You will pay, and you know why.*
> *I can smell your fear.*

Sergeant Osbourne scribbled a few notes, then turned to the envelopes. 'No return address,' he muttered. 'The postmark's English.'

'That's right.'

He put his pen down and looked across the table at her. 'England? That's a long way away.'

'I know.'

'Who's Angie Smith?'

132

'Angela Smith. Someone I knew at the very beginning of my career.'

'Did you piss her off? Do you think she's writing the letters? Or do you suspect somebody else?'

'I...look, I have no idea who's sending them,' she said honestly. 'I've made a lot of enemies.'

He smiled, wrinkling his nose. 'Really?'

Clearly, he couldn't imagine it. She had been quiet, almost reclusive, in her time out here. She had deliberately kept a low profile, precisely because of her past. Now it was catching up with her and she didn't know what she was most afraid of: the idea that the letter writer might hurt her, or the possibility that a bright light would be shined on her again, just when she was learning to inhabit the quiet, dim corners of existence.

Sergeant Osbourne leaned back in his chair and gazed up at the ceiling, choosing his words carefully. 'Look, I'll file a report and keep an eye on the situation but... You want my advice? Go home, stop worrying about it. You were famous once, and famous people attract the occasional harmless loon. For this person to hurt you – if that's what's intended – he or she has a long way to come. We're miles from anywhere, remember? Nobody's going to find you.' Now he leaned forward, the grin returning. 'Tony McGregor's wife's taking orders for a pie drive. You interested?'

As she turned into her long, dusty driveway later that afternoon, she felt very alone and vulnerable. Of course, Sergeant Osbourne made a certain kind of sense, and she tried to reassure herself with his words. But still, she knew that she had brought this anxious situation on herself. For the millionth time, she wondered why on earth she had done what she did. At the time it had seemed so straightforward; now she knew with fatal certainty that she had made all the wrong decisions.

ELEVEN

*P*enny waited, sitting on her suitcase at the Montoya train station, as the afternoon shadows grew long and the hazy sunlight dimmed from yellow to golden. On the plane trip from London, the express train from Madrid, and the slow, regional service down from Cordoba, she had been accompanied by a six-and-a-half-foot security guard who made little conversation. But now he had disappeared on the return train and her lift to her next destination hadn't arrived yet. She was angry at George for not organising it better. She understood that there were only two trains to Montoya a week, but why couldn't the security guard just stay a few days? It was better than leaving her here, vulnerable and exposed.

Though she had to admit she didn't feel frightened. She gazed at the sleepy town assembled beyond the train station. A dirt road running off towards a post office, a dozen shops, a tiny paved town square, and pretty painted cottages beyond. For the first time in six weeks she couldn't readily imagine something terrible happening to her here. She had finally arrived *nowhere*.

A shiny black car came into view at the end of the road, and Penny knew it was her ride. She stood to wait, suitcase clutched in her hand and tote bag over her shoulder. Soon, the car had slid up to the station, and a matronly woman with silver-grey hair got out.

'Penny?' she said.

'Yes.'

The woman beamed and said, 'I'm Estrella. I'll be taking care of you for the next few weeks.' Her accent was light, and she had obviously learned English from a plummy native. Her words were very precise, almost clipped. She gestured to the passenger door. 'Please, get in. I will manage your suitcase.'

Penny settled in to the car, and within moments Estrella was back at the wheel, pulling onto the road.

'Señor Fellowes has told me all about you,' she said, lowering dark sunglasses against the setting sun. 'I hope you will enjoy your stay.'

'How far is the house from here?'

'Not far; perhaps twenty minutes. Relax. Would you like me to put some music on?' Estrella indicated the tape player, but Penny shook her head. She turned to the window instead, watching the golden light bathe the road and the trees as they sped past. She was suddenly, acutely, so glad to be out of London that she might have wept. Estrella's words returned to her: *I'll be taking care of you for the next few weeks*. Was a few weeks all she could hope for? George had suggested she stay as long as she need to... Did he really mean it? The tour dates hadn't changed, the album release couldn't be put off forever.

'We'll stop at the village to buy something for dinner,' Estrella said, breaking into Penny's anxious reverie. 'What do you like to eat?'

Penny shrugged. 'Anything.'

Estrella smiled at her. 'What would you cook for yourself at home?'

'I don't know. Fish fingers and mash?'

Estrella's smile dimmed at the corners. 'I'll decide then,' she said. 'You're too thin anyway.'

Estrella stopped in front of a tiny store on the side of the road. Penny waited in the car while she went in. The village was little more than a tiny collection of houses with shingles out front. A general store, a bakery, a pub. The sun had slipped over the horizon now, and soft dusk hung over the land. Estrella was back, loading two string bags of food into the rear seat. Then they were on their way again.

A short time later, the car pulled into a long driveway. This was it: the place George had described to her. A white stuccoed villa with a high verandah, rust stains artfully hidden by overgrown window boxes, narrow shuttered windows, a cat sleeping on a high-up balcony railing, the tinkle of a fountain in the distance. Penny climbed out and breathed the mild autumn air. This place belonged to an old business associate of George's. He lived here only two months in every year, in the summer. The rest of the time Estrella lived here by herself, keeping it tidy and maintained.

'It's lovely,' Penny said, really meaning it.

Estrella smiled proudly. 'Let me take you inside, make you comfortable.'

The interior of the house was all high wooden beams and tiled floors covered with bright rugs. Estrella grew a leafy plant in almost every spare corner. She showed Penny up to her room. Up here the floor was carpeted in modern, thick carpet. The exposed bricks of the wall were decorated with paintings, the bed had a soft throw folded casually over its foot. A double glass door led out onto a tiled balcony, a profusion of long-limbed plants growing over it. Penny took in the view, over treetops and towards blue mountains in the distance. A bird whirred past overhead. Inside, Estrella put down her suitcase.

'Come, Penny.' She showed her through to the adjoining bathroom. The deep bath beckoned. 'Would you like to freshen up?' Estrella asked, reading her mind.

'I'd love to.'

'There are bath salts in the cupboard. I can unpack your things for you.'

'Thank you.'

Penny closed the door behind her and ran the bath. The bathroom smelled faintly of bleach. She sank into the bath, and closed her eyes. Her muscles began to unbunch, one by one, and with them, her overtired mind. Only one cold, tight thought recurred to her. The rehearsals for the tour… She would have to go back, and sooner than she would like. It stopped her from relaxing completely, and she knew for certain that she had to let George know, that she had to pull out and allow herself to recover properly.

Outside, night fell. When the water had gone cold, she was forced to get out and dress. The aroma of cooking food wafted up the stairs, and her stomach grumbled. But she had work to do: she found a notebook in the bottom of the dresser, and sat cross-legged on her bed with a pen to write a letter to George.

Dear George…

Here she stopped, chewing the end of the pen. How on earth was she going to word this? She knew in her heart that she should phone him, talk to him, but he was so persuasive. He'd talk her around. She tapped the pen on the notebook, then tried again.

I have only been here a few hours, but I am already feeling very relaxed.

No, that was no good. She didn't want him thinking that all she needed was a short break. She needed a long break. She tore out the page and crumpled it, then started again with purpose.

Dear George, I don't want to come back. I don't want to do the tour.

Again she crumpled the page and started again.

Dear George, I'm sorry but I'm not coming back.

A knock at the door. Penny stashed the notebook back in the bottom of the dresser and called, 'Come in.'

'Dinner is ready,' Estrella said. 'Come down when you're ready.'

Writing the letter was hard work. Perhaps she would think about it the next day. She followed Estrella downstairs, where only one setting had been laid for dinner.

'Aren't you going to eat with me?'

'I've already eaten. I never dine with the guests.' She offered that warm, beaming smile again. 'I hope you like what I've made. It's a traditional dish in my family. *Pollo al chilindrón*.'

The food was wonderful – succulent chicken legs in tomato and capsicum – but Penny felt very odd eating it alone in the big echoing dining room. With the fall of the sun, the warmth had fled. She wished she'd worn a jacket. The single lamp on the sideboard that Estrella had switched on did little to chase away the shadows, especially those gathered high up in the ceiling.

After dinner, Estrella gave her a stack of English magazines and told her to have an early night. 'The travel must have tired you out,' she said. 'I'll have your breakfast ready at eight in the morning.'

Estrella was right. The travel had wearied her. She slipped into the warm bed and drifted off almost straightaway, rocked to sleep by the remembered motion of the long train ride.

The dream sneaked under her defences in the coldest part of the morning. The dark room, the hole in the floor, the hot breath of her pursuer. She woke, heart pounding, in a strange place.

For a few moments she didn't know where she was and the disorientation made her panic. But then, remembrance came. The villa. She was on holiday. There was nothing to fear. Still, she switched on her light, reaching unconsciously for the bottle on her bedside table.

There was no bottle. She hadn't unpacked it. Estrella had unpacked for her. Perhaps she'd left the tablets in her suitcase. Penny rose and switched on the lamp, pulled out the suitcase. Empty. In the drawers then, among her clothes. She crossed the room, ploughed through underwear and shirts and neatly folded skirts to no avail. Now her pulse was picking up. Without the pills, how was she to get back to sleep? The nightmare had charged her heart, she felt jittery, unable to focus.

Once again she went to the suitcase. The drawers. Now the wardrobe, checking pockets of coats, feeling along the high shelves. She even checked the bathroom, though she knew Estrella had not been in there, had rather left her toiletries lined up neatly on top of the chest of drawers.

There was only one thing for it. She would have to wake Estrella and ask her. It was the housekeeper's fault she couldn't find her pills – important medication – so she would just have to live with being woken in the middle of the night.

Penny opened her door and padded down the hall, wondering which of the many bedroom doors was Estrella's. In the end, it was none of them, and she went instead downstairs. Beyond the sitting room, a dark wooden door. She cracked it open, could immediately hear light snoring.

'Estrella?' she said softly. 'Estrella, it's me. Penny.'

Estrella roused, sat up and turned the lamp on. She looked bleary and confused.

'Penny? What's wrong?'

'I had some pills in my suitcase. Where did you put them?'

Here Estrella sighed, smoothing her long grey hair off her face. 'They're gone.'

'What do you mean?'

'I've flushed them down the toilet.'

Penny felt a stab to her heart. Was it rage or fear? 'What? Why?'

'Señor Fellowes was very clear in his instructions to me. No pills.'

'But a doctor prescribed them. I need them to –'

'Hush!' Estrella said sharply, and the beaming smile was nowhere in evidence. Suddenly, Penny felt eight years old again, receiving an admonishment from her mother. 'And listen. I've had other young ladies in my care in the many years I've worked here. I do my job well. You must learn to trust that I know what's good for you.'

'What are you – ?'

'I'll not hear another word of it. Now go back to bed.'

The finality in her voice caused Penny to back out of the room and close the door. The light extinguished under the door. Penny hesitated, heart thudding, her feet growing cold from the tiles. *Other young ladies in my care?*

What kind of place had George sent her to?

At breakfast, Estrella was back to her usual smiling self, bustling around and plonking a plate of bacon and eggs in front of Penny. She began to wonder if she had imagined the harsh tones Estrella had used deep in the night. Penny hadn't slept again; rather she had lain there until dawn bled into the sky and she could finally, thankfully, get up. She was tired, dead tired, and longed for the jazzy bump of the uppers. But the uppers were gone.

'I'm doing laundry this morning,' Estrella said. 'If you have anything for me to wash, just bring it down.'

'Estrella,' Penny said slowly, 'about what happened last night...'

'Oh, you'll forgive me, won't you?' Estrella said, leaning over to stroke Penny's hair softly. 'I get cranky when I'm woken up.'

Penny swallowed her next sentence. This was easily fixed. She would go to the village, see the doctor – George had given her a Spanish phrasebook before she left – and get some more pills. Then she would hide them from Estrella and have them there if she needed them. She did intend to give up, of course she did. But gradually. She still needed help settling into her new environment.

With Estrella ensconced in the laundry, Penny dressed in jeans and comfortable shoes and headed down to the road. She couldn't remember seeing a doctor's surgery in the village, but there was bound to be one. And if not, then Montoya was probably only an hour or so walk. What else did she have to do with her time? Maybe she would look up the train schedule while she was there, just in case...

The morning was still cool, but the sun would soon grow warm so she stuck to the shade. A pair of woodchats sat in the low branches of a lime tree, looking at her curiously through the falling leaves. She could hear birds chirping, the occasional breeze softly singing in the upper branches, and the crunch of her own footsteps in the gravel and leaves. London was so different, with its noisy incessant traffic. She hadn't realised before how much she had grown to dislike it. Not just the noises, either. The alienation as people moved past each other day after day, all of them strangers despite their proximity.

The village came into view at the bottom of the next hill. She was growing warm from walking, and was grateful to step inside the interior of the general store. The bell over the door sounded. She lifted her sunglasses onto her head, noticing her hands were shaking slightly.

An aged man with a hooked nose shuffled out from his back room and peered at her curiously.

'Hello,' she said, reciting the limited Spanish she had learned. 'I'm looking for a *médico*? *Aquí*? *En poblado*?'

He shook his head, letting loose a rapid-fire stream of Spanish. She shrugged and held her hands apart to indicate she hadn't understood. He said, slowly in English, 'No doctor in village. Doctor in Montoya.'

She backed out, smiling. 'Thank you. Thank you. *Gracias.*'

He didn't smile in return, rather watched her with suspicious eyebrows lowered. The door closed behind her, she was once again in the warm sunshine.

Montoya. A lot further to walk. A dull nausea grew inside her, and sweat prickled across her ribs and her palms. Was she really so unfit that a long walk could make her feel unwell? She stared off down the road a few moments. Better to keep moving before lethargy set in. A couple of uppers would have helped, if Estrella hadn't flushed them away…

Penny kept moving, allowing herself for the first time to feel genuine anger towards the housekeeper. Estrella's broad smile, her bustling motherliness, were very endearing. But she had no right to interfere in Penny's business. George would be appalled when he heard. As soon as she had the thought, she doubted it. George had made it clear he wanted her off the pills. But he was overreacting, they were all overreacting. She used the pills because she needed them. When she didn't need them any longer – when the quiet of the villa had done its work and the ordeal in London had been forgotten – she'd be fine to come off them. It wasn't as though she was a desperate junkie, hooked on street drugs. She pressed her hand to her forehead, lifting her fringe off her sweaty brow. Now she was feeling distinctly unwell. The nausea was sharpening, her head was beginning to throb, and exhaustion was creeping into her muscles.

The sound of a car engine behind her. She glanced over her shoulder. It was Estrella.

'What the hell...?'

Estrella pulled up beside her and got out. 'You should get into the car, Penny,' she said.

'I'm going for a walk.'

'Señor Ramos called me from the general store. He said you looked ill, and you do. Do you really think you can make it to Montoya?'

Penny hesitated. No, she didn't really think she could make it to Montoya. In fact, she wanted to find somewhere cool and dark to lie with a damp cloth over her head, and wait for this rolling nausea to pass. 'But I have to go to the doctor.'

'You should have asked me,' Estrella said, and some of the sternness of the previous night worked its way back into her voice and her expression. 'I am here to look after you. The doctor can come to us, I need only to make a phone call.'

Still Penny stood on the side of the road. She wanted very badly to get into the car, to be driven home and taken care of in her soft, quiet room. But she was wary of Estrella now.

Estrella set her lips. 'I will count to ten. If you don't get in, I'll drive off and you'll have to walk back. One...two...'

Dimly, Penny remembered her mother using a similar method of discipline when she was a small child. It insulted her. But her muscles felt as though they were turning to mush and she didn't want to walk any further. She opened the door and got in.

A moment later, Estrella was sitting in the driver's seat, beaming at her. 'Good girl. Now, let's get you home. You'll feel much better.'

Estrella put her to bed, with a cold compress on her head and a glass of lemon and water for her stomach. Penny asked when she would call the doctor, but Estrella was evasive. She wasn't sure if he worked on Fridays. She'd see if Penny was well after lunch. Penny had to bite her tongue so she didn't blurt out, *I won't be well after lunch unless I get my pills.* She had to play it cool. If Estrella refused to call the doctor, then Penny would call George and get him to sort it. She wondered if he was back from Germany yet. For now, she was grateful to be lying still and quiet, riding the rolling waves of nausea and pain.

She dozed, on and off, and her sleep was punctuated by bad dreams. Not the usual nightmare, nothing so coherent or ordered. Just snatches of anxious and ill thoughts: a ball of knotted string unable to be unravelled by her nauseous fingers; a black stain growing on the carpet beside her bed, hissing and whispering; an old cupboard full of junk that dated back centuries, ugly dolls and dusty cases that contained evil secrets. After a few hours of this, she woke with such acute nausea that she had to get up immediately and run for the bathroom to vomit.

Afterwards, she sat on the cool tile floor of the bathroom and cried. Her head was throbbing, her hands were shaking, every muscle in her body ached. She couldn't remember ever feeling so ill. Estrella couldn't refuse her. She intended to march downstairs and demand that the housekeeper call a doctor.

Penny cleaned herself up as best she could, splashing her face with water and changing her shirt. Then she went to the door of her bedroom. It didn't budge.

She had been locked in.

Ellie tried not to stare too hard. She had never seen anything like London. The streets were alive with traffic, moving, changing constantly. The urban grey was punctuated by the bright red of buses, the gleaming black of taxis speeding past buildings so famous – Big Ben, St Paul's Cathedral – that they seemed to be made of mist and vapour, like structures in dreams. Even Bremen had not had the density, the layers of buildings, people, odd fashions, traffic... Parallel rows upon rows of houses and shops crowded in on George's car – a black Mercedes with gleaming chrome fins – as he made his way through the city and towards her new home: an apartment in Chelsea where she would live alone. At first she had been taken aback, assuming that she would stay with George for the three months. But he was very keen to raise no suspicions at all. If she was to become Penny Bright, she had to live Penny Bright's life from dawn until nightfall, every single day. She was overwhelmed, but she wouldn't let George Fellowes see it. With a profound sense of self-preservation, she reminded herself that she must keep her head at all costs. Bad things happened to farmgirls in big cities full of the wealthy; Ellie Frankel vowed to stay in control.

George had the Penny Bright cartridge playing in the car's eight-track, so she could learn the songs. It was unnecessary; she had learned them in the two days between George's visit to the farm and her departure. In truth, there wasn't much to learn. The tunes were simple, the lyrics facile. The hardest part was going to be singing them in the disconnected tones of pop music. She'd practised a little, out in the cowshed when she was sure nobody could hear her, and it had provided nothing close to the joy of singing opera. There was a challenge in copying the real Penny's intonation, her unconscious vowel modifications, her stop-start breathing patterns; but she drew the line at copying the occasional flat note. Penny Bright might get away with singing out of tune, but Ellie Frankel refused to do so.

Everything had happened so quickly it still felt as though it wasn't real. The shock of trading farm life for London life, poverty for financial security, was acute but thrilling. She half-expected to wake up and suffer the disappointment of this opportunity melting back into dreamland; the way her first opportunity with the West German Opera had. The only thing that told her she wasn't dreaming was the rumble and cramp of her stomach: hunger pains. Penny Bright was much slimmer; Ellie had barely eaten in three days.

'We'll park here,' George said, expertly backing the big car into a tiny spare space. 'The apartment is around the corner, but it's impossible to park outside.'

Ellie was amused to think that people in London had cars that they couldn't park near their homes, and she thought about the rusted-out utility truck on the Neumanns' farm, where the chickens sometimes roosted. George let her out and took her suitcase, leading her around the corner to a newly built pebble-brick apartment complex. He let them both in, and they went up in a lift to the third floor. Once there, George handed her a key and let her unlock the door to her new lodgings.

'My business rents this for Penny,' George said as she pushed open the door. 'So you needn't feel that you're trespassing on her property.'

Ellie stepped into a plain, clean living room, with thick shag carpet, a big television and a shiny record player. George's words provoked a question that had occurred to her once or twice, but which she hadn't dared yet ask.

'Does Penny Bright know I'm here?'

George smiled. 'Not exactly. Well, in fact, no. But Penny is not well, and I'd rather she concentrated on getting better.'

'What do you mean by "not well"?'

He chose his words carefully. 'Penny has recently been through a traumatic event. She became rather too reliant on prescription medication.'

'Drugs?' So the things they said about English pop stars were true.

'Nothing illegal,' he said quickly. 'She's a good girl.' He strode to the record player, calling over his shoulder that she should look at the rest of the tiny flat: a tidy bedroom with quality linen, a small bathroom with brand-new fittings, a kitchen with a laundry built into its corner. Everything smelled new. She thought about her converted storeroom at the Neumanns' house, the woody, fresh-laundry scent of it, and felt her first pang of homesickness.

Music played: George had put the Penny Bright tape on again. She joined him in the living room.

'I thought you should listen to this again. You'll need to learn the songs very quickly.'

'I've already learned the songs.'

George's serious eyebrows shot up. 'Not just the singles. The others too.'

'I've learned all of them. Everything on the tape.'

'Already?'

'Already.'

His lips curled up in amusement. He switched off the tape and nodded towards her. 'Go on, then. Let's hear one.'

The needle of pressure was comfortingly familiar. She knew what to do with pressure, turning her mind with steely determination to the task at hand. Picking up at the phrase where the tape had cut out, she began to sing.

It was a science for Ellie. Cover the note here, cut the vowel short there, add a slight nasal tone, breathe in the middle of the phrase. All the components of bad singing in her opinion, but the sum of it was that she sounded precisely like Penny Bright.

George listened to the end of the song, lips slightly parted in wonder. 'That was truly...remarkable,' he said.

'Papa always said I had a good ear,' Ellie replied, and the thought of Papa, of what he'd make of this latest venture, cast a little cloud over her exciting day.

George checked his watch. 'I've got a hairdresser coming by in half an hour,' he said. 'I've made space in Penny's room for your things, if you'd like to unpack.'

He helped Ellie with her suitcase, then returned to the living room to make a phone call while she unpacked. She had very few things, and most of them faded clothes not fit for a pop star. Six of Penny's outfits had been left in the wardrobe: she suspected they were the more generous ones. As she was folding away her underwear, she found a manila folder taped to the bottom of the drawer. She peeled it off: inside were an overdue electricity account, a warranty for the record player, a driving licence, and an envelope with a window and a solicitor's address on the front. She closed the folder and took it out to George, who was just finishing up his phone call.

'I found this,' she said. 'Some of the papers look important, I wouldn't want it to get misplaced.'

George flipped through the things inside. With a frown, he turned the envelope over, tipping out the letter inside and scanning it quickly. Ellie went to the kitchen and searched the cupboards for a glass. She was starving, but dared not eat. Instead, she gulped down a drink of water to douse the hunger pains. A buzz at the door sounded, and George called out that he was going down to let the hairdresser in. Alone for the first time, Ellie took a deep breath. Soon there were voices in the hallway, and George brought in an elderly, overly made-up woman with a big shoulder bag. She took one look at Ellie and stopped, gaping.

'Oh, my God!' she squealed, reaching out a plump hand to take Ellie's. 'Penny Bright! I *love* your songs.'

George looked stricken. Obviously he hadn't thought a woman of such advanced years would have heard of Penny Bright, let alone recognise her.

Ellie, too, took a moment to understand that she had been recognised as the pop star. An odd sense of dislocation, of not knowing who she really was, suddenly gripped her. She fought it down and produced a calm smile, taking the woman's hand. 'You know my name, but I don't know yours.'

'Barbara Murray,' she said brightly. 'I can't wait to tell my daughter. She's just bought tickets for your show. She wants me to go with her, but I think I'm too old for a pop concert.'

'Not at all,' Ellie replied. 'I think you *should* go.'

George intervened. 'Mrs Murray, Penny and I have another appointment shortly. Could we get started?'

She nodded decisively. 'Of course. What are you having done?'

George handed her the same glossy photograph he had shown Ellie back in Kokondorf. 'Exactly like that.'

Barbara Murray eyed the picture, then Ellie's long black hair. Clearly, the disparity had now occurred to her, and Ellie's heart picked up a beat. 'But I saw you on *Top of the Pops* not long ago...your hair has grown very quickly.'

'Oh, that was filmed ages ago,' George said. 'That's the way it is with television.'

She seemed excited to be let in to some kind of inside information about the life of a pop star, nodding enthusiastically as she unpacked her shoulder bag onto the dining table. 'Of course. And I must say, you look a lot better with some flesh on your bones, too.' She produced a pair of gleaming scissors. 'Right, let's get started.'

Penny's body was falling apart. It shuddered and it shook. Her skull felt as though it had been sandpapered to a rough texture on the inside, and her brain no longer fitted right. She sat on a wrought-iron chair on her balcony, hoping the evening air would help. Three days had now passed since Estrella locked her in, and each day she felt sicker than the day before. The headaches and nausea she could almost manage, but the disturbance to her sleep was unbearable. Sleep only came periodically, in three- or four-hour snatches. But when it came, it took her down to unmined depths where it wasn't safe for anyone to reside. Her dreams were confused horrors, like the feverish dreams she'd experienced as a child. She'd struggle to wake up, be wide awake for hours, terrified to sleep again, then finally be reclaimed back into those nightmare vistas.

Time passed, making little sense. On one occasion she sat on her balcony watching a group of birds clean themselves in a nearby tree. She thought she had watched for five minutes, but was surprised to find an hour had passed. On another occasion, she had tried to distract herself flipping through one of the magazines Estrella had given her, to pass a few hours that way. But only ten minutes had passed, and the long emptiness of time panicked her. How long before Estrella let her go?

Penny had begged repeatedly for the chance to phone George and talk to him. Estrella had refused her, saying he was in Germany and she couldn't contact him. But Penny didn't believe her. Why would George be in Germany? Why wouldn't he tell her if he was going abroad? Or perhaps he had told her...past conversations became tangled up with conversations in her dreams. Confused, nonsensical.

The worst aspect of her imprisonment was that she had no idea why she was so sick. Estrella told her repeatedly that it was the drugs leaving her system, that in a day or so she would start feeling better than she had for a long time. Penny didn't believe this either. She was no fool, of course: she knew she relied a little too heavily on her uppers and downers. But they had been prescribed by medical doctors.

Sure she exceeded the dosage, but the dosage was designed for average people. She had more problems than average people; average people weren't pop stars who had to be sparkling performers at a moment's notice. Cold turkey was for heroin addicts, desperate losers. No, she was convinced that she had contracted some other illness, something that required immediate medical attention. And Estrella refusing it was endangering Penny's life.

A knock at the door. Penny didn't know why Estrella bothered knocking. The keys rattled on the chain, the door opened, a tray of food was slid in and the door locked again.

Outside, the night was very soft and cool. Crickets chirped, the half-moon sat low. Penny's stomach grumbled. She stood shakily and went inside, picked up the tray and took it to her bed. The food smelled delicious, her mouth watered. She loaded a forkful of rice and it was halfway to her mouth when a thought popped wholly formed into her mind.

She's poisoning you.

Penny froze. A grain of rice dropped off her fork and into her lap. She threw the fork back onto the plate, pushing the dinner tray away and leaping to her feet. Of course! That's why she was so sick. How had she been so stupid not to figure it out before? Estrella was lacing her food with poison, and every day she would get sicker and sicker and eventually she would die. Benedict might have threatened to kill her by violence, but Estrella was killing her by stealth. Maybe Benedict had put Estrella up to it. Or maybe one of her other enemies.

Maybe George was her enemy.

Maybe this whole trip had been a way to finish off quietly what Benedict had attempted to do quickly.

Penny's heart was pumping so hard in her chest she thought it might burst. This panicked her all the more. Was this a symptom of it? She ran to the bathroom and gulped down a big glass of water. She had to flush her system of the poison. The water hit her stomach then began to rise. Good, she was going to vomit. She leaned over the toilet and let it all come out, feeling vaguely satisfied that Estrella's plan wasn't going to come to fruition after all. She stood, looked at herself eye to eye in the mirror.

'You need to get out of here.' She tried to force her thoughts into straight lines. All she had to do was get out of this room, make her way to Montoya. She had plenty of money for a hotel until the train came, and then she could get back to London, tell George everything...

George. Was he in on it? He had left her in this place, defenceless. He hadn't called to check once. She shook her head. Of course he wouldn't want to hurt her. He loved her.

Or did he? Perhaps he only loved what she could earn for him. The tour was in jeopardy...maybe he had some kind of insurance policy on her life. George was an astute businessman, that would make sense.

She sagged against the mirror and tears squeezed out of her eyes. *Betrayed.* She had been betrayed by the only person in the world she was close to. The tears turned into sobs, her chest shook, her face grew hot. Her loneliness weighed on her, crushing her, and she caved in underneath it, sinking to the bathroom floor and sobbing.

Time passed. Minutes or hours.

She knew she had to do something. She couldn't just wait here for Estrella to finish her off. With purpose, she took to her feet. She found her tote bag, her passport, her purse. She counted her money. There was plenty of cash, and her chequebook. She threw in a few items of practical clothing. Jeans, long-sleeved T-shirts, socks, a pullover. Hesitating, she snatched up her make-up bag too. There were colours there she was really fond of, and could only get in London. She laced on her gym boots, pulled on a jacket and a scarf. She walked onto the balcony.

A cold breeze tickled the treetops. She shivered. Looked down.

It was too far to jump, and impossible to climb. She dropped her bag and returned to the bedroom. She stripped the sheets, tied them in tight knots, one to the next. With the long rope of linen, she returned to the balcony to fasten it to one of the iron bars. Tested the knot. Tight enough.

Bag over her shoulder, Penny threw her legs over the railing. The toes of her shoes balanced on the outer edge of the balcony. She squatted, grabbed the rope. Tried her weight on it. It held. She began to lower herself slowly, heart thundering under her ribs.

A tearing sound. Something gave. Her hands gripped the sheet hard, she stifled a shriek. As she dangled, too far from either the balcony or the ground for safety, her escape revealed itself to be a very bad idea.

Another rip. The air collapsed beneath her back. Before she had time to scream, the ground had rushed up to meet her.

TWELVE

*I*t was nine in the morning when George let himself into the theatre at Leytonstone, Ellie Frankel in tow. With her hair newly cut in Penny's style, and her eyes rimmed in kohl and glitter, the resemblance to Penny was breathtaking. There were differences of course: no two people in the world were identical. Ellie was taller, he suspected, the impression of her being heavier probably a result of a more imposing stature than Penny's slender frailty. Ellie's face, too, was fuller, with more prominent cheekbones and a stronger mouth. Penny, despite her height, was almost elfin, whereas Ellie was bordering on statuesque. But then, the similarities overrode any of these differences. The eyes were identical in colour and shape, and were spaced precisely the same. The smile, when it came – Ellie, he was learning, was very serious – was beguiling in its girlish uncertainty, just like Penny's. While he missed Penny, he was strangely reassured by Ellie's presence. He found himself wondering if he would eventually become as close to Ellie as he was to Penny.

'This is where we rehearse?' Ellie asked, taking in the long rows of empty seats and the cleaner sweeping up near the edge of the stage.

'Twice a week now for the next few months. The band won't be here until ten, I wanted to run a few things through with you first.'

He led her to a big black desk, covered with coloured knobs, right in the centre of the room. He leaned over and flicked a switch, and power hummed on. 'This is a mixing desk,' he told her. 'The sound goes through here and back into the speakers.'

The cleaner, alerted by the sound, lifted her head and saw them. She waved. Ellie waved back.

George frowned as the cleaner approached. 'What does she want?'

'I don't know, but she seems to know me.'

'Good morning, Penny,' the cleaner said. 'You're here early.'

'We have a lot to do today,' Ellie said, not skipping a beat. George was amazed once again at her ability to be completely comfortable adopting Penny's persona. 'I'm sorry, I've forgotten your name. I meet rather a lot of people.'

The young woman blushed. 'It's Gloria. I shouldn't have presumed –'

'Not at all. It's good to see you again.'

George leaned across the desk. 'Gloria, what time do you finish?'

'Nine-thirty.'

'Go home early today.'

'But I haven't done the –'

'I'll call the theatre owner and let him know. Penny and I need some time alone.'

Gloria looked to Ellie, who nodded reassuringly.

'Mr Fellowes is a man of his word,' she said. 'Have an early finish.'

Gloria packed up her things and left, while George fiddled with the mixing desk. When they were alone, George turned to her.

'Penny called me George,' he said.

'All right, George,' she replied, smiling.

'There's an art to singing into a microphone,' he said.

'Oh?'

He could tell she didn't believe him. He could tell she didn't believe there was an art involved in anything to do with pop music.

'Yes, and as much as being able to sing just like Penny, you have to be as comfortable as her on the stage and with the equipment.

That's why we're here before the band. To make sure they don't suspect anything.' He waved her towards the stage. 'Go on, up you go. Take the microphone in the middle.'

She strode off with purpose.

'Ellie,' he called. 'Don't stand up so straight. Penny didn't.'

Without turning around she slumped her shoulders forward a fraction. George smiled to himself. She was a quick student.

She lined herself up at the middle microphone, and George called out to her, 'I have to adjust the levels. Can you make some noise?'

'Hello, hello,' she said.

'I mean sing something,' he said.

She took a breath and opened her mouth. Opera. An arpeggio that went to the moon. It was a hundred times louder than what he'd anticipated, shrieking through the speakers and sending him scrambling for the volume. She alarmed herself, pressed her hand over the microphone, making it feed back loudly. The speakers screamed again, George flattened the channel.

'Ellie,' he called, 'don't ever cover the microphone with your hand.'

She nodded, chastened.

'And don't sing so loud.'

'You asked me to sing.'

'Not like that. Sing like Penny.'

She stepped back in front of the microphone and started again. George adjusted the volume, the reverb, calling out instructions. 'That's better... Keep your lips nice and close to the mic... Good... You don't have to hide your breathing, the breathy sound is part of the effect... That's excellent. Now, relax your knees a little, drape your hand more casually over the stand. You're doing a fantastic job.' The casual stance didn't come easy to her: she was awkward, but that was to be expected. But he talked her through it, and she responded quickly and calmly, assuming a semblance of pop-star cool in short order. He began to understand that she was highly intelligent as well as highly motivated, and he almost wished he wasn't an atheist because he'd like to thank God for her. It was clear that she disdained pop music, but perhaps it was that very disdain, that refusal to be seduced

154

by the fantasy of being a pop star, that made it so easy for her to impersonate one.

The door to the foyer opened and George looked around. Musicians here early? Impossible. The theatre door swung in, and James Powell stood there, dressed in a smart business suit, grinning his usual inane grin.

'Hello, George.'

George's heart picked up a beat. 'James...' He turned to Ellie. 'Take a break, Penny.' Then back to Powell, 'I wasn't expecting you.'

'That's the point,' Powell said. 'Harry and I wanted to drop in on a rehearsal, make sure everything's up to scratch.'

'You're early. The band won't be here for another half-hour.'

'I can wait.' He nodded towards the stage. 'She's put on some pounds in rehab.'

George frowned, irritated by Powell's cockiness, but also feeling a twinge of worry for the real Penny. He hoped Estrella was treating her kindly. 'I told you, she wasn't in rehab. She's had a viral infection, she's —'

'Get her to come down. I'd like to chat with her.'

George's blood froze. It was too soon. He hadn't coached Ellie enough yet. He hadn't warned her about the financiers, their suspicions, how important it was for her to be convincing, professional, knowledgeable about her own career.

'We're just in the middle of something important,' he hedged.

'Bring her down.'

George turned to Ellie, who waited, rather too straight-backed, up on the stage. 'Penny, could you come down here for a moment? There's somebody I want you to meet.'

Ellie came. She held out a hand for James Powell, smiling. 'Hello, I'm Penny.'

'I'm James,' he said, taking her hand and kissing it. Ellie, a little taken aback, withdrew her hand too quickly.

'James is one of our financiers,' George explained quickly. 'The tour wouldn't be going ahead without him.'

'Then I'm doubly pleased to meet you,' Ellie said, without missing a beat. 'Will you stay and watch us rehearse?'

George was floored. How could she be so confident?

James Powell seemed equally surprised. 'I'd really like that.'

'Why don't you make yourself comfortable and wait?'

Powell found himself a seat a few rows back from the mixing desk, opened his briefcase and lost himself in some paperwork.

Ellie leaned close to George, dropping her voice to a whisper. 'He's important, I take it?'

'Very. Very, very.'

'Don't worry. I can do this.'

He hoped she was right. She waited quietly on a seat next to the mixing desk while he prepared for the rehearsal. Soon, the musicians started arriving. He noticed they barely glanced at Ellie, and certainly nobody seemed suspicious that she looked or acted different. He was sweating so hard he had to shrug out of his jacket. His palms were moist, but he couldn't show James Powell that he was worried. So he kept pretending everything was all right, while Ellie kept pretending she was Penny Bright; and nobody seemed any the wiser about either of their pretences.

The moment of truth arrived half an hour later, with the band finally set up, James Powell alert in his seat with his briefcase packed away, and Ellie returning – with sufficiently slumped shoulders this time – once more to the stage. Everything was poised to go for rehearsal; George's anxiety peaked.

Then the drummer counted the band in, the first four bars of the song played, and Ellie began to sing.

Thank God. It sounded exactly like the record. There was no audible difference between the new Penny Bright and the old one. Ellie stood, relaxed, hand casually resting on her mic stand, looking for all the world like somebody she wasn't. The song ended, the next one began. Again, Ellie's performance was uncanny. It was almost as though Penny had never left.

James Powell was at his shoulder, nodding enthusiastically. 'You've put my mind at rest, George.'

'I'm glad,' George said, trying desperately to cover up the intense relief that was flooding through his veins, making his knees sag and his shoulders collapse.

Powell turned his gaze to the stage and watched a little while, a smile on the corners of his lips. 'She's good, isn't she?' he said.

George watched Ellie, hiding his own smile. 'Oh yes,' he said. 'She's amazing.'

Alone in her luxury apartment, the stress of the day finally caught up with Ellie. As she stood in the gleaming kitchen, waiting for the toaster to pop, she felt a sense of growing emptiness, of coldness and estrangement. She tried to reassure herself that she was just tired, but the feeling unsettled her. She sat at the table with her toast and ate it with a meagre smear of marmalade, longing for Frau Neumann's honey-roasted pork, for cabbage stewed with onion and apple, and potatoes whipped with horseradish and cream.

After the long rehearsal, she was exhausted. The pressure of pretending to be somebody else, the mind-bending task of speaking English constantly, and then all the new faces, new experiences to process. Singing like Penny Bright was the easy part; the rest was taxing her. Even standing right was difficult, let alone dealing with the hangers-on who dropped in and out of the theatre: musicians' girlfriends in floppy felt hats and big sunglasses, unwashed road crew who puffed cigarettes – *Cigarettes!* – while she was trying to sing, record company people on invented business who stayed for the entire rehearsal, friends-of-friends-of-friends whose eyes lingered on her hungrily, who laughed too hard and listened too intently...It had tested her concentration to its limit and now she longed for the familiar and the comfortable. Even when George had given her the first half of her money, it hadn't managed to ease her homesickness. The cash lay in a thick envelope on the table, ready for her to take to the bank. But it meant little: money was cold, and she was too tired to think of what she might do with it when these few months were over and she returned to her normal life.

Ellie finished her toast and wiped the crumbs from her fingers. Her stomach rumbled in protest: she was still hungry. But she wouldn't eat. George said there was a magazine interview coming up, a photo shoot. She had to get a slender edge on her figure before then.

She eyed the telephone on the kitchen bench. Would it be permissible for her to use it, to phone Dieter? She suspected that, even if it wasn't, she could offer to pay George back for the cost. She had no idea how much money George had, but knew that rich people were often miserly. Hesitantly, she called the operator and asked for a line to Germany.

At the other end, the phone rang and rang and nobody answered. She checked her watch. They should be home. They should all be sitting around the dinner table in the cosy house, surrounded by smells of cooking and the quiet sounds of the rural night. Where could they be? Frustrated, she hung up.

Ellie picked up the envelope and peered in. All that money, more than she had ever seen. But right now, she just wanted to be home where people knew who she was and loved her.

Damp cold on her back. Aching bones. Hot pain in her head. Her eyes fluttered open. Disorientation swooped down on her. Beneath her, wet grass. Above her, looming like a shadow from a nightmare, was a tall house. A sheet tied to the balcony fluttered in the breeze. Something about the sight of the house sent ice to her heart.

You have to get out of here.

She struggled to her feet. A bag lay next to her, its contents half-tumbled on the grass. What on earth had happened to her?

You have to get out of here.

The urgent message hammered at her brain. Quickly, she collected her things and began to move. A low fence separated her from a wide field. Beyond it, a forest. The sky was clear and dark, the moon gave only a little light. She dashed across the field, her ears ringing and her head pounding. Once she was in the cover of the trees, she sat on a flat rock and tried to think.

Her thoughts were in disarray. How had she ended up outside that house? She tried to work backwards, but found in her memory only a dark shadow. So she tried to stretch back further. Where was she? Again, the shadow. Panic gripped her. She tried to breathe through it. With trepidation, she asked herself the most fundamental question there was: Who was she?

Only shadow.

Her heart began to pound. Clearly, she'd taken a blow to the head. When the pain had subsided, she'd remember again. *Don't panic, don't panic.* Maybe she just needed a little prompting. She riffled through the bag, pulling out clothes and cosmetics. Crumpled tissues, mint wrappers and bits of paper spilled out. Here was her purse. No driving licence. Her hand closed over a dark blue booklet.

'My passport,' she murmured, nervous fingers flipping it open. She peered into the dark, trying to turn the pages towards the weak moonlight.

Angela Annette Smith.

She waited for the shadow on her memory to move. It didn't.

'Angela Smith,' she said, trying the name on. But it was just a name, it didn't feel like *her* name. It didn't feel like it was connected in any way to this body, which felt completely familiar. She turned her hands over in front of her face. Short, well-kept nails. A single silver ring on her right hand. None of this surprised her, none of it moved under the shadow. They were her hands and she knew them. She tried to remember where she had got the ring, focusing down hard on it.

More shadows.

She picked up the passport again, examining it more closely in the moonlight. She recognised the crest on the front as British. So she was British? That felt right. But it didn't mean she was in Britain. If she had her passport, she might be travelling abroad. She flipped through the pages, but couldn't make out the stamps in the dark. Instead, she turned back to the page with her photograph again, that name that she felt disconnected from. She read the other details as best she could in the dark. Date of birth was listed as 21 January 1955. That made her twenty. But how did she know that, how did she know with certainty that it was 1975? She concentrated again, hoping that one memory might unlock another.

It was futile. Again, thoughts slipped under shadow, and she was completely disconnected from herself, except for her body and the pain in it.

A light from nearby caught her attention. She looked up and across the field. Lights had come on in the tall house. Her heart skipped a beat.

They're looking for me.

She didn't know who *they* were or what they wanted, but she knew she couldn't let them find her. Jumping to her feet, Angela Smith scooped up her bag and began to run.

Dieter helped his mother out of her coat and hung it behind the front door. Her shoulders were slumped forward under her brown cardigan, and she put him in mind of a moth. The last awful hours had dulled her, made her small.

'He'll be all right, Mama,' Dieter said, one arm around her tired shoulders. She turned to him, allowing herself to be folded in his arms.

They had spent two days at a hospital in Bremen. The horrible dream had begun yesterday – Was it only yesterday? It felt like a million years ago when Dieter's father had gone out to fix the tractor engine. The engine had been running, the bonnet open, when somehow the gears had slipped and the machine had lurched forward, crushing him against the wall of the barn. An ambulance had been called, Dieter's mother had been convinced her husband was dead, but they had carefully removed him and rushed him to intensive care in Bremen. Dieter and Mama had followed in his car, silent and panicked. By the time they arrived, Papa was already having emergency surgery. They paced, unable to find a word to say to each other. Finally, he emerged, unconscious and attached to many wires and machines. For Dieter, it was surreal. His father, always so robust, reduced to this. They sat with him, his mother twisting a handkerchief between her hands. Hours passed, a parade of doctors and specialists passed too. Bland reassurances were offered, but eventually, after the long sleepless night and the hallucinatory following day, a kind doctor told them to go home.

'It will be some time before he becomes conscious. We expect him to recover fully, but slowly. You should get some rest.'

Now, Dieter stood back and led his mother to a chair at the kitchen table. 'I'll make you something to eat,' he said.

'I'm not hungry.'

'You must eat.'

'What will I do if he dies, Dieter? He's everything to me. Life without him would be too long, too empty.'

'Hush, Mama. He isn't going to die.' He sat opposite her, alarmed by the dark circles under her eyes. 'If you're sure you aren't hungry, then I think you should go to bed. Neither of us has slept.'

Her eyes welled with tears. 'I've never slept a night apart from him since we were married.'

He stood, helping her to her feet. 'Go on, rest. Perhaps it won't seem so awful in the morning.'

When she had gone to bed, Dieter fixed himself some soup and bread, and began to eye the telephone. He put his dishes in the sink and found the phone number Ellie had given him on the morning she left.

'This is where I'll be staying,' she'd said. 'Don't hesitate to call.'

But Dieter hesitated. Of course he wanted to speak to her. The sound of her voice was only small compensation for the loss of her presence. Yet, he didn't want to burden Ellie with his anxiety. The news would make her feel worried and far from home. If he called, it could only be to ask her how she was enjoying her adventure, how she was coping with homesickness. He'd have to bury all of his own feelings for her sake. But just to hear her voice would ease his mind. He drew a chair up to the bench and began to dial.

Despite his promise not to worry her, he was defeated at the first hurdle. She said, 'I phoned last night. Where were you?'

He didn't know whether it was his natural aversion to lying, or simply that he had to unburden his heart, but the story came out in a rush. It felt good to talk about it finally. She knew just what to say, reassured him, made sympathetic noises, and her gentle practicality was a balm for his ragged nerves.

'Dieter,' she said quietly, when he had finished. 'If your father can't work, what's going to happen to the farm?'

'I'll have to work harder, I suppose,' he said, frowning. He'd been so tired, this hadn't yet occurred to him.

'Let me send you some money.'

'No, Ellie. The money is yours.'

'You'll need to hire somebody. You won't manage otherwise.'

'I won't take your money.'

'Why not? I've taken yours, your family's. It would make me so happy to repay you.'

Dieter couldn't think of what to say. Ellie raised a valid point; how were they going to manage if Papa was sick for a long time?

'I'm sending you a cheque,' she said, with finality. 'I have plenty of money, now. I'll still have a lot left over.'

He could see there was no point in arguing, so he simply said, 'Thank you, Ellie.'

He asked about her, then, about London and what she'd been doing, but she was noncommittal, guarded. Perhaps she was holding back on her own feelings, out of consideration for his. In any case, when she finally reminded him that the phone call was costing a lot of money and he should get some rest, he agreed with her.

'I still love you,' she said.

'I'll never stop loving you,' he replied, thinking of his mother and father, and how they had never slept a night apart until now. 'I can't wait to be with you again.'

Then he had to say goodbye and hang up. The house felt very silent, and very empty.

Ellie was nervous. Singing, she was good at. But being interviewed was completely new to her. To have to answer questions about her own life would be difficult, but to provide details about another woman's felt impossible.

George had coached her, of course. 'Remember,' he kept saying, 'this wasn't Penny's real life either. She made it all up, all you have to do is stick to the story.'

Ellie had read every article about Penny that George had given her, and he'd coached her through at least half-a-dozen mock interviews. But now the pressure was really on.

The interview was to take place at a radio station in south London. She waited in a drab, overheated lounge room while George paced. She was starting to get the hang of the hair and make-up. The secret was masses of hairspray, and glitter everywhere to hide uneven lines or poor shading. Her silvery-blue blouse was clinging to her armpits, and she tried to will herself not to sweat. The radio played in the lounge room – a lot of talking, very little music – and Ellie twisted a tissue between her fingers and deliberately kept her face neutral. Autograph seekers from among the staff stopped by, and Ellie practised her new skill: forging Penny Bright's signature. It was difficult, the real Penny was left-handed, but she thought she had just about mastered the odd slope, the narrow loop on the bottom of the 'y' and 'g'.

'I wanted to ask you about the B side to the last single,' one young man with a twitching left eyelid said. 'What are the lyrics about?'

Ellie was stumped. She wasn't even sure what a 'B side' was. 'Oh, you know, love…girls and boys…relationships.'

He nodded as though he'd been given the divine secrets of the universe. George shooed him off. 'Haven't you got somewhere else to be?'

Ellie smiled at George after the young man had left. 'What on earth was he talking about?'

'The track on the other side of the record. It's actually about snow. Penny wrote it when we were driving up in the north country one January.'

'Snow? I'll have to remember that.'

Finally, the DJ came through to find them. 'Reggie Bones, they call me Doctor Bones,' he said with a laugh disproportionate to the humour of his nickname. He had a big square head and a sandy moustache. 'Come on through.'

'Come with me, George?' she said on impulse.

He seemed relieved to be asked. They followed Reggie Bones down a corridor lined with records in frames, and into a recording booth. Ellie was given a seat, a set of padded headphones, and shown her microphone. Levels were adjusted, lights blinked, a producer twiddled dials. George sat next to her and made off-air small talk with the DJ. Ellie hadn't slept well the night before. After Dieter's phone call, and with the pressure of the interview in the morning, sleep had eluded her until well after midnight, and then had been full of half-dreams that jerked her awake periodically. She stifled a yawn, making the dozens of thin bangles on her wrist clank against each other, and tried to gather her thoughts.

'Okay, Penny,' the DJ said. 'We're on in five.'

She nodded solemnly, took her courage in her hands and waited for the first question.

'Welcome back, listeners. We have, here in the studio with us, pop's newest princess, Penny Bright. Welcome, Penny.'

'Hi, Reggie.'

'Ah, my friends call me Doc. Doc Bones!' Here he pressed a button and a sound effect – rattling bones – echoed loudly in her ears. He laughed as if it was the funniest thing he had ever heard. 'First, let's talk about your upcoming tour. Can you tell me what audiences can expect?'

Solid ground. George had practised this question with her over and over, so she was easily able to answer questions about the stage set-up, the light show, the music, the venues. Holding firmly to the crisp English tones she had learned from her mother, she forced herself to relax and answered the questions confidently. She warmed to her topic, and found herself almost regretful that it wouldn't actually be her going on the tour: the real Penny would be back by then, and the fun would all be hers.

'Now, let's talk a little about your background,' Reggie Bones said, managing flashing lights and coloured dials without even glancing at her.

Ellie shifted in her seat, leaned forward on her elbows, preparing herself.

'You're only twenty, but you've achieved quite a lot.'

'I started singing very young.'

'Who taught you to sing?'

This hadn't been in any of the practice sessions. 'My father,' Ellie answered, after the silence had drawn out a little too long.

'Oh?' The DJ glanced at his notes. 'I thought your father was a bus driver?'

'He loved music.' She glanced across at George, who nodded almost imperceptibly. 'He had once been a musician of great promise himself, but when that didn't happen, I think he poured all of his ambition into me.'

Again he checked his notes. 'It says here that both your parents are dead.'

'That's right,' Ellie answered. Penny had insisted on dead parents in all her interviews, she had once told George that live parents would just create problems. Ellie wondered where Penny's parents really were, and if they were worried about her.

'If they were alive today, do you think they'd be proud of you?'

No, Papa would be horrified. 'My mother would have been proud of whatever I did,' she said slowly. 'My father was a little harder to please.'

'Really? He wouldn't be proud that you became a singer, after he taught you how to sing?'

Papa's voice was in her ears now, as clear as if he was sitting right next to her, spitting in disdainful German. 'Singing? That's not singing. You sound as if you are being strangled! There's no timbre, no colour, your voice is collapsing on itself.' Momentarily confused, Ellie had missed the DJ's question.

'I'm sorry?' she managed.

'I said that surely he'd be proud. After all, he taught you to sing.'

'It's comp...' *Kompliziert*. Only the German word would come to her. How could this be happening? She was fluent in English, had been thinking in English for days. *Kompliziert, kompliziert*. She reached for a synonym, but now language had stopped signifying at all. Time ticked on in the dark, quiet booth. She froze.

George intervened, leaning across to speak into her mic. 'Penny would rather not talk about her family,' he said sternly.

'Complicated,' she gasped. 'My feelings about my family are complicated. George is right, I'd rather not talk about them.' She recovered now, smiling. 'I'd just like to leave the past behind me, look towards the future. Let's talk about the album.'

Reggie, ever aware of dead air on the radio, quickly turned to his next question. Then it was time for a commercial break, and the DJ left them alone for a few moments.

'What happened?' George asked, in a low voice.

'My English failed. Just for a second.'

'We got away with it, I think.'

'Perhaps we'd better wait another week or so before we do any more interviews. I need to settle in, I need to...' She pressed a hand to her forehead, disappointed in herself. She would have to do better.

George sensed her frustration, and he tapped her on the shoulder: a gesture that couldn't decide if it was affectionate or impersonal. 'I think that's a good idea. I'll reschedule Friday's, and we'll just concentrate on the rehearsals.'

Reggie Bones re-entered the booth, chuckling. 'You wouldn't believe it,' he said. 'There's a crowd gathering outside the station. They heard the interview was live and came straight down. You might be signing a few autographs on your way out.'

George smiled at Ellie, who felt a wave of tiredness.

'Let's play your new single,' the DJ said, and cued up the song to play directly after the commercials.

Ellie waited, and Papa's voice came back to her. By an effort of will, she banished it.

I'm sorry, Papa, she said in her mind, *I can't listen to you now.*

The phone call came in the early hours of the morning. George woke, his heart jumping. Only bad news came at that time of day.

Aila sat up sleepily. 'Is that the phone?'

'I'll get it,' he said, stumbling out of bed. 'Don't worry.'

In the living room, he turned on the light and scooped up the phone.

'Hello?' he croaked.

'Señor Fellowes, it is bad news.' Estrella. His blood dropped two degrees.

'What's wrong?'

'Penny's gone.'

'What? How?'

'I think she climbed off the balcony.'

'Climbed off the...' He lowered his voice to a harsh whisper. 'Estrella, it's twenty feet high.'

'There were sheets in the garden. She tied them together. I don't know which way she went, it's dark...What do you want me to do?'

George's mind circled crazily. Penny was gone? It was impossible.

Aila stood at the threshold of the room, looking pale and curious. He covered the receiver with his hand and said to her, 'Go back to bed. It's business.'

'It's three a.m.,' she said, the faintest note of suspicion in her tone. 'Is that Penny?'

'No, it's someone else,' he said. 'You know this industry never shuts down.'

She pulled her lips into a tight line, but turned and left the room anyway. He returned his attention to Estrella. 'Find her. Get everybody you know to help. She can't get far without being seen. Find her.'

'I'll do my best, Señor Fellowes. But you have to come.'

'I'll get the earliest flight I can. Estrella, you weren't cruel to her, were you?'

'I did what I had to do,' she huffed, defensively. 'And she was getting better. Another three or four days…'

George sighed, this was no time for remonstrations. 'Just find her. I'll be with you as soon as I can.'

He hung up, and went to pack his bags for a trip to Spain.

THIRTEEN

*L*ondon was daunting without George.

Ellie consulted her carefully drawn map again and set off up Sydney Street. George had called her just an hour ago, from a payphone at the airport.

'I can't pick you up for rehearsal today. I've urgent business to attend to. Do you think you can manage to get there yourself?' He'd given her instructions to organise the limousine service then, at her blunt refusal, given her the number to phone a taxi. But she thought it would be better to catch the Tube. She knew so little about London, and here she was pretending to be somebody who had lived here for years. She had hidden herself under a floppy hat and big sunglasses, and consulted the Underground map, making a list of which trains to catch, and where to change.

She had experienced London so far as a series of trips in George's Mercedes, or from the windows of her apartment, high up above it all. Down here on the cold street, it was different. The city smells – exhaust fumes, coffee being ground, wet pavement, stale perfume on musty coats – were stronger. The city sounds – traffic growling street by street into the distance, machinery, buskers, sirens – were louder. She tried to enjoy it, but found that her senses weren't used to the layers of impressions. She felt disconnected, alien.

Still, she only had to get herself as far as South Kensington underground, then change at Holborn for Leytonstone. It was all written on her piece of paper, and she clutched it tightly in her right hand.

Two stops in the wrong direction from South Kensington, she realised her mistake and got off the train. Changed platforms. Was on her way again. The carriage was so crowded she couldn't get to the door in time at Holborn and had to get off at Chancery Lane. No connecting trains from here. Back to Holborn. Waited for what seemed like forever, aware that it would probably be bad to be late for this rehearsal. People everywhere, and she began to grow afraid that she'd be recognised despite her attempts to disguise herself. She'd been mobbed at the radio station after the interview, and hadn't liked it at all. The fans had called out that they loved her, but it was more like they wanted to pluck pieces of her flesh away for keepsakes. Finally she climbed aboard the train to Leytonstone and stood uncomfortably close to a stooped businessman who insisted on reading *The Times* with one hand, so that the edge of the paper kept drooping into her cheek. People behind her and beside her, nowhere to move to. She took a deep breath and closed her eyes, tried to conjure up the wide fields of the farm in her imagination. But all she could smell was newsprint and all she could hear was the clatter of the train.

The carriages slowly began to empty out, and soon she was at her destination. The theatre was a brisk ten-minute walk, and then she removed her hat and glasses so Gloria knew her to let her in. While she was relieved that the journey was over, she had the whole new challenge of getting through a rehearsal without George there to manage everything. She hoped she wouldn't have another episode like the day before, when her English failed her. Perhaps if she looked unfriendly enough, nobody would try to talk to her at length. She had the distinct impression already that the band didn't like her, and she wondered what Penny had done to get them offside so quickly.

Ellie was the first one there. As Gloria finished mopping the foyer, Ellie stood on stage and remembered her old fantasies. She cautiously imagined this was a rehearsal, not for a pop band, but for a grand opera. One of the majestic bel canto tragedies, *Lucia*, perhaps. Or one of the rich romances like *Butterfly*. It had been so long since she sang. How she would love to sing Puccini, or Verdi with his glorious melodies. Singing Penny's tunes was not satisfying, it could only ever be an exercise in imitation, and being onstage aroused in her again her first love of opera. She had some money now, and she imagined it would give her incredible freedom. When she returned to Germany she could travel to audition, or move to Munich. Dieter would come with her.

Wouldn't he?

She dismissed the thought before it took root. They were meant to be together, so they would be together. Somehow. He wouldn't make her give up her dreams.

The door to the foyer opened, and Tony and Paul walked in, talking and laughing together. A too-thin woman in tight bell-bottoms, a tiny tank top and miles-high platform shoes accompanied them. She was obviously stoned, blowing hot breath and wet kisses into their ears and nearly tripping on a lead as she crossed the stage to perch on Tony's amplifier. The musicians greeted Ellie coolly, and she sat on the edge of the stage and waited for everybody to arrive, to tune up, to ready themselves to rehearse. The usual entourage of hangers-on dribbled in and out, and Ellie gave up the pretence of being friendly towards them or interested in what they had to say. Pop stars were supposed to be sullen and egotistical: let them think that's what she was.

Preparations to play took a lot longer without George there, and the band's slowness irritated her: it was they who needed to rehearse, not her. Her stomach grumbled, the tiny breakfast she had eaten having already slipped through without making an impression. Finally, they were ready. The drummer counted in, and they launched into the first song, Penny Bright's latest single.

But something sounded wrong in the chorus.

Ellie turned around, holding her hand up to stop them. The music clattered to a halt.

'That's wrong,' she said.

Tony, eyes rounded, smiled at her. 'Wrong?'

Ellie had the suspicion that his smile was insincere. She scanned the faces of the other band members, and her suspicion grew. Was this some kind of joke? Surely not: professional musicians wouldn't behave that way. She'd noticed at their first rehearsal that they were always making mistakes, playing without being properly tuned, not forcing their lazy, fumbling fingers into precise patterns. This was probably just another instance of their inadequacy.

'Yes, it's wrong,' she said slowly, as if explaining to a simpleton. 'The second bar there changes from A minor to D minor, not C-sharp minor. That makes no harmonic sense, and it makes me sound like I'm singing out of tune…which I'm not.'

They were all silent, staring at her.

Her stomach rumbled again, and she was suddenly very tired of this. She despised carelessness and mediocrity in music; especially when she was working so hard. George wasn't strict enough with them. 'Let's do it again, and let's do it right this time. And, you,' she said to Tony with a peremptory point of her finger, 'your guitar is out of tune.'

The groupie on top of his amp stared at her, mouth open, nearly toppling off her seat. Tony parted his lips to say something, then thought better of it and quickly tuned up. The drummer counted them in again and this time it sounded right. Ellie was satisfied for now, but she would have to watch them. She couldn't have anybody else making her sound bad.

It was midmorning when George finally slid into Estrella's car at Montoya station.

'Have you heard anything?' he asked breathlessly.

She shook her head and his heart fell. All through the long journey he'd fantasised about arriving to find Penny safely returned, sheepishly admitting that she'd made a silly mistake, feeling better and ready to return to work. But she was still missing; disappeared into the dark.

'You've put out the alert?'

Estrella drew out into traffic. 'Everybody on the road in and out of the village has been told to look for her. Certainly, somebody will have to see her. I left her description with the stationmaster here, so if he sees her he'll call me immediately. It's her only way back home.' Here she dropped her voice. 'That is, if she intends to go home.'

George knew what she meant. Penny could be anywhere. He felt acutely the world's vastness, the way it stretched off in a million directions from every point. And Penny was heading off in one of those directions. How would he ever find her? 'Is she very sick? Could she be in danger?'

'She was very close to being well again, Señor Fellowes. My guess is that she was quite well when she left. Feeling well may have made her leave.'

'What do you mean?'

She slowed to steer around a family of ducks crossing the dirt road. 'Let me ask, Señor Fellowes, why would a girl of such a young age have already developed such a dangerous habit?'

'In response to a traumatic event. I told you that.' But even as George said it, he knew that Penny's problems with the drugs had started well before Benedict Marten had abducted her. She was highly strung, she kept to a punishing schedule. Penny had a tiger on her tail: her past had been tough and that desperation to escape it, to make something else of herself, meant it was impossible for her to relax. Coming here, unwinding, glimpsing another kind of life... now George saw Estrella's point. 'So you think that once she felt normal again...?'

'She couldn't bear the idea of going back to the situation that created her addiction.'

'But that means she'll never come back.'

'She may. She likes being a pop star, yes?'

'I think so, yes.' But, again, he wasn't sure. Did he really know so little about Penny? He turned to watch out the window, as the morning sunshine poured over the broad golden fields on either side of the road. 'I don't like this, Estrella,' he murmured. 'It reminds me of that other time...'

'That was long ago,' she said, and he wasn't sure if she was reassuring him or herself. 'And this is completely different.' Her voice dropped, and George heard her say, 'This time, there are no innocent victims.' He didn't answer.

Soon, the villa came into view. The trees had grown since last he'd been here, and now towered over the roof. Estrella's employer was an old friend of George's, going back to his early days in the business. Over the years, George had made use of the house on a number of unhappy occasions. The last time had been after Aila's final miscarriage when they'd come together to convalesce, to school themselves to a life as a couple without children. But it had also become a favoured, discreet destination for record industry contacts worried about their unstable artists. It was not unusual for a manager or producer to sidle up to him at a party, enquire in an urgent whisper about 'the house in Spain', and then ask George to organise a 'holiday' for a pop star suffering from nervous exhaustion, or trying to get off booze or drugs.

He opened the car door and stood, peering off into the distance. On the other side of the house's low fence, there was a field of yellowed grass with an old tractor rusting on its side. Beyond, trees stretched away.

'Have you checked out there?' he asked Estrella.

She shook her head. 'Not yet, I've been busy driving up and down the main roads.'

'But if she's trying to run away, if she's afraid of you...'

'You go on. I'll make you some lunch. You must be hungry.'

He was, but it was hardly important at the moment. Still, he nodded and strode off towards the fence and across the field.

'Penny?' he called, heading out of the sunlit field and into the shade of the wood. 'Penny, it's George! Are you in here?'

His eyes scanned the ground, looking for disturbances to the thick layer of leaves. He picked up a stick and weaved slowly through the outer edge of trees, poking at odd objects carefully. Mostly stones and twigs and skulls of long-dead birds. Then he came to a flat rock, and his eyes lit on a scattering of junk: tissues, mint wrappers, a bent train ticket. He swooped on them. The mint wrapper he recognised as Penny's favourite brand: she'd often asked him to find a store on the way home from a meeting or interview so she could buy them.

But the train ticket was absolute confirmation. Cordoba to Montoya, dated with the day she had arrived.

'Penny!' he called again, louder this time. His voice alarmed birds perched quietly nearby, and they took off in a flurry of anxious wings. 'Penny! Penny, where are you?'

Galvanised, he plunged further into the trees, calling and calling. But there was no response except for the crickets in the shade, and the peep of birds too far away to be alarmed by his shouting. Something about seeing actual evidence of her being here had woken new alarm in his heart. It hadn't been that long since somebody with evil intent had snatched her away: Could she be so unlucky for that to happen to her again? He knew so little of her past; could somebody else have followed her here, waited for the right moment to make his move...?

'Señor Fellowes!' This from the distance, behind him.

He hesitated. Perhaps if he kept moving into the wood, she might be just around the next tree.

'Señor Fellowes!' Estrella's voice was urgent. George admitted he had no idea how deep the wood was, or what was on the other side. He turned and headed back. Estrella was halfway across the field, and he met her by the shade of the overturned tractor.

She flapped a piece of paper at him, panting. 'I found this, in her room.'

George frowned and took the paper from her, reading the single line inscribed on it. *Dear George, I'm sorry but I'm not coming back.*

His head spun. Not coming back? But she had to come back. He read the line again, then grew curious. Why wasn't the letter signed? Why were there no explanations, no mention of her plans?

'Is there anything else? This looks unfinished.'

'It was still in the notepad. It probably *was* unfinished.' She touched his arm softly. 'It might have been a very difficult letter for her to write.'

George shivered faintly with relief. At least she had left willingly, on her own. 'Estrella, what's on the other side of the forest?'

'Farms.'

'Roads?'

'Local roads.'

'Do they lead to Montoya?'

She pursed her lips, considering. 'Only back through the village. Somebody would see her.'

George shook his head, his eyes going to the horizon. The angle of the sun on the grass, the smell of the air, the shadow of the villa behind him: all reminders of another time. He was in a turmoil of unpleasant emotions. Worry for Penny's wellbeing, guilt for sending her here in the first place, anxiety over the future of the tour, and other feelings...feelings he thought he'd dealt with long ago, and had hoped never to experience again.

George's first job in the industry was in the mail room at Falcon Records, an ambitious new label started by young entrepreneur Warren Barker. George showed his wit and determination at every opportunity, and was gradually promoted through the small company. Within eighteen months, he was the youngest head of division at Falcon. George's great skill was in reading the market, identifying the talent that would hit the spot and finding the right song. He signed the casts of three popular musicals, and was credited with discovering England's first 'teen idol': seventeen-year-old Timmy Starr. Warren Barker began grooming George for an executive position. George wanted nothing of it: it was too much paperwork. He wanted to learn the technical side of recording and production, but Barker wouldn't allow him to. George had ideas, creative ambitions about the texture of music and how it could be manipulated. He left Falcon for a lower paid position assisting a producer with TRG, and prepared himself to start all over again.

On the Friday evening of his first week at TRG, George let himself into the tiny South Kensington flat that Aila's parents had bought them as a wedding present. Aila was waiting on the couch, her face was pink. She leapt off the couch and launched herself into his arms.

'What is it?' he asked, alarmed.

She stood back, barely able to contain her smile. 'I'm pregnant,' she announced breathlessly.

George felt a hot shock. They had been trying for a baby since their wedding night; it was Aila's dearest wish to be a mother. But as more than a year passed with no result, George had begun to think it would never happen. His reaction to their inability to have children was mixed. For Aila's sake, he was sad. The way she fussed over other people's children, the silly tearfulness she fell to when she spoke about babies, was as endearing as it was painful to watch. For his sake, he was relieved. He hadn't forgotten Mr Lewins's words: he had to guard himself against repeating his own father's mistakes. And though he'd never had the slightest predisposition towards mistreating anyone, let alone children, he couldn't help but fear that deep down he was blighted. Never having to become a father meant that he would never have to face that possible darkness inside him.

He closed his arms around Aila and breathed the warm scent of her hair. She shook with happy sobs and he held her as tightly as he could.

'Just think, *Lemmikki*,' she said, her voice muffled against his shirt. *Lemmikki* was her pet name for him: Finnish for 'darling'. 'By this time next year, our lives will be completely different.'

Aila was wrong. She miscarried six days later.

Now that she knew she could fall pregnant, she became determined to fall again. Every night, no matter how late he came home or what mood he was in, she would urge him to make love. Their lovemaking had never been spectacular – his feelings for her had always been more about the tenderness of the heart than the passions of the body – but now it became a duty. A terrible routine evolved in their lives: long months of disappointment, then a brief few weeks of joy and hope. Then Aila would miscarry again...and again. George felt keenly his inability to comfort her. The only thing that could bring her happiness, he knew, was a baby. But there was no baby. There was money, there was a new house being built, there were shoes and dresses and parties with the rich and famous, but there was no baby.

And there never would be.

FOURTEEN

ngela Smith spent the night in a barn on the other side of the forest. It was impossible to sleep. She kept trying to stretch the edges of her memory, her body and brain throbbed with pain, she dropped in and out of nightmares – meaningless, savage – then finally woke in the warmest part of the morning to noise outside. She rose and peered out through the barn doors. A lorry idled nearby, its driver just closing up the tray and getting into the cabin. She snatched up her bag and began to run, waving and calling, 'Wait!' The lorry stopped, she ran to catch up with it and opened the door.

A very fat woman, dressed in man's clothes, peered down at her. For an instant, the trace of an old memory laid itself over this image, and Angela froze, trying to recall it to her tired mind. But it slipped from her grasp, and the woman was speaking to her in Spanish.

Spain. She was in Spain. She concentrated hard: did she speak Spanish? Words squeezed into consciousness, but not Spanish. Greek. No use to her, here.

'Do you speak English?' she asked, desperately.

'Yes, a leetle.'

'I need a lift to the nearest large town.'

'I go to Montoya.'

Angela turned the name of the town over in her mind, checking it for any sense of foreboding.

'You come?' the woman asked.

'Yes,' Angela said decisively, climbing into the seat. 'Thank you.'

The woman nodded, and the rest of the journey was passed in silence. When they arrived in the town, Angela started to feel the first stirrings of unease. Vaguely familiar sights prickled at her memory. The front of the train station came into view and she instinctively sank down in her seat.

'Stop here!' she said breathlessly.

The woman stopped. Angela reached into her purse for a handful of coins to give her. 'Thank you, thank you.'

The woman took the money and threw it on the dashboard, her lips not once curling into a smile. She jabbed a stubby finger at the train station. 'Cordoba or Granada. Last trains for two days. They go this morning.'

Angela understood, and climbed from the cabin cautiously. Keeping to the shadows of trees and buildings, she made her way towards the train station. The sight of a big, black car parked in the turning circle outside had her ducking into an alley between two buildings. She peered around. Why did the car frighten her? Was she being paranoid? It waited, engine idling. Angela waited too, trying to scour her mind for any shred of memory about the black car. Nothing would come, and the frustration made her want to weep. Was this going to be her life from now on? Her head was pounding and she felt sick and achey. She should really see a doctor, but she had the awful conviction that she had to get away from here as soon as possible.

A tall man, dressed in black, emerged from the train station and approached the car. Recognition glimmered. Angela almost called out to him, but the name wouldn't find its way onto her tongue. She knew him, he was important somehow...but was he a friend or a foe? She searched herself, found no bad feelings. Maybe he could help her remember herself. She was a moment from stepping out of the cover of the alley and running towards him, when a woman emerged from the car and moved to the boot to open it for him. At the sight of the woman, Angela's blood froze. A flash of memory flickered through the shadow and then was gone before she could catch it. But it was nasty, and it involved this woman. The word 'poison' lodged itself in her mind with chilling sharpness. Angela flattened herself against the wall, not even daring to peek out now. She waited a few minutes, heart pounding, then looked around to see the car was gone.

Angela ran for the train station. Cordoba or Granada? Neither name meant anything to her. A train was waiting on the platform. She checked the sign. It was leaving for Cordoba in five minutes. She went to the ticket booth. A friendly faced woman took her money, said something to her in Spanish that she didn't understand, and waved her back towards the platform. Another train slid into the opposite platform. She realised she was desperate to use the toilet, and found one behind a door with peeling green paint, just off the platform.

Her face in the mirror was familiar, and she took a moment to look at it closely, seeing if it would trigger any memories. Again the horrible, panicked frustration.

I don't know who I am.

A train whistle blew. She hitched her bag over her shoulder and headed out to the platform. As the door closed behind her, she almost ran into a tall man in a blue uniform. He stood back to apologise, looked at her, seemed to recognise her. She kept her head down and moved away, heart pounding. Behind her, she heard his hurried footsteps. She glanced over her shoulder, expecting to see him following her. But he was heading towards the station office. Before the door swung shut behind him, she saw that he had scooped up the phone.

Angela knew he was calling the woman in the black car. *She knew it.* She hesitated, about to step onto the train to Cordoba.

No, nobody could know where she was going. She began to run, up and over the concourse, down the other side to the Granada train. She hurried into a carriage and sat at the very back, sliding down in the seat and pulling her collar up over her ears and hair. At last, the train creaked into life, and began its slow but steady rhythm down the track. Away from Montoya, away from the woman in the black car. Into mysterious realms.

George pulled Estrella's car in at a crazy angle outside Cordoba train station. Once the stationmaster's call had come, there had been no other remedy available. He had to drive to Cordoba, beat the train there, and intercept Penny before she got any further away from him. The train was already ahead of him, but George knew just how slow and rattling the regional service was, so he still held out hope of beating it. Estrella had been protective of her car, had never driven it so far herself, but her guilt over losing Penny meant she let it go with little prompting.

He ran past the station's front gates and through to the concourse. Which platform? He checked the boards, found that the Montoya train was only two minutes from arriving. He made his way down to the platform to wait. The noisy station bustled on under the huge arched roof, people hauling cases, greeting loved ones, wandering confused, looking for their trains. George was oblivious to it all, chewing the inside of his mouth and jiggling his right leg. What could he say to her to change her mind? Should he be hard, cruel even? To cancel the tour, he could tell her, would signal the end of her career. Without her career, he couldn't allow her to remain in her apartment, she wouldn't have an allowance for clothes and records...she'd be back where she started. Or should he try the softly-softly approach? Tell her to relax, that she'd feel better in a few weeks, that he would make life as easy for her as he possibly could?

The train drew into the station. His eyes scanned it carriage by carriage, but he didn't see her. Still, he wasn't alarmed. He waited. A parade of people climbed out, to be greeted by their loved ones or to walk to the concourse on their way to their next destination. No Penny.

George frowned, waited. Strode up to the first carriage to peer in through the door. Empty. The next carriage. Also empty. He began to run now, down through the carriages, clattering the doors between them open and calling, 'Penny? Penny?' A conductor nearly collided with him, said something unintelligible in Spanish.

George turned to him, panicked now. 'A young woman, very pretty, dark hair? Have you seen her? Have you seen her?'

The conductor shrugged extravagantly, indicating he had no idea what George was saying. George went all the way to the final carriage. Penny was nowhere in sight. He climbed back down to the platform, disbelieving. The stationmaster at Montoya had been so certain: Penny had bought a ticket to Cordoba that morning. But the facts told another story. She had either alighted early, or had never been on this train at all.

Which meant that George had no way of knowing where she was now.

Once the train was rattling along briskly, Angela finally took the time to think through her situation. Nausea rolled in her stomach, and her head stung with pain. An elderly couple sat opposite her, talking softly to each other in Spanish. He had a folded newspaper on his lap, she had a bag of knitting. Apart from that, the little compartment was empty. She hefted her bag up onto the seat next to her and began methodically to go through it, looking for clues that might jog her memory.

Clothes... fairly casual ones. Jeans, long-sleeved T-shirts. Did this mean she was the kind of woman who wore casual clothes? Or was this just what she had packed for her escape from the villa? She concentrated hard, but nothing came. A make-up bag. She unzipped it, saw kohl pencils, glitter eye shadow, dark lipstick. Did she wear make-up often? These colours were very dramatic; in fact, she could hardly imagine applying them to her face. She put the little bag aside and kept looking. Her purse was next.

A few coins, some local currency. She unzipped a side pocket, and gasped.

A stack of British pounds. Why on earth was she carrying all this money? Was she rich? Or had she withdrawn all her savings to come to Spain? A chequebook was folded and shoved in the side of the purse. Only two cheques left. She flipped carefully through the stubs, reading the dates and the purchases. Learned that she wasn't the best of record-keepers. The ones that were filled in gave little away: electricity bills, purchases at Selfridges, one cheque was made out for thirty-three pence for bread. She flipped to the last stub, eyes widening again as she saw how much money was left, by her calculations, in the balance column. The name on the last two cheques was *A. A. Smith Account 1*. How many accounts did she have? Why did she have so much money?

She sat back, closing her eyes and taking a deep breath.

Remember, remember.

But the shadow moved wherever she focused her mind, and nothing would come to her. Perhaps she had been saving for a trip to Spain. She opened her passport, trying to follow its pages for clues.

The pages were largely empty. She had travelled twice to France, both times within the last year. Then there was an immigration stamp for her arrival in Madrid. Angela peered across at the old man's newspapers, noting the date and then comparing it to the stamp. She had been in Spain a week. Why had she come? Why was she at the villa?

Again, she concentrated her mind on these questions. This time, the edge of the shadow lifted. But rather than images and ideas, all that came to her was a terrible, bone-chilling sense of fear. Without prompting, her heart began to race and shivers ran up her spine. *Something awful happened to me.* A black hole of panic threatened to open up inside her, so she pulled back from that memory, and had to take a moment to look outside the train window, at the hills in the distance, the burnished gold and olive landscape, the clear autumn sky.

When she felt her equilibrium returning, she turned once again to her passport. No dependants: good, at least she wasn't leaving a child behind. She glanced at her left hand, suddenly afraid she might see a wedding ring. Nothing. The facts on the final page of her passport gave away little. She peered at the photograph. Most of the dramatic make-up was in place, her hair was blow-dried, not just hanging limp and pulled back in a band as it was now. Looking at the photo gave her a comforting sense of familiarity, so she stared at it a long time. She was *someone*. Even if she couldn't remember precisely who right now, it would come to her. It had to.

Angela put her hand to her head. She felt terribly ill, and lay down on the seat to rest. Shivers raced over her body, the train continued on its way. At length, she fell into a doze.

She woke when the woman opposite her shook her gently, saying something unintelligible in Spanish. Angela looked around blearily. They had arrived in Granada.

Her bag over her shoulder, she stumbled out of the train and through the concourse where she stopped and thought, while people jostled past her. Where to now? She had to go somewhere that she might be able to find herself. Back to England? Her name was Smith. How on earth was she supposed to find her family with so common a surname? Millions of people lived in England. Besides, the edge of cold fear she had felt earlier was associated with England.

She remembered, then, about the Greek words that had come to her mind. Was she Greek? Her colouring suggested she might have a Greek heritage even if her passport insisted she was British. A surname like Smith would stand out in Greece.

There was nothing stopping her going to Greece. She could certainly afford a plane fare.

She realised she was standing outside the door of a shop selling papers and books. Inside, she found a dim corner full of travel guides to different locations. The one on Greece was very dusty. She pulled it down, sneezing, and flipped through to the map.

Angela scanned the names of the locations to see if any aroused familiarity in her. Athens...no. Thessaloniki...no. Her eyes were drawn down to the islands. One tiny speck caught her eye. Petaloudos. It meant 'Butterfly Island' and she could see immediately that it was the butterfly shape that had given it its name. Something about the idea of butterflies appealed to her. They forgot themselves too, emerging as something completely different after a long time in darkness.

But did her pleasure in the name come from memory or imagination? Was Petaloudos a place that she knew?

There was only one way to find out.

Angela flipped the book closed. She might not know who she was, but now, at least, she knew where she was going.

Ellie pulled a chair under one of the windows of her apartment, and sat to watch the sky struggle towards dawn, and the London traffic begin its stuttered parade. The double glazing kept most of the sound out, except for the occasional siren. Headlights and tail-lights bloomed white and red in the semi-dark; and as day struggled to break a miserable November rain began to fall, making the streets slick, dirty mirrors for reflecting the lights. She was lonely and bored, and missed Dieter. Missed his warm, smooth skin. Missed his liquid, hazel eyes. Missed his spicy, clean smell.

She didn't have to be lonely, of course. Now she was in England, it would make sense to contact her mother's family, but Ellie kept pulling back from taking that step. Her father had fallen out with them, there was bad blood there. And she wasn't sure how she would explain her situation: they would have heard of Penny Bright for certain and George was insistent about keeping quiet about their deception. So she settled, instead, for learning to be on her own.

The buzz of the doorbell jolted her out of her reverie. She leaned out to open the window. Bitter cold flooded in. She peered down. George waited below, illuminated by a sputtering streetlight. She knew he had a key, but perhaps he hadn't wanted to frighten her by barging in so early in the morning.

'Come up,' she called. He disappeared under the doorway, and a few minutes later was taking a seat in the kitchen. The only light was from her bedroom, so he was almost in the dark. But she could tell from the angle of his neck, the way he thrummed his fingers on the table, that he was anxious. Her skin prickled lightly. Was she in trouble?

She sat opposite him, almost afraid to ask. 'What's wrong?'

'Penny's gone.'

Her tired brain couldn't process this. 'What do you mean?'

'She's run away. She's left us. Me. She's left me. She's...she doesn't want to do this anymore.'

'Why not?'

'That's all I know. She left a note, a short one, and she disappeared. I've no idea where she is.'

Ellie took a moment to think all this through.

'Ellie, the tour has to go ahead,' George said. 'I'll be frank with you, if the tour is cancelled I lose a lot of money. A *lot* of money.'

The gears in Ellie's mind turned. She suspected he knew where he was going with this, and she had to make sure she concentrated. 'You want me to stay on?' she said slowly. 'A little longer?'

'I want you to stay on. Indefinitely.'

Ellie leaned back in her chair and took in the dimly lit surroundings. She liked living in a fancy apartment in London. She liked being on stage, she was even starting to like – just a little – some of Penny's songs. And the thought of big crowds of people applauding her...it wasn't precisely the same as her fantasy. No Puccini, no soaring voice lifting the roof off a luxuriously decorated opera house. Still, it was a version of the fantasy.

But most of all, Ellie liked having money. To wake up in the morning without the spectre of poverty hanging over her was a kind of bliss to which she had rapidly become accustomed.

She knew that she had to deal with George Fellowes very carefully, now. She couldn't let him take advantage of her. He had said he would lose a lot of money if the tour was cancelled, so that meant he would be willing to pay a high price to keep her. 'Indefinitely?' she said. 'What do you mean precisely? Until she comes back?'

'I don't know if she's ever coming back.'

'But if she does?'

George pushed his lips together, making his usually stern face look almost petulant. 'That will depend on what Penny wants.'

Ellie was wary. 'But Mr Fellowes, if I'm Penny Bright for, say, a year. If I do the tour, if I record the next single, if it's *my* voice, *my* performance that brings the success, how can it possibly be fair for me simply to step aside if she comes back?'

She could see that she had angered him, although he was trying to control it.

'I take your point, Ellie, but you must remember that Penny – the real Penny – did all the work that got us here in the first place. *You* didn't.'

'It seems to me that the real Penny has walked away from any of the benefits she might be due.' Ellie kept her voice even, cool.

'All right, then,' George allowed. 'Let's not talk about "indefinitely". I'll pay you another five thousand marks to do the tour, and then we'll review the situation.'

'Are you sure you want to risk that, Mr Fellowes? What if she doesn't come back?'

'Then you can stay on.'

She shrugged, feigning nonchalance. 'I might not want to. Then you'll have no Penny Bright at all.'

A long silence drew out between them. George scowled, Ellie didn't flinch.

Then, he broke into a smile, a disbelieving laugh. 'Ellie Frankel, your spine is made of steel,' he said.

'I'm simply protecting myself.'

'Tell me what you want,' he said.

At that moment, when she knew he was going to concede, doubt crept in. Dieter, the farm, home. She hesitated. Then pushed on. With enough money, any difficulty could be overcome: she knew it in her bones.

'From this date forwards, I will be Penny Bright,' she said. 'I will be paid her earnings, not a portion of it meted out by you. It will be my career, and I will be involved in the decision-making – with your guidance as my manager of course.'

George nodded. 'As long as you realise that, under those terms, you share in any failures as well as the successes.'

'There won't be failures, Mr Fellowes.'

'Stop calling me Mr Fellowes,' he said. 'I've told you, Penny called me George.'

She took a moment's pause, thinking about Penny. Was she doing the right thing? But she dismissed her doubts. Penny had walked away. Ellie decided she was picking up a dropped opportunity, just as somebody had picked up hers after her father had died. She held out her hand. 'Do we have a deal, George?'

He reached across and grasped her hand firmly, shaking it. 'Yes, Ellie. We have a deal.'

FIFTEEN

*I*t was late afternoon when the supply vessel, the only route to and from the island of Petaloudos, finally angled towards the pier that pointed like a long finger out of the sweeping curve of the harbour. Petaloudos was one of a chain of small islands between Naxos and Amorgos in the Cyclades, southeast of the Greek mainland. Angela was tired from two days of travel: by land, by air, by land again, then finally by rolling sea. But despite the tiredness, she felt better than she had since she woke up in the garden outside the villa. Her headache and nausea were gone and she was somehow clearer of thoughts, cleaner of body. Memories still eluded her, but she believed they would come back in time, now that she was well again.

Her grasp of Greek, she was discovering, was not particularly wide or accurate. But the captain of the supply vessel had spoken enough English for them to get by.

'Petaloudos? No tourists.'

'I'm not a tourist. I'm looking for somebody over there.'

'Boat only three times in week.'

She'd accepted this, and presumed that she'd find somewhere to stay – a *domatio*, or a room above a taverna – while she asked about her family.

'Do you know,' she'd asked him, 'how many people live on the island?'

He pursed his lips, thinking, then said, 'Maybe only two hundred. Maybe less.'

Two hundred people. She'd be bound to find somebody who knew who she was; it would almost be possible to talk to them all. She hadn't allowed herself to consider the possibility that her dim glimmer of feeling about Petaloudos was imagined.

As the boat slowed and bumped to a standstill against the pier, she took in the vista of the island's coast. The harbour was dotted with fishing boats. Goats roamed on rocky hills that rolled down towards unspoiled beaches. Little whitewashed houses crowded together behind, on cobbled alleys overflowing with fishing nets and baskets.

The captain was at her shoulder then, smiling down at her. 'Is beautiful?'

'Yes,' she said.

'Good luck finding your somebody. The main village is up the hill: Agios Manolis is called.' He tipped his hat. 'Boat comes again on Thursday, if you need to go home.'

She wanted to say, 'I don't know where my home is,' but he had already turned away and was shouting orders to men on the pier. She hitched her bag over her shoulder and made her way down the gangplank to land. The clouds had darkened to slate. She cursed herself for not buying an umbrella in Athens. It simply hadn't occurred to her. Since she'd woken without her memory, the weather had been fine. Was it possible to forget about rain as well as who she was and where she came from? She remembered rain now, of course, and hurried her steps to stay ahead of it.

The pier led off to a circular road that led uphill. A few old cars and a van were parked on the dirt shoulder. She followed the road around to the south, and found herself heading towards the cramped village square of Agios Manolis. A disused fountain, streaked with dirt, marked the middle of the square. Shops and whitewashed houses with brightly painted shutters overhanging narrow alleys surrounded it. The only building that had any space was the round Orthodox church with its weathered cross standing tall and brave against the grey sky. Alleys led off the square, stone stairs winding upwards to houses and businesses, jumbled beside each other. Two little black-haired girls played with jacks nearby. Angela struggled to read the signs around her, which were written in Cyrillic letters. The scruffy white building with the blue doors was the taverna. The dark arched doorway led to the chemist. The freshly whitewashed plaster and azure shutters of the bakery looked inviting. Her stomach rumbled, and she decided to make this her first stop.

A bell over the door chimed as she went in. The shopkeeper, a thin woman with very dark eyes, looked up curiously from her magazine.

'Um... hello,' Angela said.

The woman smiled, transforming her face. Now she seemed girlish, friendly. Angela spotted a glass case full of cheese pies and honey-soaked pastries, and pointed at the kataifi. 'One of these, please,' she said in Greek.

As the woman pulled out the pastry and slid it into a paper bag, Angela gave her a coin and asked, 'Do you know if there is a family named Smith on the island?'

The woman looked puzzled and responded in rapid-fire Greek. Angela had trouble keeping up.

'Slowly, please,' she said.

'I know of nobody,' the woman replied. 'Are you expected by them?'

'I... Never mind,' she said. 'Thank you.'

She stepped outside the bakery to discover it was drizzling. She dashed across the square to the taverna, closing the rain out behind her. Inside, it was dark and cavernous. Crowded booths sat under a huge stone arch, noisy laughter rose, two men hunched over a backgammon board at the end of the long bar. The smell – stale beer and cigarettes – touched her memory, and she stopped for a moment, concentrating, trying to follow the feelings back to their roots. Unease, a panicky flutter in her chest. She pushed it away, and the memory disappeared with it.

A young woman behind the bar was looking at her expectantly.

'Hello,' she said. 'I'm looking for a family named Smith.'

She was beginning to think her Greek pronunciation must be terrible, because this woman also looked baffled. She shook her head.

'The Smith family?' Angela pulled out her passport, opened it to the last page and pointed out her surname. The young woman peered at it, confused. Perhaps she couldn't read the English letters.

The young woman pointed to a bar stool and said in Greek, 'Sit down, I know who you need to speak to.'

'Thank you,' she said, gratefully taking the weight off her feet. 'Thank you very much.'

She waited in the silence for a few minutes. Music played, voices echoed. She bit her lip, wondering if it had been foolish to come here. *Butterflies.* What nonsense. Then the young woman emerged again, with an old man. He was at least seventy, his long white beard a distinct contrast against his deeply tanned skin and his sharp black eyes. The young woman pointed Angela out to him, and he approached.

'Hello,' he said in lightly accented English. 'My name is Silas. My granddaughter seems to think I can help you.'

Angela was relieved to be able to speak to somebody easily. 'Yes, I'm Angela Smith. I have a feeling I might have family here.'

'Smith, you say?'

Angela pulled out her passport again and showed him.

He peered at it closely, frowning. His eyes flickered almost imperceptibly, then he shook his head. 'There is nobody of this name on the island.'

'Are you sure?' she asked, disappointment making her heart heavy.

'I've lived here nearly my whole life. I was certainly here in January 1955.' He jabbed a finger at her birthdate on the passport. 'No Smiths. I'd remember.' The old man touched her shoulder lightly. 'Why did you think they would be here? Did your parents tell you to come?'

Angela shook her head. It was too complicated to explain. 'I just hoped...It was silly.' She shrugged. 'Do you know somewhere I could stay a few nights on the island? Until the boat comes back?'

Silas frowned again, his eyes darting to his granddaughter. 'We've only one room here and it's full. There's nowhere else.'

'Nowhere?' Angela was taken aback. 'But where do people stay when they come here?'

'Usually they only come here to visit friends or family. They stay with their loved ones.'

Angela remembered the captain's words: *Petaloudos? No tourists.*

'If you are quick,' Silas continued, 'you can make it back to the pier before the boat leaves.'

'Yes…thanks.' Angela hitched her bag on her shoulder and began to run. The drizzle still fell lightly, misting her with cold. All that travel to get here, all those hopes, dismissed in a few words from Silas. *There is nobody of this name on the island.* So it had been a wild-goose chase after all: Petaloudos meant nothing to her other than a pretty name. It became achingly clear to her that she didn't know what to do next, where to go, who to speak to. But she knew she had to catch the boat, so she hurried. Back through the village square and down the road, nearly getting knocked over by a van heading up from the pier. Her heart was thumping and her breath caught. She skidded around the corner only to see the boat pulling away, men winding up ropes.

'Hey!' she shouted, pounding down towards the road. 'Hey, wait! Come back!'

Her voice was lost at this distance. The boat had already slid out onto the water.

Angela stopped, bending over and resting her hands on her knees, gasping for air. Then she straightened her back, watching the boat disappear. The rain intensified. The pier had emptied of people. She wiped her wet hair out of her eyes.

What now? She was stuck here for at least two days, and Silas had told her there was nowhere to sleep. She was cold, wet, dislocated…

She turned and began to walk back down the pier. The clouds lowered, the rain deepened, thundering on the wooden boards. The deserted road was growing muddy, and looked very slippery. This time she followed it around to the north, where the road was in better condition. This time she saw the house up on the bluff.

It was odd, up there by itself. Large, rambling; whitewashed stone; peeling blue windowsills and shutters; contained within a sagging barbed-wire fence. The road skirted past it, almost as if avoiding it on its way back to the village. The door hung open. It looked empty, deserted.

But the roof looked intact, and she needed somewhere to shelter.

Angela dashed up the hill, nearly sliding on the wet grass. She carefully picked her way through a gap in the two rows of wire, managing only to catch the cuff of her jeans on a barb. She wondered guiltily if the barbed wire was a sign that she should stay out, but the fence was poorly maintained. She doubted anybody had been here in years.

Finally, she reached shelter and closed the door behind her. The house was dark, musty. She held onto her bag tightly as she browsed through. A huge kitchen, with spiders living in the sink. Bare, dusty floorboards. A little lounge room with a boarded-over fireplace. Here a half-broken floral couch had been left to gather dust and mould. A dining room faced the kitchen across the hallway. Five empty rooms that must have once been bedrooms. Discolourations in the wallpaper showed Angela where paintings might once have hung. A bathroom, nearly black with years of mould, finished the end of the hallway. Angela left wet footprints behind her as she returned to the lounge room. She eyed the fireplace. If she pulled off the boards, she might be able to burn them... No, if the chimney hadn't been used in years she'd probably just end up filling the house with smoke. Besides, she hadn't any matches to light the fire with, and she wasn't going to head back up to the village until the rain stopped. Instead, she decided to try to get dry.

Angela stripped to her underwear and used her unwashed clothes from the previous day to dry herself. She hung the wet clothes in the kitchen, and put on fresh jeans and a pullover. Wrapping herself in her jacket, she tucked herself up on the old couch and ate the pastry she'd bought earlier at the bakery.

Outside, night gathered. She was still cold, but at least she was dry and not hungry. Using her bag for a pillow, she lay down on the couch and tried to think things through. She began to calm for the first time in days. At least here, in a deserted house on a tiny island in the Cyclades, the woman in the black car couldn't find her. The thought cheered her, and she made herself as cosy as she could. Exhaustion overtook her senses, her thoughts flickered and she fell into a deep sleep.

'I don't see why I have to learn to dance,' Ellie huffed as George led her up the stairs to a dance studio in Soho.

'Because you have to be comfortable on stage while performing.'

'I am comfortable.'

They stopped on the landing, outside a frosted glass door. A poster, a purple figure of a man in mid ballet leap, had been taped to the glass.

'I'll be honest with you, Ellie, you're a little square.'

'Square?'

'You could loosen up a little. You need to own the stage, you need to strut like a pop star. At the moment, you just stand there.'

'I have to dance?'

'No, you have to *move*. It's different. But Sacha will be able to help.' He pushed the door open.

They entered a brightly lit room with mirrors lining one wall. Nine little girls in pink tutus did pliés at the barre while a woman played an out-of-tune piano. Within a moment, a lithe man was striding towards Ellie and George, pushing long blond curls behind his ears. She deduced this was Sacha, the dance teacher. He took Ellie's hand. He was dazzlingly handsome, with strong full lips and warm skin.

'Penny! You are more beautiful than your photographs,' he said in a thick eastern European accent, and kissed her hand before dropping it. She could still feel the heat of his lips long after they had left.

The nine little girls broke formation and she was surrounded by a swarm, squealing her name. Sacha indulged them with smiles for a few minutes, but then shooed them away.

'Go now, little ones. Miss Bright and I have work to do.'

George leaned down to whisper in her ear, 'Will you be all right?'

Ellie, whose eyes hadn't left Sacha, nodded dumbly.

Sacha led her into a private room, with a parquetry floor. This one had a mirror wall too, but there was only one window so the light was dim.

'Now, Penny,' Sacha said, pressing his lips together in puzzlement. 'I have seen you on the television. Why does your manager think you need movement lessons?'

She shrugged out of her cardigan and hung it by the door. 'The tour. It's a big stage,' she said, as George had instructed her. Then she added, 'He thinks I'm "square".'

Sacha laughed. 'What nonsense.' He pulled up close to her, pressing his palm into her solar plexus. 'It's all about grace, Penny, and confidence.'

She gulped. 'I see.'

He started her with simple movements to loosen her shoulders and hips. She could see herself in the mirror, and it made her feel even more awkward. Even after losing all that weight, she still felt big and clumsy. Her discomfort was made worse by the proximity and scrutiny of Sacha, whose hot Slavic eyes never broke her gaze.

The hour sped by. As a final exercise, Sacha had her close her eyes and raise her arms at her sides, holding perfectly still.

She did as he asked. Moments passed, she could hear him breathing close by. Then his arms slid around her from behind, and his hands closed over her breasts.

Ellie yelped and brushed him off, turning in anger. 'What the hell are you doing?' She could hear her German accent break through, and bit back further reproaches.

He held her in his gaze, unruffled. 'Giving you what you wanted. I saw the way you looked at me.'

Her mind reeled. She remembered Dieter, and wanted to tell Sacha he wasn't half the man. But at the thought of Dieter, she realised she had been flirting with Sacha. Silently, perhaps, but certainly, with her eyes. Guilt soured her stomach.

'I'm sorry,' she said tightly, 'but you've misunderstood.'

Sacha sniffed. 'No need to apologise. I've had plenty of beautiful women.'

Ellie pulled her cardigan on again and hugged it about her tightly. She should have been used to this by now: everybody wanted a piece of her. Sacha was no different. For all that she kept telling herself to keep her head, she had nearly lost it in one hour with his smouldering gaze.

A soft knock on the door alerted them to George's return. He peeked in. 'Everything go well?' he asked.

'I'm sorry, George,' she said in a haughty tone, 'I can't work with this person.' She flounced past, leaving Sacha to explain.

Ellie cursed herself as she made her way down the stairs. What a fool. What a silly, little girl. If she was to survive here in London, in the music industry, she had to be made of much stronger stuff. She had to be continually on her guard, and as hard and cool as diamonds.

She is in a dark room. She can't make out shapes and she knows somewhere around here there is a hole in the floor. If she steps through it, she will fall forever and forever. She moves hesitantly, toes stretched ahead of her. But then she hears him behind her. His hot breath. She must move quicker, he mustn't catch her. She must get back up the stairs and out the door. The room swells and grows, she can't find her way. He draws closer, terror crushes her ribs, she begins to run. Her foot sails into a void, the ground disappears beneath her and she pitches forward, falling and falling into nothingness . . .

Angela woke with a start, her hands clutching at air unconsciously. Pale morning light, her neck cramped uncomfortably. Where was she?

She sat up, remembered the previous day. She felt displaced, lost. The dream returned to her: with dread conviction, she knew that something about it was remembered.

'What happened to me?' she whispered to herself, but she was suddenly terrified to know. It wasn't just the woman in the black car, something else had befallen her, some dark awful stain lay upon her life; a man…a knife…

Angela leapt to her feet and began to pace, for the first time pushing the memories away, dragging the shadow back over them. She didn't want to remember; she feared that if she did, it would drive her mad. Gradually she calmed. Began to take stock.

She couldn't stay another night in the damp, grimy house. She needed running water, a soft pillow. Her hopes of finding her identity here had been thwarted. She had to find a way off the island. There were plenty of fishing boats in the harbour. Perhaps she could persuade somebody to take her to the next island in the chain, to find somewhere to stay there. Just until she could decide what to do. Return to England? The thought terrified her. She didn't know who she was, but somebody else might. Somebody dangerous…

One thing at a time. She packed her clothes – not quite dry, but close enough – and headed down to the harbour.

Dawn had only just broken, a stiff wind rattled around her. As she walked down towards the pier, her eyes scanned for boats. Most of them had already left for the morning. Nobody was in sight. At the end of the pier, a dog barked madly. At first the sound didn't register with her, she was too busy working out where she might find a kindly fisherman. Then realisation came: the dog was agitated. A little wooden dinghy bobbed about on the choppy waves, a small white-clad figure in it. She started up the pier. The dinghy was rocking madly. Inside was a child, trying vainly to row to the pier.

Anxiety woke inside her. Where were the child's parents? Did they know he was out there on the rough sea? She looked around her. The dirt road was free of traffic. The closest humans were out on their boats. Her heart thudded. Should she run back to the village and raise the alarm?

A big wave came along, thrusting the dinghy hard against the pier. The child flailed, the dinghy sucked backwards. The child was in danger, and she realised with alarm that she was the only one who knew. The only one who could help.

Without a second thought, she dropped her bag and pelted up the pier, the wind whipping her hair into her mouth. The dog barked madly. The dinghy struck the pier again and this time the front of it cracked and it began to sink. The child, a little boy of about seven she could see now, began to scream. She kicked off her shoes and ran, heart pumping, muscles protesting. At the end of the pier she cast herself onto her stomach, grazing her elbows and throwing out her hands.

'Here, grab on!'

She knew he probably couldn't understand English, but he could understand her gesture. His hands flailed. His dark eyes were panicked. He couldn't reach her. He began to scream at her in Greek. The dinghy was sinking. The child sobbed and began to call, 'Mama! Mama!'

Angela stood and dived into the water. A thought flashed across her mind: *You don't even know if you can swim.* But she could. A wave picked her up and slammed her against a wooden pylon. The water, sunless for hours, was freezing. She fought for air, swallowing a mouthful of salt water. The little boy launched himself at her; she caught him around the wrist and dragged him towards her, bundled him under her arm and fought vainly to make her way back to the pier. Now there were other voices, other people on the pier. A woman shouting, 'Christos! Christos!'

Angela assumed this was the boy's name, that his family had noticed his little bed was empty. The old man from the taverna, Silas, was there a moment later, kneeling on the pier and holding out his walking stick. Angela grasped it. Two men knelt with Silas, helping him pull the stick towards the pier. Angela passed little Christos towards them. He was quickly pulled from the water and pressed against the sobbing woman's bosom. Then the two men with Silas reached for her, dragged her from the sea. She was freezing and soaked, out of breath and had a belly full of sea water. She flopped onto the wooden boards, panting. A whirl of unintelligible shouting surrounded her. Finally, Silas helped her to her feet, speaking to her in English.

'You are an angel,' he said. 'You have saved the life of my great-grandson.'

She tried a smile. 'He's yours?'

The shouting continued. Christos was sobbing again, the dog was jumping up, whimpering.

'He is mine. He's visiting for a few weeks. He wasn't supposed to be down here.' Silas turned to give the child a stern look, which was duly ignored. He turned back to Angela. 'I did not know when I first saw you that you would be a blessing to our village. Please, come back to my home and I will find you warm dry clothes.'

Angela nodded, finally catching her breath. 'I'd like that.'

An hour later, when all the commotion had died down and Angela was drinking hot soup in the warm, cluttered dining room of Silas's home, she finally started to relax. Christos and his mother went home, and she was left with Silas, who smoked his pipe and drank his soupy black coffee and watched her.

'This is good soup, Kyrios Silas,' she said.

'I am a good cook.' He smiled, his eyes crinkling at the corners. 'You'll find out if you stay a while.'

'Just until the boat comes back.'

'You're welcome to stay as long as you like. Are you in a hurry to get home?'

She shook her head, putting down her spoon. 'No. Not particularly. I...' She pressed her lips together, trying to stop tears.

'Angela?' Silas said gently. 'What's wrong?'

'I don't know who I am,' she said. The story came out all at once, and Silas listened, nodding and puffing his pipe.

When she had finished, he said, 'My dear girl, I'm so sorry for your distress. But whatever set you on the path that led here, I'm glad you came. Without you, Christos would have drowned.'

She smiled, taking comfort from his words. Then she dropped her voice low, trusting him completely. 'The worst thing is,' she said, 'I think that I'm running from something awful, someone who wanted to hurt me...and I don't know where I'll go next or what I'll do. I'm not even sure if I'm safe.'

He shook his head, perplexed. 'Isn't it clear? You'll stay here with us. We'll look after you.'

'We?'

'The island. The community. You have blessed us, you are one of us now.' He spoke calmly, matter-of-fact, and Angela felt a profound connection to his words. All at once, whatever she was before ceased to matter.

'Well?' he said. 'Will you stay?'

Angela nodded. 'Yes. Yes, I will.'

He raised his coffee cup with a mischievous smile. 'So. Here's to your new life.'

Dieter put down the receiver of the phone and turned, his shoulders sagging. Waiting in the dark threshold was his mother. He felt a quick flush of guilt. He had been talking to Ellie, and had hoped that the late hour had given him secrecy.

'Mama, I didn't know you were there,' he said.

His mother sighed, wrapping her robe closer around her waist and tightening the belt. 'Sit down, Dieter. Tell me what's going on.'

Dieter sat at the kitchen table in the dark, and Mama sat opposite. The only light was from the moon through the window. Outside, cold wind rattled the bare branches, throwing shifting shadows over them.

'It was Ellie,' he said.

'I know,' she replied.

'She and I…' To confess to their affair would only reveal how deceitful he had been until now.

'I know,' Mama said again. 'I'm not a fool, Dieter. I know that you and Ellie…'

'We're in love,' Dieter said.

'Your father and I love Ellie too,' she said. 'It's all right. We've known for a long time.'

Dieter felt ashamed, like a little boy again.

'You miss her, don't you?' Mama said.

Dieter turned this thought over in his head, as he remembered their phone call. She was staying in London, indefinitely. George Fellowes was throwing money at her, making her promises of stardom on the stage. Always Ellie's weakness: Dieter could never see why a little wasn't enough for her. He blamed her father, his rapacious ambition which he had sowed like a seed in his daughter's heart.

'But what about us?' Dieter had asked her, trying to keep his voice calm.

'I'll wire you some more money. You can come to visit. You'd love London.'

'Ellie, my father is still recovering from his accident. He can't work. I can't leave Mama to run the place herself. I have to stay here.'

'He'll be well again soon, surely.' She'd sounded less certain then, young and perhaps even regretful. 'I'll phone you every day.'

But phone calls weren't enough. He needed to see her, to hold her.

'Dieter?' his mother said, breaking into his reverie.

'I'm losing her, Mama,' he said. 'I know it, and there's nothing I can do about it. I'm losing her.'

'Read it again,' Silas said, tapping the page with his pen. 'Remember, the stress falls on the accent. It's so English of you only to stress the first syllable.'

She read the line again. Silas had decided that her poor Greek vocabulary and even worse Greek grammar meant she had learned in childhood, so he had made it his project to help her master the language. His method was painful: reading Greek novels aloud then translating them into English. She much preferred to pick up new words by listening, trying them on her own tongue. Every day she heard new words and expressions repeated: in the morning at the markets, on the radio in the kitchen of Silas's taverna while she washed dishes, from one of the old-timers in the bar drinking his thick black coffee and smoking his thin rolled cigarettes. From context, she would figure out the meaning. Slowly, the vocabulary was dropping into her mind and lodging there. But Silas was insistent: if she wanted to learn the grammar, the range of the language, she had to do it from books.

'Can we stop now, Kyrios Silas?' she asked, in Greek. 'I'm tired.'

'It's only been an hour since we started.'

But he didn't understand. It wasn't just an hour a day she struggled with the language, it was *all day*. By nightfall, her mind was limp with weariness.

'I need to go for a walk,' she said, back in English now. 'I need to clear my mind.'

'Very well.' Silas hurrumphed and reached for his pipe, and she pushed back her chair and let herself out of the warm, smoky house and into the fresh sea air.

Every afternoon in the weeks since she'd arrived, she'd taken this walk to clear her head. The mind-bending work of studying Greek and the dislocation of her memory's dead end made her feel tense and overwhelmed. She was slowly getting used to it, and the fresh air and dusk sky certainly helped. She could imagine a time, when she had built enough new memories here on the island and had mastered the language, when she might feel calm and settled. It was just around the corner, gleaming in the sunshine.

She followed the path up the hill and stopped at the cliff above Halki Beach. A perfect pebbled curve, not a single soul on it or in the glassy water. A hidden paradise. To the north, fishing boats came and went between the curved hands of the harbour. Angela sat down and closed her eyes. The salty air was moist in her nostrils, a little cool on her skin. She breathed deeply, and let go of verb tables and the differences between *dimotiki* and *katharevousa*. When she opened her eyes, evening had crept up on her. The sky had changed from pink to purple, and she could see lights glowing on the next island in the chain. A stiff breeze gusted over her, and she thought she could hear music carried on it: the clamorous *lyra* and the rhythms of the *toumberleki*. She stood, stretched, ready to head home.

Footfalls nearby attracted her attention.

A lone figure, a slender woman with long, unbound hair, about two hundred feet away on the edge of the cliff. For one awful moment, Angela thought she was going to jump off. But she didn't. She stood perfectly still, gazing out at the water. She seemed unaware of Angela's presence.

Angela watched her a while, and an inexplicable prickle shivered across her skin. The woman was so very still, that she began to think it wasn't a woman at all, but a statue. Then the breeze picked up again, lifting the woman's hair. Angela realised from her posture, her movements, that the woman was crying.

Without thinking, she approached.

'Hello?' she said in Greek.

There was no response.

'Hello?' She drew closer, wary now. Perhaps the woman didn't want anyone to talk to her. Perhaps she had come out here to cry alone. Angela hesitated.

The woman turned, saw Angela, and broke into a slow smile. It was almost beatific, that smile, giving Angela the impression that the sun was still shining somewhere on the world.

'Hello,' the woman said.

'I heard you crying,' Angela managed, in very bad Greek indeed, her tenses completely muddled.

The woman said something – too quiet and too fast for Angela to understand – then turned and began to hurry away.

'Wait,' Angela called, though she didn't know why she was calling after her. It must have been that smile, as though she knew her. Perhaps the woman had heard the stories about Angela rescuing Christos. Then why didn't she stay and talk? Angela watched her until she disappeared over the rise, the odd sense of unease recurring to her. She wouldn't be surprised to hear that the island had a ghost, and that Angela had just met her. The woman was so beautiful and sad and strange…

Angela turned back to the harbour, its water reflecting the evening sky now. Time moved very slowly, but perhaps that was because she had nothing to compare it to. Eventually she would learn of everyone on the island, learn its secrets and its mysteries – ghosts included. She had plenty of time. Would she stay weeks or months or years? It didn't matter. She had nowhere else to go. For now, she would concentrate on capturing each moment as it arrived, each day as it dawned.

SIXTEEN
1976

Ellie watched herself in the mirror of her dressing-room, backstage at the East Ham Odeon. A soft knock at the door. George came in.

'Are you ready?' he asked.

'One minute,' she said.

He backed out respectfully.

Opening night of the tour. The final soundcheck had been performed that afternoon. Her voice had boomed out of the sound system, clear and echoing in the empty hall. George had scribbled out setlists and taped them to the foldback wedges at the front of the stage. The band, seemingly shocked into obedience by the size of the venue, were in tune and free of both groupies and bags of cocaine. She had to admit that the soundcheck had awoken an acute excitement in her. She imagined the venue filling up, the coloured lights playing on her, her silver and glitter clothes gleaming in the dark... Now she gazed at her reflection, dripping with silver jewellery, every brushstroke of make-up perfectly in place. She could already hear the rumbles and cheers of the crowd who waited. For her.

It was the culmination of four months' hard work. The rehearsals; the diet and exercise; the movement classes with another, safer, teacher. And as the months had passed, she had settled more and more into the role of the English pop star: handling interviews with aplomb, scribbling perfectly forged autographs at a record signing on Oxford Street, adopting the hip-dislocating pop-star stance at industry parties, tossing her hair nonchalantly through photo shoots, using the lingo as if 'valve amps' and 'phase cancellation' were concepts learned at her mother's knee. The music she still didn't care much for, the fame she found amusing; but the money was intoxicating. Ellie didn't like to spend it, she just liked to have it.

So far, it was mostly unearned. Tonight, her first performance, was the biggest test of all.

A flutter in her stomach. Butterflies. She wasn't concerned by them: Ellie Frankel's great gift was being able to make butterflies fly in formation. Without fear there was no fire in performance.

So why the delicate thread of regret, curling into her heart? Perhaps it was just that she'd imagined a glorious debut for her whole life, but it had always been an opera debut. She listened to the crowd calling again, and tried to smile; tried to take comfort in the fact that no opera audience would ever behave like that. And just because she sang pop, didn't mean she couldn't enjoy opera. She had been toying with the idea of getting some lessons, just for the pure joy of singing; and to honour her father's memory.

Ellie sighed, inserting a pair of oversized hoops through the new holes in her earlobes. How she wished Dieter could have been here tonight. She had struggled to organise it, he had been receptive, but at the last minute a crisis at the farm had arisen, and his father still wasn't able to manage by himself. If she admitted it, his failure to show up had irritated her. Of course she understood that his family was important, but she had made it so easy for him – money to hire help, a plane ticket – and he had still said no. It made her feel as though what she did was frivolous, unimportant; but then, perhaps she was overreacting. She still held out hope that he would make it to one of the later shows. It had been so long since she had seen him, that she had almost forgotten what he looked like. The two-dimensional snapshot she kept next to her bed had taken all the warmth and depth out of his features. Daily phone calls weren't really enough, and she was aware that long separations weakened relationships, no matter how loving they were.

A knock at the door again. 'Minute's up,' George said.

'I'm ready,' she said, pressing her palms against her dressing table to push herself up.

Through the darkened corridors to the stage striding comfortably in her platform shoes. She let the band go, one by one, ahead of her. As each member took to the stage, there was a roar from the crowd. Soon, it was her turn.

George hesitantly put his arm around her shoulder. They didn't share the most comfortable of relationships. His affection, which she guessed stemmed from Ellie's similarity to his much-loved Penny, made her prickly. Her prickliness made him wary of her.

'You'll be wonderful,' he said. 'I know you will.'

'Thanks.' She nodded once, then strode out to the stage. The screams were deafening, the monstrously loud music could barely drown them out. The first song began, and Ellie was on her way.

Angela waited on the pier, shifting from one foot to the other with excitement. The supply vessel docked, the deckhands took their time tying it tightly to the pylons at the end of the pier. Captain Lianis, whom Angela had got to know well over the few months she had been working at the taverna, emerged from his cabin to smile at her.

'Ah, Angela. I thought I might see you today.'

'Is it here?' she asked.

'I picked it up this morning. I'll get the boys to unload it first.'

Angela clapped her hands together. Back up on deck, two men wheeled out from behind a cargo container a red moped. Carefully, they managed it down to the pier where Angela took the handlebars.

'Thank you, thank you.' The last of the wad of cash she'd had in her purse had gone towards the moped, that and two months of strict saving. One of Angela's favourite things to do on Petaloudos was to walk every afternoon, around the winding paths and dirt roads of the island, taking in the glorious scenery. But she longed to go faster, to wheel up the steep paths to the summit instead of walk them, puffing and gasping, to feel the wind in her hair. And so she'd enlisted Captain Lianis's help to find her a second-hand moped on the mainland. He, always obliging, had located a suitable one just the week before.

'I love it!' Hardly a scratch marked the bright red paintwork, the chrome was still shiny.

Captain Lianis jumped down from the gangplank. 'But can you ride it?'

Angela shrugged. She had no idea if she'd ever ridden a moped before. 'It doesn't look that hard.'

Captain Lianis showed her how to start the engine, where the accelerator, gears and brakes were, and told her to ask him next time she saw him if she needed any help. Then she was pushing it down the pier to the road, eyeing the bright blue sky for any clouds that could ruin her day's outing. There were none.

It was siesta time now on Petaloudos, nobody would reopen their stores until five that afternoon. In her bag, she had stashed a picnic lunch, organised earlier: cheesy *tiropitakia* from the bakery, cold *keftedes* from the markets, rich with the aroma of rosemary and thyme, and a flask of *retsina* she had filled from Silas's wine stores. She flipped up the top bar of the carrier and snapped her bag into place. Then she started the noisy engine and, finding her balance, revved the bike around the bluff and up the dirt road towards the far western side of the island.

It was a beautiful day. The clear sky seemed transparent, the sunshine wide and white. She left the crowded village behind and headed out past the olive groves, up into rocky hills where the sun baked the slopes and the cliffs dropped away to sheltered beaches and blue sea. The shoosh and suck of the waves below echoed up on the breeze, gulls riding currents hung in the sky. The wind was in her hair and stung her eyes, and she felt a surge of liberty that reverberated all the way down to her toes.

She rode up towards the huge whitewashed mansion that sat near the island's highest point. The road ran out here, but a dusty, potholed track swerved past the imposing iron gates. Angela took it slowly, curious. But the gates allowed only the barest glimpse through to dense gardens before the tall plastered walls blocked all else from view. A gentle decline started shortly after, down to the other side of the island, where the prevailing winds blighted the soil with salt. Angela had never seen this side of the island, and took her time coasting down the rutted track, before finally stopping to lay out her picnic.

The grass here was toughened and yellow, the ground rocky and uneven. She found a flat place and spread out the rug she had packed. From here, she could see the misted outline of the next island on the horizon, and two ships reduced to tiny slow beetles by distance. She could hear the waves crashing on rocks below, a harsher sound than the rhythmic heartbeat on the beaches around the other side. The smell of salt and seaweed was so thick she could almost feel it on her tongue. She unpacked her lunch and gazed over the sea as she ate it. Sweet, ineffable happiness. She mused, not for the first time, on how happy she had been since she let go of her own mysterious past, since she had stopped worrying about who she was and what she had been through. Sometimes, she had the strong conviction that her life had once been very complicated, and the memory of those complications were still locked in her nerves and cells. So now, those ordinary pleasures of life – work in the quiet taverna, making new friends, today's outing – brought her a relief that she could not feel consciously, but which registered strongly in her body. Most of her memories still resided under the blanket of shadow. If it lifted its corner, even for a moment, Angela blocked the dim images that threatened to creep out.

After she'd eaten, she lay down on the blanket and looked up at the sky. The sun warmed her face and the sea breeze danced across her skin. She daydreamed for a while, then packed up to head back to the village. The flat roofs came into view, and she mused on this strange little island. No tourists. It was too small, Silas had told her. But she didn't believe it. She thought that perhaps the villagers were too small-minded, and didn't see the benefits that might arise from a steady, but modest, inflow of tourist money. The village square could be restored, Lilika Stathakis who ran the bakery could feel confident enough to bake her pastries daily, Silas could increase his dinner trade at the taverna, and even Captain Lianis could benefit by selling a few of those passenger berths that, for the moment, were being used to store the crew's bags and coats. If she could organise something to attract the tourists, it would be a wonderful way of paying back the community that had embraced her so warmly.

Angela checked her watch. She was due at work in a little over an hour. Not that anyone expected her to turn up on time. The people of Petaloudos called punctuality 'being English'. No shop ever opened on time, no appointment was ever strictly kept. She was learning not to mind. She cruised down towards the bluff from the northern end of the island, past the abandoned house she had sheltered in on her arrival. The front door, usually left hanging open, was closed. The shutters too. Curious, she parked the moped next to the barbed-wire fence and stepped off.

She knew from experience that nobody could live there. It was too cold and damp. Her little room at Silas's house was a thousand times more comfortable. But somebody had been here, had locked it all up since last time she had seen it. Perhaps there was somebody there... Perhaps she should just go and knock to say hello, to say thank you... She moved towards the fence to climb over.

'Angela!'

Angela stepped back and spun around to see Silas approaching up the path. She waved, and waited for him. Despite his advanced years, he was very fit. The incline didn't bother him at all, and he barely needed the walking cane that he kept close by at all times.

'You should stay away from here,' Silas said, with only the hint of a gasp for regular breath.

Angela was surprised. 'Really? Why?'

He lifted his cane and jabbed it towards the house. 'The person who owns this property is not a nice person. If she knew you were snooping around in there... She's dangerous.'

Angela glanced from the house to Silas, trying to decide if he was genuine or if this was one of his mischievous jokes. 'Seriously?'

'Very seriously.'

'I stayed here, the night I arrived. It was the first dry place I came to.'

'That was very foolish,' he said, with a stern downturn of his mouth. 'You were lucky she didn't find you.'

'Who owns it?'

'*Mia Trelos*,' he muttered.

Angela translated, 'Crazy Mia? That's her name?' She had a vision of an old witch, hunched, straw-haired, like something out of a children's book.

'That's what we call her in the village.'

'Does she live here?' Angela asked.

'No, no. This place is empty.' He gestured towards the unsheltered side of the island. 'She lives in the big house, you would have seen it.'

'Is she really crazy?'

He nodded. 'Oh, yes. She comes to the markets maybe once a fortnight, late in the day, with her sunglasses on and her hair under a scarf as though she thinks she can disguise herself. She invariably upsets somebody.'

Angela was intrigued. A woman lived in the big house alone? She'd assumed it was a wealthy man with a large family.

'She must be very rich,' Angela said, 'to own such a big house, and this one too.'

'Mia is not short of money,' Silas huffed. 'Nor is she averse to reminding us all.' He stretched, one hand pressed into the small of his back. 'You'll excuse me. I'd like to continue my walk. It keeps me well.'

'I'll walk with you, Kyrios Silas,' she said impulsively. 'I've had an idea.'

He inclined his head slightly. 'As you wish.'

Leaving the moped parked beside the fence, she fell into step beside him. 'Remember the day I arrived here? I asked if you had a room at the taverna to stay in and you said it was already taken?'

Silas's mouth turned up at the corners.

'Well, I know now. You never let out that room. It's full of old furniture.'

'I wondered when you'd catch on.'

'Why did you turn me down? It was raining, I was stuck on the island...'

'Because we have no way of catering for tourists. I would have had to move all that furniture, just for two nights of rent...it was too much trouble.' He shrugged. 'I thought you'd make it back to the boat on time.'

'Kyrios Silas, would you let me clear out the room? Set it up like an English bed and breakfast room? Then you could rent it out. I'd take care of it, the breakfasts, everything. Just as an experiment?'

'Why would anyone come here?'

'Petaloudos is so beautiful,' Angela said. 'It's a little piece of quiet paradise. Tourists would love it.'

'Psh. There's nothing to see or do.'

'But there is. I could rent out my moped, get Lilika to put a picnic basket of local delicacies together. We could charge what we wanted.'

Silas pursed his lips, considering. 'You only have one moped. What would you do if a couple wanted to come together?'

Angela pondered this. She had no more money to buy another. What was left in that cheque account was no longer accessible: it had been risky enough cashing a cheque for her plane fare back in Madrid. To disappear completely meant leaving the money untouched.

'You know,' Silas said, stroking his white beard, 'I think my son has an old moped in his garage, on Paros. It's in need of repair, but perhaps Markos at the petrol station could be persuaded to fix it cheaply...'

Angela grew excited. 'So you *do* think it's a good idea?'

'Only if you do all the work.' He grinned. 'I'm too old.'

Her imagination filled with ideas. 'I could paint the room, couldn't I? Put up some nice pictures. There's a lovely view from up there, it's a shame nobody sees it. Maybe I could – ?'

'Now, now, don't get too far ahead of yourself. Keep your goals modest, then if nothing comes of it, you won't be too disappointed.'

Angela adopted a suitably sober expression, but she was excited nonetheless and couldn't wait to start work on her new project.

George was shaving when the phone rang. He wiped his face with a white hotel towel, and went to answer it.

'George Fellowes,' he said, noticing a drop of toothpaste on his black skivvy. He thumbed at it with his free hand.

'George, it's Alice from TRG. How's the weather in Liverpool?'

George flicked the curtain aside to gaze down onto a rainy street. 'Miserable. How's London?'

'The sun's shining today here at the office. It's good news.'

George tried not to hold his breath.

'Penny's got a number one album on her hands.'

He was so conflicted that he couldn't feel the excitement. *Penny*. It wasn't even Penny he would be delivering this news to. It was Ellie in the next suite at the Adelphi Hotel. Prickly Ellie, with a detachment that bordered on arrogance, a young woman he simply could not get to know. She was protecting herself, he understood that. He sometimes wondered about her past, and suspected it had been as harsh as Penny's. But he didn't sense her vulnerability, only her determination. Ellie would never succumb to drugs the way Penny had; that glacial mind would weigh the benefits against the deficits and reject the notion. But it was that vulnerability that he missed: Penny's hesitant affection, her silly fear of being late, her slavish addiction to eye make-up. He wondered for the millionth time where she was, and if he'd ever be able to contact her to let her know she had a number one album. And that he was proud of her.

'That is fantastic news,' George said to Alice. 'I'll let her know.'

'Give her my love,' Alice said before hanging up. She had been the only person at the record company to show any signs of suspicion about the new Penny Bright. He hadn't realised that Penny and Alice had developed a friendship that went beyond nodding acquaintance. But even Alice had been won over in the end, with Ellie apologising for not being herself since her 'illness'. It was amazing, really, the way that Ellie had stepped into Penny's life with so few problems.

Of course, why would anybody have the need to question whether or not the person they were talking to was the same person they had always known by that name? The most basic assumptions of human nature were on his and Ellie's side: people saw precisely what they had always seen.

Any pressure exerted on their deception came from only one quarter: George's guilty conscience itself. He knew it had the power to undermine them seriously, and he kept it in check the best he could. But he had already made some bad decisions. Ellie had offered to rerecord the vocal track on the album, but George had refused. Not because of the extra expense – the whole album had been recorded in his home studio, after all – but because he missed Penny and wanted the original vocal track to remember her by. Now, on the back of somebody else's work, this number one album would eventually make Ellie a wealthy woman. Penny had also written more than half of the songs, so publishing royalties would be forthcoming. Unearned by Ellie but pouring straight into her bank account. Everything went through George's hands first and he knew it was fraud. He knew that he and Ellie were crossing a line that hadn't been crossed in the original deception. Then it had been a simple exchange: a delimited sum of money for playing a part. Now, they were on the wrong side of the law. If Penny ever came back...

George admonished himself. Penny wasn't coming back. Her long silence was proof of that. He'd tried to trace her through her bank account. Her last transaction was a cheque for cash in Madrid. He had no idea what she'd used it for, where she'd gone next. She could be on the other side of the world for all he knew.

He returned to the bathroom and finished shaving, changed his shirt and locked up his suite behind him to visit Ellie. It was early, but he had to make sure she was awake anyway. There were interviews scheduled with the Liverpool press today, then a soundcheck for tonight's performance at the Empire. He knocked firmly. A few seconds later she was there.

'Good morning, George. I'm just making coffee. Would you like some?'

George preferred tea, but he accepted anyway. 'I have news,' he said, following her into her suite. She was dressed and had already made her own bed, but wore no make-up yet. She looked much younger without it. 'You know, you don't have to make your bed.'

'I know, but the room's so untidy otherwise, and it only takes a minute.' She had a coffee pot and a drip filter in her room, ordered up from the front desk when she arrived yesterday. 'Besides, I do it better than the maid. White with two sugars?' she asked.

'That's right,' he replied. 'You know, Penny Bright has the number one album in the UK this morning.'

She barely glanced up, but she broke into a broad smile. 'Will there be more money?'

'Well, yes, but it's more than that. It means you're a star.'

'I feel very little difference. Except I'm more tired.' It had been a gruelling last few weeks, but she had coped admirably, never complaining once about the late nights, the frantic mornings packing and driving, the endless interviews and soundchecks, the constant round of hangers-on to deal with. 'Perhaps all stars are tired,' she said, handing him a mug of coffee. She took one for herself and sat down at the small square dining table tucked into the corner of the suite.

He sat opposite, and he noticed the shadows under her eyes. 'Are you sleeping all right?' he asked, a shade of the old panic about Penny returning. That's where it had all started: sleeping pills for sleepless nights.

She sipped her coffee. 'I find it difficult to calm down after a performance. All those people cheering for me, then back to an empty hotel room...' She shrugged. 'Thanks for your concern, but I'm sure I'll manage.'

'Only three weeks to go.'

Setting her mug on the table, she leaned forward. 'What then, George? What does an English pop star do when she's not rehearsing or performing?'

George rubbed his newly smooth chin. 'You can have a break. But there will be things to do. More interviews, maybe. We'll need to start working on the next album, write some songs, rehearse them.'

'But the pace won't be so frantic?'

'No.'

'I'd like to take some time out for voice training.'

George didn't understand. 'But you already sing fine.'

She smiled, glancing away, and looked so much like his Penny that it made his heart twinge. 'I mean *real* singing.'

'Opera?'

'I need to spend some time retraining my voice. It's been a long time since I've worked with an expert, and I'd like to return to peak condition.'

'You are talking about opera, though? Not pop music.'

'George, pop music presents me with very few challenges.'

'But Penny Bright is a pop singer, not an opera singer.' He shook his head, confused. 'What are you thinking, Ellie?'

He sensed a sadness in her, stiffening into anger. 'Are you saying I can't get lessons?'

'You can do what you like in your spare time,' he said grudgingly. 'But you need to put aside any notions that you're going to be singing at Covent Garden. We haven't invested all this time and money to turn our backs on success. Nobody listens to opera.'

'Plenty of people listen to opera,' she replied, swiftly and hotly.

He tried to smile, to defuse the situation. 'All right, all right. Plenty of people listen to opera, but your album isn't at number one because of those people. Can't you be happy with what you have? There are girls who would kill to be in your shoes.'

She raised one eyebrow. 'I'm not just any girl.'

'I know that.' Sincerely.

'Opera is art, George. It transcends our petty existences, it is magnificent, sublime, it is the closest we can get to God on this earth.'

He had never heard her speak so passionately. Her German accent had crept back into her words.

She leaned back in her chair, nursing her mug in her long fingers. 'Pop music is rather base and soulless by comparison.'

George bristled. 'Then you've misunderstood it. Pop music is *all* soul. It's the folk music of a culture, it's the way we understand ourselves. And it takes a lot of skill to write something that sounds so simple, but that stays with listeners for their whole lives.'

'You don't seriously think that any of these Penny Bright songs will stay with people for their whole lives?'

He nodded. 'Music means different things to different people, Ellie. Just because you'd rather listen to *Lady Butterfly* –'

'*Madama Butterfly*,' she corrected him.

'Plenty of others would rather listen to the Rolling Stones, and will still be listening to them when they've got grandchildren.'

Ellie met his gaze squarely. 'So let me get this clear: Are you forbidding me from taking singing lessons?'

'No. I'm forbidding you from singing opera as anything but a hobby. You are Penny Bright, the pop star. That's that.'

Her mouth tightened. It wasn't an expression he'd ever seen on Penny, and he felt alienated from Ellie: she was a cuckoo in the nest.

'I see.' She checked her watch. 'What time are we heading to the radio station?'

'Ten.'

She stood and turned her back, taking her mug to the bench. 'I'll come to your suite when I'm ready.'

'I'll see you then.' He rose and left the room, trying not to be anxious about where Ellie's stubbornness might lead.

It was a quiet night at the taverna. Now her Greek was improving exponentially, Silas allowed her to work one night a week behind the bar. It made a welcome change from washing glasses in the tiny, dark kitchen; and she needed the money to get her picnic tour project off the ground.

Silas was there when she arrived, reading a book at one of the tables, his pipe in its habitual lodging place at the corner of his mouth. She approached him as she tied her apron on.

'Kyrios Silas, can I ask you something?'

He held up his hand. 'Greek, please,' he said with a stern glance.

She switched languages, on less steady ground but still certain she could make herself understood. 'I saw a woman this evening. It's the second time I've seen her, the same time of day, the same place.'

He raised his eyebrows, his dark eyes curious. 'Yes?'

'She's very beautiful, in her late forties I suppose. She looks very sad, but when I try to talk to her she runs off.' She couldn't put into words – not in Greek, at least – how unsettled seeing the woman again had made her feel. This time there had been no benevolent smile, and Angela had been strangely disappointed. Instead, the woman had given her an icy glare before she left. The half-light, the woman's strange beauty: she couldn't shake the feeling that she wasn't real at all, but some kind of spectre.

'I don't know who you mean,' Silas said. 'There are many beautiful women here on Petaloudos. The most beautiful in the world.'

'There's not a... ghost on the island, is there?'

Silas threw back his head and laughed until he shook. 'No, no. No ghosts. What an idea, Angela!'

'She just seems so strange.'

Silas shrugged. 'Perhaps you interrupted her while she was trying to have a quiet moment. Be careful now, you don't want a reputation as a busybody. Reputations last for centuries on this island.'

She returned to the bar, relieved that Silas had dismissed her fears, but wondering all the same about the woman, and what her sad secret might be.

Dieter let himself into the house, and dropped the string bag of oranges onto the kitchen table. He couldn't hear his mother or his father anywhere in the house, so he walked through to the back door and out past the shed. His parents were deep in conversation with a tall, gaunt man, down by the vegetable garden. The tall man had a young woman with him, and Dieter couldn't tell at this distance if she was his daughter or his wife.

'Mama?' he called, curious.

His mother looked up and bustled over, leaving his father still in conversation with the tall man.

'Dieter, come and meet Herr Podolski,' she said in a bright voice.

'Who is he?'

Here her smile wavered. 'He...ah...he's looking over the farm.'

Dieter shook his head, confused.

'Your father is thinking of selling.'

'Selling the farm? Why?'

She dropped her voice. 'Please, Dieter, just come and meet him and be nice, and we'll explain later.'

He followed her, and was introduced to Herr Podolski and his daughter, a pretty blonde of about his age named Ingrid. They exchanged pleasantries, and all the while Dieter's mind was reeling. Sell the farm? Why hadn't they mentioned it to him before now? Papa was recovering, they made a good living, the farm had belonged to his grandfather. Dieter had assumed this was where he would always live.

Papa offered to show Herr Podolski the back fence of the property, and Dieter lagged back, hoping to return to the house. They began to move off, but then Ingrid held back too, joining Dieter as the others began the long walk down through the corridors of newly planted maize.

She smiled at him sympathetically. Her eyelashes were so pale it seemed, at first glance, as though she had none at all. 'I take it you don't want to sell the farm?'

Dieter was wary. 'Papa has his reasons, I'm certain.'

She glanced around, the smile still in place. 'It's so beautiful here. Very calm and restful.'

'It's hard work. Certainly too much for one man.'

'My father has no intention of doing any hard physical labour. He'll hire somebody.'

'Then why buy a farm?'

Here the smile faltered. 'My mother died a year ago. He had always promised her that we'd leave the city one day, go and live on a farm. But Papa's job was very demanding, and he left it too late. I think he needs a place to go to remember her.'

'Has he looked at many properties?'

She cheered again. 'Oh, dozens. He says he'll know when he sees the right one.'

Dieter allowed himself to relax. Podolski had looked at many farms and hadn't bought one yet. Perhaps this occasion would be no different.

'I'm sorry,' she said. 'I didn't catch your name.'

'Dieter,' he said.

'And your wife's name?'

Dieter was momentarily puzzled, then realised she was trying to find out whether or not he was single. He felt his body language become guarded. 'I'm not married,' he replied. 'Not yet.'

'But there's somebody?' Unblinking, unashamed to ask.

'She's in London for a little while.' He kicked the dirt, embarrassed to meet her eyes. 'I'm going over to see her very soon.'

The rebuff didn't perturb Ingrid. 'London's a big dirty place. Do you speak English?'

'I've been practising very hard.'

'Good, because none of the English speak a word of another language. Or if they do, it's so mispronounced you haven't the faintest idea what they're saying. I can't say whether they're stupid or arrogant...' Here she stopped herself. 'I'm sorry. Is she English?'

'Half,' he replied. 'But she grew up here in Kokondorf.'

'I didn't mean to insult her,' she said. 'Oh, I think Papa's calling me.'

Dieter glanced up. Podolski was gesturing theatrically. 'You'd better go.'

'Will you walk with me?'

'I have things to do in the house.'

'Ah.' She produced that smile again, and Dieter was struck by how very pretty she was: in a transparent, girlish way. 'It's been lovely to meet you, Dieter.'

220

'The same. Goodbye.' He returned to the house, hoping he might never see her or her father again.

When the Podolskis had left, his parents came to find him. He was hosing the cement floor of the tractor shed. His mother gestured for him to turn off the hose. Neither she nor his father were wearing boots, so he dropped the hose and moved to the dry portion of cement to talk to them.

'I'm sorry about that,' Papa said.

Dieter wanted to be angry with him, but he looked so small and grey, with his thickly knitted cardigan hanging from newly thin shoulders.

'Why didn't you tell me you were thinking of selling the farm?'

'Because it was only a thought,' Papa said. 'And Herr Podolski only called this morning. There was no time to tell you before he got here.'

'When you say it was only a thought...?'

Here, Mama interjected, fierce as a tigress. 'It's too much for your father, Dieter.'

Dieter turned his eyes to Papa, and thought he saw a wince of shame. 'But you're nearly well again. Aren't you?'

'He nearly died,' Mama continued. 'Don't you remember?'

'Of course I remember,' Dieter said hotly.

Papa held up his hands, trying to calm them both. 'The truth is this: I'm not the man I was. I'm fifty-four, it's foolish to think I'll ever fully regain my health. You are a wonderful help to me, Dieter, in fact you've nearly run the place single-handedly the last few months. But spring is here. There's a lot to do, and we can't afford to put somebody else on. Nor can we accept any more money from Ellie,' he said firmly. 'If we sell the farm, we can buy a little house in the village and I can do something else. Odd jobs, repairs... I've always liked tinkering with things.'

Dieter wanted to say, *Where does this leave me?* But he didn't. He was twenty-five, and men his age were supposed to have left home long ago. But he had left home once, to join the army, and he'd hated it. When he'd returned, he'd thought it was for good, to play his part in the family business, to secure his inheritance, raise his own family.

Instead, he said, 'And if Herr Podolski doesn't buy it? Do you still intend to find somebody else who will?'

His parents exchanged glances. A silence, made to seem longer by the significance of his question, lingered. A sudden wind made the door on the shed swing all the way open, letting in a band of sunshine.

'Papa?' he prompted.

But it was his mother who answered. 'Herr Podolski has already made an offer,' she said. 'I'm sorry, Dieter. The farm is no longer ours.'

SEVENTEEN

Three times a week for two weeks, Angela had waited hopefully at the end of the pier. Beside her, propped up with a block of wood, was a small blackboard she had painted herself, with *Petaloudos Picnic Tours* written on it. Three times a week for two weeks, Captain Lianis had shaken his head at her sadly. Nobody had come. Even though she had advertised in the tourist information brochure near the docks on the mainland, even though she had made Captain Lianis promise he would personally try to drum up business.

So, on the Tuesday of the third week, she waited but was not hopeful. She chewed the edge off one of her fingernails, and cursed the sky for being so clear and fine when nobody who mattered would be here to see it. The supply boat was late today, a distant speck on the sea.

She wondered how long Silas would let her keep trying before he wrote off the money he had loaned her to repair the second moped; or before he demanded his spare room back. At the moment, the old furniture from it was stored in his car shed, and his car was parked on the street. But she knew that he had been impressed when he saw what she had done with the room. Every inch of the tiny bathroom had been bleached and scrubbed, the brass polished and gleaming. She had invested in new towels and bath mats, thick, in rich colours. The room she had painted herself, pale apricot, and hung a wallpaper border of white flowers. The old bed had already been in the room, and she had oiled the springs, beaten and turned the mattress, cleaned and re-hemmed the sheets and bought two new bedspreads. The shutter that looked out to the sea was repainted gaily, and she had hand-sewn curtains and a pelmet. The carpet, which had been stained and old, she'd ripped up and thrown away, to reveal dark floorboards beneath. They were cleaned, but she'd had no money for polishing. Instead, she'd covered them with bright rugs from the markets. The overall impression was one of a bright, clean room. She hoped that any residual shabbiness would be interpreted as ethnic charm.

As the boat came closer into view, she realised Captain Lianis was waving to her with both arms. She shielded her eyes against the afternoon sun and waved back. He hitched his thumb at two people who stood leaning on the railing at the stern of the boat. Her heart picked up a beat as she caught his meaning.

Somebody had come!

Her body was suddenly erect, her fingernail pulled from her mouth, her clothes smoothed with nervous hands. Her first customers were about to arrive; she wanted to make a good impression.

They were Swiss, a young couple from Lucerne. They didn't speak a word of Greek, but their English was superb. She took them to the taverna and showed them their room, told them where they could find food and gave them a hand-drawn map of the island.

She promised to return at eight in the morning to fetch them for breakfast. 'At around eleven, I'll bring your picnic lunch and you can take the mopeds wherever you like,' she said.

The young woman thanked her profusely, told her the room was 'charming', and Angela left them alone, very pleased with herself.

Silas met her on the stairs.

'All settled in?' he asked, and she realised for the first time that he was as nervous as her. This almost made her laugh: Silas was usually so unflappable.

'They seem to be. I'll be back for my shift at five, but if you need anything before then...'

'I can manage,' he said. He touched her shoulder lightly. 'Good work, Angela.'

'It wouldn't have been possible without you. The room, the moped, the translation of the insurance policy...' She shook her head, remembering the nightmare of paperwork that had characterised the past month. 'So thank you.' Impulsively, she leaned up and kissed his leathery cheek. As she left, she was sure she saw him blushing.

Walking home up the narrow cobbled lane, an afternoon sea breeze lifted her hair and filled her nostrils with the scent of salt and seaweed. There was that sensation again: deep, peaceful happiness. The irony was not lost on her: she had come to this island an unhappy woman, determined to know about her past. But in cutting off from that past – whatever it was – she had found a different happiness, one she wasn't even looking for. Simple, easeful. The pleasure of making something out of nothing, of creating a bed and breakfast room out of a storeroom, a nascent tourist business out of moped parts and a grand idea, was deep and satisfying. As she let herself into the dark stairwell that led up to her tiny room, she had the distinct feeling that anything was possible for her, precisely because she had no idea who she was.

'So, George, are you going to tell me what we're doing here?'

George stole a quick glance at Ellie before returning his eyes to the road. How was he supposed to answer her: *We're here to commit fraud.* She had been a good sport so far. The tour had been over for only two days, she was probably sick of being driven around the English countryside, but this morning he'd picked her up for a drive to Silkfield, just outside Trowbridge, promising explanations on the way. He had handed her Penny's driving licence, in the name of Angela Smith, and told her to practise the signature. She had scribbled on a notebook on her lap for half an hour, then pleaded a headache and dozed the rest of the way.

Here they were pulling into the high street and he still hadn't outlined his plan, though she must have suspected it was something illicit. A row of stone shops lined the dark road. The pub grew ivy up its walls, a week-old newspaper headline rattled in the breeze outside the general store, and a thin woman with a broom swept the front step of the post office.

'Well,' he started, indicating to pull into an empty space on the side of the road, 'I need to pick up some documents. I mean, I need *you* to pick up some documents.'

'For Penny?'

'Yes, and no. They were in her real name: Angela Smith.' He switched the engine off and turned to her. 'Hence the driving licence. She hated driving, but I made her take the test. She never used it.'

Ellie flipped open the booklet and studied the signature again.

'I expect they'll need identification,' George continued. 'You sign for it and open the safe-deposit box, get me the documents, and we head back to London.' If the documents were still there; if Penny hadn't already been to collect them, and by that learned something that was keeping her far, far away.

'This feels...illegal,' Ellie said.

'And nothing else we've done so far feels that way to you?' he said, shortly. Then, calming his voice, 'I'm going to take them for safekeeping. One day she'll be back, and she'll want them. Do you think you can do it?'

'Of course. I've been forging her handwriting for months now.'

'I mean, do you think you can do something so overtly illegal?'

She considered this, gave a little shrug. 'If it's part of being Penny Bright I'll do it. That was our deal. You'll come in with me?'

George unbuckled his seatbelt. 'Absolutely.'

He took her to the queue with the oldest male teller, hoping this might mean an anonymous transaction. Of course, he was foiled the instant a young woman watering indoor plants caught sight of Ellie.

'Penny Bright!' she squealed, hurrying over. 'It's got to be!'

Ellie turned to her and smiled, while the elderly teller frowned over the top of his bifocals.

'Oh, my God, I'm so excited to meet you!' She forced her hand into Ellie's. The tag on her uniform said her name was Helen. 'What are you doing out here?'

Ellie glanced at George and back to the young woman. George intervened. 'Helen, we're here for a confidential transaction, and Penny would appreciate your discretion.'

Helen nodded secretively, dropping her voice. 'Right. I'll take over. Come down to counter three.' She pulled out a set of keys and let herself in behind the counter, meeting George and Ellie at the third window. George produced the solicitor's letter and Ellie produced Penny's driving licence. Helen, after expressing surprise that Penny Bright was not a real name and swearing her secrecy on her grandmother's grave, organised the paperwork, signatures and, finally, the key.

'Meet me at the security door,' she said, indicating a metal and two-way glass door at the end of the counter. She led them through it and down a linoleum corridor that smelled of rising damp and bleach. More keys were produced, she opened the door to a lightless vault.

'All right, then,' Helen said, as the fluorescent tubes overhead flickered into life. 'Box number C184 is a very old one. Probably from the fifties.' She rolled her eyes, as though 'the fifties' were centuries ago. George tried not to take offence. She marched down to the back of the room, squatting and muttering to herself, then pulled out the box and handed it to Ellie. 'Here you are, Angela.'

'I prefer Penny,' Ellie replied, without glancing up.

'Of course. Sorry, Penny. There's a bureau to work on back near the entrance. I'll leave you in peace.' She indicated a panel by the door. 'Just buzz when you want me to let you out.'

Then she was gone, locking the vault behind her.

Ellie turned to George and handed the box over. 'Go on. It's yours.'

'It doesn't belong to either of us,' he sighed, guilty and unaccountably fearful. 'But she gave you the key.' He held the box out, and she slid the key into the lock. It took a little fiddling before it popped. Certainly, the box had been sealed a long time; Penny hadn't been here looking for it.

He lifted the lid and inside was a large envelope, yellowed by time. He took it, and handed Ellie the empty box. She locked it and left it on the bureau. George realised his heart was pounding. He tucked the envelope under his arm.

'Are you going to see what's in there?' Ellie asked.

'I think I might already know.'

Ellie looked puzzled.

'Penny had a past.'

'So now you have her past.' She indicated the envelope. 'And I have her future. I hope she's hanging on tightly to the present.' She turned and pressed the buzzer. Eager Helen returned, having dug up a Box Brownie camera and a sheet of paper for an autograph. George refused the photograph, but Ellie happily signed the paper as Penny Bright. Then they were back in the car.

George started the engine and Ellie reached for the radio while he stored the envelope in the glove box. She was always fiddling with the radio, chasing snatches of music and chatter across the dial until she landed on a classical music station, where she would resolutely stay put beyond the point where George could scream if he heard another meandering french horn concerto.

Opera this time, and he knew he was doomed.

But then he turned to her, saw that her wrists were covered in gooseflesh, her eyes misting into middle distance.

'Ellie? Are you all right?'

She broke from her reverie, and he realised tears were welling. 'I... this aria...'

'What is it?'

'*Un bel di.*'

'In English?'

'*One fine day* from *Madama Butterfly*. Puccini.'

'Why are you crying?'

'The words... it's as though I'm hearing them for the first time.'

'Wait... you speak French?'

She smiled slightly. 'It's Italian.' She turned the radio up. 'Cio-Cio-San has faith every day that her beloved will arrive...Listen... "See you, now he is coming".' Her voice caught here, and George wanted very badly to touch that cool hand that had come to rest in her lap, squeeze it and tell her everything would be all right.

'It's about Dieter, isn't it? The young man back in Germany?'

Ellie nodded, pressing her lips together. 'It's ridiculous. I'm not Cio-Cio-San, he's not Pinkerton. His father has been ill, he hasn't been able to get away, but...'

'But when you love somebody, you're always afraid of losing them.'

'Precisely,' she said, reaching into her handbag for a tissue. 'I've lost nearly everyone dear to me, George. I've often wondered if it's my own fault. Perhaps I'm careless or cold or...'

George released his seatbelt and reached across to hug her. To his surprise – and, he suspected, hers – she encircled his neck with her arms and let him hold her briefly. The first thought that occurred to him was how little she felt like the real Penny. Penny's embraces were soft, as though she was happy to collapse into his arms; but Ellie was stiff, straight. She might have been able to impersonate Penny in every other way, but here in this one, crucial way, she was profoundly different. Then she was pulling away, straightening her back, getting her tears under control.

'Put it on another station,' she said. 'English pop music. That could never make anyone cry.'

Instead of his usual irritation with such a dismissive comment from her, he smiled, reaching for the radio dial. 'English pop music it is.'

Ellie had George drop her off at Leicester Square, and she immediately went in search of records to play at home. She had been long enough without that wonderful music. George could say what he liked about pop music, but she knew it was ephemeral and transient. The great opera arias glittered like magnificent jewels, growing more precious with every generation. She found a dusty second-hand music shop off Charing Cross Road. The large man behind the counter was whistling along enthusiastically with a bebop jazz record that blasted through the speakers positioned at the front of the store. She browsed a few minutes, found a Maria Callas collection on an LP and took it up to the counter to pay.

'You're Penny Bright,' the man behind the counter said as he slid the LP into a paper bag.

'No,' she said. 'Though I hear that all the time.'

Then she was gone, and hailing a taxi before anyone else could recognise her.

At home, she put the record on loud and sank into the couch with her eyes closed. One by one, she listened to the songs. Sublime. Her throat ached from holding back tears. The soaring notes pierced her heart. *I want to sing.*

She opened her mouth and joined in.

Only it didn't feel right.

Of course, she hadn't warmed up, her throat was constricted from crying. She was foolish to think she could launch right into the middle of a duet with Maria Callas. But the hoarseness troubled her. As though a layer of phlegm covered her voice, making it impossible to work properly. Touring, late nights, singing with poor habits. Certainly, she had been paid handsomely, but here was the real cost.

Her father's voice was suddenly in her ears, chilling her blood. 'You have ruined your instrument.'

George sat at his writing desk in his warm, woody studio, and fiddled with the edge of the envelope. He had come this far, finally working up the nerve to pick up the documents; was he really going to let something so minor as breaking the seal stop him?

No. He tried gingerly to peel up the edge, but it wouldn't budge, so he took out a letter opener and split the envelope open, spilling out the collection of papers within.

He glanced through them, and his heart tightened with guilt. A soft knock on the door made him jump, and he hastily shoved the papers under his in-tray, so they weren't visible.

'Come in.'

Aila opened the door. '*Lemmikki*, I need your opinion on something.' She held in her hands a tiny pair of patent leather shoes. Her fingers closed around them gently, almost possessively. 'I'm afraid I've got myself in a bit of a flap and...' She trailed off, and George tried to put the papers out of his head, to give her his full attention.

'What is it?'

She offered the little shoes into evidence, her voice shaking almost imperceptibly. 'It's Julia's baby's christening on Sunday. Do you think... they're old, but not used. So pretty. It's a shame to have them locked up in a cupboard.'

Immediately George understood. During her third pregnancy, the one that had lasted for twelve awful hope- and fear-drenched weeks, Aila had bought baby shoes. In the whirlpool of despair that had attended the miscarriage, he hadn't given the shoes another thought. But of course she had held onto them all these years. A sad reminder of what wasn't to be. He felt angry, tired, guilty, wanted to hold her and wash all her sad feelings away. He pulled her down on his lap and kissed her soft neck. 'Aila, if you want to keep them, you can.'

'I don't think I should.'

'Then give them to Julia. She'll love them.'

She smiled at him. 'Thank you.'

'We should go somewhere this weekend,' he said. 'Paris, maybe? It's an age since we did something nice together.'

'I'd love that. But the christening...'

'The weekend after then. I'd like to take you out and spoil you.'

She laughed softly. 'And I'd like to be spoilt.' She slid off his lap and moved to the door. 'I'm glad the tour is over. It's nice to have you home.'

'It's nice to be home. Would you put the kettle on, Aila? I'm nearly finished here.'

As soon as she was gone, speed returned to his movements. He hurriedly stuffed the papers back into their envelope, his heart thudding. What to do with them? He couldn't destroy them: Penny might return one day, he would have to give them to her... He shoved the envelope deep in the bottom of his filing cabinet, locked the cabinet and, finally, his office.

It was vital to keep those papers in the shadows.

Ellie was at the TRG office, picking up copies of her latest press clippings, when she saw Ivan Hamblyn.

He was beautifully dressed as always, spine very erect, moving down the corridor to his office. Magpie-eyed Alice, who was in the middle of a sentence, stopped to watch Ellie stare at Ivan.

'Seen something you like?' she joked.

Ellie laughed self-consciously. 'I...no, seeing Ivan made me remember something. Do you mind? I might just go and speak to him.' She was trying not to let her recent realisation that she was losing her voice haunt her. All she needed was to work with a good teacher, one who understood her voice and what she had to put it through. She was in London: great teachers lived in big cities. She only needed to find one.

Ivan Hamblyn, who had seen her audition in Bremen, who managed classical music for TRG, would know a teacher. She was certain of it.

Alice was checking the diary. 'Well, his lordship is free for another ten minutes,' she said, tapping the page. 'Then he's due in a sales meeting.'

Ellie thought this was an odd choice of nickname for Ivan, who had seemed quite humble and approachable on the few occasions they'd met.

'Come on,' Alice said, crooking her index finger. 'I'll take you down there.'

'Thank you.' A guilty conscience made Ellie too garrulous. 'I'm trying to get tickets to the symphony for an old friend,' she said, to an uninterested Alice. 'You know, just exploiting my contacts.'

'Mm-hm,' Alice said, stopping outside a closed door with Ivan Hamblyn's name inscribed on a large gold name badge. 'Here we are. Perhaps later we could catch up for that cup of tea you keep promising we'll have together?'

Ellie nodded enthusiastically. 'We will, we will. But not today. I'll have to dash off after this.'

Alice smiled, a little tightly, and left her. She knocked on the door and was called in.

'Penny?' Ivan Hamblyn said, dropping his pen on his desk and rising to take her hand. 'This is a pleasant surprise.'

Ellie closed the door behind her. He wore a dove-grey suit, with a blue silk cravat. Turning down the volume on his record player he invited her to sit down.

'Bach's Brandenburg Concertos,' he said. 'I always work better with baroque music playing.'

She settled across from him and flicked her hair out of her eyes in her best impersonation of Penny Bright. 'It's lovely,' she said. It was on the tip of her tongue to make a comment about how little she enjoyed baroque music, how the sweet torment of romanticism was more to her taste. But she couldn't, because she would simply give too much away. Penny knew very little about music. Ellie started to feel the edge of a dangerous tide that she was inching towards. She cleared her throat, unsure how to proceed.

'How can I help you, my dear?' he said, meeting her eyes with his clear blue gaze.

'I have a friend who would like to learn to sing. Opera.'

He nodded. 'I see.'

'I said I'd find out who the best teachers in London were. I thought you might know where to start.'

He was already reaching for his battered address book. 'Would she prefer a female teacher?'

'She's a soprano.' Ellie shrugged, mock-dumbly. 'Whatever that means.'

'The English voice is quite different from the European voice,' Ivan said. 'Many prefer European styles, such as Russian or Italian. Do you think your friend would rather learn with an English teacher?'

Ellie answered guardedly. She knew of this distinction: English voices were trained with a lighter tone. She didn't want that. She wanted somebody who could be as good as her father. 'I'm certain she'd rather learn with a European one if there is somebody in London.'

'Then you want Dobryna Grusova. Madame to her pupils. She's Russian, but she's lived and worked all over Europe, and has trained some of the most famous voices in the world. She coached for a little while at the English National Opera, but her style didn't suit them. She has a reputation for being volatile, even cruel, but she gets results. I know she's very, very good, the best. I presume your...friend has sufficient money to pay for the very best?'

'She does,' Ellie said, fighting her excitement. Madame Grusova sounded perfect.

He dictated the spelling of the name and the phone number while Ellie scribbled it on the back of her chequebook.

'If it doesn't work out, give me a call,' he said. 'I have other names.'

Ellie tucked the phone number into her bag and stood. 'Thank you very much. One other thing, I'd prefer if you didn't tell George I've been in.'

The corner of his mouth twitched up. 'I see. That's fine.'

She moved towards the door.

'*Viel Glück,*' he said.

Ellie froze. He had spoken to her in German. She turned, forcing a smile. 'I'm sorry, what did you say?' Her heart was pounding. What should she do? Continue to pretend she hadn't understood? Come clean and beg him not to tell anyone? He suspected her, that was the only reason he would have said what he said. In an instant she saw it clearly: it had been too dangerous to come to him. He met her first as a young aspiring opera singer; he tipped off George about her whereabouts; and now she had come directly to his office, talking about opera singing with some lame excuse about a friend...

'It's German,' he said, 'it means "best of luck".' His expression gave nothing more away.

She feigned confusion. Best not to give him an inch of encouragement. 'Oh. Thanks, I guess.'

'If your friend is ever interested in signing with England's finest classical label, I would hope she'd give me a call.'

'I think she's a long way from that kind of success,' Ellie said.

He parted his hands and gave a shrug. 'Goodbye then, Penny.'

'Thanks,' she said. 'See you around.'

She barrelled down the corridor, head down, called out a gruff farewell to Alice then was back outside in the fresh air. Her heart raced, but she didn't know if it was the excitement of returning to her true passion, or the fear of wondering whether she had just survived a close call.

EIGHTEEN

'*I*'m proud of you, you know.'

Angela looked up from her vantage point, kneeling on the bathroom floor, scrubbing the toilet before the next couple of tourists arrived. Silas wore a serious expression. She laughed. 'You're proud of me for cleaning the toilet so well?'

Silas smiled, folded his cane under his arm and sat on the edge of the laundry basket. 'You know what I mean. And you must know, by now, that it's hard for me to say such things, so...'

'Yes, I know. Take it with good grace.' She dropped the scrubbing brush in the bucket with a clatter and peeled her rubber gloves off. 'Thank you, Kyrios Silas. It *is* going well, isn't it?'

'Lilika at the bakery thinks you're a genius.'

'That's because she's charging a fortune for the picnic lunches.' She washed her hands and dried them on her jeans. 'Come with me, I need to ask you about something.' Silas followed her to the bedroom, where she opened the shutters, and started making the bed.

'What is it?' Silas asked.

'Lilika's not the only one who's pleased,' she said. 'I had a long chat with Captain Lianis the other day. He told me something very interesting.'

'Leo Lianis is full of ideas that don't come to fruition,' Silas cautioned. 'What has he told you?'

Angela ignored his warning note, and spoke while she worked. 'He told me he's had to turn away people on four occasions now, because we only have one room. He told me that if he could book three couples on the boat, instead of one, he would make enough money to bring the boat over one extra trip a week. Just think: the whole island would benefit. Every business would have more access to supplies, every resident would have more opportunities to cross to the mainland.' She smoothed the covers and plumped the cushions, then sat on the end of the bed.

Silas looked puzzled. 'We can't accommodate six people here.'

'I know.'

'Then what are you thinking?'

'A dedicated bed and breakfast hotel. On the island.'

'Where?'

'Crazy Mia's empty house, down on the bluff.'

Silas puffed out his ample bottom lip and made a noise of derision. 'That is a very silly idea.'

'Why?' she asked, not in the least deterred by his scepticism. 'She's not using it, it's the right size, it's soundly built. All you need to do is go and ask her what rent she'd be willing to charge and –'

'*I'm* not going anywhere near that woman.'

Angela was taken aback as she realised that Silas had grown very agitated and angry. 'I'll ask her then. But I can only do this if you're willing to help me.'

'This argument is pointless. She'll never agree.'

'She might.'

Silas breathed out noisily. 'I advise you very strongly not to go near her. No good will come of it.'

Silence fell. A stiff sea breeze rattled against the windows and Angela glanced out over the rooftops. Clouds were moving in. She knew instinctively that Captain Lianis would be bringing no tourists today. The weather was about to turn bad. Perhaps Silas was right; perhaps it was foolish to try to expand the business beyond what it was.

'Is she really so dangerous?' Angela asked.

'She could be.'

'Why is she so rich? If she's crazy? Crazy people are usually poor, they live in cardboard boxes.' A flash of memory slid out from under the shadow; unpleasant, cold. She hastily pushed it away.

'She was rich before she was crazy. She bought the house years before she came here. People say she was a wealthy socialite in Europe, that she fell in love and he broke her heart. Ancient history now.' He waved his hand. 'She lived on the bluff while she had the mansion on the hill built. Hardly anyone ever saw her. Everyone says the broken heart had sent her mad.'

'Perhaps she's not mad. Perhaps she's lonely.'

'Lonely people don't poison their neighbours' pets; they don't shout obscenities at strangers in the marketplace; they don't lock themselves up alone in dusty mansions and threaten the postman with a gun.'

Angela turned these images over in her head. She knew that Silas would never approach Mia on her behalf, so did she dare approach the old woman herself? She imagined the house on the bluff, newly painted and decorated, bustling with activity, a half-dozen shiny new mopeds parked out the front. The fantasy was too appealing to deter her from at least trying to meet Mia... Perhaps Silas was exaggerating. That was the way in small communities; once somebody had become a pariah, the tall tales about that person would grow taller with each passing year.

'What are you thinking?' Silas said, eyes narrowed suspiciously.

'I'm thinking I'd better get down to the pier to see if Captain Lianis has brought me any new guests,' she said with a quick smile.

'Angela, don't take my warning lightly.'

'Thanks for your concern, Kyrios Silas.' She lifted herself off the edge of the bed and stretched her back. 'You're right. Approaching Mia is probably too much trouble.'

The rain started then, misting at the window, and she vowed that on the very next fine day, she would go up to the mansion and introduce herself to Crazy Mia.

Ellie walked up from the bus stop towards Madame Grusova's address. She wore a scarf over her hair, a big pair of sunglasses, and was deliberately dressed down in a loose dress and flat shoes. Nobody had recognised her on the trip out to Greenwich. Of course she could have called a taxi, but it would have been expensive and Ellie was frugal. She loved watching the numbers build up in her little bank-book, and felt a real wrench every time she had to withdraw some and see the numbers go down again. With those numbers behind her, the old fears of the dark chill of poverty eased. She felt safe, for the first time in her memory. Her one indulgence was her phone calls to Dieter; and to pay for them she skimped with the cheapest food, used as little electricity as she could, and rarely bought new clothes. Buses and trains were cheap, she could get places with spare change. So she disguised herself and risked it whenever she could.

She had not yet spoken with Madame Grusova. On the phone, the singing teacher's assistant had answered and organised the interview. She only took new students after an interview; it mattered nothing to her how much money they could afford, the assistant had said, Madame cared about voices, not money. If she believed somebody was not able to sing, then she wouldn't take them on. Ellie was both galvanised by this challenge, and a little intimidated. Ivan Hamblyn had said she was the best. Ellie wanted the best.

She had imagined a tall, imposing house for Madame, but instead found a white semidetached with a brown tiled roof and a neat garden. Ellie walked up the front path and rang the doorbell. A middle-aged woman answered.

'Madame Grusova?' Ellie asked.

'No, I'm Clare, her assistant. You must be Penny.'

'That's right.'

'Come in. Madame is just finishing her tea.' Clare let her into a brightly lit hallway. There was a strong smell of medicine and disinfectant. A piece of medical equipment that Ellie couldn't identify – a trolley with an oxygen cylinder and some tubes hanging from it – took up one corner of the living room. Ellie assessed Clare's plain blue dress and flat shoes, and started to wonder if she was a nurse as well as an assistant. Perhaps Madame was ill.

Clare led her through to a music room, with a wooden floor and a narrow window covered by a dark brown curtain. A grand piano took up most of the floor space. Clare indicated a threadbare armchair. 'Wait here, Madame will be along shortly.'

She left, but Ellie didn't sit. She went to the window and drew the curtain aside a little to let the light in. Down on the street, cars went past, made silent by the double glazing. Ellie unpicked the knot in her scarf and tucked it in her handbag with her sunglasses. There was a noise by the door.

'You are Penny?'

Ellie turned. Madame Grusova was simply the oldest living person Ellie had ever seen. Her back was shaped like a question mark and her face was a network of deep lines that obscured her features. She had to be at least eighty; Ellie wouldn't have been surprised if she was ninety.

'Yes, I'm Penny,' Ellie said, striding over and extending her hand. 'I'm very pleased to meet you.'

Madame looked at Ellie's hand and wrinkled up her nose. 'I'll see how pleased I am after you've sung.' Shuffling to the piano, she indicated that Ellie should stand at her right side. She sat heavily on the stool and flipped up the lid.

'I trained to sing opera when I was a teenager,' Ellie started to explain, 'but lately I've been –'

Madame cut her off with a gesture of her right hand. 'I don't want explanations. Explanations mean nothing to me. I only want to hear you sing. Voices speak to me, your voice will tell me everything I need to know. So!' She bashed out a loud chord, then started to play arpeggios.

Ellie took a breath and started to sing along. It all came back to her, the correct way to support her voice, the vowel modifications necessary for transition through her registers, the techniques for placing her highest notes. She was proud of herself, as her voice soared again. Certainly, there was a hoarseness there, a breathiness that hadn't been there before, but she was sure Madame would hear through those things to the voice beneath.

After five minutes, Madame stopped playing in the middle of an arpeggio. Ellie fell silent. Madame turned to her and eyed her sharply, her lips twisted to one side. Ellie waited, her pulse thumping in her throat.

'I won't take you,' Madame said at last.

'What? Why?' Ellie protested.

'Bad habits, terrible habits. I can't fix them.'

Wounded pride made her speak too plainly. 'But I'm a good singer. Can't you hear that?'

'You might have been once, but your voice is damaged.'

'Damaged?' It was as though ice had been poured into her heart. 'What do you mean?'

'Your vocal folds are swollen. You've treated them poorly. They don't seal properly.' She held out her two index fingers to demonstrate, bashing them against each other. 'Your breath escapes, you sound hoarse. Eventually, they will grow calloused – if they aren't already – and they will become hard and inflexible. I don't want to start down this road with you now. You are less than a year away from losing your voice.'

Ellie was speechless with horror. She'd had no idea she could damage her voice so easily and with no warning.

Madame moved to stand, but Ellie said, 'No, wait!'

Madame sat again, eyebrows drawn down in irritation.

'Tell me, apart from the hoarseness, I have a good voice under there. My father trained me. You may have heard of him. His name was Kasper Frankel, and he was the star pupil of Franz Auerbach in the early 1950s.'

Madame shrugged. 'It's clear that you've trained, you may have had potential once.'

'That's why I'm here. To reverse the damage, to get my voice back.'

'You're willing to do whatever I say? To stop doing whatever it is you do that has caused this problem?'

'I…'

241

'I didn't think so,' Madame said with a dismissive tone.

Ellie thought quickly. Rehearsals for the new album wouldn't start for another six weeks; she wouldn't have to sing any pop music at least until then. She could get a lot of early nights, rest. She could start lessons with Madame, and see how things went. After that... she would worry about that later.

'Yes, I'll stop,' Ellie said. 'If you take me on. I'll do whatever you say.'

Finally, Madame smiled, and revealed a perfect set of false teeth. 'Good girl. I will see you Tuesdays and Thursdays at three o'clock sharp. I don't tolerate lateness. Leave your address with Clare and she will post you an account for your first term.'

Ellie left Madame's house feeling excited but uncertain. For a few weeks, at least, she'd be able to work on getting her voice back. But what then? She had insisted on becoming Penny Bright, but now she wasn't sure if she wanted that anymore.

Not if Penny Bright was losing her voice.

George left the record company building and made his way down the road and across the square towards his car. The little patch of green was sunny, and he paused a moment to watch two pigeons pick around in the grass for food. He could hear the traffic roaring out on the street, though it was muffled by the tall trees that stood all around.

'George!'

The pigeons took flight, wings whirring. George turned in surprise to see Ivan Hamblyn, sitting on a bench with a lunchbox on his lap. He waved cheerily, and George waved back.

'Come over!' he called.

Curious, George wandered over and sat next to Ivan on the wooden bench.

'Lovely day,' Ivan said, crunching on a piece of celery.

'Do you always have lunch in the square?'

He nodded. 'On fine days. On rainy days I stay in.'

George nodded in return, folded his hands between his knees and leaned forward, wondering why Ivan was being so friendly.

They'd had very little to do with each other over the years. Silence stretched out between them, broken only by the sound of the occasional lorry going past, and Ivan crunching on his celery.

George was about to stand and make his farewells, when Ivan said, 'George, I know.'

At first, George didn't understand him. 'I'm sorry?'

Ivan snapped the lid back on his lunchbox and turned his eyes up to the cloudless sky, and continued to speak in a casual tone. 'I know about Penny. Ellie.'

George's heart charged, an electric shock. Words were stuck in his throat, unable to make it to his tongue.

'Don't worry, I have nothing to gain from telling anybody.' He met George's eyes and smiled. 'But I have to ask, where is Penny? The real Penny?'

A full ten seconds passed before George could bring himself to answer. *Ivan knew.* Where would this lead? Then he gathered himself; he had been asked a question. 'I don't know,' he said helplessly. 'She ran away. The last I heard, she cashed a cheque in Madrid. Where she's gone is anyone's guess.' George shook his head. 'But how did you figure it out? Ellie's stepped into the role so well, I thought that –'

'I doubt that anybody else would have twigged, George. I just happened to have the right information at the right time.' He leaned forward. 'Last week, Ellie... Penny...' He shrugged, laughed it off. 'She came to see me, to ask me where in London she could get opera lessons. For "a friend", she said, right before she asked me not to tell you she'd been in. The mention of opera, and remembering how you'd grilled me at that party last year, when I mistook Penny for Ellie... well, I would've been a fool not to figure it out.'

George recalled their conversation of all those months ago so differently. In his imagination, he had been very cool and casual, had asked for little more than the girl's name and an idea of which part of Germany she lived in. But then, how could he have been cool and casual, given the intensity behind his questions. Ivan Hamblyn had always been a risk. He should have foreseen this and managed it better.

'The proof, though, was right there in front of me,' Ivan continued. 'She wrote Madame's number down with her right hand. Penny was left-handed, like me. I remember her signing autographs at the party.'

'What will it take?' George spluttered, breathless. 'What do you want me to do so you'll never mention this to anyone? How much do you want?' Already he realised he was defeated: everyone knew that Ivan was a wealthy man.

'George,' Ivan said, offended, 'I've no way to benefit from telling anyone. You've gone quite pale; I want to reassure you, the secret is safe.' He winked broadly now. 'Though when she decides she wants an opera career, I hope you'll give me the first opportunity to record her.'

'She's not going to pursue an opera career. She's Penny Bright, and Penny Bright sings pop.'

'If you'd heard her sing...'

'Then, if she was so good at the audition, why wasn't she singing opera when I found her? Why was she working on a farm?'

'Her father died that evening, she didn't return for the entry interview. By the time we found out, it was too late. We'd offered the position to somebody else. But she was a phenomenal talent, she made us all sit up and gasp.'

'Still, she's made her choice now,' George said. 'I've just come from a meeting. The album will be released in the United States in two months, and I'm taking her over there on tour. Fifty-eight dates already pencilled in. I'm going to make her a superstar. No time for opera.'

'There are opera superstars.'

'Name one.'

Ivan rattled off a list of names – Callas, Angelis, Sutherland – George recognised them but waved a dismissive hand nonetheless. 'It all comes down to money,' he said. 'She wants it, a lot of it; I'm good at making it. We're a perfect partnership. She'll forget about the opera.'

'I hope you're right. Nothing so difficult as a reluctant superstar.

Sounds like you've already had one get away from you.' He checked his watch. 'Back to the grind. It's been nice chatting with you.'

'Ivan,' George said, as his companion stood and made to leave. 'I can count on your discretion?'

Ivan smiled his lopsided smile. 'Don't waste another thought on it.' He shook his head, laughing again. 'What a news story it would make, eh?' Then he was off, striding back across the square towards the office.

George sat a long time after his departure, fighting with his feelings. Despite the gorgeous blue sky and the warm sun, he felt cold and unsettled. Was it because Ivan knew? Maybe, but George trusted him. There were few men as decent as Ivan Hamblyn. Was it because Ellie was so determined to take her opera lessons? He had to nip that situation in the bud, before the new single, before the US tour, well before Penny Bright became an international superstar and George had a lot more to lose.

Dieter was overwhelmed by the airport. Concourses led in all directions; a sea of people flooded past, coming, going; and Ellie was nowhere in sight. Everyone spoke in a babble of English. He sat hesitantly, with his small bag between his feet. Mama had tried to insist he take a large suitcase, but he hadn't much to bring with him. A few clothes, the coat he wore hung loose over his shoulders, an English phrasebook for difficult moments when Ellie wasn't there. Like now.

He glanced around, eyes searching for her familiar features. It had been so long since he'd seen her, held her, that the pressure of knowing that moment was only a few heartbeats away made him anxious and afraid; though he couldn't put his finger on what, precisely, he was afraid of. Perhaps he was just afraid of everything being different... but, in truth, it had been different since she left.

'Dieter!'

Then she was there, waving, pushing her way through the crowd. She was much slimmer, her body had taken a sleek edge that matched the studied hairstyle, the well-fitted clothes. The awkwardness of the farmgirl was completely absent; she looked like a picture in a magazine, and he became keenly aware of his crushed clothes, his messy hair. He stood and hurried towards her, nearly tripping over his bag. A moment later, she was in his arms, and the smell of her was familiar and comforting. She was Ellie again. *His* Ellie. He closed his eyes and pressed her close, and time stood still. Then a male voice spoke, very near to them.

'Miss Bright, we need to get moving.'

Dieter stepped back, and noticed for the first time the tall man in a grey suit that stood behind her shoulder.

Ellie offered an apologetic smile. 'Security,' she whispered in his ear in German. 'It's hard for me to go out... I get recognised. I would have come in disguise but I wanted to look nice for you.'

Dieter looked around, and saw immediately what she meant. Two girls were snapping pictures of Ellie; a little further off a group had gathered to watch her; a man was calling out, 'Penny!' as he hurried over, brandishing a pen. The man in the grey suit fobbed him off and Ellie, gripping Dieter's hand tightly, led him away. Now, she wasn't *his* Ellie at all. She belonged to the thronging crowd, the security guard, the shining limousine she had ordered for them; and a sense of alienation and estrangement crept over him, making him feel cold and lost.

NINETEEN

After four days of rain, the cobbled roads were drenched and the air was heavy with the smell of damp earth and seaweed. But today the sun shone brightly from a clear, washed sky, and it was early when Angela set off to see Crazy Mia.

She took her red moped and started up the road. It was the first time she'd ridden it for many weeks. Usually, she left it free for tourists, but nobody had come to the island on a picnic tour for the duration of the rain. She cruised up the hill, the gleaming sea on her right and the sun low and white. Her stomach jittered a little with anxiety as she approached Mia's mansion, the vision of a witch returning to her. She parked the moped on the grass, and crossed the muddy road to the iron gates that stood in the long, plastered wall. Through the bars, she viewed the house, a spectacular mansion in gleaming whitewash, the morning sun dazzling off its azure roof. The gardens were wild and overgrown, as though nobody had been in them for a long time. The impression was fairy-tale-like: a castle where everyone slept, perhaps, and wilderness had enfolded it for a hundred years. It was quiet, almost serene. Nothing about it matched with Silas's description of Mia as a gun-wielding, dog-poisoning, foul-mouthed shrew. But still, she was on her guard as she tried the gate.

Of course, it was locked.

Angela looked around for a doorbell of some sort, but there was nothing. She circled the property, searching for any way of letting Mia know she was outside and wanted to come in. Arriving back at the iron gates, she pondered what to do next.

She wasn't going home and giving up.

'Mia!' she called loudly. 'Hello? Is anyone there? Mia!'

Then she waited. The house was large, and she could only see one window open in a downstairs room. Mia probably wouldn't hear her. She sighed, thought about shouting again, then decided against it. Turning away, she saw a letterbox; perhaps she could just leave a note. It wasn't ideal, but it was a way of making contact. Either that, or she would have to keep an eye out at the markets for a woman in a scarf and big sunglasses, a woman whom nobody talked to.

'What do you want?'

Angela whirled around. Standing on the front path, beyond the gate, was an impossibly slender woman with long dark hair and black eyes. In a second, Angela realised it was the woman she had seen on the edge of the cliff at twilight. Not a crone at all. She wore a champagne-coloured silk dressing-gown and her feet were bare. 'Are you Mia?' she asked.

'Yes.'

Angela collected herself. 'I'm sorry,' she said, indicating her clothes. 'Did I wake you?'

Mia shook her head. 'I've been awake for hours. The birds woke me. They are happy that the rain has stopped.' She spoke precisely but quickly, and Angela had trouble keeping up with the Greek.

Mia didn't seem to be as hostile or crazy as the stories about her held her to be. 'My name is Angela. Can I come in to talk to you?'

'No.'

'I won't take up much of your time.'

'I have plenty of time. I just don't want to talk to you. Time is not anything, time is everywhere and sometimes it runs through my fingers all day.'

Angela worked hard to decode what she meant, wondering if she'd mistranslated the Greek. But then she remembered that the woman was known as Crazy Mia and stopped expecting her to make perfect sense.

'Goodbye,' Mia said, and turned to go.

'Wait.'

'I don't like waiting.'

'I mean, stop. I really need to talk to you.'

Mia hesitated and turned back, then addressed Angela in English. 'You're the new girl, aren't you? The one I hear them talking about in the market. The English girl with the big ideas.'

'I...yes,' Angela said, relieved to be back in her native tongue.

'That's why you're here. Because you're new. Because you don't know about me and you're not afraid.'

'I've heard about you,' Angela conceded. 'I don't know how much I believe. And, no, I'm not afraid.'

For the first time, Mia smiled. Under it, Angela could see the echo of that smile she had witnessed on the cliff top, but today there was a crueller edge to her mouth. 'Perhaps I should frighten you on purpose,' Mia said.

'Please, can I come in and talk to you?'

'Nobody has been in my house for a long time.' She bit her lip, momentarily looking like a nervous teenager. 'It's a mess.'

'I only want to talk. I won't judge you.'

'Yes, you will. Everyone judges.' As she spoke, she approached the gate and unlocked it.

Angela hid her surprise: she'd thought she was getting nowhere. 'Thank you,' she said. 'I appreciate it.' She wished she'd brought something, some baklava from Lilika's bakery, or a bunch of wild sea-daffodils from the calm side of the island.

Mia swung the gate open and turned to lead Angela up the path and into the house.

Inside it was dark, dusty and smelled of cat urine and old potato peelings. They moved through the spacious foyer while two cats wound their bodies around Angela's legs, as though they were trying to trip her on purpose. She paused to scratch their ears.

'Come on, hurry up,' Mia said from the dining room.

Angela joined her. Mia had pushed a chair out at the dining table for Angela to sit on. The table was thick with dust, and a candelabra in the centre was strung with cobwebs. Books were piled in untidy stacks along one side of the table. Mia went to the blind and drew it, letting in the sunshine. One of the cats jumped up onto the table and sat there in the dust, eyeing Angela.

'I don't use my dining table,' Mia explained. 'I don't have guests.'

'How many cats do you have? Just these two?'

Mia held up four fingers as she pulled out a chair and sat next to Angela. 'But the other two are wild. They live in the garden, they don't come in.'

On cue, the second cat jumped into Angela's lap and began to knead her with its paws. She sat very still and waited for the cat to lie down.

'It's lovely of you to come and visit,' Mia said, but her anxious expression was at odds with the perfunctory politeness of her tone.

'I wanted to ask you about the house on the bluff,' Angela said.

'Should I make coffee? Or tea? You English like that muck.'

'Don't go to any bother. Perhaps another time I can come for coffee, and bring a cake?'

'You won't come back. Once you've got what you want. You're all like that in the end.'

Angela struggled to keep up; Mia's thought processes were unpredictable. Gently, she tried to turn back to her reason for being here. 'The house on the bluff, Mia?'

'I haven't been there in years. Things happened there.' Her eyes went to the window as though she could see the house, but beyond the glass was only the tangle of the garden. 'Oh, I go down there every now and again to chase out the swallows.'

'It's a lovely house. Very big.'

Mia sniffed, derisive suddenly. 'Not as big as this house. You know I have nine bedrooms? I sleep in a different one every night, sometimes I change halfway through the night.'

'Would you consider renting the house on the bluff to me?'

Mia snapped her attention back to Angela, drawing down her brows. 'Do you want to live there?'

'I want to convert it into a bed and breakfast hotel.'

Mia smiled, and Angela was encouraged to blurt out the rest of her plan. 'We would work out an arrangement where you took a percentage of the profits every week. I'd take care of everything, I'd raise the money to clean it up and paint it and furnish it. All you'd have to do is agree to a nominal rent until it opened.'

Still smiling, Mia said, 'No.'

The cold, flat refusal caught Angela by surprise. 'Take some time to consider it –'

'No, no, no. No. You are a strange girl, Andrea. You make me laugh.'

'Angela.'

'Such big ideas on such a small island.'

'It's actually a very modest idea. I've managed to build the picnic tour business to such an extent that –'

'You wouldn't ask if you knew what happened.'

'I'm sorry?'

'You wouldn't ask. If you knew what happened to me there.' She turned her eyes down and started picking anxiously at her fingernails. 'All those years ago. No. You wouldn't ask.'

Angela took a deep breath and told herself to be patient. Mia was not in control of her faculties: her mind darted all over the place like a skittish kitten. 'What happened there?'

'I lost somebody.'

Angela remembered the story about the broken heart that had caused Mia's descent into madness. 'I'm very sorry.'

'It wasn't your fault.'

'I mean, I feel sorry for you. It's hard to lose somebody.'

'Do you really know?' Mia took on a defiant expression. 'Have you ever lost anybody?'

Angela faltered. 'I... I don't know.'

'What do you mean, you don't know?'

Something about Mia's vulnerability, her scrambled thoughts and her fading beauty, made Angela speak the truth. 'I don't know. I woke up six months ago with no memory of my life before that moment. I don't know if I've lost somebody. I don't even know if I had somebody to lose.'

Mia fell into a long silence, staring at Angela unabashedly. Her lips moved, but no words emerged. Angela tried not to feel disconcerted. At length, Mia said quietly, 'You are very lucky to forget. I wish I could forget. I wouldn't feel as though...as though I hadn't done enough...' She stood, and put her hand on Angela's chair. 'You can go now.'

'Will you consider my offer?'

'No, I won't.'

'Please.'

'Don't plead. Go now.'

'Can I come back again? To talk?'

'No, I don't want to see you again. You have to go.' She rattled the chair. 'Come on, stand up. Go home.'

This was more like the Crazy Mia she had been told about. But it didn't make Angela angry. She felt as though she had encountered the real Mia out there on the cliff top – her beauty, her benevolent smile – and found she could be patient with her.

Mia stood at the front door and shooed Angela down to the gate. It locked with a clunk behind her.

'If you change your mind,' Angela said, 'or if you just want to talk...' But Mia had already gone inside and closed the door.

Some days, working in his downstairs office in the corner of his studio, George felt claustrophobic. There were no windows to let the sun in, so he had only harsh fluorescent light to work in. He didn't mind so much if he was recording, because then music warmed the space and he had company to distract him. But by the end of a day sitting at his desk, making endless phone calls about finance, the concept of money became alien to him: just numbers with no corresponding significance. It made him headachy and a little breathless.

Already he was on to his sixth phone call for the day: making a deal with the devil. Or, at least, a deal with Packenham and Powell who, after the success of the Penny Bright tour, were keen to provide finance for the proposed US tour. George was very excited about this tour; it was a lucrative market and already a number of contacts were falling into place, offering money or column inches or airtime. TRG in New York were talking Penny up in a big way, and the first single was due to be released in six weeks. Expectations were high: Penny would sweep through America. Together, she and George would make a lot of money. Not that he had told Ellie about this yet. He was avoiding her, and he knew it. Still angry about her going to see Ivan Hamblyn and giving the game away. How he would relish giving her a sixty-date US tour to prepare for: see her try to keep up with her opera lessons then.

The phone rang. He scooped it up.

'George Fellowes.'

'Hello, Mr Fellowes, it's Natalie here from Barnes Bank at Leicester Square. I have that information for you.'

'Go ahead.'

'The money you deposited into that account has remained untouched.'

'How long since there's been any activity on it?'

'Six months. Would you like us to draw you a cheque for the amount of the deposit?'

George considered this. At the time, it had seemed the right thing to do. As the royalties from Penny's number one album had started pouring in, he had quietly siphoned off a small percentage to deposit in the real Penny's – Angela Smith's – bank account. He presumed she'd see it, guess what it was for and where it was from, and then use it gratefully. Maybe – in his fondest dreams – call him to thank him. But a bank account untouched for so long meant only one thing: she didn't want to be found at any cost; she didn't want his money. She really was through with him.

She really wasn't ever coming back.

'Yes,' he said, finally. 'Yes, draw me a cheque. I won't be making any more deposits. I don't need you to watch that account any longer.'

With a heavy heart, George finally admitted to himself that it was over. He would probably never see Penny again.

TWENTY

*D*ieter stared at the menu, feeling puzzled and embarrassed. He hadn't a clue what most of the items were, while George and Ellie had long since made their decisions and placed their menus confidently at their elbows. Dieter didn't like this restaurant; he didn't like the overly mannered waiter, the private table tucked in a dim corner of the cavernous room, nor the harsh stop-start music of the jazz pianist who was playing. Above all, he didn't like that, despite his earnest practising of English for the last three months, he couldn't read the damn menu because it was in French.

'I'll have what Ellie is having,' he said at last, putting the menu down.

'You don't like fish, Dieter,' she said, touching his elbow.

'It's fish?'

'Try this one.' She pointed out an item on the menu, then switched into German briefly to say, 'It's duck with an orange sauce; it's very nice.'

He nodded, and George beckoned over the waiter. They placed their order, and soon a bottle of wine had arrived. As the waiter filled their glasses, George spoke.

'Are you two enjoying the first day of your holiday?'

Ellie glanced at Dieter with a hesitant smile on her lips. 'Oh, yes,' she said. 'Though we haven't been much out of the apartment yet.'

Dieter blushed, and changed the subject. 'Are you on holiday too, George?'

George shook his head. 'No rest for the wicked. This industry is a beast, and it needs constant management.' He sipped his wine then put the glass aside and leaned forward. 'In fact, Ellie, I've some news for you.'

'Good news, I hope?' she said.

'Very good news. It involves travel, money, fame... Interested?'

'Go on.'

'A US tour. Sixty dates. Late autumn.'

Ellie's smile froze on her face. Dieter's gaze went from George to Ellie, but he said nothing.

If George noticed her reluctance, he didn't show it. 'We'll probably have to start rehearsals before too much longer. I'm getting together some serious money for a big stage show, and I'll probably go over in the next few weeks to meet with some people and make some preliminary arrangements. What do you think? Exciting?'

Ellie produced a glorious smile. 'Very exciting. How long have you known, George?'

'I've been thinking about it for months, but it's just come together in the last few weeks. I wanted to make sure it was definite before I told you.'

Dieter found it difficult to keep up with their conversation, but he tried not to let it dissuade him from talking at all. 'Will Ellie have a chance to come home for a little while before then?' he asked.

'Home? Oh, to Germany.' George shrugged. 'We'll have a look at her schedule.'

Now Dieter turned to Ellie. 'And will you come home after your tour? Really come home? For good?'

Ellie glanced from Dieter to George and back again. 'Maybe. I... This isn't just for a few months anymore, Dieter, I told you that. It's a permanent arrangement.'

'But you have to live somewhere.'

'It's best for Ellie to be where the business is,' George said.

'London is where I'm based for now,' she said simply. 'You understand, don't you?'

He didn't understand. Dieter felt, not for the first time since his arrival that morning, that he was missing a vital piece of information. In all their phone calls, Ellie had talked about missing him, missing the farm and the village, being homesick. And yet, he was starting to realise, none of that talk translated into an actual plan to be at home. What was going on?

Ellie rose, dropping her napkin on the table. 'Excuse me a moment,' she said, before disappearing towards the powder room.

Dieter looked into his wine glass and waited, uncomfortable. As soon as Ellie was out of earshot, George said, 'I'd appreciate it if you didn't talk about "going home".'

Dieter looked up, puzzled at his clipped tone. 'I'm sorry?'

'I know that Ellie is already conflicted about her career. Talk of returning to Germany doesn't help her.'

Dieter took a moment to translate this properly, to understand fully what George meant.

George smiled, a sudden friendly gesture. 'I'm sorry, Dieter. I don't mean to be rude. You are always welcome here, but I don't want Ellie running off back to the village. She doesn't belong there anymore.'

'She will always belong there,' Dieter said. 'It's her home.' George was shaking his head, and Dieter filled up with annoyance. 'You'll excuse me, but I know her better than you.'

'Do you? Do you really? She's not a farmgirl. She's a superstar in the making. She's beautiful and talented and she wants to be richer and more famous. She won't get that back in Kokondorf.'

'Yes, she is beautiful and she is talented. But as for rich and famous: that's not what Ellie wants, not really.'

'Then you haven't spoken to her lately.'

Dieter shook his head vehemently. 'If you think that's what she wants, you aren't listening to her. You are listening to her father, speaking through her.' Dieter watched George, hoping that his English had been understood.

George took a sip of his wine. 'Her father?'

'He was an ambitious man. He sowed seeds, not all of them flowered as brightly as her beautiful voice.' Here, he struggled for words. It would have been so much easier to express this in his native tongue. 'He made Ellie feel as though she was not important unless she performed brilliantly. This is why she is good at everything she does. It is also why she will never be happy until she understands that what she *does* is never as important as who she *is*. With my family, on the farm, she was closer to understanding that. Here, in London, her father is still pulling all the strings.' Dieter glanced at his wine glass again. 'You are pulling the same strings.'

'I don't know if I believe you,' George said. 'She adored her father, she clearly misses him.'

'She remembers only the good in him, what little there was.' He looked up, met George's eyes. 'One time I was in the village, and he was leaving the pub, drunk as always. He fell down, grazed his hands and elbows. I helped him up and offered to walk home with him. I still remember his exact words to me.' Dieter closed his eyes to concentrate on the translation. '"You must not feel superior to me, Dieter Neumann, when you are so very low, when you have no education, when you do not know art, when you are a pig-stained idiot like your parents."' He glanced around now, keeping an eye out for Ellie. 'I never told her,' Dieter said quickly. 'I never told her any of the rude, cruel things he said to me or to my family. She loved him and he died, that was enough.'

George's voice lost its hard edge, now, and Dieter saw for the first time beneath the businessman's exterior. 'Whatever you think,' he said, 'whatever is driving her, you must understand that she can't go home to Germany. Not now. She can't go back to her old life, too much has changed. I know she cares about you; perhaps you should think of moving here.'

Dieter had, of course, already considered this. The farm would be gone soon, he didn't want to live with his parents in a small house in the village. The idea of being cooped up in the London apartment, with only traffic noise and English babble around him, made him feel he couldn't breathe properly. But if that's what Ellie wanted…

'You could go on tour with her. See the world.'

Dieter shrugged and didn't respond. He'd be more persuaded by these words if he didn't think that George's only interest was George himself. Of course, Dieter had his own interest in Ellie's future. He wondered what Ellie wanted – *really* wanted – and realised it had been a long time since he'd asked her.

Then she was there, looking beautiful and elegant and so far beyond his reach. Dieter took her hand and squeezed it, tried not to hold on too tightly.

Angela waited on the pier while Captain Lianis pulled the boat tight into the pylons. The English couple who had spent the last two nights at the taverna eyed the greying sky warily.

'Don't worry,' Angela said. 'It won't rain until you're on board, I promise.'

The middle-aged man nodded, his wife relaxed a little. Angela moved to the side of the boat and gave Captain Lianis a hopeful lift of the eyebrows.

'Sorry, Angela. Nobody for you today.'

Her heart sank, as it always did on rainy days. The problem was that the picnic tours weren't enough. Who wanted to come on a picnic when the weather looked bad? She needed Silas to put on entertainment at the taverna. She needed Lilika to open up the front of the bakery and start serving thick coffee and sweet pastries under umbrellas on the warm cobblestones. She needed Magda at the local art society to organise the art gallery and to raise the funds for the refurbishment of the town museum, which had a small collection of Cycladian figurines – little bulls and round-bellied fertility goddesses – carved from ancient Parian marble. She needed somebody to take tours down to the caves. But to persuade people to do all these things, she needed a proper bed and breakfast with a steady influx of tourists.

Captain Lianis had lowered the gangplank, and Angela moved to guide the couple onto it.

'You know, I've been meaning to ask you…' the wife said, turning to Angela with an embarrassed smile.

Angela waited, puzzled. 'Yes?'

'You're not related to Penny Bright, are you?'

Penny Bright. A corner of the shadow lifted, a shiver of unpleasant feeling washed over her. 'Who's Penny Bright?' she managed, almost dreading the answer. A swirl of hot panic threatened her. Was this it? Was this her past finding her?

'The pop star. Oh, she's very big back home,' her husband said. 'I've read about her in the papers. Only, you look so much like her, it's quite uncanny.'

Angela's tongue was paralysed: she didn't know whether or not she was related to Penny Bright. For all she knew, she could *be* Penny Bright.

'Though I've read she has no siblings,' the wife offered helpfully. 'Only child, daughter of a Wiltshire bus driver. Done very well for herself, she has.'

Angela was pulled by two simultaneous impulses. The first was to find out everything she could about this Penny Bright; the second was to shut down all those pathways in her brain immediately. 'She's still in England, then?' she asked cautiously. 'She hasn't…left the country or…?' She wanted to say, 'disappeared', but it seemed too ridiculous to ask.

'Well, who's to say where a pop star is? They've so much money, they're probably always on the beach in southern France. But I heard her interviewed on the radio a couple of weeks ago and that was live.'

Angela nodded, relieved. Just a coincidental resemblance then; not a link to her frightening past.

'Anyway, thanks again. We'll let our friends know about your business.'

'I'd appreciate it,' Angela said, forcing a smile. Captain Lianis helped the couple on board, and Angela turned back towards the road, feeling troubled and uncertain. The sight of a slim figure waiting at the bottom of the pier drove all other thoughts out of her mind. A woman, wrapped in a navy raincoat, wearing large sunglasses.

Mia.

She lifted an arm to wave to Angela, and Angela hurried towards her.

'Mia?' she said as she stepped off the pier. 'This is a surprise.'

Mia pushed her sunglasses up onto her head, pinning her dark hair back from her face. She seemed even more slight out here in the open air, with the sea breeze whipping at her clothes.

'I need to talk to you,' Mia said.

'Do you want to come back up to the taverna?'

Mia shook her head. 'What, with old Silas hanging around like an ageing basset hound?'

Angela stifled a laugh.

'No, here will do,' Mia said. 'I'll be quick. I thought about what you asked me, and I changed my mind.'

Angela's heart leapt, but she reminded herself that Mia was crazy and perhaps meant something other than the obvious.

'You'd have to transform it though. Everything.'

'What do you mean?' Angela said cautiously.

'I don't want it to look the same. New paint, new curtains. Like it was never mine, like those things never happened there.'

Angela nodded slowly. 'Mia, can I just clarify what you're saying to me? You want to rent me the house on the bluff for a bed and breakfast?'

'Yes.'

She couldn't hide her smile. 'Thank you. Thank you so much.'

'But it all has to change, do you see? It all has to be different in there.'

'I understand, but I must tell you that I'll be working on a limited budget so –'

'No, you won't. I'll give you all the money you need.' Her hands moved nervously through the air. 'Change it all. You understand? No limited budget. Change it all.'

'If you're certain.'

'I'm certain.' Mia lowered the sunglasses again. 'I'm going home now, I see the way Leo Lianis looks at me.'

Angela glanced over her shoulder. Captain Lianis was nowhere in sight. She turned back to Mia. 'We'll need to make arrangements, draw up a rental contract...'

'Come to see me tomorrow morning. I'll sign anything you need.' Then she pulled up the hood of her raincoat and walked swiftly away.

Angela watched her go. The first spit of rain fell but she hardly noticed. She didn't know whether to be joyful or apprehensive: it looked like she was going into business with Crazy Mia.

Ellie stepped out of Madame's house and into a waiting taxi. She was struggling with feelings of happy satisfaction and niggling worry. The lesson, her tenth with Madame, had gone particularly well. Finally, the hoarseness had disappeared. Finally, her voice – Ellie Frankel's voice, not Penny Bright's – was back in full, glorious form. Madame, not an easy woman to impress, had raised her eyebrows after Ellie's performance of an easy Mozart aria, then gone riffling through her music stand for something much more challenging. *Come scoglio* had emerged, that bête noire of Ellie's youth. She had sung it with ease.

Madame hid a smile. 'I think we're getting somewhere, Penelope,' she had said. Madame had taken to calling her Penelope; she said nobody should be named after a form of currency. 'I think we are getting somewhere very good indeed.'

As London streets sped by, Ellie closed her eyes and leaned her head back. Now her voice had returned, she had reached an impossible junction in her career. She didn't want to sing like Penny Bright anymore, and ruin her voice. The deep joy of singing opera satisfied her as nothing else could. In those moments, when her voice was soaring, when she was completely in control of the powerful music within her, she felt connected to the heavens, to her dead father, to her destiny. But how could she get out of the tour? The rehearsals?

The recording? She felt trapped, and it made her want to cry with frustration.

Then she remembered what Ivan Hamblyn had said to her, when she suspected he knew of her true identity: *If your friend is ever interested in signing with England's finest classical label, I would hope she'd give me a call.* Why couldn't she simply change musical direction? Why couldn't she be Penny Bright, opera star? Her name was known, she had access to record company contacts, she had the best manager in the business...

As she thought of George, her heart sank. He would never let her do it.

She opened her eyes. They were stopped at lights. A woman in tight PVC pants, held together at the seams with an untidy row of safety pins, was crossing the road. Her hair was dyed bright purple, her lipstick was black. This was precisely the problem Ellie had with the music industry: what was popular one moment was reviled the next. Punk rock had started to move into the London clubs, leaving no room for pop; who knew if Penny Bright would even be relevant by the time she returned home from her tour? Opera endured. And George wasn't her boss.

She grew excited as she thought this through: there was no formal agreement between her and George. The shady circumstances surrounding their deal had precluded a legal contract. Of course, she would have to forgo some income for a brief time, but she had a decent buffer of money behind her. Ellie almost laughed, the trapped feeling evaporating as she realised she had mis-thought the whole situation. *He couldn't stop her.* Certainly he would be angry, but then he had committed no money yet. Anyway, there was money to be made in opera, too, and she'd need a good manager.

Ellie was on her path: she felt it in her nerves and sinews. It had been a roundabout route to get here, but here she was on the brink of her true destiny at last. And she vowed that nothing – *nothing* – would get in her way.

She paid the taxi driver outside her building, and glanced up to see if Dieter was watching for her out the window. He spent a lot of time gazing down into the street. But his familiar face wasn't there. He would be waiting inside; perhaps he was even cooking her a hearty German dinner. She got the feeling he didn't like her new, slender look. She got the feeling he didn't like a great deal about her new life – especially London – but she was just so glad to have him here with her that she fought her impatience. She couldn't wait to get inside and tell him her new plan.

When she let herself into the flat, Dieter was pacing. He almost jumped on her.

'Ellie, I'm glad you're back,' he said, too quickly. 'I've had a call from home.'

Ellie dropped her keys in the little dish by the door, a spike of disappointment touching her heart. She put her excitement aside for a moment. 'Is everything all right?'

'I'm not sure. Papa has had to return to hospital. They suspect a mild stroke. One of the seasonal workers fell through, and he's had so much to do getting the farm ready for the sale.'

Ellie could have wept. She knew what was coming next. 'You have to go back, don't you?'

He caught her hands and stroked them gently. 'I'm sorry. But the sale goes through in one month, and then I will be free again.'

'I understand.'

'I know you do.'

Ellie dropped her hands and moved to the phone. 'I'll call the airline, I can get you back there tomorrow.' She was pulling out the phone book, flicking through its thin pages.

'Ellie, wait.'

'There's no problem with the money. And I'll have the limousine take you out there.'

'Ellie, wait,' he said again, and this time she turned.

'I have to ask you something,' he said, quickly, all on a breath.

'What is it?'

A silence ensued, and for some reason Ellie shivered. Her feeling of euphoria was evaporating. She sat down and he sat opposite.

Dieter's expression was serious. He took a deep breath. 'Ellie, I have always loved you. First as a child does, then as a man does. I know you better than anyone; I believe I know you better even than you know yourself.'

She tried a smile. 'Oh, really?'

He smiled in return. 'Yes. Really.' He shook his head, spread his hands in front of him. 'Another separation waits for us. I can't go home without saying this. I want you to come back. I want you to sing in your own voice, in Germany. I will be right there beside you, I'll support you.'

'Dieter, I –'

'I want you to marry me. I want a family. I want the life for us that I've dreamed of for so long.'

Ellie's head spun. Was that really all he dreamed of? *Anyone* could marry and have a family. And of course she intended to, one day, and of course it was Dieter she wanted to share her life with. But his timing was terrible. Moments passed.

'Ellie,' he said, nervous laughter underlying his voice. 'This isn't quite the response I'd hoped for.'

'We can get engaged, certainly,' she said guardedly. 'But I have to stay in London.'

He frowned. 'But London's not you, Ellie. You're pretending to be somebody else here, you don't even like pop music.'

'Yes, but Penny Bright has no profile in Europe. I do intend to sing in my own voice, to go back to opera using the contacts and knowledge I have now. But those contacts are here. In London.'

Dieter looked away, running a hand through his hair. 'I don't want to live in London.'

How infuriating. Was he not listening to her at all? Her career was here, her future. 'That much is obvious, Dieter. You make me feel bad about being here every day.'

'I don't make you feel bad.'

'Maybe not on purpose, but you do. You're always criticising one thing or another. Why are you really so reluctant to be here? What do you really hate so much about London?'

He shrugged, obviously considering this question for the first time. 'I don't like it because it's not home.'

One of her father's criticisms of the Neumanns came to mind unbidden: *They're ignorant farmers, they've never even been out of the pigsty.* 'Were you like this in Munich, too? The homesick farmboy?' She regretted the insult, realising immediately that it would escalate the argument.

Understandably, he bristled. 'What is so wrong with wanting to be where you belong?'

'There is so much to see and experience in this world, Dieter. There is life beyond the village.'

'That's unfair. I have to be in Kokondorf at the moment. My father is sick, my parents are getting older...'

She dismissed his comment. 'Your father will be fine as soon as the farm is sold, and they'll both live another thirty years at least. Admit it, you don't want to live in London because you're afraid to try something different.'

'That's not it,' he said forcefully. 'I don't like London because it's an insincere place, full of insincere people. There are lies in everybody's eyes here. Look at you: you're pretending to be somebody else. You *are* a lie.'

Dimly, Ellie became aware that some long-repressed resentments were being aired, and that the end result could only be explosive. They knew each other too well; it was too easy to hit where it hurt. 'I'm not doing it because I want to be dishonest. I'm doing it because I'm making so much money. For us, for our future.'

'Don't pretend it's for us, Ellie. You know money is nothing to me.'

Ellie sniffed. 'People say that, but they don't mean it.'

Dieter's face flushed. He pulled out his wallet and opened it, shaking the wad of notes she'd given him on the floor. 'Don't tell me what I mean or don't mean. Money is nothing.'

Money is nothing. Only a person who never had to worry about money would say that. She had stood on the edge of the abyss; he had grown up with parents who owned a farm, a business. She struggled to find the way to communicate this without offending him. 'You have the luxury of saying such a thing because you've always had money,' she said. 'Your parents looked after you.'

'They looked after you, too. Or had you forgotten?'

'Of course I haven't forgotten,' she said quickly, ashamed for a moment then angry that he had made her feel ashamed. Hot steam gathered behind her eyes, and it was rapidly becoming impossible to control her tongue. 'But they made me work for it.'

He shrugged. 'Everyone has to pitch in on the farm.'

'I am better than a cook and a maid, Dieter. Is that what you want for me?'

'No, of course –'

'Because I am a musician. I am an opera singer. I am going to be the best.'

'Better than everybody else?'

'Yes.'

'Now you sound like your father.'

Papa. How dare he bring him into the argument? 'Is that meant to be an insult?'

He hedged, perhaps aware that he had gone too far. 'No, no. It's just that…sometimes he speaks through you. Perhaps you should question what he taught you.'

'Question what he…? He taught me *everything*. He learned from one of the greatest teachers in Europe, and he passed it all on to me.'

'You learned other lessons from him besides music.'

'Yes, such as dignity, how to value oneself –'

'Self-value? The man hated himself so much he had to be drunk all day.'

Ellie's fists clenched unconsciously. 'Papa had a great sadness in him,' she said. 'His dreams had been dashed, he drank for comfort.'

'It's easier to believe that, isn't it? That he was a great man, a hero, that coming to the village was a step down for him…but none of it was true, Ellie.'

'Don't pretend to understand him.'

'Why? Am I so far beneath him in your opinion? Do you think he was a better man than I am?'

Her ribs tightened with rage.

'I can tell by your silence that you think so,' he said.

'This is ridiculous.'

'He was the one who made you poor, Ellie. He tried to drink your future.'

'You are wrong,' she said slowly. 'Without my voice, I had no future. You can't see that because you haven't the education or imagination to see beyond the limited circle of your own experience.'

A vacuum of silence followed her words, and she immediately wished she could recall them.

'Your father spoke like that to me too,' Dieter replied, anger making his voice shake. 'He taught you well. And as long as you are still repeating his lessons, we are destined to misunderstand each other.'

'He was a good man.'

'He was an arrogant drunkard!' Dieter shouted, slamming his hands on the table.

Ellie recoiled, ice turning her heart hard. 'Go,' she said. 'Go back to the village, it's over.'

He rose. 'If that's what you want.'

'It is.' She scooped a handful of money off the floor and threw it at him. 'Take the money, buy your own damn plane ticket.'

He brushed it off. 'I don't need your money.' He disappeared into the bedroom, leaving Ellie at the table, fighting angry tears. Moments later, he emerged, his little suitcase hastily packed. 'Goodbye then,' he said, hand on the door.

'Goodbye.'

There was a pause, an expectant moment in the thread of life, where she could have said, 'Don't go, let's work this out,' or he could have said, 'I'm sorry, how can I make it up to you?' But a long separation had weakened the structure of their relationship from within: the moment passed in sad silence, and then the door was open, and then he was gone.

Sobs threatened to shake her to pieces. Ellie took a deep breath, pressed her palms down hard on the table. Anger and pride forbade her from going after him, but somewhere inside her was a girl, aching with mad love, desperate to hang on.

Ellie stood and paced. It wouldn't do to cry: once she started she mightn't stop. So instead she began to sing. Scales at first, forcing her breathing into regular patterns, keeping time with her footfalls. Then an aria, the sublime notes of Saint-Saëns...but two bars in her voice stopped in her throat and the silence that rushed in was cold; a coldness that she knew would follow her for years to come.

TWENTY-ONE

*G*eorge parked his car and considered taking his golf clubs out of the boot, then decided not to. It had been a long time since he had played, and now he ached all over. Aila would laugh at him; he found it amusing himself. As though his body, unaccustomed to recreation, was protesting an afternoon in the clear air.

He let himself into the house. The smell of roasting beef made his mouth water. She had spent the day at housework: the faint odour of furniture polish clung to everything, the brass fittings all gleamed.

'Aila!'

She emerged from the kitchen. Her hair was tied loosely at the nape of her neck, soft strands escaping. Her pale beauty, as always, took his breath away. 'I've made your favourite,' she said. 'Roast beef, gravy, Yorkshire pudding…'

'What's the special occasion?'

'Golf day.'

'That's a special occasion?'

'It's a special occasion when you take some time off work to do something for yourself.' She stood on tiptoes to kiss his cheek. 'Dinner will be ready in half an hour.' She moved away, heading back to the kitchen.

'Did anybody call?' he said, shrugging out of his coat and hanging it in the hallway cupboard.

'Of course they called,' she responded from the kitchen. 'They don't stop, but all of them were happy to call back tomorrow. Except Penny.'

George peered around the corner into the kitchen. 'Penny?'

'She was agitated. Wanted to speak to you urgently. I said you wouldn't be back until late.' Her mouth tightened. 'You certainly earn your money working with her, don't you?'

George had deliberately kept Ellie and Aila apart since Penny's disappearance. Aila had spent too much time with Penny, she might have suspected something was different. Unfortunately, Aila grew suspicious anyway, wondering why George didn't bring his young star over for dinner anymore, perhaps even wondering why Penny wasn't as friendly or warm on the phone as she had once been.

'This isn't an ordinary business,' he said dismissively. 'No real days off.' Ellie was agitated? The thought troubled him. 'I'll give her a call,' he said.

'Don't be too long.' She gestured towards the oven. 'Yorkshire pudding, remember? We don't want it to get all rubbery.'

George descended the stairs to his office and switched on the light. He dialled Ellie's number and waited for her to pick up.

'Hello?'

'It's George.'

'George, thanks for calling back. I need to see you.'

'Now?' He thought of Aila's roast beef dinner, and knew that he couldn't take care of any business tonight. 'I can't come now.'

'Soon, then. Tomorrow morning.'

'Can't you tell me over the phone?'

'No. In person. We have things to work out.'

'Ellie, you're making me worried.'

'You shouldn't be worried. I know what I'm doing.'

This made him even more worried. 'Is this about the tour?'

'It is. That's part of it. It's about everything, it's... Look, we need to speak, face to face. First thing tomorrow morning.'

Damn this restlessness in her. Damn her for being a German farmgirl with delusions of grandeur. 'It's Dieter, isn't it? He's persuaded you to do something foolish. He's –'

'Dieter's gone home,' she said simply. 'We can discuss this in the morning.'

'Ellie...'

'Shall I come to you? Is ten o'clock too early?'

'Not early enough. I'll meet you for breakfast. The little café on the corner near your place. Make it eight.'

'I'll be there.'

Then the line went quiet, and George was left staring at the telephone, wondering what on earth was going on. Fearing the worst.

Dusk was gathering in the arch of the sky, the first pale stars glimmering weakly, as Dieter made his way up the hill from the train station and to home. The yellow lights glowed inside, and he remembered a lifetime of returning to the house, of leaving the cold dew of the fields behind for the warm smells of cooking. It was impossible, surely, that it would all change.

But, of course, it already had. Papa was in hospital, Mama was a spectre of her old self, worn down by worry. As much as Dieter hated change, he had to accept it. There would be no cooking smells. He would be eating cheese and bread for dinner tonight.

He came in through the front door, where his mother waited with her arms open.

'I'm so sorry, darling,' she said, very close to his ear. He had phoned her from the train station in Bremen, told her everything. Then wished that he'd held back a detail or two, so that his mother didn't turn on Ellie the way he knew she would. 'But you're probably better off without her. She's changed.'

Dieter reflected on this, eyes closed as he bowed his head onto his mother's shoulder. He didn't believe that he would be better off without Ellie; but he did believe that she would be better off without him. In the end, letting her go hadn't been about her anger or their childish argument. It had been about recognising that she had become something else, a glamorous creature inhabiting a different world from his. Without him, those ties to her old life would be cut; she could move forward. He vowed that, if his heart ever recovered, he wouldn't choose a woman like her again.

He opened his eyes, looked around him. Most of their things were packed now, only the major pieces of furniture were left. There was too much space.

Mama stood back. 'I'm sorry, Dieter, but there's no dinner for you. I'm just going out to the hospital to see your father. Will you come?'

'I've been travelling for two days. I need a long bath. Tell him I'll come to see him in the morning.'

She nodded, smoothing his hair. 'Herr Podolski is coming tonight to measure the windows for new curtains. He has a key, but if you do see him, can you be nice to him?'

Dieter nodded, and watched as she pulled on her coat and hat before leaving. He took his suitcase to the laundry, unloaded his dirty clothes there. He heard a sound at the front door, and went to greet Herr Podolski.

Only it wasn't Herr Podolski, it was his daughter, Ingrid, closing the door behind her.

She smiled broadly, lighting every aspect of her pretty, freckled face. 'Hello, Dieter.'

He smiled guardedly in return. 'Hello, Ingrid,' he said.

Angela's arms ached, and perspiration ran off her forehead, despite the cold, inclement weather outside. It was after eleven p.m. Her shift had finished at the taverna and tonight, like every other night this week, she had come straight down to the house on the bluff to scrape wallpaper off.

She paused, wiping her face on the shoulder of her shirt. Outside, a storm had blown in off the sea and was rattling the windowpanes. She worked by the light of an old lamp – having the electricity reconnected and the locks replaced had been her first chores – and the yellow glow kept the shadows and booming thunder at arm's-length. Angela stood back to look at her handiwork. She was nearly finished this room, the second bedroom. Of course, she could have paid somebody to do this for her. Mia had made it very clear that she wasn't to spare expenses. But the painter she'd contacted on Naxos couldn't come for three weeks, and she was keen to get started. Besides, she enjoyed the work. Transforming this old wreck of a place into something clean and fresh and colourful... it was so gratifying. She wanted to be involved at every level.

A boom of thunder shook the walls, and she picked up her scraper again. She was right in the middle of one long peel of wallpaper, when lightning flashed directly overhead and her lamp went out.

'Damn,' she muttered, dropping the scraper and waiting a moment for her eyes to adjust to the dark. There was a fuse box out behind the kitchen door, but she would get soaked going out there. Perhaps she should just wait... doss down on the old couch tonight and continue tomorrow.

But tomorrow she would probably have guests arriving for a picnic tour. She was so close to finishing the room. All she needed was a little light to work by. Maybe it was as easy as flicking a switch...

Angela made her way out to the back door.

She stuck close to the wall, hoping the eaves would protect her from the worst of the rain. But the gutters were overflowing and cold water trickled down her back as she opened the fuse box and peered in. A torch would have helped. A flash of lightning illuminated the scene, but she had to admit she didn't really know what she was looking for within. Perhaps the blackout was general all over the island. She went back inside, slamming out the rain, and made her way to the front door, from where she hoped to see the village.

Under the front entrance, she was better protected from the rain. No lights on in the village. She wouldn't be finishing her work tonight.

Just as she was about to go back inside, lightning flashed again and she caught sight of a figure, standing a little way off on the headland, looking towards the house. Her heart jumped, but then she recognised Mia.

What on earth was she doing out in the storm?

'Mia!' Angela called, beckoning her with both hands. 'Come out of the rain!'

The figure didn't move and she began to doubt that she had seen it at all. She took two steps out into the rain and peered into the dark. Another flash of lightning. It was definitely her.

'Come on!' she called over the howling wind and the booming thunder. 'Come inside, get dry.'

Mia moved. Slowly, as though she hadn't even noticed she was getting wet. Angela shivered, damp now and feeling the cold. She waited under the gabled entrance. When Mia was close enough, Angela bundled her frail figure into the dark house.

'You're soaked,' Angela said. 'You must be freezing.'

'What are you doing here every night?' Mia asked.

Angela tried to focus on her in the dark. Her eyes were wild and glistening.

'You've been here other nights?' Angela said.

'What are you doing?'

Angela hesitated. Had Mia forgotten their deal? The contract they had both signed? 'I'm scraping off wallpaper,' she said simply. 'I'm getting the house ready for the painters.'

'Can you show me?'

Angela took Mia's elbow. 'In the bedrooms. Come on.'

She led Mia to the bedroom she had most recently been working in. The curls of wallpaper on the ground were like ghostly scrolls in the dark. Mia bent to pick one up.

'I chose this pattern,' she said.

'I'm sorry. It's not that I don't like it –'

'No, no. I said I wanted it all to change. I meant it. I was a different woman when I chose this. I had...different dreams.' She clutched the scrap tightly, held it against her chest. It took Angela a few moments to realise that she was weeping.

'Mia?' she said softly.

'Life is so brutal,' Mia managed.

'Do you want to tell me what happened here? What you're so sad about?'

Mia shook her head. Her soft hiccoughing sobs continued, and Angela didn't know what to do other than to gather Mia into her arms and hold her. 'There,' she said. 'There, let it all out.'

Mia, soaking wet, pressed her face into Angela's shoulder and wept.

'Mia, if it's too much for you to come here...'

'It is,' she said. 'But I wanted to see.'

'You can see it when it's finished. This past that makes you so unhappy, it will be gone. Everything will be newly painted, it will be completely different.'

Mia pulled herself away, her eyes going towards the storm outside the window. 'Like you,' she said. 'The past erased. Only the new.'

Angela smiled. 'Yes, a bit like me.'

'All right. All right, I won't come again until it's done. But you must come to see me, once a week, and tell me how it's getting on.' She still clutched the scrap of wallpaper, and Angela reached out to prise it from her fingers.

'Come on, then,' Angela said. 'Let it go.'

Mia let the scrap fall, and Angela took her elbow. 'I think I should walk you home.'

'The storm...you'll get wet.'

'It's blowing over now. We'll be wet together. I'll have a hot shower when I get home. I'm not getting any more work done tonight in this blackout.'

Mia nodded and let Angela lead her from the house.

Ellie waited at a booth near the window of the café. The morning was empty, drained of colour. Dieter was gone, and this time there would be no late-night phone calls to ameliorate his absence. She had woken with regret in her stomach, almost picked up the phone to call him...and then remembered what he'd said about her father. More than just a terrible insult, it demonstrated how little he understood her, how he could never support her absolutely in her ambitions. She had vowed not to let anything stand in her way; how could she continue in a relationship with somebody who would eventually undermine her, intentionally or otherwise?

She smiled grimly to herself. That left George to be dealt with. *Be calm, Ellie.* She was doing entirely the right thing, George would simply have to accept her decision. It was her voice, her life. He didn't own her and, she hoped, eventually he would see that she was right. There was no future in pop music: it was transient, today's hero all too quickly slipped into obscurity. The real path to ongoing stability and success was in an art form that endured, where a career could span into one's thirties and forties. And Ellie had set her sights on the most enduring career of them all.

The smell of frying bacon filled the air. Ellie tapped her fingers on the table, then realised it betrayed her anxiety, and stopped. George came into view, all in black, with an expression to match. He pushed open the door to the café and hung up his coat, his eyes narrowing almost imperceptibly as he greeted her.

'Good morning, George,' she said as he slid into the seat opposite her.

He picked up the menu, scanned it and called the waitress over. 'Our first priority is coffee. Are we agreed?'

'Agreed,' she said, thinking that perhaps it might be all they agreed on this morning.

They placed their orders, and George leaned back in his seat. 'So, what did you want to talk to me about?'

Ellie took a deep breath and plunged in. 'I don't want to go to America.'

He didn't miss a beat. 'You have to go to America.'

'How far committed are we?'

'We're committed. I have promoters, venues lined up. You have to go.'

She steeled herself. Of course this wasn't going to be easy. 'Financially. How much of our money?'

He raised an eyebrow at her use of the term 'our money'. 'I'm about a week away from nailing the deal with the financier.'

'Don't make the deal.'

George was shaking his head, his pale skin growing flushed. 'Ellie…'

'I'm not doing it. I nearly ruined my voice forever on the last tour, and it was much shorter.'

'You didn't ruin your voice. You sounded better at the end of the tour than at the start.'

'Breathier? Huskier?'

'That's sexy. Pop music is meant to be sexy.'

'And when I'm not sexy anymore? When I'm old hat, when I lose my looks, what do I do for a voice then?'

The waitress arrived with her coffee pot, and they both sat silently until she had left.

George scowled. 'Is this about opera?'

'It's about my deepest passion, George.' She let her words stand for a few moments, before adding, 'You know you can't stop me.'

'We can scale the tour back,' George said, a note of desperation creeping in. 'I'll get a specialist for your voice. We can concentrate on recording.'

'No, George. No tour. No album. At least, no pop album. Penny Bright is changing direction. I know Ivan Hamblyn would sign us, I know it would work.'

George put his head in his hands and groaned with frustration. When he looked at her again, she could see the effort it required for him to keep his voice even. 'You know *nothing* about this business.'

'I'm learning every day.'

'You have a huge audience now. None of them will want to hear you sing opera.'

'I think they will. And I think that opera audiences will like me too. I'm good, George. You don't even know how good.'

'I don't really care if you sing like one of God's angels. You are Penny Bright. Penny Bright sings pop.'

Ellie gripped the underside of the table and made her voice very cold. 'I am Ellie Frankel. Whatever ridiculous name I have been saddled with, Ellie Frankel sings opera.'

'It will be the end of your career. It's my moral duty to forbid you from going down this path.'

'You can't forbid me from anything, George. You don't own me. I'm not Angela Smith. I'm not some drugged-up fool who does whatever you say.'

Thunderclouds gathered on his brow. 'Don't bring Penny into this. You didn't know her.'

'And in the end, she didn't want to know you. She ended it.'

'So that's what you're doing?'

Ellie shook her head, reminding herself to keep him onside if she could. 'I want you to manage me still. You're a good business-man, and I'd like to have you work for me.'

George snorted a disbelieving laugh.

'Are you interested?' she said, keeping her voice deliberately neutral.

She could almost read his mind. He was interested, of course he was. But part of him wanted her to fail, wanted it so badly that he'd never be able to willingly take over the next phase of her career.

'I don't know what to say,' he replied. He leaned forward, pressing his index finger hard into the table, right in front of her. 'Listen to me: *This will fail.* You are making the biggest mistake of your career. You won't make any money out of it, and I know how important money is to you.'

'You would say that, wouldn't you? You have an interest in keeping me where I am.'

He shook his head, a cruel smile touching his lips. 'I'm not warning you out of self-interest. I'm warning you for your own good.'

'I don't believe you.'

He spread his hands. 'Perhaps I should speak to my solicitor.'

It was an empty threat, and Ellie knew it. 'George, we are complicit in a vast deception, engineered by you, that involves a lot of money.' She sat back, sipping her coffee. 'Don't threaten me with the law.'

The fury in his eyes was so intense that Ellie felt a glimmer of fear. Then it was gone, a coolness in its place. 'There are some uncovered financial costs,' he said. 'Money spent in the early stages of setting up the tour.'

'Of course.' Her blood dropped a few degrees. How much money was he talking about?

He clearly enjoyed seeing her discomfort. 'I'll need you out of the apartment by the end of the week. Given that you haven't performed as Penny Bright in over a month, I'll be withholding any earnings from that period. And, of course, any ongoing earnings.'

Now he was deliberately trying to frighten her, so she kept herself calm, refusing to let him see her anxiety. She reminded herself that she already knew there was a financial risk involved, but she had hardly spent a pound so far. Her bank balance was healthy enough to see her through.

He rose. 'I'll have a look over what else you might owe me and send you an itemised bill.' He dropped fifty pence on the table. 'That's for the coffee. Goodbye.'

He grabbed his coat and left. Ellie stared at his untouched coffee, her stomach swirling with fear and guilt.

Then she cheered herself. It was done. She had severed another tie that was holding her back. If she was to stay true to herself, to her passions, to the memory of her beloved father; then it was the right decision.

It was the *only* decision.

It had been a long time since George had felt such rage.

He passed Aila wordlessly, taking refuge in the soundproofed studio. On his desk was the paperwork for the tour. He swept it to the floor with violent hands. Unsatisfied by the whispering of papers, he began to throw empty tea cups. The bang and smash helped. A poster of Penny Bright on his wall fell into his hands, and he was about to tear it when he stopped himself, unable to remember for a moment if this was the real Penny, or Ellie. In that moment, Aila knocked and entered without waiting for an invitation.

'What on earth is wrong?'

'She's left me.'

'I beg your pardon?'

'Penny. She's broken it off.'

Aila arched an eyebrow. 'George, you make it sound like you were a couple.'

He didn't have time for her jealousy. 'You know what I mean. She's dissolved our business relationship. She wants to do something different. She wants to sing opera.'

Aila stifled a laugh. 'I didn't know Penny liked opera.'

George found himself about to tell Aila all about the Ellie Frankel deception, then stopped. Too many suspicions would be raised. 'She can sing,' he conceded. 'Ivan Hamblyn sent her to a teacher.'

Aila shook her head. 'Why did she need to fire you then? She'll still need a manager.'

'Aila, she'll need a bloody miracle.' He toed a piece of broken cup.

'Don't swear, *Lemmikki*,' she said, bending to pick up the pieces. 'I must say, I'm rather happy she's gone. She was hard to look after, wasn't she?'

An understatement. First Penny with her anxieties and her drugs, then Ellie: stubborn, treacherous Ellie... At least he would have the satisfaction of watching her fail.

At that thought, the first note of regret sounded amongst his anger. Where had such a cruel thought come from? Why could he not be more forgiving? Especially of Ellie?

Especially when he had so many sins of his own to forgive.

TWENTY-TWO

*T*he early fifties were a bittersweet time for George and Aila. On the one hand, George thrived in his work. He loved the studio, the technicalities, the potential for using music and sound creatively. He started to dream of building his own studio, like Sam Phillips's Sun Records in Memphis, and producing different types of music. From across the Atlantic came the new sounds of rockabilly and Chicago blues. The first time George heard the Delta Cats, chills had run over his spine. There was a revolution in music coming, he knew it, and if he could only be involved in that, he could be happy. He began to trawl the dingy clubs of regional England, looking for a band that could replicate that electrifying black style. Aila accompanied him, her ladylike dignity always at odds with the smoky spaces, the rawness of the young men full of fire and passion, but who could barely play their instruments properly.

The downside of this time in their lives came in the form of dashed hopes about babies. Aila had now suffered through six miscarriages in just under two years, and was beginning to give up hope of carrying a child to term. Instead, her parents gave her money so she could employ a solicitor to organise a private adoption. Within two months, they had a telegram. A six-week-old baby boy, Birmingham. George's heart pounded through his chest throughout the entire drive. Aila was white, teary. They stopped on the way to buy six nappies, and she twisted them in her hands for the rest of the journey, speechless with hope and excitement.

The awful obliteration of those hopes was, at least, mercifully swift. The family of the sixteen-year-old birth mother had refused, at the last moment, to sign the paperwork. George wasn't sure what hurt Aila most: the disintegration of her fantasies, or the fact that teenagers could so casually do what she could not. She dismissed the solicitor the following week.

'I won't go through that again, George,' she said. 'I won't rely on strangers for a baby. We'll just keep trying.'

So they did, with no success.

George had ambitions and TRG were not always supportive of them. As long as he made their latest popular ballad a hit, they weren't concerned to discover a local version of American music. He knew he had to make his dream a reality: build his own studio – sixteen tracks – under their new house at Lambeth. It would be hideously expensive, but he started off small and slow, knowing it would be seven or eight years before he had everything the way he wanted it. Her parents offered to loan them the money, but George had his pride. When he was offered a promotion at TRG, out of production and into administration, he considered it very carefully. By his calculations, the extra money would mean he could finish the studio within three years. Then he would achieve the career autonomy he'd long dreamed of. Perhaps it was worth the sacrifice.

'There's only one catch,' the chief executive told him after outlining the terms of the promotion, 'it's abroad.'

'How far abroad?' George asked warily.

'The European office. In Vienna.'

'I see.'

'And it's with the classical division.'

George sighed. Popular music was his passion. 'I see.'

'Go home, think about it.'

Aila loved the idea. She'd always wanted to live abroad, and Vienna was a romantic city. George did his sums, decided it was worth the risk. They started making their plans, ready for an adventure overseas.

Two nights before they were due to leave, Aila was folding up clothes to go into storage and prattling merrily about how a change of scene might help them fall pregnant again, when the phone rang. She answered it innocently, but within moments George saw her face fall.

'But how could we not have known?' she was saying. 'How long has she been ill?' Then a long pause and a mournful, 'How much longer does she have?'

Her mother, who had always seemed in the most robust of health, had been diagnosed with a brain tumour. She had only a few months to live.

Of course, Aila couldn't go. But George had accepted the new job and had to. And so, for the first time since they had been married, they prepared themselves to be apart.

The morning of their parting dawned cool and cloudless. George waited on the footpath for the taxi to the airport; Aila leaned into him, her hand firmly in his. Since the news about her mother, she had worn a distracted, resigned expression. He wanted very much to be here with her while she went through this terrible sadness, but the job in Vienna would not wait.

The taxi rounded the corner. She slid her arms around him and began to cry.

'Aila, Aila,' he said, smoothing her hair. 'I can stay. Just say the word, and I'll stay.'

'No, you have to go. I'll join you eventually. After...' She couldn't bring herself to talk of her mother's impending death. 'You have to go,' she said, simply. 'It's the right thing to do.'

The taxi pulled up and now George wanted to cry, too. To stop himself, he began to talk too fast. 'I'll write every day. I'll send photos. It will be like we're not apart at all.'

'You'll be busy. I understand.'

'I won't be too busy to tell my wife I love her.' He tried a smile. 'I'm forever yours, Aila.'

'And I'm forever yours.'

He extricated himself from her desperate embrace and opened the door of the taxi. The driver was already loading in his suitcases.

'Goodbye,' he said.

'It will be over soon,' she said. 'This nightmare, this sadness. Then everything will be back to the way it was.'

'Of course,' he said.

The driver closed the door for him, and soon they were pulling away. He watched Aila waving until she disappeared from view, and then he turned his eyes ahead of him.

'Where are you flying to today?' the taxi driver asked.

'Austria,' George said, 'Vienna.'

'Going for long? Your girlfriend looks upset.'

The driver's overfamiliarity irked him. He adopted an icy tone. 'I'm taking a job there. My *wife* has to stay here with her sick mother.'

They were stopped at lights. The taxi driver gave him a broad wink. 'Better make sure you behave yourself then,' he said.

George turned his gaze to the window, ignoring him. Only a fool who didn't understand about love would make such a comment. He nursed his pain at their parting, truly believing that he would 'behave' in Vienna.

But perhaps he didn't know himself as well as he thought.

At first, George didn't want to explore his new home. It seemed unfair to Aila, to go out and see the magnificent Imperial Palace and the gothic grandeur of Stephansdom, or ramble through the art galleries that lay within the Ringstrasse. But after two days, the excitement of being in a new city caught him, and he spent an hour after work every day wandering the streets of Vienna, no longer wondering why it was thought to be one of the most romantic cities in the world.

His cramped apartment on Schellingstrasse was close to everything important: the Vienna Staatsoper, which was the centre of classical music in the city, and the TRG European office, which was above a block of shops on Kaerntnerstrasse. George knew almost nothing about classical music, but that didn't matter. His job was administrative: budgeting, accounting, hiring and firing, approving expenditure. Very little about the post interested him, but the salary was good and the apartment was paid for, so he lived on a shoestring and squirrelled all the money away for his home studio.

The first month passed quickly. Every morning he would make tea and toast for breakfast before taking the brisk walk to the office. He worked until six, then took an hour to wander through the city, stopping at a café on Spiegelgasse for a thick hot chocolate. Two nights a week he attended German lessons, but he wasn't a good student and found most people he needed to communicate with spoke perfect English anyway. He talked to Aila on the phone once a week, and wrote her a lot of letters. Without her, he felt as though he was only marking time until life started again for real.

Her voice was mock-cheerful on the morning of his birthday. The operator connected her and she began to sing straightaway, in Finnish.

'What a beautiful way to wake up,' he said when the song ended, carrying the phone as far as the cord would allow it and sitting on the end of the couch.

'I miss you,' she said, her voice trembling.

'And I miss you.' He paused. 'Is everything all right?'

'It's Mama,' she said, emotion turning her voice to a whisper. 'She's very bad, *Lemmikki*. She's...she's not herself.'

Aila described watching her mother's personality changing as the tumour pressed its insistent roots into her mind and memory. One moment calm and positive, the next bad-tempered and swearing, forgetting words, forgetting her chidren. Aching to hold Aila, George began to regret the distance between them.

'She's already gone,' Aila said through sobs. 'Everything she was... vanished inside herself.'

'Do you want me to come home?' he asked.

She took a deep breath. 'Yes, I do. Of course I do. But don't come back, stay in Vienna. It's for your future, our future. I've got a good feeling about you being there. As though it's meant to be.'

He dropped his voice low. 'I wish I could hold you.'

'I can feel you holding me, *Lemmikki*. I'll be fine.'

So George stayed, clinging to Aila's assertion that he was meant to be in Vienna, that somehow their future together would be served by this time apart. Then, on the first day of spring, one of his artist and repertoire managers named Karl approached him to approve a huge advance.

'She's been recording with DG,' he explained. 'But she's looking for a smaller label, more control. We're perfect for her.'

'This is big money,' George said.

'She's a big star.'

George knew the classical record industry worked very differently from pop. While a popular record could outsell a classical album one hundred times over in a first week of release, a classical record might go on selling for decades. He usually trusted the A & R department's instincts, but he was hesitant to commit this much money.

'Come and see her,' Karl urged him. 'She's performing tonight at the Staatsoper. Perhaps you'll understand then.'

George phoned Aila before he left for the concert. It would have been easier for him not to hear her voice, not to have the wound picked open again. But she needed him to listen as she vented all her sadness about her mother's worsening condition. Tonight, though, the operator couldn't get through.

Later, he wondered if it was some kind of sign.

ACT III

Farewell to the past,
To beautiful laughing dreams...

Addio, del passato, FROM *La traviata*, GIUSEPPE VERDI

Review of Penelope Bright's *Butterfly* by *Classical Monthly*,
19 May 1978

It is difficult to know what to make of this recording. Erstwhile pop
chanteuse, Penny Bright, has reinvented herself as Penelope Bright,
opera singer. The boldness (some may say the cheek) of the move
cannot help but irk the listener: here is Bright singing great arias
from Puccini, Verdi, Bizet... and all without having ever set foot on
the opera stage. With no pedigree, it feels very much as though the
carriage has been put before the horse. Certainly, Bright has a tolerable
enough soprano voice, though a little too heavy-handed across the
passagio and with far too much steel in the upper register for her
young years. Such ambition does not become her. Without an
apprenticeship behind her it is all a little too much like gimmickry
for this listener. There are many other fine voices who have not had
the luxury of a major recording deal and album release; and certainly
many much finer voices than this girl. She may be Bright, but she's
far from brilliant.

Review of Penelope Bright's *Butterfly* by *London Music Mag*,
24 May 1978

What was she thinking? Penny Bright, husky-toned darling of the
pop scene, has lost her mind. Instead of putting out a follow-up to

her fabulous eponymous debut, she has decided to release an opera album. It's hard to imagine who she thought would buy this: certainly all but the most diehard fans will be extremely disappointed as she warbles through some fusty old pieces, sounding for all the world as though she has a stick rammed firmly up her jacksy. The only reason to buy this is if you're curious to hear what career suicide sounds like.

Review of 'Mia's Place' by *The Good B&B Guide*,
eleventh edition, U.K. 1978
Proprietor: Angela Smith
Address: Agios Manolis, Island of Petaloudos

This sharply run establishment, the only place to stay on the tiny but beautiful Petaloudos in the Little Cyclades, is low on cost but high on quality. The four rooms are cosy and pretty, with a slightly dishevelled charm. The shared bathroom facilities are spotless. Full English breakfast is served daily, with lovely touches such as home-made marmalade and hand-embroidered linen. The owner will help you organise a picnic tour of the island by moped, or dinner with live entertainment at the local taverna, or a tour of the village's highlights with an ageing but sprightly tour guide full of colourful stories. The place is always full and the boat only plies from the mainland four times a week, so do call to book in advance. You don't want to miss this one!

TWENTY-THREE
1978

*E*llie's voice soared. It was a pity that her only audience was the reflection in her bathroom mirror. She had taken to practising in the bathroom of her dingy little ground-floor flat in Ladywell, ever since the tobacco-reeking Mr Pope, whose wall adjoined hers, had started complaining about the noise.

'Planes take off quieter than you sing,' he had said, and Ellie finally understood why the English had a reputation for complaining.

So she had taken refuge in the bathroom, and sung to her own reflection for nearly two years now. Surrounded by the corroded mirror, the cracked tiles and the tiny pink enamel bathtub, she tried not to think about the apartment in Chelsea that George had evicted her from. Her new home was far, far cheaper. She'd thought at first that she'd only be there a month or so, while she found somewhere else nicer. But she feared the erosion of her savings; and after the first year without earnings, necessity kept her there.

It wasn't that she hadn't properly thought through her switch from pop to opera; it was just that she'd assumed things would happen much faster. Ivan Hamblyn had done his best for her, but he wasn't a manager like George. He didn't move, and he didn't shake; and when he'd come to her with a May 1978 release date for her opera record, she had just had to accept it. No more of Penny Bright's earnings came to her, and she could hardly go and work in a dress shop with her high profile. So, while she waited for fame and fortune as an opera singer, she eked out a living on her ever-dwindling savings. Rent, food, singing lessons. No telephone, no new clothes. All that would be ahead of her. What did it matter if she had no money? She had been poor before. What did it matter that the split with Dieter had broken her heart? She had suffered through loss and survived. George had once said her spine was made of steel, and she felt that: an unbreakable but slightly chill rod that helped her hold her head high. Ellie responded to life's challenges by turning inside herself and doing what she did best: she sang, she studied scores, she practised her languages. She made herself ready for her glorious debut.

But things hadn't gone quite to plan.

Ellie paused between arpeggios and heard a loud knock at the door. She sighed, pushing her hair back off her face and catching it in a ponytail. It was a warm day, and the bathroom was growing stuffy. Should she answer the door? It was probably just Mr Pope again...she wasn't in the mood for another of his lectures about neighbourly responsibility.

Then she heard a voice accompanying the knocking, 'Ellie, are you there?'

It was Ivan. She hurried through the dim lounge room to the front door.

'I'm sorry, Ivan,' she said, 'have you been knocking long?'

'Just a few minutes. I could hear you practising so I waited for a break.' He smiled and held out a magazine. 'A good review.'

Ellie steeled herself. The reviews had been universally bad, and Ivan's idea of a good review differed vastly from hers. At the very best, she had been damned with faint praise. At the worst, she had become a laughing-stock. Nobody in the opera world could bring themselves to admire her because of her lack of pedigree; nobody in the pop world could understand her. She had dreamed of catching a wide audience, crossing over between the popular and classical worlds. Instead, she had fallen down the crack between the two. So far, she had sold fewer than a thousand records.

'Come in, then,' she said to Ivan, taking the magazine. 'Let's have a look at it.'

The review was short but blunt: whatever one made of Penny Bright's puzzling switch from pop to opera, there was no denying her voice was superb.

'Superb,' Ivan said. 'That's good, isn't it?'

Ellie flipped the magazine back to its front cover. *Future Tense*, an alternative art magazine, probably with a circulation of twenty. She flopped into a threadbare armchair with a sigh. Of course her voice was superb; she had been working on it for years. Why, then, couldn't the more influential critics admit it? It was discrimination, plain and simple.

'Ivan, I need to get roles. Then they have to take me seriously.' So far, her search for roles had been fruitless. At first, nobody believed she could sing. Then, when they heard her, they would either decline (nobody wanted to lose credibility by employing a pop starlet in a major role), or offer her roles so small that it insulted her.

'I know, I know,' he said, running his hand through his thin fair hair. He wasn't George, he had few skills in management, he had other artists to look after. But he tried, and for that Ellie was grateful. He sat opposite her, on a vinyl dining chair. 'That's the other reason I'm here. Westminster Opera Company has employed a new musical director. His name is Andre Anderson, he's young, so he's not stuffy; and he's been in Europe the last five years so he'll love your voice. And I know that he's preparing to stage *La traviata*.'

Ellie leaned forward, excited. Violetta was a role to die for. 'Can I audition for him?'

'Better than that, I think. My family knows his. I've invited him for dinner on Thursday night, at my home. Would you care to join us?'

'I'd love that. Thank you. Shall I prepare an aria?'

He shook his head. 'Let's not be too forward. We'll approach this gently.' He fished in his pocket and pulled out a five-pound note. 'Here, for a taxi to my house. I'll write the address down for you. I'm at Marylebone, just down from York Gate. Try to be there by seven.'

Ellie was curious to see Ivan's home. Because the studio was in George's home, she had had a window into his personal life that she didn't have with Ivan. It wasn't that Ivan was unfriendly – on the contrary he was always polite, smiling, solicitous – but he had maintained a respectful distance. Whether it was for his own sake or hers, she didn't know.

Ivan stood, smoothing his trousers over his long legs. 'Very well, I'll see you on Thursday.'

Ellie saw him out, then returned to the bathroom. New determination filled her. She left off from her arpeggios and launched into Violetta's *Addio, del passato*, a song that appeared on her record. Closing her eyes, she shut out the depressing surrounds and conjured in her imagination the stage, the audience, the lights. A rush of new hope lit all her senses. This time it would work out; Andre Anderson would hear her, he would give her the role.

He had to.

Angela had only put mascara on one set of eyelashes when the phone rang again.

'Damn it,' she muttered under her breath. She hurriedly finished with her mascara and raced for the front desk. It was Silas's seventy-fifth birthday, and the party at the taverna had started five minutes ago. She had done everything she could to organise the b & b so that she could take off for a couple of hours, but her refrigerator had stopped working that afternoon and she was desperately trying to organise for somebody to come as soon as possible to fix it. She couldn't have all the bacon and milk go off before breakfast.

'Mia's Place,' she gasped into the phone. 'Angela Smith.'

A stream of fast Greek. After more than two years here, she still had trouble.

'Slower, slower, please,' she said to him.

'It's Nick Savadelis, the electrician,' he said. 'I can come by now if you still need me.'

Angela's heart fell. She didn't want to miss the party, but she needed the repair done. 'That would be good, thank you.'

So she waited. Half an hour passed. She phoned Nick Savadelis back, he was just on his way. Another half an hour. It was seven o'clock. Finally, he came. Within minutes, the fridge's motor was in pieces on the formerly spotless kitchen floor.

'How long will it take?' she asked, tapping her foot.

He looked up at her and shrugged.

'Would you mind…? I have to go out.'

He urged her away with his big, hairy hands. 'Go on, I don't need you here. I'll leave the bill on the bench.'

She raced away, nearly colliding with an English tourist in the hallway.

'Miss Smith,' she said in clipped tones, 'I haven't had fresh towels today.'

Angela took a deep breath. 'I only provide fresh towels every second day,' she said. 'To save water.' This wasn't entirely true: on top of the cleaning, the cooking and the paperwork, the laundry had been killing her.

'Well, I'd like a fresh towel tonight.'

Angela clenched her teeth and pulled out her keys. 'Certainly. Follow me.' She led the tourist to the linen cupboard, handed her two fresh towels and finally, finally, escaped into the evening cool.

The season was turning towards summer, and the air grew softer. Angela took a deep breath. The world was filled with layers of scent: damp earth, flowers, the sea and, as she drew closer to the taverna, the smell of hot oil and spices from the new exhaust fan. The steady stream of customers to the b & b had to eat somewhere, and Silas had extended his dinner trade enough to build a new kitchen and dining area. Angela's shoes clicked on the stone pathway leading up to the taverna, and now she could hear music from inside, and laughter. She had missed the start of the party, but it sounded like it would be a long time before the finish. She pushed open the door and was overwhelmed by light and smoke and sound. Lilika Stathakis's teenage son, Mitros, had set up with his band in the corner diagonally opposite the entrance. They were four good-looking boys, not one of them past his eighteenth birthday. Mitros had a cigarette jammed between his lips, and was concentrating very hard on playing the *bouzouki*. The music was rough, but played enthusiastically. More than two dozen people had linked arms to dance the *kalamatianos* to the clamorous rhythms of the *toumberleki*. Their shining faces, and red-cheeked laughter suggested they had already drunk too much. Silas watched from the sidelines with his customary expression of amused disapproval, his pipe hanging from his bottom lip.

Angela approached him and leaned in for a kiss. 'Happy birthday, old man,' she shouted over the music.

He raised his hairy eyebrows and withdrew his pipe. 'You're still too new to the island to tease me, you know.'

'I've been here more than two years.'

'You'll be an outsider until you've been here twenty,' he said.

'Then why does everybody like me so much?'

Silas grinned. 'Because you're making us all a lot of money.'

Angela laughed and scanned the room. Close to a hundred people were here, laughing, drinking, smoking, shouting to each other over the music. The room pulsed with warmth. Angela shrugged out of her cardigan. Mia wasn't here, of course. No matter how much the community appreciated Angela's efforts in bringing tourist money to the island, nobody wanted to hear how Mia had made it possible. The animosity towards her ran too deep. Most people in the village could not bring themselves to use the words 'Mia's Place' and settled instead for calling it 'the hotel'. Angela took a secret delight in using the correct title as much as possible, just to see them flinch.

The loathing between Mia and the community was mutual, with Mia determined to stay confined to her big, dark house, nursing her old secrets and sorrows. On Angela's invitation, she had been down to the b & b half-a-dozen times. The day that it had opened, when all the renovations had been finished, Mia stood in the sitting room and wept, open-mouthed like a child, for twenty minutes. Since then, she hadn't again mentioned the past unhappiness that had taken place at the house on the bluff. She would come for a cup of coffee (which she never drank), then leave hurriedly if somebody from the village stopped by. Angela frowned as she thought of this: she hadn't seen Mia for nearly three months. It was probably time she went up there to check on her.

The band thundered to the end of the song, and everybody cheered and clapped. Angela caught sight of a face she didn't recognise in the crowd: a tall man with long sandy-brown hair standing by the bar with his arms folded over his chest. He wore a loose, button-up white shirt and jeans that looked like they had seen better days.

'Who's that?' she asked Silas.

Silas followed her gaze. 'Tourist.'

She bristled. 'If he's a tourist, where's he staying?'

'With the Theodrakises. Apparently he'd been travelling with their son in Germany and Italy, and was told if he was ever on Petaloudos, he could stay with them.' Silas smiled wickedly; he wasn't fond of Antonia Theodrakis, who was an uptight, insincerely polite woman. 'He's been here a week already, and Antonia can't bring herself to tell him to go. So she hints constantly but he's either too stupid or too smart to get it.'

'I've got a vacancy from tomorrow. I wonder if he'd like the room.'

'I doubt it. Antonia said he has no money.'

'Still,' Angela said. 'It's worth asking. Is he English?'

'Australian. His name's Jerry Robbins.'

Angela patted Silas's shoulder and headed to the bar. She bought a gin and tonic then sidled up to Jerry Robbins. 'Hello,' she said, 'I'm Angela.'

He turned with a dazzling smile that nearly took her breath away. 'I'm Jerry. Nice to meet you.' He grasped her hand for a firm shake, and his fingers were warm and strong.

She gathered herself, dropping her hand. 'I run the b & b out on the bluff. Word is that you're looking for a place to stay.'

'No, I have a place to stay.'

'We have very reasonable rates.'

'The place I'm staying is much cheaper. It's free.'

'But perhaps they won't be able to accommodate you much longer...'

The music started again, and Jerry leaned in close to answer her. His hot breath tickled her ear. 'She'll kick me out eventually, then I'll head off the island.'

Angela nodded, sipping her drink. 'I see. Well, it's been nice to talk to you.'

He resumed his position at the bar, arms folded. She hesitated, then moved back towards Silas. He was now deep in conversation with his granddaughter, so she found a place to sit alone and sipped her drink thoughtfully. The music whirled on, people danced past. For some reason, hearing music played live like this always unsettled her, made her feel anxious. She was always waiting for it to stop.

Angela lifted her eyes. Jerry was looking at her. She tried not to smile, averted her eyes. Mitros's band launched into another tune with a traditional folk sound. Angela could only make out a few words of the lyrics: something about love and loneliness... She could feel Jerry's eyes on her, and she had to laugh to herself. A flush of desire was spreading up through her, just thinking about those warm, firm hands, that easy smile.

She looked up. He grinned at her. Knowingness passed between them.

'Angela?'

She was distracted. It was Nick Savadelis, the fridge mechanic.

'Oh. Nick,' she said, pulling her mind back to practical matters.

'I thought I'd find you here. I've fixed it for now, but you'll probably need a new compressor. Do you want me to order you one?'

'Will it take long to come?'

'I can get one over on the next boat.'

'Then go ahead. I can't be without my fridge.'

'Of course not. I left the bill on the kitchen bench. I can call you when the part arrives.'

'Thanks, Nick. And thank you for coming out so quickly.'

Nick left, and she turned her attention back to Jerry. The space he'd occupied at the bar was empty. He was gone. Trying not to be frantic, her eyes scanned the crowd. Nowhere.

She drained her drink and went to the bar for another, feeling strangely disappointed.

Ellie was puzzled when the taxi driver pulled up outside a beautifully kept townhouse.

'This is it?' she asked.

'Number fourteen,' he said.

She checked Ivan's address, written on the back of his business card. 'And it's the right street?'

'Yes.'

Ellie paid the driver and stood for a moment on the footpath, looking up at the neatly painted sills in the dormer windows, the dutch gables, the stained-glass fanlight above the door. How did Ivan Hamblyn afford such a house, in such a neighbourhood? Even George's house wasn't as big. She had been expecting a little flat. Not this.

Perhaps she was mistaken. Perhaps he rented a room in there.

She ascended the stairs, running her fingers idly over the wrought-iron banister, and rang the bell. Inside, she could hear a small dog yapping. The door opened, and Ivan stood there. He was dressed much more casually than she had seen him before, in jeans and a loose button-up shirt. He held a tea towel with one hand, which he flicked gently at the dog – a Yorkshire terrier – to make her stop barking. Glorious smells of roasting meat and vegetables wafted out. Behind him, she had the impression of gleaming honey colours: parquetry, well-made furniture.

'Ellie, come in. Right on time.'

She followed him inside, hanging her coat on the rack by the door. The entrance hall was tiled in black and white, the walls pale cream with gold flocking. Inside the house, she gazed around. Everything was beautiful: the paint and wallpaper, the lovingly polished knick-knacks, the rows of elaborately framed paintings that lined the walls. Bizet played from the record player.

'You have a lovely home,' Ellie said, her voice stuck in her throat. It was more than lovely, it was incredible. Ivan Hamblyn, who, so

301

far as she knew, was on a modest artist-and-repertoire manager's salary, lived in the deepest luxury.

'Thank you. Off the couch, Mimi!' At this, the little Yorkshire terrier went yapping off towards the kitchen. 'I'm sorry,' he said to Ellie, 'she gets excited when there are guests.'

'Andre isn't here yet?'

'He won't be long. He's very punctual. Can I get you a drink of something?'

'Just water.' Ellie still believed she might sing for Andre tonight, and didn't want to dehydrate with alcohol. 'Thank you.'

He moved towards the kitchen and Ellie, curious, followed him. Her suspicions were confirmed: the beautiful objects and tasteful decoration were not just limited to one room.

'How long have you lived here?' Ellie asked. She had never been particularly interested in Ivan's personal life, but now she needed some insight.

'Hmm...about eight years now, I suppose.'

'You live...alone?'

'Yes and no. I have a maid, she stays from Monday until Wednesday here, then goes up to my other place for the rest of the week.'

'Your other place?'

'I have a cottage. In the Cotswolds.'

Ellie was just working out how to word her next question – nothing so blunt as, 'Why have you got so much money?' – when the doorbell rang.

Ivan handed her a glass of water. 'That will be Andre. Come back into the sitting room.'

Ellie perched on the sofa, taking a deep breath. She had to make a good impression on Andre Anderson, but had little idea of how to do this without actually singing. *Just be yourself.* Ellie nearly laughed out loud at this thought: she had been pretending to be somebody else for more than two years.

Ivan returned with a short, neatly bearded man. 'Penelope, meet Andre Anderson.'

Ellie leapt to her feet and extended her hand in greeting. Andre's fingers were very pale and smooth, almost feminine. He smelled strongly of aftershave. 'It's a pleasure to meet you,' she said.

'And you, Penelope. Ivan speaks very highly of you.'

While he settled in the armchair opposite her, Ivan surreptitiously moved to the record player and put her album on. Ellie tried not to become self-conscious. Ivan and Andre fell into relaxed conversation, including her where they could. After half an hour, Andre nodded towards the record player and said, 'Who is that, Ivan? I've been trying to pick her voice since I got here.'

'It's Penelope,' Ivan said, hiding his grin behind the rim of his whisky glass.

Andre turned surprised eyes to Ellie. 'Really? I hadn't heard you, but what I'd heard *of* you would never have hinted at how good you are.'

'The critics were very harsh.'

He shrugged, as though it didn't matter at all. 'It's understandable. In this business, the voice isn't everything. It's who you know, what you've done. You'd understand that. Pop music must have been the same.'

Ellie didn't tell him that, actually, everything had been a lot easier when she'd sung pop music. She had been spoiled, and it had made her naïve. 'Ivan says you're casting *La traviata* soon,' she said.

Ivan gave her a warning glance, but Ellie didn't see the point of waiting and hoping.

'I am,' Andre said. 'And I think I might have something for a soprano with your kind of talent. But let's not discuss business now, let's enjoy our dinner.'

Ellie smiled. So it was going to be that easy after all.

She was very relaxed over dinner, laughing and making jokes, joining in the conversation as though she had known Andre for her entire life. She felt light, relieved. How much would she get paid for a major role with the Westminster Opera? Such a prestigious company would surely pay well. She could start saving again, build her bank account up once more…

Andre didn't mention *La traviata* again until he was leaving.

'Penelope,' he said, shrugging into his coat, 'if you give me your phone number, I'll call you tomorrow about that role.'

'I don't have a phone...' she started.

'I'll call Ivan then.' He gave her a smile and a warm handshake. 'I think you'll make a perfect Annina.'

Annina? Ellie was stunned into silence. He wanted to cast her as the maid? A tiny role with no great aria, no grand entrance or tragic exit?

'Goodbye, Andre,' Ivan was saying. 'It was lovely to spend some time with you.'

'And you, Ivan. Pass on my regards to Lord Dovercourt.'

'I will, and give my best to your mother.' Ivan closed the door behind Andre and turned to Ellie. 'Ellie? You don't look happy.'

'Annina.'

'It's a role with a major opera company.'

'It's beneath me.'

'I know that, but –'

'Don't you see, I can't take it. The role is too small, it will seem like I'm taking it to please my critics. I've already released an album, I'm already famous.' She heard the shrillness in her voice and hated it.

'I still think you should consider the offer.'

Ellie folded her arms and sighed with exasperation. She was convinced that to accept the role would be a step backwards, but at the same time it was the only role with a major opera company that she was being offered. Cool air from the doorway touched her skin, bringing her out in goosebumps.

'Sleep on it,' Ivan said. 'Do you want me to call you a taxi?'

She turned to him, suddenly realising what Andre had said as he was leaving. Ivan's wealth was beginning to make sense. 'Who's Lord Dovercourt?' she asked, though she suspected she already knew.

Ivan blushed and averted his eyes. 'My father,' he mumbled.

'Your father is a Lord?'

He nodded.

'What does that make you? Are you a Lord as well?'

He shook his head, and seemed relieved to say, 'No, no. But I am supposed to inherit his title one day.'

Ellie gestured around. 'So...all this...?'

'Belongs to my family, yes.'

Ellie was staggered by the thought. A family with money...the jealousy pinched her hard. 'What else will you inherit with his title?' she managed, then regretted the question immediately.

'I said *I'm supposed to* inherit his title. I might not.'

'Why not?'

'My parents, they don't...they want me to marry and have children. I'm forty-one and still not... They worry that the family line will stop with me.' He laughed, rubbing his fingers over his smooth chin. 'You know, I think they're of the opinion that my younger brother might make a better sixth Lord Dovercourt. He has a brood of robust little boys.'

Ellie stopped to process all this. She had thought until now that Ivan Hamblyn was ordinary, perhaps even boring. Alice had once called him 'his lordship' and Ellie had thought it a joke, a send-up. But it was no joke. 'Why do you work for TRG?' she asked. 'Surely you don't need to work.' She realised immediately it was a rude question, but Ivan answered anyway.

'I don't need to work for money, no. But I need to work. I've seen how being idle poisons people. It's good for one's spirit to work, and I do love music. I do love my job so very much.'

A lorry rumbled past outside, and Ellie realised Ivan was waiting for her to leave: he still hadn't closed the front door. She wanted to ask him a thousand more questions that manners prevented her from asking. Why wasn't he married? How much did he have? How much did he stand to inherit? But she held her tongue, and tried to check her envy. Instead, she forced a smile. 'You'd better call me a taxi.'

As she pulled away from Ivan's house, the injustice of life struck her keenly. Here she was, considering taking a role far beneath her in the hopes that she could pay the rent on her miserable little flat for another few months. Ivan Hamblyn who had never had to work particularly hard for anything, lived luxuriously in two houses. Assured of a stream of money that would never run out. The unfairness made her ache. She felt once again like she had the night of the singing competition: her teenage self desperate and hopeful in her darned tights, while the polished girl from the wealthy family waltzed in with ease and confidence, to steal away Ellie's prize.

TWENTY-FOUR

Angela rummaged through the baskets under the bench, cursing that she didn't have enough storage space at the b & b: there was one tiny linen cupboard, an overcrowded bookshelf in the lounge and another in the dining room, the oversized corner unit in the kitchen that she was forever banging her spine on while cooking breakfasts, and this narrow bench in the entrance hall that served as her front counter. All kinds of things ended up in the baskets beneath it: invoices, lost property, spare change, stationery, old magazines...all jumbled together in no particular order, because she never had time to sort them. A loose thread on one of the bedspreads had sent her looking for the scissors. She knew they were in there somewhere.

The counter bell rang, startling her. She bumped her head on the underside of the counter, nearly falling over backwards.

'Sorry,' a male voice said. 'Didn't mean to frighten you.'

Angela looked up. It was Jerry. At once she was self-conscious. Her hair was scraped back, she had no make-up on. She struggled to stand and tried a smile. 'Oh, hello. How can I help you?' She presumed he had changed his mind about taking a room, and became uncomfortable at the thought of him being so close, sharing her bathroom.

'I came to help *you*,' he said with a grin. 'Does your boss ever give you time off?'

'I work for myself,' she said, irritated. This was a common assumption that people made: she looked too young to be running such a successful business.

Jerry just laughed. 'It was a joke,' he said. 'Your boss. You. Do you ever give yourself time off?'

Angela's face flushed. 'Oh. Sometimes.' The truth was, she rarely left the b & b. There were always chores to be done. And if she did leave, it was to go to the markets to buy food for her customers, or to the taverna to organise dinners and tours with Silas, or to the pier to greet new guests. But she didn't admit this. She suspected she already seemed uptight to Jerry: she didn't want to seem boring as well.

'Good. I'd like to take one of those moped tours. And I'd like to take you with me.'

A hundred things that she had to do that morning flitted across her mind. But it was a beautiful day; the mopeds were available; Jerry was standing here smiling at her like he knew some secret about lovers that nobody else knew.

'That sounds wonderful,' she said.

She grabbed a picnic basket off the kitchen bench and they took off.

The sun shone on the blue sea, dazzling her eyes. On the edge of the cliff, he stopped and she pulled over next to him. A sea breeze made her hair tickle her face, and she was glad that she'd come out.

Jerry took a deep breath of the fresh air. 'Take me somewhere that nobody else goes,' he said.

'The island's pretty small,' she replied.

'There's got to be somewhere.'

'I doubt that many go to the bottom of this cliff,' she said. 'There's no beach to speak of, no interesting caves, only rocks and tide pools.'

'How do we get down?'

'There's a path, an old fishermen's route.'

He pulled the picnic basket and rug off the wire rack on the red moped. 'Show me.'

She led him two hundred feet along the cliff's edge. Between the waving, yellow grass, she found the stone pathway. It led down steeply. Large pebbles became slipping stones, and she had to steady herself a few times when she lost her footing. Jerry was behind her, carrying the basket, picking his way carefully. As they got closer to the damp rocks at the bottom, they moved out of the sun and it grew chilly.

She took a quick glance backwards to see how far behind Jerry was. Her foot slipped and she pitched backwards.

In the split second after she started to fall, an awful feeling of dread washed into her mind. An image formed, and she was inside it. Her hands were tied, she was in a cold dark place, despair and fear gripped her... But then Jerry caught her, stopped her from sliding down the slope on her back.

'Are you okay?'

The memory slid under cover, leaving only an echo of the dread behind. She forced a smile. 'I...'

He helped her to stand, and she looked around her for reassurance. The blue sky, the sparkling sea, Jerry with his gorgeous smile gazing at her. Slowly, she began to relax. 'I'm fine,' she said. 'Let's keep going.'

Soon they had reached the bottom of the path. The smell of seaweed was stronger down here, and Angela started to wonder if this was the best place for a picnic.

'Phew!' Jerry said, confirming her feelings. 'What's that smell?'

'Seaweed,' she said. 'And rock pools.'

Undeterred, he said, 'There's a big flat rock over there we could sit on.'

They picked their way over rock pools and seagull droppings to the flat rock. Angela spread out the rug – half in the sun, half in the shade – and they sat down. The waves broke gently on the rocks just a few feet away.

'It's not as nice as the beach,' she said, 'but it has its own charm. Maybe we can go and have a look at Halki Beach afterwards. It's very beautiful. Just a little further north.'

'You should see the beaches back home,' Jerry said, eyes going out to the ocean as though he was trying to see home right now. 'White sand for miles.'

'Where do you come from? I mean, I know you're from Australia.'

'I've lived all over. I grew up at a place called the Sunshine Coast. My parents still live there, but I haven't been there in a while.' He turned his gaze to her. 'You know, over here people say it's a sunny day and I think, mate, you haven't seen sunshine until you've seen Queensland. The sky's so blue and big it makes your eyeballs ache, everything is drenched in light, and the trees are vivid green, *rudely* green. It's bloody beautiful.'

She smiled at him, surprised and charmed by his passionate disclosure.

'How about you? Where are you from?'

Angela hesitated, not sure of what to tell him. She had no idea where she was from.

'Let me guess,' he said, saving her from having to answer. 'I spent a year in England, and I'm getting pretty good at telling the accents apart. You're not from up north, I know that.'

'No,' she said.

'You've been to a good school, I'd say, but not a real posh one.'

'Mm-hm.'

'And you've spent a bit of time in London, but west, not south. Definitely not south.'

'You're really very good at this,' she said. 'I am from London, but I much prefer it here.' As she said this, a statement that she had conjured up purely to satisfy his curiosity, she recognised it as a very important truth about herself. She didn't want to stay on this topic. 'Shall we eat? Lilika's picnics are wonderful.'

'Yeah, great,' he said. 'I'm starving.'

She unfolded the linen over the basket, and began to unpack Lilika's bakery treats. Two seconds later, a big wave broke on the rocks, showering their picnic with salty water.

'Oh!' Angela exclaimed, leaping to her feet. Water had soaked the right leg of her jeans.

Jerry broke into easy laughter, and a moment later Angela was laughing too.

'I'm sorry,' Jerry said, gasping for breath through his laughter. 'You're all wet, I shouldn't be laughing.'

'It's not your fault.'

'It is. Here I was trying to be fascinating, leading you down here...' Another burst of laughter. The sun shone on his sandy hair, and Angela's heart lurched a little in her chest.

'Angela,' he said, forcing his tone to be even and climbing to his feet. He took her hands and lowered his voice, finally getting his laughter under control. 'Angela, maybe I should just dispense with all this romantic bullshit and tell you this. I'm leaving the island on Thursday. But I think you're pretty and I'd like to kiss you before I go, if you'd let me.'

Angela realised she didn't know if she'd ever kissed anyone before. She presumed she must have, but what if she didn't know what to do?

He misread her moment of hesitation. 'I'm sorry, am I being too forward? You English girls –'

'Yes,' she said quickly. 'I mean, no. No, you're not being too forward. Yes, to...the other part.'

He smiled. He curled a warm hand around the back of her head and drew her gently closer. His lips were hot, firm, melting against hers. She sighed into him: his warm, slightly rough maleness was profoundly reassuring, awaking deep longing in her. Then another wave came, soaking their shoes.

'Damn it,' he said, pulling away, laughing again.

'Come on,' she said. 'Let's go back to the b & b and dry off. I'll make you some lunch. I've been experimenting with traditional recipes and I'm getting quite good.'

'You can cook too? Bloody hell, you might just be perfect.'

She hid a stupidly flattered grin, thinking exactly the same thing about him.

⦂∞⦂

'That's a take, Charlie,' George said. 'Come on through and we'll listen back.'

Charlie Crowe, George's new project, nodded and put aside his headphones. George turned to Aila, who sat very quietly on a stool at the back of the control room, and raised his eyebrows. 'Well? Is he worth the trouble?'

She nodded enthusiastically. 'I love this song.'

George was bemused. She never usually ventured down here to the studio, but she'd taken an interest in Charlie. Certainly, the young man was very charming and funny, with his broad cockney accent and his endless stream of anecdotes; but usually Aila left the business to him. He suspected she was trying to get more involved, so a repeat of the last disaster didn't happen.

Ellie's betrayal had awoken a deep resentment that still had the ability to keep him awake at night. After their relationship had broken down, he had turned inwards, become cold. Aila had begged him to forgive Ellie and move on. But every phone call he'd had to have with concert promoters, foreign record labels, marketing teams and publicity machines had caused him pain. He felt embarrassed, stupid. He felt like a failure. He berated himself for not forcing her to stay somehow. And when the first inklings of her new musical direction had become known to the press, and the first derisive comments had begun to circulate, he had taken devilish pleasure in them, had leaked a few details of his own: she was an egotist, she saw herself playing the great roles, she thought all her fans would love her and she'd gain thousands of new ones. Aila had told him he was becoming cruel.

Then, a year ago, he had walked into a smoky pub near King's Cross station and found Charlie. With just a guitar and a microphone, he was hypnotising the tiny audience with a blue-eyed charm and a bourbon-soaked voice that could bruise hearts. George could not understand why this talent, at twenty-eight years old, had never been signed before.

Six weeks into their working relationship, he figured it out. Charlie was lazy, couldn't turn up anywhere on time, was rude to the media, and far too fond of a drink. But George needed a new star to help him forget the old one, so, at Aila's urging, he had stuck with Charlie. Now, after a first single that had made it to number eleven, they were working together on his second single; and Aila was keeping an eye on them both.

Charlie slouched out, closing the door to the recording booth behind him. 'How did I sound?' he asked.

'I think you sounded marvellous,' Aila said with a sweet smile.

He gave her a wink. 'Thanks, darlin'. How 'bout you, guv? Did you like it?'

'I said it was a take,' George grumbled. 'I would have made you do it again if I didn't like it.'

'That's my George, always generous with his praise.' Charlie reached into his pocket for tobacco and paper, and rolled a cigarette between stained fingers. 'Tell me,' he said, holding the cigarette between his lips to light it, 'is it too early in the day for a Scotch to celebrate?'

'Yes,' George said. 'We have more work to do before you get on the sauce. The backing vocals, for starters.'

'I'll make tea,' Aila volunteered, sliding down from her stool.

'Don't go to any trouble, darlin',' Charlie said, but George knew he didn't mean it.

The tape rattled back on the reel as Aila left and Charlie smoked. George pressed play and they listened to the song, George's expert fingers dancing over the mixing desk, adjusting levels, dropping channels in and out; all the while his mind working: perhaps a little reverb here, perhaps double the piano track there, perhaps hire some female vocalists for a backing to the chorus... Charlie sucked on his cigarette, filling the tiny room with smoke. The end of the song came, George faded it out, and Charlie gave a self-satisfied grin.

'Not bad, not bad, eh, guv? I reckon this one might just go to number one.'

His cockiness irritated George, despite the fact that he too wanted it to go to the top of the charts. 'We'll see. There are a lot of factors at play. You'll have to tour, you'll have to be polite to the media.'

Charlie waved away his concerns, accidentally flicking ash all over the mixing desk. 'I know it, Georgie.' Calling him 'Georgie' was only one of Charlie's irritating habits. 'My old gran's a fortune teller, you know. When I was four she told my ma that she knew I was going to have my picture in all the papers one day.'

George didn't point out that criminals sometimes had their pictures in the papers.

Aila had re-entered with a tea tray. 'Is that right? Your gran was a fortune teller?'

Charlie smiled his cheeky smile. 'Well, she charged five quid to tell fortunes, but whether or not she was the real thing or a shyster...' He shrugged theatrically. 'Who's to know?'

Aila laughed politely, tapping George's shoulder. 'There's a delivery at the front door, *Lemmikki*. They want you to sign for it.'

George was glad for the distraction. As he left, Aila poured tea while Charlie butted his cigarette on yesterday's saucer. The smoke-free air in the upstairs of his house was welcome. At the front door, a courier in a red uniform waited patiently with a large carton between his feet. George signed for it, then brought the carton inside. Curious, he picked off the tape and opened it.

Tapes in big grey boxes. They were labelled in his handwriting. *Penny Bright, recording session, July 1973*: the original Penny's original recordings, returned from the pressing service with a note about lack of storage room. George sat back on the thick carpet, one of the tapes between his hands. That first recording session had been a lifetime ago, it seemed. Penny, hopeful but wary, had played and sung for him one of her own songs. He remembered clearly the surprise and delight on her face when she'd emerged from the booth to listen back. Not the assured cockiness of Charlie Crowe, nor the satisfied indifference of Ellie. Penny had been shocked.

'Do I sound like that?' she'd asked.

'You do.'

'But it's...good.'

He'd wanted to gather her up and hold her then, moved by her wounded innocence, her uncertainty about herself despite her beauty and talent...

George stood, dropping the tape back in the box. He hadn't room for all these tapes either. Would he destroy them, then? His heart said no. Maybe Aila wouldn't notice if they were in a corner of the garage for a while.

Thoughtfully, he descended to the basement. He opened the door, and was confronted by a sight that pulled at his heart. Charlie had Aila's hand, palm up, in his, tracing it with his fingertips. Aila was gazing at him as though mesmerised, he was smiling at her in a way that could not be described as anything but seductive. Within a half-moment of his entry, they had jumped apart. And Aila wouldn't meet his eyes.

'Charlie was reading my future, *Lemmikki*,' she said quickly. Too quickly.

'Something I picked up from my gran,' Charlie said, without any hint of guilt or apology in his tone. 'She's going to live a long life, your missus.'

The explanation did little to ease him. If their exchange was so innocent, why was she blushing? In more than twenty-five years of marriage, he had never seen her look like that.

'Well, I'm pleased that she'll live a long time; but we have only a short time to get this recording finished,' he said gruffly. 'No time for nonsense, Charlie. We've got plenty more work to do today.'

'Sure thing, guv.' Charlie stretched, winked at Aila and returned to the recording booth. George rewound the tape again, fighting the jealous feelings and promising himself never to leave Aila alone with Charlie again.

Ellie waited in Madame's music room, her forehead pressed against the glass of the window as she gazed out at the street. It had been confirmed, Andre Anderson was offering her the role of Annina in the Westminster Opera's production of *La traviata*. Ivan thought she should take it; she had said no. Now she wondered whether to tell Madame or not. Would the old teacher agree with her decision, or call her a foolish snob and tell her to take work wherever she could?

It was always hard to predict Madame, who was as changeable as the weather.

The door opened, and Ellie turned, dropping the dusty curtain back into place. Madame shuffled across the wooden floorboards, sat at the piano. Her customary way to begin a lesson was to play a scale for Ellie to sing, without so much as a nod of greeting. Today, she sat very still and considered Ellie with pursed lips.

'What is it?' Ellie said at last. 'Don't you want me to sing?'

'I am trying to decide whether to bother with you.'

Ellie was puzzled. 'I don't know what you mean.'

'Your last cheque bounced. You cannot afford to see me any longer.'

Panic seized Ellie's heart. 'It bounced?' She kept such meticulous bank records; how could that happen? Were her funds really so low?

'I think perhaps you are worth the trouble, Penelope, but I grow old. You should not take advantage of me.'

'I'm not, I didn't,' Ellie replied, flustered. 'I'm so sorry; I'll write you another . . .'

'In my experience, when a bank account is empty it remains empty until more money goes in. Have you made any more money since Tuesday?'

Ellie shook her head.

Madame held up four withered fingers. 'I will give you four more lessons, and then if you still have no money, that will be the end of our relationship.'

She wanted to cry, she wanted to rage. Instead, she bowed her head and said, 'Yes, Madame. Thank you for your generosity.'

Madame's voice became soft. 'Come here, child,' she said, patting the space on the piano stool next to her. 'I need to tell you something.'

Puzzled, Ellie approached the piano stool. Madame had never asked her to sit with her before; she always protected her personal space ferociously. Ellie slid onto the stool, careful that her arm didn't touch Madame's body. Up close, she could smell the old woman's powder and shampoo. Musty roses.

Madame met her gaze evenly. 'Yesterday, I was fortunate enough to have lunch with an old, dear friend. One I have not seen in more than fifteen years.'

A short silence ensued. The muted sunlight from behind the curtains was very still.

Madame continued. 'His name is Franz Auerbach. I know that you know of him. The first time we met, you told me he trained your father.'

A keen stab of sadness went to Ellie's heart. Papa. She no longer thought of him every day, but when he did come to mind, the sense of loss was never far behind.

'He did,' Ellie said. 'Papa spoke very highly of him.'

Madame smiled tightly, and Ellie thought she detected a shade of pity in the expression. 'Penelope, you told me your father's name was Kasper Frankel. Is that right?'

'Yes.'

'I'm sorry, but Franz says he has never met anyone by that name.'

The shock was like a bolt of light; her lips started moving without her brain's permission. 'Then he's forgotten. It was many years ago.'

'I remember very clearly you saying your father was Franz's star pupil. He would not forget that.'

'He's old...he's...' Ellie realised she was being rude and stopped herself. 'He must be mistaken. He *must* be.'

Madame patted Ellie's knee. Under other circumstances the gesture would have been astounding, but Ellie was too busy fighting with the revelation about her father to notice it.

'I know that you must be disappointed,' Madame said.

'But why would Papa say that if it wasn't true?' Ellie didn't need Madame to answer that. Her father had always needed to be thought special, better than everyone else. 'Who did he train with, if not Auerbach?'

'Somebody competent, I imagine,' Madame replied with a grudging shrug. 'You were well-trained, he passed on good-enough skills.'

Ellie was lost in thought. If Papa had lied about that, what else had he lied about? Had he really had a promising career? Was his failure really due to illness? Or was he only ever an amateur, one of a million aspiring opera singers with grand dreams of adoration, the kind of man who was so bitter or embarrassed about his failure that he had to tell his daughter untruths? Tears sprang to her eyes, and Ellie quickly stood and moved away from Madame.

'I can't accept your offer of free lessons,' she said, squaring her shoulders and picking up her music from the top of the piano. 'I'll call you when I have the money.'

'Penelope, there's no need to be ashamed.'

'Ashamed? Ashamed of what?'

'Of your father, or yourself.'

'I'm not ashamed,' Ellie said, though perhaps she was. 'Papa was a fine man and he taught me well. He would have had good reasons for what he did.'

Madame sniffed. 'I imagine it was pride. Perhaps he taught you that, too.'

Anger needled Ellie's stomach. Without a word, she walked out.

It was only on the street, with the warm sunshine on her cheeks and the summer breeze in her hair, that she realised that her anger was because Madame had homed in on the truth. She *was* too proud; and it was certainly something her father had taught her.

'Damn her for being right,' she muttered, fishing in her pocket. She pulled out a few coins and went to find a phone box. She had to ring Ivan; she had to see if Andre's offer still stood. She had to start somewhere.

TWENTY-FIVE

*P*erhaps Dieter could have done better for his new bride than dusty plastic flowers in cheap vases, and generic piano music on a tape. Perhaps he could have chosen a more romantic place to celebrate his marriage than this faintly musty office with its worn carpet and its overly polite celebrant, whose smile didn't quite make it to his eyes. But Dieter was just giving Ingrid what she wanted: an invisible wedding.

'But don't you want to wear a white dress? Have your family there?' he had asked.

She had patted her still-flat belly. 'My father is disappointed enough in me already, without me making myself into a spectacle in front of his relatives. And white is for virgins.'

Ingrid's father being 'disappointed' by her unplanned pregnancy was an understatement. His anger had driven them both from Kokondorf and into the city, where they were renting a little flat at Gröplingen in the short term. His own parents had not passed judgment: he was a grown man after all. Ellie was gone, and they had long ago resigned themselves to his relationship with Podolski's daughter. One night, Dieter's mother had asked if his intentions towards her were genuine.

'What do you mean?' he'd replied.

'It's not just another way for you to keep the farm?'

Dieter had been horrified at the suggestion, then later wondered if, deep down, part of Ingrid's attraction to him was the connection to his childhood home. He'd remembered Ellie's words: *There is life beyond the village.* Was he afraid of change? The idea that she might be right appalled him so much, that he'd started to make plans to move far away. He'd applied for an assisted passage to Australia. The approval had come through yesterday, the day before his wedding.

Their vows were exchanged in front of two old school friends of Ingrid's. The ceremony was necessarily anticlimactic. Soon the celebrant was showing them which forms to sign. The piano music scrambled, and the tape cut off.

'I do apologise,' said the celebrant with a flash of his big white teeth, hurrying to the tape player to fix the problem. Miles of unwound tape spewed out onto the burnt-orange carpet.

Ingrid signed her name neatly and decisively. Everything about her was neat and decisive. The last two years, he honestly had to admit, she had given him little trouble. She wasn't bossy, or clingy, or cold, or stupidly ambitious. Certainly she had a fiery temper, but his wasn't the type of personality that roused it. Their relationship had been pleasant. Whenever she said she loved him, he would happily tell her he loved her too. No, he'd never expected it to last forever. Did he still hope that one day Ellie would come back to him? Only a fool would cherish such a hope. Still, the finality of marriage – through necessity, rather than choice – brought Ellie to mind again, and Dieter took the pen hesitantly.

'Go on,' Ingrid said, her pretty face puzzled. 'Dieter?'

'I'm sorry,' he said. 'Did he say I have to sign both forms?'

'Both,' she said. 'Here.' She smiled at him and pressed the pen into his hand with her warm, soft fingers.

Dieter took the pen and a deep breath at the same time. He did what he had to do.

Angela loved the heady sensory impressions of the markets. Mouthwatering aromas of sizzling *doner* competed with the more

320

subtle smells of the fruit stalls: capers, rosemary, sage, lemons. Laid out around her were all manner of cheeses, crayfish and whitebait on ice, tubs of oil, buckets of olives and pistachios, tempting trays of *dolmathakia* and oily cheesy pies. Three times a week the town square was filled with bright stalls and the whole community came out under the sunny sky to do their shopping, to gossip and chatter, or to sit at the long tables and enjoy their soupy black coffee, or paper cups of orange squash.

Usually she was here on a Tuesday to shop for the b & b. But today was a Thursday, and she had quite a different purpose. Jerry was leaving today. They'd spent the last few weeks in each other's pockets, but right about now he'd be packing his backpack, thanking a relieved Antonia Theodrakis, and getting ready to catch the boat back to the mainland. Angela was due to meet him at the pier to say goodbye, and she wanted to give him something. He was travelling light – with nothing more than a backpack and a broad-brimmed hat – so she couldn't give him old books or antique-framed pictures. Instead, she was busy choosing handmade treats from Sofi Nikolaides's sweet stall, to tie in a linen bag and squeeze into the side of his backpack. Perhaps he would only remember her as long as the sweets lasted, but that was all right. He'd made it clear that their time together was fun but not forever. Angela smiled wryly to herself: she'd hardly given him any incentive to stay. Kisses were all she'd offered him, despite his insistence. Anything beyond that frightened her: she'd no idea whether she had any sexual experience or not, and could hardly admit that to him.

She already had pieces of *mandolato*, honey chocolates and stone toffees, and surveyed the rest of the stall. 'What are these like?' she said, pointing to the sign that read *koufeta*.

'Try some,' Sofi said expansively, wiping her hands on her ample bosom and reaching for the scoop.

Angela picked one of the sweets out of the scoop and popped it into her mouth. An explosion of sugar and almond. She nodded enthusiastically. 'Yes, a scoop of those too. I really should get you to supply some bags of sweets to the b & b. The guests would love them.'

Sofi poured an extra scoop of *koufeta* into the linen bag. 'I'd be very interested to talk to you about that proposal.'

Angela smiled. 'We could –' A cold hand on her wrist stopped her mid-sentence. She turned with a start to see Mia, huge sunglasses making her face seem thin and pinched, standing nervously beside her.

'Mia!' she exclaimed.

Sofi crossed her arms and adopted a disapproving frown.

'Not here,' Mia hissed, pulling on Angela's arm.

'Wait, I have to pay for –'

'Pay me later,' Sofi said. 'It's fine.'

Mia led her away from the markets. Angela crammed the sweets into her handbag as they walked. Even though she knew Mia was disliked, it still alarmed her to see the scowling faces that watched them go. Couldn't they be more forgiving? Mia held her head high, but when they reached the edge of the square she turned and spat on the ground and Angela thought that perhaps she was too hard to forgive.

'What's going on?' Angela asked, switching to English as much to hide their conversation as for ease.

'I need to talk to you privately. Here.' She pulled Angela up the alleyway beside the bakery. The buildings were only a few feet apart, and the smell of baking bread was strong and warm. Mia stopped and removed her sunglasses with a flourish. 'I think I'm terribly sick,' Mia said. 'I think I might die.'

Angela felt a pulse of alarm, and realised that she had become much more fond of Mia than she knew. 'What do you mean?'

'I have a lump. Here.' Mia took Angela's hand and, without embarrassment or hesitation, pressed it firmly into her left breast.

Angela tried not to be startled. She felt for the lump.

'See?' Mia said. 'It's big, isn't it?'

'I can't feel anything.'

'Try harder.' Mia pulled open her blouse and dug Angela's fingers into the flesh above her bra. 'How can you not feel it? It's huge.'

'I can't...' Angela gently withdrew her hand. 'When did you find it?'

'This morning. I dreamed last night of children, babies. I dreamed I was nursing them at my breasts. I woke and found the lump.' Tears sprang to her eyes. 'I never nursed babies, Angela. That's why I'm being punished with this awful cancer.'

'You don't have cancer.' She stopped herself from saying, *You don't even have a lump*, because clearly Mia thought she did have one. 'I'm sure you'll be all right.'

'It's easy for you to be sure,' Mia snapped. 'You're not dying.'

Angela adopted her most patient voice. 'If you're worried, you need to see Doctor Moscopolos.'

'I won't go near that old fool!' Mia shouted, then sagged against the wall, dropping her eyes. Her next question was almost a whisper. 'Or do you think I should?'

'You should. He can examine the lump, he might be able to put your mind at ease.'

'He might be able to tell me how long I have left, I suppose,' Mia sighed. Her head rose hopefully and she met Angela's eyes. 'Will you take me?'

Angela knew better than to check her watch. Anyway, she could sense that midday was well behind, that afternoon was full upon them. She knew that Jerry would be getting on the boat within an hour. But she hoped that she would be able to take Mia to Doctor Moscopolos and still make it to the pier on time.

'Of course,' she managed to say. 'Of course I'll take you.'

They wound up the hill and through the maze of streets. The sun didn't quite make its way into these alleys, and Angela felt a chill. The weather-beaten shingle was the only indication that the small, white-plastered house at the end of the street belonged to a medical practice, one of only two on the island. Angela pushed the door open, but Mia hung back.

'What's wrong?' Angela asked.

323

'He hates me.'

'I'm sure he doesn't.'

'I once called his wife a fat nanny-goat.'

Angela had to stifle a laugh. Emalia Moscopolos did, indeed, resemble an overfed goat. She forced a serious expression. 'No matter what has happened between you two in the past, he's a doctor and he's duty-bound to see you.'

Mia pushed her sunglasses back on. 'You go in first,' Mia said. 'Everybody likes you. You go in, and you ask him if he'll see me.'

Angela sighed. 'Mia...'

'Please,' Mia said, suddenly desperate. 'Please, Angela, you're my only friend.'

The shingle flapped in the breeze, its chain chinking on the pole. Time was speeding by; Angela decided to take the path of least resistance. 'All right, then. Wait here.'

Inside the warm of the doctor's office, Angela approached the reception desk and rang the bell. A short, beak-nosed woman bustled out, an armful of medical records spilling out of her grasp and onto the desk.

'Can I help?'

'I need to speak to Doctor Moscopolos.'

'He's in with a patient, but he won't be long if you'd care to wait.' She indicated the long, vinyl-covered bench seat against the wall. Angela eyed it, glanced at the clock, then sat down.

The magazines were years old, and she still had trouble reading the Cyrillic alphabet so she didn't bother to pick one up. Instead she stared at the wood-panelled walls and tried to ignore the ticking of the clock. Captain Lianis often ran late and, besides, if she could be out of here in twenty minutes she'd still make it. Easily. She felt the little bag of sweets in her bag and smiled, thinking of Jerry. If only he could stay a little longer...

Five minutes later an elderly woman emerged from the doctor's office, and Doctor Moscopolos himself appeared. The receptionist explained that Angela was here to see him, and he invited her in.

'I don't need to see you for myself,' Angela explained. 'I came to ask if you'd see Mia.'

Doctor Moscopolos frowned beneath his big moustache. 'I really am very busy this afternoon...'

'Please. She's found a lump in her breast and she's afraid that she has cancer. I know you don't like her, but as a doctor you can't refuse to treat somebody who's ill.'

The receptionist adopted a sour expression, but Angela pressed on.

'It will only take a few minutes of your time, and she'll pay you just like any other patient.'

Doctor Moscopolos parted his hands, a gesture of surrender. 'Very well, send her in.'

'Thank you,' Angela breathed, and she really meant it. Now all she had to do was deliver Mia into the doctor's hands, then dash down to the pier.

Outside, though, Mia was nowhere in sight.

'Damn,' Angela muttered, turning in a circle. She spotted Mia, on her way back down the hill. 'Mia, wait!' she called.

Mia began to run.

Angela thought about abandoning her. She thought about letting her retreat to her grand, grimy house. She thought about Jerry's strong arms and warm lips. But what if Mia really was sick? She'd never forgive herself. She began to run after her.

Angela caught Mia at the bottom of the hill. She grasped both her arms firmly.

'Mia, stop. He says he'll see you.'

Mia's sunglasses were awry, giving her face a lopsided appearance. 'No. He'll see my breasts, he'll tell everybody.'

Angela relaxed her grasp. 'He won't tell anyone. He can't, he's a doctor.'

Mia began to sob.

'Mia, you have to see him. To put your mind at rest.'

'He can't put my mind at rest. I *know* I'm dying. I can feel it. My skin is shrinking around me.' She wrapped her arms over her shoulders.

Angela took her hand. 'Come on.'

'I'm frightened.'

'I'll wait in the waiting room for you.'

'No, come in with me. Hold my hand.'

'All right, then.'

As they walked back up the hill, Angela still hoped she might make it to the pier on time. She was only half-concentrating on the doctor's examination of Mia in his sterile-smelling consultation room.

'I can feel no lump,' he said at length.

Mia huffed. 'I can.'

'Come back in six weeks and I'll check again. Put your mind at rest.'

'It's my fault, isn't it? I'm being punished.'

The doctor shook his head, chuckling lightly. 'Mia, cancerous lumps aren't sent to punish the wicked.'

'Do you think I'm wicked?'

He met Mia's gaze very evenly, his brow stern. Something passed between them, but Angela wasn't sure what it was. She realised that Mia knew Doctor Moscopolos better than she let on.

'No, Mia, I don't think you're wicked. Though you've done many things to upset the good folk of this island.'

Now Mia was all bluster as she buttoned up her blouse. 'Good folk? Ha! You all think you're too good for me, don't you?'

Angela intervened. 'Come on, Mia. The doctor says you're fine, we can go.'

Mia was still spitting venom as they left the doctor's surgery, but Angela wasn't listening.

'I'm sorry, I have to dash,' Angela said. 'I'm seeing somebody off on the boat.'

Mia waved her away and trotted back towards her home as though nothing had happened. This left Angela running as hard as she could for the pier. Grey clouds gathered overhead.

She could already see, as she rounded the bluff, that the boat had untied its moorings and was heading out. She wasn't going to make it in time to give him his present, but perhaps he would be up on deck, watching for her. She pelted down the pier, manoeuvring around Nick Savadelis, who was struggling with a carton he'd loaded off the boat. She pulled up on the last plank, searching for his face on deck, but it wasn't there. Two of her guests, on their way home, waved at her. She forced a smile and waved back. Maybe he hadn't gone. Maybe he'd decided to stay.

Nick Savadelis was at her elbow a moment later. 'The Australian man asked me to give you a message before he got on the boat.'

Her heart fell. 'He did?'

'He said to expect a Christmas card.'

'Anything else?'

Nick shrugged. 'No. That's all.'

That's all. Angela watched Nick go, then turned back as the boat shrank into the distance.

Ellie met Nancy McKenzie for the first time backstage at the Geminus Theatre – home of the Westminster Opera Company at Milbank – on the first afternoon of blocking out *La traviata*. Nancy, who was to play Violetta, was an international star and had been away touring in America for the first month of rehearsals. Her understudy had sung the role for those early, note-bashing practices on the floor of the theatre, where everybody had learned the score. Ellie, of course, had learned her own part before the first rehearsal, and was astounded by the range of indolence, apathy and carelessness displayed by other members of the cast. The weak-chinned Lex Honeydew, who was to play Alfredo, was still mispronouncing his Italian six weeks out from the performance. Andre was forever losing his temper, shouting at them all – despite the fact that Ellie never sang a note out of tune, nor mangled one Italian vowel – and threatening them with public humiliation on opening night in December.

When she'd asked the accompanist whether Andre had hired a troupe of amateurs with no work ethic, he'd merely laughed and said, 'It will surprise you how it all comes together in the end.' So far, she was yet to be surprised.

So now she leaned against a chair in the wings, gazing out past the big empty stage of the Geminus – scarred with eighty years of dramatic footprints, spotted with pieces of dirty masking tape and the occasional cigarette burn – to the round auditorium. Rows of old seats rose in tiers from the floor and around the back wall; but the seats on the floor were yet to be put in. The overhead lights – bright, square spotlights – were on, making the mock-baroque decorations on the stalls look old and tired. A cleaner was mopping the floorboards with something that smelled faintly of lavender and bleach. But Ellie knew that when the time came, when the lights were dimmed and the well-heeled opera lovers began to slide and whisper into their seats, when the stage lights flared and the orchestra played those opening chords of Verdi's beautiful overture, the magic of the theatre would return.

The piano was now in the orchestra pit, and the accompanist idly played scales with his right hand. New, different people milled about. Costumiers, set builders, technical staff, members of the chorus. Ellie had not bothered to introduce herself to any of them. In their glances, their occasional knowing smiles, she read their disdain for her past as a pop singer, their familiarity with the bad reviews she'd received, their hungry expectation that she would fail in her first test on a real opera stage. Ivan, when she told him this, suggested she might be imagining the hostility. But she wasn't. These people could never be her friends, so there was little benefit in learning their names.

A short stocky woman with a square face approached her as she stood there. She narrowed her eyes to peer at Ellie in the backstage shadows.

'Excuse me,' she said, 'are you Penny Bright?'

Ellie nodded.

The woman broke into laughter, and Ellie wasn't sure how to respond so she said nothing.

'Well, don't you see?' the woman continued. 'Don't you see what a great joke it is? You used to be a pop star, you were famous. My sister used to love watching you on *Top of the Pops*. And now you're my maid.' With that, she strode out onto the stage and took her place at its centre, and Ellie realised she'd just met famed diva, Nancy McKenzie.

'You have me for two hours,' Nancy called to Andre, who stood in the pit next to the piano. She tapped her watch and held up two fingers. 'Make good use of your time.'

Ellie boiled inside with rage and jealousy. Even more so when Nancy began to sing and Ellie knew – she *knew* – that her own voice was far superior. Nancy's voice was silvery in the upper register, but the middle was muddy, imprecise. She modified her vowels too radically, losing the sense of the words. Ellie fought with her feelings of injustice, then decided that she couldn't watch, and moved backstage. One of the rooms had been set aside as a tea room, with a creaking old urn and a set of matching teacups in a bland shade of brown. Plastic chairs lined the walls. Ellie searched for instant coffee, but could only find a glass jar with a few grounds left. She inspected them uncertainly, then decided to try anyway.

'Penelope?'

She turned from the sink to see a young man standing in the doorway. He was very handsome, with dark hair and smoky eyes. And he was smiling at her genuinely, not as though he thought her a sideshow act.

'Yes?' she asked, warily.

'I'm Damien.' He moved forward, offering her a hand which she shook. 'I'm in the chorus. I have your album. The album of arias, I mean.'

One of the few, she thought, suppressing a wry smile. 'It's nice to meet you, Damien.'

'I love it. You have a voice...' Here he kissed his fingertips. 'It's delicious.'

Now she was warming to him.

'Thank you,' she said. 'I work very hard.'

'This role, Annina. It's beneath you. You should be Violetta. Not that old harpy.' He laughed then stopped suddenly. 'Oh, sorry. Perhaps you're friends with Nancy.'

'I'm not.' She gestured at her coffee cup. 'Would you care to join me?'

'Is that all right? They're always telling us in the chorus not to bother the principals.'

'I don't mind.'

So he made himself a cup of tea and sat with her – praising her some more, telling her unflattering gossip about Nancy McKenzie, Andre Anderson and just about everybody else in the Westminster Opera – she began to feel the pull of attraction to his grey eyes and his ready smile.

'I wonder,' he said, when she had truly warmed to him and let her guard down, 'what you can tell me about Ivan Hamblyn?'

'Ivan?'

'He's your manager, isn't he?'

'Not really, though I have a good business relationship with him. He's the person who signed me with TRG's classical division.'

'Yes, that's right. Ivan is one of the most powerful people in classical music, but he's impossible to meet. He doesn't get out to the performances much. He goes to industry parties, but it's hard to get an invitation...'

Slowly, it dawned on Ellie that Damien's interest wasn't her, it was the much greater prize: making contact with Ivan. A cold sensation passed over her skin, as her defences were once more raised.

'Is that true?' he continued. 'Do you know of anywhere he might go regularly, any meetings or parties where a young tenor with recording aspirations could meet him?'

Her voice was chilly. 'Ivan keeps very much to himself.'

Damien laughed, either oblivious to her tone or cheerfully ignoring it. 'I have an idea,' he continued blithely. 'Maybe you could introduce me to him?'

Ellie stood, placing her unfinished coffee on the bench. 'I can't help you.'

In a moment, his friendly smile had disappeared. 'Can't or won't?'

'You didn't really buy my album, did you?'

He shrugged. 'Nobody did.'

A sharp knock at the door grabbed her attention.

'Miss Bright? Miss McKenzie wants you on stage for the duet. Now.'

Wonderful: no doubt she was in for more ridicule, more derision. She took a deep breath and gritted her teeth. 'Certainly,' she said. 'I'm ready.'

When Ellie let herself into Ivan's office, he was on the phone. He smiled at her weakly then turned his back to finish the call. The cord pulled the phone to the edge of the broad oak desk, where it sat precariously while Ivan spoke. 'Yes, Mummy... No, I wouldn't... If you want me to be there, I will...'

Ellie was awkward witnessing the conversation. She would have waited outside, but Alice had told her to, 'Go right in, he's expecting you'. She averted her eyes, gazing instead around the office, with its tasteful prints, its four gold records in glass cases, and its towering bookshelves stacked vertically with records. The call continued. Ellie considered standing up and leaving, but then Ivan said, 'Look, I have to go. We'll talk later... Yes, I promise I'll work something out. Bye.'

He dropped the receiver into the cradle with a sigh of relief, and turned his attention to Ellie. 'I'm very sorry, Ellie. I shouldn't have taken the call. I knew you'd be here right on time.'

'No, I'm sorry, I should have waited outside.'

'Oh, it was just my mother,' he said, dismissing her apology. 'She gets a little tense in the lead-up to Christmas... especially this year. Daddy isn't well and... it's irrelevant. We're here to talk about you.' He steepled his hands and leaned forward with a kind but sad smile. 'I think you know what I'm going to say.'

Even though she'd been expecting it, her heart still sank. 'They aren't going to sign me again, are they?'

'Not yet. They will, I'm sure. Just not yet. The first Penelope Bright album did very poorly and they want to be sure that next time they put out a recording, it will work. I told the sales team about your engagement with the Westminster Opera and they asked me to congratulate you, and to tell you that you're on the right track now.'

Ellie bit her tongue so she wouldn't ask him whether anybody had brought up the possibility of her recording as Penny Bright, pop star, again. She was desperate for money, and was afraid she might consider it.

'I hope you will keep in touch, Ellie,' Ivan was saying. 'No matter what your sales were like, you are one of the finest talents I've had the pleasure to work with.'

Ellie felt a jolt of sadness. Or was it loneliness? She had been cut adrift. Without a TRG contract, Ivan was no longer involved in her career. 'I will keep in touch. Of course. Perhaps we can meet once in a while? I could take you to lunch, to thank you for all you've done.'

Ivan suddenly adopted a thoughtful expression. His eyes went to the telephone. 'Ellie, I've just thought of... I don't want to insult you.'

Ellie was puzzled. 'I'm sorry?'

'It's only... I've just thought of a way that you *could* thank me. It would involve me taking you to lunch though. Somewhere a bit stuffy.'

'Of course.'

'Wait, I need to explain.' He smiled sheepishly, a blush creeping up his neck. 'It's very silly. My mother... I told you, didn't I, that my parents see me as a risky heir?'

Ellie nodded.

'They fear I'll never marry. My father, especially, fears it. He's sick, now, and may even die in the next few months.'

Ellie was surprised that Ivan could talk about such things without the slightest hint of sadness in his voice. 'I'm sorry to hear that.'

'Mummy wants me to make an effort to meet somebody. A girl.' He laughed, blushing again, and Ellie began to worry. Was he going to ask her out? He was much older, and she'd certainly never found anything attractive about him. His skin was too milky, his neck slightly hunched, his hands always moist.

'I'm afraid I'm just not interested in all that nonsense,' he continued, and Ellie hid her sigh of relief. 'I have my work, my art

332

collection... I'm quite happy with my life the way it is now. But she thinks it would cheer Daddy greatly if I brought somebody...a girl...along to our family Christmas party. He wouldn't need to know the truth.'

From this sputtered, bashful confession, Ellie managed to deduce that Ivan was asking her to attend a family gathering as his date, but not a real date. She fell silent, wondering if asking for a fee would be too close to prostitution.

'I'm sorry, I've insulted you,' he said, when her silence had extended a little too long.

'No, not at all,' Ellie said quickly.

'The party's on Christmas Day. I can't say that you'll have a good time, but there will be a lovely lunch, and Mummy will buy you some expensive treat as a Christmas present. You'd be able to look at the family estate. It's nearly two hundred years old and quite beautiful.'

Curiosity took over. 'I'd love to.'

Ivan's face grew serious. 'Just so that we're very clear, you will have to pretend that you and I are...in a relationship. Not that I expect...displays of physical affection aren't really welcome around my mother anyway.'

Ellie had to laugh, and Ivan laughed too. It relieved the tension of the awkward situation. 'Ivan, it's fine. I've nowhere else to go at Christmas.' The truth of this statement made her smile freeze on her face. She couldn't go on being alone all the time, and vowed to make contact with her mother's family here in England soon despite her misgivings. 'It will be fun.'

'Good. Good.' He tapped his desk with his knuckles twice. 'That's a relief.'

Alice leaned in through the door at that moment. 'Ivan,' she said, 'Donna Jones from sales is on the line.'

'Thank you, Alice. We're done here.' He turned his gaze to Ellie. 'I'll see you soon, in any case. Opening night is only two weeks away.'

'That's right.'

'And you're getting on all right?'

Ellie didn't bother telling him about how much she hated the rest of the cast, how Nancy McKenzie treated her with contempt, how painful it had been to see her name left off the billboard and misspelt as 'Penlope' in the program. There was nothing he could do, after all. 'Everything's fine,' she said. 'Perfectly fine.'

TWENTY-SIX

Every blow of the hammer made Angela's head throb. She'd
barely slept the night before: the four Scottish backpacking
girls who were sharing the smallest room had decided to sit up all
night in the lounge, smoking and drinking and laughing loudly.
From her bedroom, Angela could hear it all. Even with a pillow over
her head. She must have drifted off around four, only to be woken
at six by the Italian man with the big moustache who demanded
breakfast early.

'I always eat at six,' he said in broken English.

She'd climbed out of bed and made him breakfast, then made
breakfast one by one for the others, then stripped the beds and
started the laundry, then the workmen had arrived to pull out the
eastern wall. Her business was growing, so the b & b had to grow
as well. Now the low season was nearly upon her, the disruption
wouldn't cost her so dearly. A new bathroom was going in, a storeroom,
and an additional two bedrooms with views out over the sea. She
was very tempted to move into one of the new rooms herself, but
knew that part of the reason her business was returning such a good
profit was the fact that she was careful with money and didn't take
up too much space.

So now, as the hammers thudded out the back, and she tried to wrap her aching head around the end-of-week figures at a dining room table, the last thing Angela was prepared for was a sudden flash of memory.

She was naked, and somebody had a camera trained on her. She felt vulnerable, exposed. 'Angie,' a male voice said, 'you're just beautiful.'

Then it was gone again, just as quickly. Angela dropped her pen, closing her eyes and pinching the bridge of her nose. She hated to be called Angie: Was this why? What had she done? But then, before her brain helpfully provided the answers, Angela shut down the memories again. *I don't want to know.* Irrational anger boiled inside her. How dare these memories come back unbidden? A long time had passed since her accident in Spain, and she had begun to think that she would never remember, that she would remain at peace. It bothered her that she couldn't control her memories, make them stay beneath the shadow forever.

She opened her eyes and was alarmed by a dark figure standing near the end of the table. It was only Mia, unannounced as usual. She stood very still, her large sunglasses in place.

'Hello, Mia,' Angela said, grateful for the diversion. 'Is everything all right?'

Mia shrugged silently. Angela searched under her papers for her chequebook. 'I have your rent cheque here. Do you want to take it now?'

Again, she shrugged without saying a word. Angela tore off the cheque and handed it to her, wondering if she'd bother to bank it: She'd only banked five so far. The last time she'd been up at Mia's house she'd found all the cheques in a pile under an empty, dusty fruit bowl.

Mia sat down, head in hands. Her voice became a whisper. 'I think I'm dying.'

Angela steeled herself. This was the fourth time in as many weeks that Mia had thought she was dying. Cancers, blood diseases, lung problems... Doctor Moscopolos, bless him, had developed a gentle sense of pity towards her, and now knew precisely what to say to reassure her. 'I'm sure you're fine, Mia.'

Mia shook her head. 'Not this time. My heart races. It skips a beat. Palpitations...'

'You're probably bringing them on by worrying.' Angela knew her reassurances wouldn't work. 'Do you want me to take you to Doctor Moscopolos?'

She raised her head, removing her big sunglasses, and Angela was alarmed by the dark rings around her eyes. 'Would you? I know he hates me. We have a past –'

'I know. You called his wife a fat nanny-goat. Doctor Moscopolos doesn't hate you, he wants to help you.'

Mia clapped her hand over her heart. 'There it goes again. It's beating too fast.' She grew pale and her eyes were panicked. 'Help me, Angela. I'm dying.'

Angela took her free hand. 'Now, calm down. Take a deep breath... There, is that better?'

Mia gulped for air. Calmed. 'Yes,' she breathed. 'But I need to get to the doctor.'

'Wait here, I'll get my coat.'

Outside the b & b, Mia stopped for a moment to watch the construction work. Her eyes were sad, distant.

'Is everything all right?' Angela asked.

'It looks so different.'

'That's what you wanted.'

Mia nodded, clearing her throat. 'Of course, of course. It's much better this way.' She pressed her hand over her heart again. 'There it goes again,' she said breathlessly.

'Let's go, then.'

The receptionist at Doctor Moscopolos's surgery was used to their regular appearances, and they only had to wait ten minutes to be seen through. Angela stood by, considering the framed photographs on the dark wood-panelled walls, while the doctor patiently listened to Mia and then checked her over. But, unlike the other occasions where he was able to dismiss Mia's fears easily, this time he frowned while listening to her heart.

'There is a slight arrhythmia,' he conceded.

Mia looked almost triumphant. 'There's something wrong with my heart?'

Doctor Moscopolos hung his stethoscope back on its hook above the oak table. It clattered against the wall. 'A very *very* slight palpitation. It may be caused by you worrying about your health. I'm sure if you can learn to relax, it will resolve itself. I don't see any need for sending you to Naxos for more tests.'

'I'm not leaving the island,' Mia replied, panicked.

'That's right, there's no need,' the doctor repeated, clearly forcing his voice to be patient. 'It's very mild, and it will resolve itself if you can learn to relax. You'll live to be one hundred if you just stop worrying.'

Mia grew thoughtful. 'One hundred is too long to live,' she muttered anxiously. 'So old. *Too* old.'

'It's a figure of speech,' he said, hiding his amusement.

Angela stepped in and took Mia by the elbow. 'Come on,' she said. 'Let me take you home.'

On the walk up the hill, Mia was quiet. It was only outside her front gate that she turned to Angela and said, 'Have you ever thought about the expression 'a broken heart'? I mean really thought about it?'

'I don't suppose I have.'

'People see it like a cartoon drawing. A love heart, cracked through the centre. But I think a heart really can be broken. I think that to love, and to lose that love, can damage your organs.' Here she beat her chest with both hands, a skinny sad monkey in oversized sunglasses. 'I think that's what's wrong with me.'

'I don't know, Mia...' Angela trailed off, realising that perhaps Mia was tired of nobody taking her seriously. 'Would you like to tell me about your broken heart?'

Her mouth trembled. 'Oh, that old nonsense.'

'I could come in and make us a pot of strong coffee. We could talk. It might make you feel better.'

Mia drew her spine straight. 'No, no. I'm far too busy today.'

'Another time, then?'

'No, I'm far too busy for that.' She was turning away, fitting the key in the lock. The gate creaked open. 'I need to go and rest, that's all. I just need to sleep for a long time. Sleep until I'm one hundred.'

Angela watched her go then made her way back down the hill. It was very sunny today, with a stiff breeze blowing off the sea. She should have been happy, but felt a vague sense of melancholy. Was it about Mia? She had to admit she'd grown to care too much, and Mia's strange moods and irrational fears were a cause of anxiety. But it was more than that. It was because Mia reminded her of what could happen to a woman if she became too lonely, if there wasn't somebody special to share life with.

She dropped by the post office to pick up her mail, then made herself coffee back at the b & b and sat down to open it. Mostly bills and booking enquiries, but a letter postmarked from Sweden caught her attention. She knew immediately that it was from Jerry.

Every time one of his letters arrived, it surprised her how thrilled she was to hear from him. She found herself thinking of him more than she cared to admit. The letters were always long, chatty, full of amusing observations and warm good humour. He finished by telling her he'd write again soon, but he never gave a return address, as he never had an idea where he was heading next. Angela put the letter down and leaned back in her chair. The bills and accounts on the dining table in front of her were momentarily forgotten as she remembered his warm skin, the clean smell of his hair, the feel of his hot breath on her throat. It was a good thing she couldn't write to him; she might be tempted to tell him she was falling for him.

She might be tempted to beg him to come back to her.

Ellie stepped off the train at Wallingham station and looked around apprehensively. All along the platform people bustled with umbrellas against the light drizzle. Ellie tried to search their faces, to look for features that might be familiar to her, but couldn't find any. Her mother's brother, Uncle Murray, was supposed to collect her, but she'd never laid eyes on him before. She hadn't expected such a crowd on the platform. People everywhere. Should she just wait? Or move down to the concourse?

'Ellie?'

Her name. She turned to see a short, plump woman with tightly-curled red hair waving to her. She wore a grey raincoat and held up a bright pink umbrella. Ellie waved back tentatively, and the woman came over and enclosed her in a warm hug. 'I'm your Aunty Bea!' she exclaimed as she stood back. 'My, what a beauty you are. Much prettier in the flesh than in the magazines.'

'Thank you,' Ellie said, warming to her aunt immediately. Ellie had let them believe she had always been Penny Bright, and that this long overdue contact had been a matter of not knowing the correct spelling of their surname. She wasn't sure if they actually believed her, but if they doubted her they were polite enough not to say so. 'And thank you for coming to pick me up.'

'Uncle Murray wouldn't have had it any other way. Taxis cost too much.'

Ellie knew this all too well. She had nearly baulked at paying for the train ticket, but her strong desire to make a connection with her family overrode her frugality. She was running out of friends. 'Where is Uncle Murray?' she asked.

'Waiting at home. The rain makes his knees ache so he's no good in the car. Come on.' She took Ellie's hand and led her down through the concourse. She indicated a new but surprisingly dirty Volvo. 'Here's your chariot.'

As Ellie got in, she had to place her feet carefully so that she didn't step on old food wrappers and junk mail. The car smelled musty.

'Oh, yes, sorry about the mess,' Aunty Bea said. 'Just kick it aside. I'll get round to cleaning it out one day.' She revved the engine loudly, indicated and pulled out, nearly wiping out a motorcyclist. He raised his fist, but Aunty Bea was blithely unaware. 'Uncle Murray's just dying to see you,' Bea said. 'And we've got our three kids, today. Your cousins. Linda, Malcolm and Paul. A real family reunion.'

Ellie found herself becoming even more apprehensive, though she told herself this was ridiculous. What was she afraid of? Being overwhelmed with feelings and memories? It would be good for her to make a connection. The fact that she had lost contact with these people at all was appalling. Of course, her father had never been fond of her mother's family. She had run away from them, in a sense, coming to Germany because of a disagreement with her brother, Murray, over an inheritance. But it was time to question her father on many fronts. Ellie took a deep breath and told herself to relax. It was only a lunch, after all. If she disliked them, she never had to see them again.

Soon, they had pulled into the driveway of a little pebble-stone cottage, identical to all the other pebble-stone cottages on the street. Before Ellie had even extracted herself from the messy car, the door of the house had swung open and an elderly man with a grey beard was limping down the front path. He closed her in a dramatic hug. Ellie tried to relax her body. He smelled of tobacco and stale aftershave.

Behind him were three other people. Brothers Malcolm and Paul, who Ellie estimated were in their early thirties, and a slightly younger woman with her mother's curly red hair but with a tall, slim figure. This was Linda. Introductions, greetings, hugs and handshakes accompanied their entry to the house. It matched the car for untidiness, but the mingled smell of old potatoes and laundry detergent was strangely comforting. This was a home, this was a family. Ellie finally began to relax.

Uncle Murray was so different in appearance from Ellie's mother that she was almost disappointed. But, every now and again, an expression would twitch his eyebrows and she thought she could see Mama after all. They were very warm with her, and she wondered how on earth Mama and Murray could have been so at odds that Mama would run so far away. An enormous pot of tea was served, with homemade jam biscuits and iced cupcakes. Hours whizzed by as Ellie was told all about her cousins: their jobs (big loud-voiced Malcolm was an ambulance driver, quiet pale-haired Paul a teacher, Linda a sales executive for a cosmetics firm), their families (Malcolm

341

was unmarried, Paul had a wife and four small children, Linda had recently become engaged), and their humiliating baby stories. She told them how her long silence from the music scene had been about a change to opera.

'My father trained me,' she told them. 'He sang opera in his youth.'

At the mention of her father, the conversation suddenly dried up. Murray muttered something about checking on the roast and limped off. Aunty Bea had a coughing fit, pressed a cotton hanky against her mouth and excused herself. Ellie sat very still with her cousins, feeling embarrassed and puzzled all at once.

'Did I say the wrong thing?' she asked.

Malcolm nodded towards Linda. 'I'm not sure. Linda knows.'

Linda shrugged. 'Dad won't talk about it. But I think there was some bad blood between him and your father.'

'Over Mama? The inheritance?'

'Inheritance?' Paul said. 'There wasn't any inheritance, was there, Linda?'

'I can't be certain what happened.' Ellie noticed that Linda wouldn't meet her gaze. 'Mum's said a few things over the years, but –'

'Nearly time for lunch!' Aunty Bea exclaimed, returning with her happy smile firmly back in place. 'Everybody wash up.'

Linda took Ellie down the dim hallway to the bathroom to wash her hands, but was careful not to mention the old family dispute.

Lunch was beautiful, and the warm conversation resumed. But it was for Ellie as though one flat note kept sounding in the symphony. She fell back into her reserved ways, and couldn't quite enjoy herself. In fact, she was relieved when Linda told her the last train would be leaving the station in half an hour.

Linda offered to drop her at the station, and made small talk on the journey. Then they stood on the platform together, waiting for the train. Night closed in, the sky had clouded over, and a swirl of wind buffeted up the tracks, tangling Ellie's hair and rattling the sign that hung outside the stationmaster's office. There was a silence between them, then Linda said, 'Look, I'm sorry about earlier. The business about your father… You must have loved him, and it wasn't right for Dad to make you feel uncomfortable.'

'I wish I knew what had happened.'

The train rattled into the station then, too loud to converse over for a moment. Finally, Linda said, 'It's complicated. And Dad's very private…' Doors on the train began to clatter open. People began to move around them. 'I'm in London from time to time on sales conferences. Can I look you up? We could go out for a drink.'

'I'd like that. But I don't have a telephone.'

'Mum has your address. It's okay.' She took a step back. 'You'd better go.'

Ellie smiled, stepping onto the train. 'Make sure you do come to see me.'

'I will. It would be nice to talk. Without my parents around.'

The conductor sounded his whistle. Ellie closed the door to the carriage and moved to a window to wave goodbye. The train chugged off, and Linda remained on the platform waving. Ellie watched her until the train rounded a bend and made its way back towards London.

The last person George wanted to see at the party was Ivan Hamblyn, dressed tidily, hands folded in front of him. Ivan didn't often come to these social events: probably thought he was too good to mingle with the masses. But there he was, smiling smugly from the other side of the function room. The TRG Christmas cocktail party always took place in November rather than December. Most of the executives were off out of the country at the end of December, chasing the sun. George would be, himself. He and Aila had organised a holiday to the Maldives. Or rather, Aila had organised it. Lately he found himself too distracted by work to plan family time.

George refused to meet Ivan's smile, instead feigning an intense interest in the Christmas decorations. The last time he'd been in this room was the night of Penny's abduction, so it held no fond memories for him. That had been the beginning of the end, though he hadn't known it at the time. At the time it had seemed like the caught breath before the thrill ride: Penny was number one, anything was possible.

He even thought that, maybe, one day, he might be able to tell her the truth about his feelings...

There were many people to blame for what had gone wrong next, of course. The wild man who had abducted her, George himself for not handling her right, Estrella for being too hard on her, Ellie for being so full of her own ambition that she couldn't keep her word to him. But right now, he blamed Ivan Hamblyn; simply because he was there, and he was easy to blame. He had discovered the Penny Bright secret, he had sown the seed in Ellie's mind, he had tempted her with a record contract. The fact that it had all gone wrong for Ellie, too, provided little comfort.

'I need a drink,' he muttered to Aila. 'More than one.'

She smiled up at him uncertainly. She wore pale pink, and a rosy-coloured lipstick that made her look twenty-seven rather than forty-seven. '*Lemmikki*? That sounds ominous.'

Ivan tried to catch his attention with a casual wave. George felt the thunderclouds gather on his brow and looked away. 'Do you want something, Aila?' he asked, his voice hard.

'Pernod, please,' she replied uncertainly.

He found a chair for Aila and left her, making for the bar. The first gin and tonic he drank on the spot, the second he nursed jealously. Aila's drink order was forgotten. Ivan stood next to him, smiling. *Smiling.*

'Hello, George,' he said, and George was glad to hear he sounded nervous.

'Ivan,' George replied gruffly, turning away.

'George, wait. I understand you're angry with me...'

'We don't have to be friends, Ivan,' George snapped, and hurried back to Aila. At first he couldn't find her, then realised that she was precisely where he'd left her, only a little crowd had gathered around her. More precisely, a little crowd had gathered around Charlie Crowe, who had parked himself on a chair next to Aila. George threw back the gin and tonic and returned to the bar for another. He joined the edge of the group around Charlie, just as Charlie delivered the punchline to one of his merry anecdotes, and everyone burst into laughter.

''Ere's me guvnor!' Charlie said expansively, holding out both arms to George. One hand held a cigarette, the other held a bottle of Scotch. He was drinking it neat.

'Evening, Charlie,' George managed. He glanced at Aila, and felt that horrible surge of jealousy again. All at once, he suspected her. She never normally came to these events, but she'd insisted tonight. She'd bought a new outfit; hell, she was even wearing high heels. He hadn't seen her in heels since her fortieth birthday, when she'd declared them too uncomfortable to bother with anymore. She wasn't looking at Charlie, but she seemed to be trying too hard *not* to look at him.

Charlie launched into another anecdote. The party was growing noisy. The main lights had been turned down so only the Christmas lights illuminated the room. George drained his drink, thought about getting another. He wasn't normally much of a drinker, and the gin was going to his head. Everything took on a surreal cast. Charlie lit another cigarette. Aila hadn't moved, hanging on everything he said.

Finally, Charlie returned his attention to George. 'Sit down with us, guv. Better protect your lovely wife from me. She's lookin' good enough to steal away.'

George set his teeth and reached for Aila's hand. 'Come on,' he said. 'I need to introduce you to somebody.'

When they were free from Charlie's coterie, George released Aila's hand and headed for the bar again.

'Who are you going to introduce me to?' she asked, hurrying to keep up with him.

'What? Oh. Nobody. I just wanted to get you away from Charlie.'

'Why?'

He faced her. Did she sound disappointed? Angry with him? 'Because... I thought...'

'And where's my drink?'

George turned towards the bar. 'I'll get it now.'

Her hand, like steel on his wrist, stopped him. Her voice dropped to a harsh whisper. 'No, George. Forget it. Forget the stupid drink and answer a question for me: Why are you acting like this?'

At that moment, the disc jockey fired up his record player. Charlie's latest single boomed through the speakers. There was a shout of delight from the corner. He turned to see Charlie doing a silly jig on his chair, while the others clapped him on. Aila watched a moment, a smile on her lips, then returned her attention to George. His jealousy must have been written all over his face.

'*Lemmikki*,' she said. 'What's going on?'

He felt confused, angry. 'I might ask you the same thing,' he said. 'What do you mean?'

'You seem quite taken with Charlie.'

Aila blinked, almost as though somebody had threatened to hit her. Deep down, George felt a swirl of guilt, but pushed it away.

'Well? Are you going to deny it?'

Two spots of red stood out on her pale cheeks, and George was dimly aware that he had rarely seen her this angry, and that if he were perfectly sober it would alarm him. 'Deny what? Are you accusing me of something?'

George hesitated, realising he had waded in too far. 'You can't deny you're attracted to him.'

'Of course, he's an attractive man. But I don't think that's the problem, here. I think the problem is you suspect me of betraying you.'

'I... No, Aila. I trust you. It's him I don't trust.'

'What nonsense. Charlie may be a little wild, but he respects you. He's a good person, *Lemmikki*. He has a good heart.'

George wanted to respond that he disagreed, that she had been fooled by his charm. But he would have sounded petulant.

Aila took both his hands. 'You've forced me to say this, but I'm going to say it. You have been different since Penny left you.'

A flare of irritation, embarrassment, resentment. He flung her hands away from him violently, and as he did so she stumbled backwards – unused to high heels – and almost fell. She caught his arm to steady herself, turning disbelieving eyes up to him. All around them, the party spun on, oblivious. Glasses clinked, music played, laughter rose in raucous bursts from around the room. His heart raced; he had been rough with her. What was wrong with him?

'Do you see what I mean?' she said. 'You used to be kinder, more forgiving. Now look at you. Refusing to acknowledge Ivan Hamblyn, snarling at Charlie, accusing me of I-don't-know-what.' She took a deep breath, then continued, 'I've often thought you must have been in love with Penny, because you were much happier when she was around.'

'My relationship with Penny was entirely business,' he replied, aware that he should rebuff the suggestion before it grew wings.

'Rubbish. You adored her.'

'I didn't... I wasn't sexually attracted to her.'

'I don't care if you were, *Lemmikki*, I trusted you not to act on those impulses even if they were present.' She straightened her cardigan. 'It's a pity you can't trust me the same way.'

George found himself battling conflicting emotions. He was frustrated that this discussion had turned around, so that now it was he who was in trouble: she was the one making eyes at a much younger man. But he also felt sad for her resigned tone, the calm way she accepted that he had spent so much time with a young, beautiful woman. One that, she was right, he adored.

'I do trust you,' he said, wondering if he meant it. He glanced over at Charlie, who was watching them. Could he tell from their tight expressions that they were arguing? Charlie raised his glass and winked broadly, and George shuddered with rage. Yes, Charlie knew they were arguing, he had guessed it was about him, and he was enjoying it.

The disc jockey had put on an old swing record, and the mood of the music was at odds with their tense exchange. Aila sighed. She pushed her hair behind her ears and fixed George in her gaze. 'I do love you, George, but at the moment you're hard to like. Penny left years ago. You must move on. You must get over it. It's ruining you.'

'Why the long faces?' This was Charlie, slapping George's back, shouting in a harsh, drunk voice. 'Come on, lovely,' he said to Aila, ''ave a dance with me.'

'Oh, no, thank you, Charlie,' Aila responded graciously. 'These shoes are hurting my feet. I can't think what possessed me to wear them.'

'Ah, come on. Just a quick spin around the room.'

George realised Charlie was goading him, and forced a smile. 'It's all right, Aila. You go and dance. I'll catch up with some business colleagues.'

Aila looked uncertainly from George to Charlie.

'Go on,' he said again.

Charlie grabbed her hand and pulled her towards the dance floor. George watched them for a few moments. Charlie whispered something in her ear, and Aila's uncertain expression was replaced by one of delight and laughter. Charlie dipped her dramatically, and they began to spin around the floor. Charlie's grace and fine footwork were a revelation. George had to look away. He spotted the bar, and found himself heading back there for another drink.

He *had* changed, he knew it. Or rather, he had *un*changed. Time was rolling backwards and he was in danger of becoming the person Aila had saved him from. Losing Penny and Ellie in quick succession represented too many bad things to him: hindering the big career success that would finally make him independent of Aila's family money, memories of ill times and dark regrets, and fears about a shadow inside him he thought he had conquered long ago, the fear that he was becoming more like his father.

No matter how much this regression troubled him, he was powerless to stop it.

TWENTY-SEVEN

*E*llie felt curiously unmoved by the audience's applause.

As she walked offstage and into the wings after the encore for *La traviata*'s opening night, she felt none of the sense of elevation and joy that she'd expected. The audience had been appreciative; an extra burst of loud applause had followed her individual bow. She had sung well, much better than Nancy McKenzie who had lost her support during *Ah forsè lui* and squawked through the famous coloratura runs. She examined her feelings carefully, as she sat in the dressing-room and began to remove her heavy make-up with cold cream. Could it be that she was too consumed with bitterness and jealousy to enjoy the simple pleasures of music? Now she couldn't meet her own gaze in the mirror, disliking what she had become.

There was a knock at the door and Ellie steeled herself. The ill will from the cast had become unbearable; she didn't want to see anyone.

'Come in,' she managed.

Andre Anderson slipped through the door and closed it behind him. 'Penelope, congratulations. You sang beautifully.'

She couldn't help but smile. 'Thank you, Andre.'

'I was told a number of times that it was a mistake to hire you, but you've rewarded my faith in you.' He pulled up a chair and sat on it neatly, his small hands smoothing his little goatee. 'I need to speak to you about next year. More work.'

Ellie's ears pricked up. She had been worried about what would happen once this season was over. 'Go on,' she said.

'I've had a word with Nancy McKenzie, who I've engaged to sing the lead in a production of *Dido and Aeneas*. She's requested you as her understudy.'

Ellie couldn't make her tongue move. Nancy McKenzie had treated her with barely contained contempt through rehearsals, criticising her for every dropped breath or covered note. Ellie's delight at being offered more work was immediately replaced by suspicion.

Finally, she managed to say, 'Nancy wants me?'

'She was insistent.'

Time ticked on as Ellie turned this over in her mind. Andre was no doubt expecting her to jump at the chance. Only one bad cold stood between her and the leading role she'd dreamed of. But something felt wrong to Ellie. Why would Nancy provide this opportunity? She thought about their first meeting, the joy Nancy had expressed that Ellie was to play her maid. And she knew: Nancy was threatened by Ellie's superior talent. Having her as an understudy kept her close; prevented her from taking other, better, work in the season; made sure she remained inferior. Nancy was gambling on not being sick, on Ellie never singing the role except in rehearsals.

But what was she to do if she didn't take this part? She had to pay her rent, and no other opera company in England would touch her. Perhaps that was the problem, perhaps she needed to get out of England. London had once been the place where everything was happening for her; now it was becoming the place where her career was stagnating, poisoned by bitchy reviewers and apathy. She had no record company anymore, she could be poor in Germany just as well as she could be poor in London. Thinking of home set her to thinking about Dieter, of the huge mistake she'd made in leaving him, in letting him go. Was it too late to go back, wipe out the last two and a half years and start again?

'Penelope?' Andre said. 'Is something wrong?'

'I won't be an understudy for Nancy McKenzie,' she said proudly. 'I'm better than her, and she knows it.'

She expected an angry retort, but Andre laughed. 'My dear, everyone knows it. But this business doesn't work like that: talent and success aren't equivalent. You have to grasp the opportunities that are presented. Don't be too proud, you're going to find it hard to get work otherwise.'

'I don't care. I won't play her game.'

Andre shrugged and rose. 'If that's your decision…'

'It is.'

'Well. Give my best to Ivan, won't you?' He made a little salute with his fingers on his brow, then closed the door behind him. Ellie quickly finished removing her make-up and changed into street clothes. Before she could think twice, she counted through the money in her purse and left the theatre to find a phone box.

Outside, a light unseasonal snow whirled in the wake of speeding cars and fell gracefully to the ground. The cold was tight and icy, and Ellie pulled her hat down over her ears. She found a phone box around the corner, under a sputtering streetlight. The door swung shut but the cold still crept under it. She peeled off her gloves and fed money into the slot. The operator helped her find the only number for Neumann in Kokondorf.

The operator connected her, and she found herself talking, for the first time in years, to Frau Neumann.

'Hello. It's Ellie Frankel,' she said.

'Hello, Ellie,' Frau Neumann replied warily.

Ellie remembered when such a guarded tone would have been unthinkable between the two of them, and ached for times passed. 'Frau Neumann, I'm looking for Dieter. Is he there with you?'

A brief silence – only a moment – prepared Ellie for disappointment. 'I'm sorry, Ellie, but he's not.'

'He finally moved out, then?' she joked, but the joke fell flat.

'You might say that. He left a week ago for Sydney.'

'Sydney? In Australia?'

'That's right.'

Ellie's head spun. Her timing was terrible. Just when she'd decided to renew contact, he was thousands and thousands of miles away. 'Do you have a contact number for him?'

'I can give you the address. He doesn't have the phone on yet.'

Ellie scrabbled in her bag for a pen and paper. 'Go on.'

As Frau Neumann dictated the address, Ellie wondered how much a flight to Sydney would cost. More than she could afford, of course. Perhaps if she sent him a letter...

'Ellie, I need to tell you something important,' Frau Neumann said. 'About Dieter.'

The snow outside intensified. 'What is it?' she asked, fearful of Frau Neumann's sober tone.

'Dieter's married now.'

The statement was like a jab to her heart. *Dieter married?* 'To whom?'

'A very nice young woman named Ingrid. They're expecting a baby in February.'

Ellie sagged against the side of the phone booth. Deep in her heart, she had always cherished the fantasy that there would be a time for her and Dieter. They were young and she knew, even though the ending had been so nasty, that he loved her. Didn't he want that too? Why on earth had he married someone else?

Perhaps it was because she hadn't contacted him in two and a half years. Because she was too concerned with her career, with money, with fame. With everything that didn't matter. Perhaps he had found somebody who, like him, never lost sight of what mattered.

'I'm very happy for him,' she managed to squeak. 'Pass on my congratulations when you next write to him.'

'You could write to him yourself,' Frau Neumann said.

'No...no. I –' With a clunk, her last coin dropped through the slot and the call cut off. Ellie gazed forlornly at the address, written on the back of a bus ticket. She folded it carefully and tucked it into her purse, before turning her eyes to the street outside. The traffic kept moving, the light above the phone box kept flickering, the snow kept falling. All indifferent to her distress.

Once, she'd believed she'd had nothing, but she'd possessed something sweeter and more precious than she'd known. She had squandered her blessings. Now she knew what true empty-handedness was.

Angela couldn't shake the blues.

This was not the first Christmas she had spent alone. For all she knew, she might have spent every Christmas alone. But this time it bothered her. She sat in the armchair in the corner of her room, idly flicking through a book by the dim illumination of a string of star-shaped Christmas lights hung on her window.

It was strange how, even without her memory, she could feel homesick at this time of year. She couldn't remember a single English Christmas, but she knew that Greek Christmas felt different: more solemn, ringing with Byzantine carols and smelling sweetly of *melomacarona* biscuits and spit-roasted lamb. Presents had been exchanged weeks ago. Christmas Eve didn't feel festive, expectant. She felt lonely. She felt lost.

She supposed she could have gone up to see Silas to spend time with him and his family. She was always welcome there, and the taverna was closed. She could have even taken the walk up to Mia's house: the older woman would probably have appreciated it. There were many ways that Angela could have found company and banished the loneliness, but she pursued none of them. Perhaps she was enjoying the melancholy too much.

Angela reached for the glass of red wine that sat on the bedside table. At least the b & b was quiet: only one guest. It was almost like having a holiday.

As soon as she had the thought, the bell at the front counter rang. She put aside the book and the glass of wine and rose wearily to her feet. Would they want more towels? A late-night snack? Or had the hot water run out?

The French tourist waited. Her Greek was terrible, and Angela struggled to comprehend her. Eventually they understood each other: she wanted a late-night snack. Angela explained she usually only provided breakfast, but offered to make some toast and tea. She went through the tasks quickly in the quiet kitchen, then returned to her room.

Almost as soon as she sat down, the bell rang again. She sighed, thought about not getting it. After all, it was Christmas Eve. Perhaps if she wrote up a sign and taped it to the counter, they would leave her alone.

The bell rang again, repeatedly, and she pulled herself to her feet. Silas was always saying that the French were rude; maybe he was right. She hurried down the hallway and rounded the corner to the entryway.

A figure, both familiar and unfamiliar at the same time, waited in the soft lamplight.

'Jerry!'

He smiled at her, his eyes crinkling up in merriment. 'Merry Christmas.' He held out a card. 'I told you to expect one of these things.'

Suddenly, she was shy with him. She approached and took the card, but couldn't meet his gaze. 'What are you doing here?'

'I wanted to be somewhere warm for Christmas. I thought the Cyclades would be nice.' He moved towards her and picked up her hands. 'I thought your arms would be nicer.'

She looked up into his smiling eyes, and her shyness seemed foolish. It didn't matter that she'd only spent four days with him, it didn't matter that all she knew about him she had gleaned from his frequent, warm and amusing letters. She felt as though she had known him forever. She threw her arms around him and he pulled her tight.

'Ah, that's better,' he said, his breath tickling her ear. 'There's been something missing since I left here, Angela. I hope you don't mind me coming back to find it.'

'I don't mind a bit,' she replied, standing back to gaze at him. 'Do you know where to start looking?'

He smiled mischievously. 'Maybe up in your bedroom?'

Angela was both thrilled to her core and desperately uncertain. She didn't know what to do, she didn't even know if she'd done this before. She thought about the awful memory, the man with the camera, but then pushed it aside. Jerry was insistent. He grasped her hand in his, and led her back up the hallway. He kicked the door closed behind them, and pressed her up against it, his hips against hers, murmuring her name against her ear. She relaxed into him, tangling her fingers in his long hair. With expert fingers, he unbuttoned her blouse, and his warm hands moved inside. Angela gasped as a hot wave of desire swept over her. The heat and firmness of his body, his intoxicating *maleness*: it was like a spell on her senses, and she succumbed to him willingly.

'The bed, the bed,' she whispered between kisses, and he scooped her up and carried her there, laying her down gently by the glow of the Christmas lights. Here, they slowed, taking their time in peeling off each other's clothes, allowing flesh to meet flesh in measured delight. Deep sensations swirled through her: she must surely have never experienced this before, because she would have remembered such pleasure, such white-hot desire blooming in her body. Jerry covered her body with his, and she said softly, 'Be gentle, I've never done this before.'

He smiled. 'I'm always gentle,' he said, and moved inside her.

It was only later, passions spent, as they lay in warm silence, that he asked her about her request. 'So, that was really your first time?'

'I think so,' she replied.

He sat up, looking down at her. His hair trailed over his shoulder. 'What do you mean?'

'I mean... I can't remember... and I'm sure I'd remember... *that.*'

Jerry was clearly puzzled, and she knew she'd have to explain to him.

'I have no recollection of my life before an accident three years ago.'

Jerry laughed, then sobered quickly when he saw no smile in response. 'You're serious, aren't you?'

'Yes.'

He gazed at her a long time, and she grew uncomfortable.

'Don't look at me like that. You make me feel like a sideshow attraction,' she said defensively.

'Oh, no. No, of course you're not.' He leaned down to kiss her collarbone. 'Babe, I didn't mean to offend you. It's just so…wild. How did it happen?'

'I don't know. I woke up in a field in Spain, made my way here… and made a new life.' She dropped her voice to a whisper. 'I think I was running from something. Or someone.'

He settled next to her on the pillow, his face very close to hers, and stroked her hair gently off her face. 'Angela Smith, you just keep getting more and more fascinating. Have you tried to remember? To find out who you were?'

She shook her head. 'I don't want to. I'm happy as I am.'

He looked as though he might say something, but held his tongue. He flipped onto his back, gazing up at the ceiling. 'You know, I could really get used to living down here on Petaloudos. You don't have a room available, do you?'

'I do,' she said with a smile. 'But you'll have to share it with an overworked b & b manager.'

'That's all right. How long is it available for?'

She propped herself up on her elbow and kissed his stubbled cheek. She was being pulled out to sea by an unrelenting tide. It was as terrifying as it was exhilarating. 'Forever if you want it.'

'I like those terms,' he replied.

And he stayed.

Ivan was awkward with Ellie on the drive southwest into the Sussex countryside. She supposed it was the strange nature of today's event, and tried to be as natural as she could to compensate.

'Do you get out here to visit your family much?' she asked, as they wound down a narrow road. Low stone fences, overgrown with moss and bare vines, lined the way. A light snow had fallen the night before, but had melted off with the fine, but cool, weather.

'I see them at Christmas, and birthdays.' He drummed the steering wheel with his fingers. 'That's about all.'

'You're not close then?'

Ivan gave her a crooked smile, then turned his eyes back to the road. 'I'm afraid not.'

Ellie wanted to ask why, but sensed it might be rude. Ivan surprised her by filling in the details without being asked.

'I was raised by nannies. A new one every year until I was seven. Then it was boarding school. I believe families need time together to grow to like each other.' The car slowed. 'Here we are.' He indicated and turned into a wide driveway.

Now Ivan's reserve, his declaration that he was 'just not interested in all that nonsense' of meeting and dating women, made more sense: a remote family, a lifetime of being kept distant from others. She almost felt sorry for him. Until they swept up the hill and she caught her first glimpse of Dovercourt Manor.

A large, beautifully kept Georgian manor house, it stood at the top of a long driveway lined by poplars encircling a dark lake. The grounds to the east extended back into woodlands as far as Ellie could see. The gardens surrounding the house itself were perfectly tidy, brimming with neat topiaries, bordered flowerbeds, rows of ancient box and a rockery extending down to the driveway. Ivan pulled up his little white Ford in the parking circle, next to a gleaming Rolls Royce. She felt unbearably intimidated.

'Ah, my brother's here already,' Ivan said, indicating the car. He reached over to the back seat for the basket of wrapped gifts. 'We'd best get inside straightaway and show you off. I'll take you down to the woodland walk after lunch.'

She climbed out of the car, hoping she didn't look as agog as she felt. She had to remember to keep her cool. Rich people believed they were better than everyone else: she wouldn't let them suspect that she believed it too.

'It's beautiful in summer,' Ivan said, gesturing towards the gardens. 'Mummy's famed for her day lilies. A shame you can't see it then.'

Ellie thought that it was a shame too. A shame that a life like this, of historic mansions and Rolls Royces and famous day lilies, should be hers to glimpse only once. She tried to push down her envy, her conviction that it was all so terribly unfair. They ascended the stone steps to the front doors, which were open, and made their way into a wide, tiled entrance hall.

'Mummy? We're here,' Ivan called, pocketing his car keys and taking Ellie's hand.

A skinny young woman in a plain black dress popped her head out. 'They're down in the conservatory, Mr Hamblyn,' she said.

'Thank you, Elizabeth. This way, Ellie.'

As they moved through the house, Ellie glimpsed room after room of rich rugs, gilded ornaments, polished antiques. But it almost seemed as though nobody lived here, as though Dovercourt Manor was a museum rather than a family home. Finally, they arrived at the conservatory. The winter sun poured through the tall glass panes and bathed the room in light. This room was more home-like, filled with green pot plants, comfortable sofas, and the laughter and shouting of children. Ivan introduced her, and she got her first glimpse of his family.

His brother, Raymond, was dark-haired with an affable smile and big hairy hands. Raymond's wife, Jayne, was a horse-faced woman with a cutglass accent who barely acknowledged Ellie's presence. Their three children – Benjamin, Alisdair and Peter – were carbon copies of their father in descending size, all with the same haircut and, cruelly in Ellie's opinion, all dressed identically. She quickly lost track of which boy was which, as they circled madly around the grand piano, or gathered solemnly under the enormous Christmas tree and its mountain of presents. Ivan's cousin Cornelia was there, a forty-something frump with a bowl haircut and a sensible cream twinset; and on her arm was her slim, pale-eyed husband Bernie whose gaze never left Ivan.

Lord Dovercourt himself must have been at least eighty, sitting tight-lipped in his rocking chair with a plaid rug over his knees. Ellie could see no outward signs of ill health, but nor could she see any signs of happiness, or an awareness of his many blessings. It was almost as though he was a painting, not part of the scene at all, but a backdrop to it. Finally, there was Lady Dovercourt, a well-preserved sixty-something with a beehive of silver hair and slender, white hands.

She took Ellie's fingers in hers and said, 'It is such a delight to meet you, my dear.' But there was a coolness behind her expression that suggested the warmth might be a performance. Ellie could have laughed: she wasn't the only person performing.

Ellie was invited to sit, and she quietly observed the family gathering, smiling in the right places, speaking only when spoken to, and all the while marvelling at the wealth that surrounded her. At the insistence of the little boys, the presents were opened. Soon the room was littered with torn wrapping paper, and the boys were despatched to the cold pathway outside the conservatory to ride their new toy cars, shoot each other with their new toy guns, and document the fun with their new instant cameras. Lady Dovercourt presented Ellie with a thin package, and she expressed her delight effusively before opening it. A canary yellow scarf and matching gloves.

'They're handmade in France, you know,' Lady Dovercourt said.

'They're lovely,' Ellie replied, half-tempted to say what her father might have: 'What makes you think the French are good at anything?'

'The colour will really suit you,' Jayne said, and Ellie wondered if Jayne had even looked at her. With her sallow skin and brown eyes, yellow was the last colour she'd choose for herself.

'Ellie, we know nothing about you,' Raymond said, refilling his glass from the whisky decanter on the sideboard and settling on the couch opposite her. 'Ivan's been very secretive,' he added with a grin. 'Do you work for a living?'

'I'm an opera singer,' she said. 'I work under the stage name Penelope Bright.'

'Ah, that's how you met!' Lady Dovercourt said. 'We had wondered.'

'You must sing for us,' croaked a voice, and Ellie turned to see it was Lord Dovercourt, a statue come to life.

'Now, Henry, I'm sure the young woman is not interested in singing for her supper.'

'I shan't hear no,' he replied. 'Go on, lass. Sing something. She says she can sing, I want to hear it.'

Ellie was unsure how to respond. She looked at Ivan who shrugged and said, 'If that's what Daddy wants.'

'It is,' he croaked, and there was such steel in his voice that Ellie jumped out of her seat and readied herself to sing.

'Wait, Ellie,' Ivan said, standing up and moving towards the piano. 'I'll accompany you.'

She was about to say, 'I didn't know you could play,' but realised it might undermine the appearance that they were a couple. 'That would be lovely,' she said instead.

'How about *Casta diva*?' Ivan said, expertly running through a scale.

It had been the third track on her album. 'Fine,' she said, moving to stand in the curve of the grand piano.

Ivan played the opening figures, and Ellie was surprised by his dexterity, his tenderness. She centred herself and began to sing. Raymond, Cornelia and Bernie watched with polite smiles, Lord Dovercourt fixed his gaze on middle distance and sat silently, almost sullenly; but Jayne and Lady Dovercourt talked to each other right through the whole performance. It was unsettling, and she felt embarrassed for being so willing to sing for a group of strangers. When she finished, only Raymond clapped his hands generously. Jayne and Lady Dovercourt continued their conversation as though nothing had happened, Cornelia turned to Bernie to ask him for a tissue, and Lord Dovercourt didn't move or make a sound. It was as though he'd fallen asleep with his eyes open.

Ivan rounded the piano and took her hand. 'Beautiful, my dear.'

'Thank you,' Ellie said uncertainly.

The three little boys burst back inside, and Elizabeth arrived at the door to tell them lunch was served. They headed into the huge formal dining room to eat.

It was only halfway through the woodland walk that Ellie realised Cornelia and Lady Dovercourt had deliberately separated her from Ivan. They worked together like hunting dogs: Ivan was waylaid by a plea from Cornelia to show her a rare old book he had mentioned;

while Ellie was drawn deep into the shady tunnel between the trees by Lady Dovercourt's insistence that she see a rare type of fern not grown anywhere else in Sussex. Clouds had rolled in over lunch, and now an icy drizzle began to fall, but Lady Dovercourt – who still hadn't offered her first name to Ellie – staunchly raised an umbrella and tucked Ellie under it with her, their arms linked at the elbows.

'You must see the fairy grotto,' she said. 'A little rain never hurt anyone.'

The rain had cleared by the time they arrived at the fairy grotto, which consisted of a ring of red-and-white toadstool seats under a weeping willow. Lady Dovercourt invited Ellie to sit on one of the toadstools, which she did. However, Lady Dovercourt remained standing.

'I had these built when Henry and I first married. I'd hoped for a little girl, but God had other plans.'

'The boys never came here?'

'Henry wouldn't have it. Didn't want them to turn out soft. Especially Ivan. He was always a sensitive boy.' Lady Dovercourt fixed her with an unwavering gaze, and Ellie was reminded of bugs on pins. 'He likes you.'

'Ivan?'

'Lord Dovercourt.'

Ellie was surprised. Lord Dovercourt had barely spoken a word to anyone at lunch, and had retired for an afternoon nap directly after. 'Did he say so?' she asked carefully.

'I can tell. We've been married forty-three years. I know what he's thinking. He likes you.' Lady Dovercourt began to pace. 'It's rare he likes anyone. God knows he hates Jayne.' She stopped and turned to Ellie with that pinpoint gaze again. 'Will you marry Ivan?'

'I... I've not thought of it, to be honest.'

Lady Dovercourt snorted. 'Oh, rubbish. You've thought of it. If not before today, you must have thought of it the moment you saw the manor. It could be yours one day.'

Ellie was momentarily overwhelmed by this thought, and Lady Dovercourt's words echoed in her mind. *It could be yours...*

'I'll be frank with you, Ellie, we need Ivan to be married. And not to somebody his own age. There must be children. You're young, his Lordship likes you, the way is clear for marriage.'

'My Lady, I –'

'Now hear me out. Ivan's a good man. He'd treat you well. He's generous, thoughtful, and I believe he's more handsome than Raymond if you look objectively. Raymond always had charm, but Ivan has a noble brow.' The drizzle had started again, but Lady Dovercourt was oblivious to it. 'You even share a common interest in music: Henry and I never had a single thing in common and we've been happy for a very long time.'

Ellie might have laughed, were she alone. Here she was, sitting on a painted toadstool in a fairy grotto in the rain, being given the hard sell on a very eligible bachelor. She wondered if she should tell Ivan.

'Well?' Lady Dovercourt asked. 'What do you think?'

'I think Ivan might have other ideas.'

'Cornelia is working on Ivan as we speak. We wouldn't leave anything to chance.'

Ellie tried a smile, but it was greeted with a stony expression. 'I think such things should progress more...naturally.'

'Nonsense. The best marriages are practical, not romantic. If you can believe that, you can be a happy woman.'

The rain intensified. Ellie stood. 'I'm sorry, can we go back? I'm getting wet.'

The umbrella was raised again, and Lady Dovercourt offered her arm. 'Just think about what I've said. That's all I ask.'

Ellie couldn't help but think about it. Lady Dovercourt was right about Ivan, and she felt she was seeing him in a new light. He played piano beautifully, sensitively. He spoke her native tongue fluently. He had always been kind to Ellie, but never overstepped any boundaries of familiarity. He was a true gentleman and, if she looked very closely, she could even see the noble brow of which his mother spoke. But why was she thinking such things? She'd never seen Ivan as more than a friend, a much older friend at that. He certainly wasn't Dieter, with his hot skin and his miles-deep eyes.

But Dieter was married. To someone else.

She felt as though she knew Ivan much better when they climbed into the car at the end of the day. The sky was growing dim, and the rain had set in. They were silent with each other as they pulled out of the long driveway and into the road. Finally, Ellie said, 'Ivan, do you really think your father will leave his estate to Raymond instead of you?'

'I don't know.'

'The manor is beautiful. You must want it.'

He didn't answer straightaway. His eyes were fixed on the road and his mouth twisted into a tight smile. 'Well,' he said gruffly, 'of course I want it.'

Ellie took a deep breath. She knew now how they could both get what they wanted. 'I think you will have it one day,' she said softly, resting her hand on his knee.

Ivan jolted, glanced down at her hand but didn't brush it off. Instead, he said, 'Maybe you're right.'

TWENTY-EIGHT
1979

*A*ngela woke one cool February morning and realised with a shock that she hadn't seen Mia in over two months.

She cursed herself for being a bad friend. But then, she had been tied up with other things. Here, she glanced across to the warm male body sleeping soundly next to her. Jerry, with his smooth shoulder exposed above the sheets, his long hair trailing over his face. Her secret lover. As soon as Silas had guessed that they were sharing a room, he had become very cold towards her and made her promise not to tell another soul.

'I am ashamed of you, Angela,' he had said, and for once his stern façade couldn't be teased away. 'Make sure that nobody else knows, for it will do your reputation great harm.'

So she pretended she had hired Jerry, that he was staying in one of the other rooms. If anybody bothered to do the maths on how many rooms she had and how many people were staying, then her secret would be out. But perhaps all that mattered was that she wasn't open about their relationship.

Angela stretched, then climbed out of bed. She would deal with Mia a little later. The breakfasts had to be made, and it was Tuesday so that meant it was her turn. Jerry was paying his board by helping out around the b & b. He did breakfast four mornings a week, had taken over the onerous laundry chores, and was slowly clearing up all the little jobs that Angela put off due to lack of time. Tap washers had been changed, scuff marks sanded off walls, hinges oiled and all the shelves cleaned and organised. She had been so used to a hectic pace, the endless round of work, that she found herself bored sometimes now. But if boredom ever set in, Jerry would whisk her off for a walk on the beach, or a drink at the taverna.

Jerry also revealed a very valuable hidden talent. Before taking off backpacking around the world, he had earned a degree in architecture, though he had never practised. He had taken one look at the plans for the extension and asked Angela, 'Is there any chance you'll ever want to build another storey on this place?' When she'd said perhaps, he'd taken his pencil and drawn all over the plans, explaining that the current rebuilding would limit any future extensions. That's what she'd been thinking about in her half-slumber on waking this morning, and that's what had made her remember Mia. Mia had to approve the plans, and of course she would. She had made it clear that the house on the bluff had to be changed completely. But Angela hadn't seen her for a long time, not since before Christmas, and in her frail state of mind it was probably best if she wasn't left alone for too much longer.

Angela took a moped up to the front gates of Mia's mansion shortly after two o'clock. The day had barely warmed at all, but Silas said it was the last shred of winter cold before spring. Angela believed him. It was as though, just behind the cool wind, was the promise of something warm and brimming with life. It filled her with a sense of hope and peace, and she wondered briefly about her life before, and if she had ever felt that way in her shadowy past. She didn't believe so; if she had, her brain wouldn't have been so ready to forget it.

She climbed off the moped and walked up to the gate. 'Mia!' she called. No answer. That was fairly typical. She waited and called again, then remembered that Mia usually took an afternoon sleep in her southern bedroom. She moved to the side wall and called, 'Mia! It's Angela. I need to see you!' Minutes passed, she tried again, and still there was no answer.

Angela frowned, the first needle of worry touching her heart. It wasn't simply that Angela hadn't been to see her, she hadn't run into her at the markets, or heard complaints about her from others in the village... Had she not been out of her home all this time? Mia spoke of being ill so often these days, that Angela didn't take her seriously. But what if she was sick with nobody to help her? Or even dead?

Angela hurried back to the front gate and sized it up. If she could climb to the highest bar, she might be able to get on to the brick arch and make her way down there to the wall. Then, perhaps, there would be a tree or something else to climb onto. She kicked off her shoes and gave thanks that she was wearing jeans. She made her way up, only just managing to haul herself onto the brick arch. Now she shinnied down the arch to the top of the wall. Five feet ahead, the bough of a plane tree stretched up over the wall. She tested her weight on it, wasn't at all sure it would hold her, but took the chance nonetheless. It began to creak, and she was suddenly overwhelmed by foreign images and sounds.

The lights on in a big house, running from somebody, a ripping noise, a falling sensation...

Angela caught her breath. Another memory, slipping out of the dark to trouble her. Underneath her, the branch was starting to give. She quickly crawled down it into the fork of the tree, then made her way down to the ground with only a ripped jacket and a grazed elbow to show for her trouble. Pausing at the bottom of the tree, she tried to hide the images away again. But she knew without a doubt that they were from the night she'd lost her memory. With an effort of mental will, she severed all the links from that memory in her head, letting the shadow fall again.

The present was more important; Mia was more important.

The front door was open. She pushed it in tentatively.

'Mia? Mia, are you here? It's Angela.'

The house was silent except for a ticking clock. The dust was thick, and the smell of cat urine was strong. Immediately, two of the cats were on her, miaowing loudly and winding themselves frantically around her legs. She gently kicked them off and headed up the stairs.

Her skin prickled and her heart was hot. She realised she was steeling herself for the very worst kind of discovery.

'Mia?'

A low groan. Angela broke into a run, threw open a bedroom door. There was Mia, a gaunt shadow, curled up on her side in bed.

'Mia, what happened? Are you sick? Shall I call the doctor?'

She shook her head. 'I'm dying.'

Angela looked at her closely. She was much thinner, and pale. 'What's wrong? Is it your heart?'

'I feel so weak.'

'How long have you been in bed?'

'Two weeks.'

'Why didn't you call me? I would have come.'

'Because I thought I'd be dead before you got here.'

Angela helped Mia sit up. 'How have you been looking after yourself? When did you last eat?'

Mia shrugged and wouldn't meet her eyes, and now Angela grew suspicious.

'Do you want me to make you something? A sandwich?'

'No,' she said. 'There's no food in the house.' Her hands fluttered in front of her like birds. 'I haven't been shopping. I can't go to town, it's full of dirty people and germs and…' Here she trailed off and shuddered.

'But, Mia, you have to eat. Your cats have to eat.'

Her eyes grew round and sad. 'The cats! My poor babies! But how can I buy them food if I can't go to the market?'

Angela kept asking questions, trying to figure out the situation. It seemed Mia had decided just before Christmas that the outside world was no longer safe for her, so she had carefully eked out the last of her food over the previous nine weeks. This accounted for her gaunt appearance. The food had run out two days ago, the cat food had run out yesterday. But she wouldn't be convinced, by any means, to go shopping.

Finally, with a sigh, Angela said, 'Would you like me to go shopping for you?'

The question wasn't even complete before Mia sat bolt upright and said, 'Would you?'

Angela thought about all the other things she needed to do, reminded herself it was low season and she was lucky to have one guest a week at the moment, and headed down to the village grocer.

On her way back up the winding stairs to where she had parked her moped, she ran into Doctor Moscopolos.

'Good afternoon, Angela. I haven't seen you in a while.' He gave her a frown of bemusement. 'Is our patient feeling well again?'

Angela knew that Mia wouldn't want her problems aired, but she figured the doctor already knew most of them. 'Actually, she's decided that there are too many germs out here and has locked herself away.' She held up a shopping bag. 'I've been elected to bring the food.'

He touched her arm. 'You're very good to her, dear,' he said. 'You know she isn't sick at all. The palpitations...she brings them on.'

'She's convinced she's dying.'

'I've seen it before, and people sometimes die simply because they believe they will.' Here he shook his head. 'Not Crazy Mia, though. She's as healthy as a horse, so don't you worry.'

'I won't,' Angela said, not sure if she meant it. She headed back up the stairs and packed the shopping bags into the basket on the back of the moped. A cold breeze chafed her cheeks. She looked back down over the village and towards the bluff, where she could see the b & b. It occurred to her that Mia's hypochondria had started around the time that the renovations had commenced. Were the two related? Mia said often that she didn't care, that she wanted all traces of what the house had been erased. But did she mean it? Was the destruction of the eastern wall akin to the destruction of some of her most important memories?

Angela turned her back and climbed on the moped, wondering again what had happened to Mia in the house on the bluff.

Ellie knew she didn't want to go to Nancy McKenzie's closing night party. She was invited, of course, albeit grudgingly. As the applause died off and the sounds of the audience leaving buzzed down through the wings and backstage, Nancy turned to Ellie and said, 'There's a party at my house. Do you want the address?' Ellie had said no. Not just because she had no friends in the cast – her fault as much as theirs: she had remained aloof for the entire run of the opera – but also because she simply didn't want to see where Nancy McKenzie lived. A house in London that was big enough to accommodate the entire cast? It would only make her jealous. Nancy was a big star with a little voice; Ellie had a big voice, and yet had watched her stardom dwindle away to nothing. The opera had had an extended season, and she was grateful for the steady income. After tonight, however, there was nothing. She would have to take a job – in a bar, perhaps, or a shop. Whether she did that in London or Munich was her next decision. In Munich, she could shake off the Penny Bright stigma, find an agent and start auditioning. But in London, there was Ivan.

Ellie and Ivan saw each other once a week on Tuesdays when she had no performances. He bought her flowers, took her to dinner. She complimented his good taste, asked after his family. He would drop her at her flat with a chaste kiss on the cheek, and a promise to come back the following Tuesday so they could do it all again. And so it had been in the weeks since Christmas. Ellie didn't find it difficult at all to like him; he was kind and personable and interested in music. But she wasn't sure if she could imagine it growing into anything else, and he was reticent about what future, if any, they had. Was he her boyfriend? She supposed he was, even though there was little intimacy in their relationship. Rather, they were like two children playing a schoolyard game: his lordship and the opera star, perfectly matched but curiously detached from one another.

Backstage, the whirl of activity and laughter slowly died away, as the cast changed out of costumes and made their way out of the theatre to Nancy's party. Ellie took her time with her make-up, and hung her costume carefully on the rack. Andre didn't come to see her, as he had on opening night, to offer her more work. There were no flowers on her dressing table as there were on the tables around her. She remembered that she hadn't yet collected a program as a memento, and made her way back across the empty stage and down through the theatre where the programs were for sale. Then she left by the front door of the theatre onto the cold street and started the walk to the bus stop. Footsteps behind her alerted her, and she turned to see Ivan waving madly.

'Ellie! Stop!'

She moved back towards him, curious.

'We've been waiting for you at the stage door,' he said, puffing, pressing a limp bouquet into her arms. His breath fogged in the air. In the streetlight, she could see he was flushed.

'We?'

'Mummy and I. We came to see your final performance. We've been waiting a long time.' He took her by the arm. 'Would you mind? Mummy wants to talk to you.'

'Of course. But let's go somewhere warm.'

Lady Dovercourt didn't look at all impressed by the interior of the café they found behind the theatre: the peeling laminate table-tops and the dusty wood panelling. But then, Lady Dovercourt never looked impressed and Ellie wondered if her face was permanently locked in an expression of mild disdain. When they'd hung up their hats and coats and found seats, she forced a smile and said to Ellie, 'You sang very well, my dear.'

'Thank you,' Ellie said. She glanced at Ivan, but he wouldn't meet her eyes. Rather, he fiddled with the edge of the table. A waitress came and took their orders for tea and coffee, and the three of them fell to uncomfortable silence.

'Well,' said Ellie to fill the silence. 'It's cold tonight, isn't it?'

Lady Dovercourt released an impatient sigh. 'Ivan has something to ask you,' she said. 'Ivan. Go on.'

Ellie was puzzled. 'Ivan?'

He tried a faltering smile. 'Ellie, Mummy and I had a long talk this afternoon, and we think it would be a good idea if you and I got married.'

And that was it. Ellie might have laughed if it wasn't such a serious moment. But then she thought of Dieter speaking about marriage: not the proposal when things were already tense between them; but the time he'd thought she was pregnant. It all returned to her in sepia-toned images. The late afternoon sunshine, the breeze flapping the clothes on the line, the wildflowers bending their heads towards autumn. Deep, unutterable melancholy washed over her. Then she regained her composure: that time had passed. She needed to think about her future. She reached across and took Ivan's hand warmly; she had already anticipated how she would answer this question. 'Yes, Ivan, that would be a good idea.'

Ivan nodded, and she sensed resignation. It mattered little: they needed each other, and many a relationship in history had started with necessity.

Lady Dovercourt took over. 'You'll have a six-month engagement and a small wedding,' she said. 'Lord Dovercourt's ill health means he can neither wait too long, nor stand too much agitation.'

Ellie wondered at whether she should be offended that her entry to the family might be considered agitating. 'Of course, I'm happy to fit in with the family's plans.'

'You'll need to give me a list of who you want invited. Very close family and friends only, please.'

Close friends? She had none. She supposed this was a failing, but she had come to England as a pop star, fawned over by shallow people she couldn't trust. And since the awful reception of her operatic album, her mistrust of those around her had grown until she'd isolated herself completely. As for family? It would be reasonable to invite her mother's family. Aunty Bea and Uncle Murray would be full of teary pride and good wishes, as they had been on the night they'd come to see the opera. They believed in love, in family, in honesty. She shrank from the idea of having them witness her marriage to Ivan. 'It's fine, Lady Dovercourt, I've nobody to invite.'

'Good then, that makes it easier. Congratulations, my dear, you must be very happy.'

Ellie reflected on this. Yes, there was a certain bright optimism about the occasion. At last she would be very, very rich. She would live in a beautiful house, surrounded by beautiful things. She would never have to worry about how to keep a roof over her head or food in her stomach. It seemed she could breathe properly again, and that did make her happy. Ivan squeezed her hand, and she tried to read his expression. He didn't seem unhappy, perhaps he was relieved too. Together they would work it out, they would make good of their situation. As long as they both got what they wanted, nothing terrible could come of it.

'I am happy,' she said. 'Of course I am.'

Jerry was indispensable at the b & b. He had taken over as unofficial supervisor on the building work, even mucking in with the builders from time to time. As the seasons turned and the bright sky grew warm, Angela became accustomed to seeing Jerry out there, shirt off, cigarette clenched between his lips, the sun glinting on his long hair. She now felt very relaxed about the extension, sure that it was planned well and being built well, all without having to struggle through difficult exchanges with Greek builders. The building was finished by the end of the low season, and the tourists began to trickle back. Then the trickle threatened to become a flood. An excellent review of Mia's Place in a popular English travel guide to Greece, meant that Angela's phone began to ring constantly. She couldn't fit everyone in, and Silas cleared out another room above the taverna and offered places for the overflow. Even so, the business was growing fast. With the extra rooms came extra work. Jerry helped all he could, but Angela soon decided to hire one of Silas's granddaughters, Delia, for the high season. Jerry began to draw plans for a top-level extension, and Angela tried to work out how she could afford to build it next low season. Captain Lianis wouldn't add any extra trips, so Angela organised for the Naxos–Amorgos ferry to make a stop at Petaloudos once a week in high season. Lilika Stathakis's sister moved to the island and opened an ice-cream and kebab shop with terrace seating onto Halki Beach. Silas, not to be outdone, also built a terrace. On any given day, there could be two dozen or more tourists in town, and they had to eat somewhere.

Angela's fleet of mopeds grew too. Jerry went to Paros to acquire them, and kept them maintained for her. He also made sure that, at least once a week, he took her with him on a ride to spend time at one of the beaches. It would have been too easy to succumb to the immense workload, and never stop. But Jerry made sure she did stop, and she was certain it kept her sane through the busiest time in her memory.

It wasn't all bliss, though. Memories were starting to creep out of the shadows. Not frequently, but regularly enough to trouble her. They were disconnected, just flashes of unpleasant sensations and scenes, but she feared that eventually they would start to join together and form sequences. Then her dreaded past would roll out all in one piece, and undo her present happiness. She had taken to saying a little mantra to herself: *Forget, forget, forget...* Usually, it worked to stop the memories forming wholly. But it frustrated and alarmed her that she wasn't completely in control of them.

She and Jerry also disagreed over Mia. Angela shopped for her weekly, then spent time up at her house cooking and freezing meals for her. Jerry thought she was too busy to bother, that it was an extra, unnecessary burden on her.

'But, Jerry,' she had said to him, 'I'm the only person on the island who likes her. I have to look after her.'

'You're not helping her by pandering to her. She's not sick. If she had to get out and do her own shopping, she'd realise that.'

She didn't expect him to understand Mia. In fact, she wasn't perfectly certain why *she* understood Mia. But deep down, she thought she knew what it was like to want to hide away from the world, to be made wheezy and breathless by open space and people.

The other note of concern Angela felt over Jerry was that the deeper she fell in love with him, the more she feared she would lose him. She could read him: he wasn't done travelling. When he spoke to the guests about the places they had seen, he would get a melancholy glaze to his eyes, and she knew that he longed to keep moving, to keep seeing things. Angela didn't feel the same. She loved Petaloudos, she loved her business, and she loved the community that had welcomed her so warmly. He may be happy for now, but she knew that eventually something would have to give. And she tried, very hard, not to love him too much.

Ellie lay, naked, under the heavy down-filled covers and listened to the shower running. It had been a long day. The wedding had gone precisely to Lady Dovercourt's specifications: it was small, brief, and caused little agitation to Lord Dovercourt, who watched with beaming pride from his chair. The garden had been decorated for the occasion, the celebrant had married them under a white marquee hung with gold ribbons and bows. Ellie wore a pale lilac dress and had her hair tied back loosely. Ivan wore a well-cut Italian suit with a blue tie the precise colour of his eyes. Everyone said they made a beautiful couple, and Ellie started to believe it.

The guests were mostly strangers to her, plum-voiced men and women who smelled of hair cream and expensive perfumes. They welcomed her warmly, some even recognised her as Penny Bright and were very interested to hear about her pseudonymous career in music, a career that they all expected her now to forswear. They ate roasted spatchcock, tiny white potatoes and artfully arranged green beans. There was a trifle for after, the sponge so soaked in brandy that Ellie was sure it would make her drunk. She and Ivan sat close, exchanging conspiratorial smiles over the painstaking airs and graces of their guests.

Evening had come at last, late and reluctantly as it does in August, and the guests had gone home. Only Ivan's cousin Cornelia and her furtive husband Bernie were hanging on, as the swarm of staff arrived to dismantle the marquee and clean up. Ivan chatted with them amiably while Ellie, tired from the day's activities, watched the cleaners and wondered when she'd be able to get to bed.

'Are you happy, dear?' Cornelia said to Ellie, a cool solicitous hand stretching out to touch Ellie's wrist.

'I am,' she said, stealing a glance at Ivan. He was deep in conversation with Bernie.

'Oh, don't worry about them. Always nattering about something.' Cornelia picked up her champagne glass, noted it was empty, then put it down again. Her face was flushed and shiny, the severe cut of her hair making her look almost mannish. 'I suppose we'd best head off shortly. But I did want to say something to you, dear.'

'What is it?'

'Love is so precious,' she said. 'Do treat him kindly.'

'Of course I will.'

'I know he'll be kind to you. A little kindness goes a long way.'

'What nonsense are you telling my wife, Nellie?' Ivan said good-naturedly, interrupting their conversation.

'Women's business,' she said with a mischievous smile. 'Much more interesting than that men's business you've been on about with Bernie.'

Ellie yawned, remembered her manners, and stopped herself.

'Ah, time for us to go,' Bernie said.

As they said their goodbyes, Ellie turned over in her head what Cornelia had said about kindness. It was such a simple idea, but so powerful. Yes, if she and Ivan could be kind to each other, it might make up for lack of real passion. She warmed herself on the thought as she followed Ivan inside.

On their way to bed, Ellie and Ivan were called into the sitting room by Lord Dovercourt, who was in high spirits and generous both with the brandy and with stories from his youth. Towards eleven, Lady Dovercourt had urged him to bed, leaving the new couple alone together for the first time that day.

Dim silence. Ivan turned to Ellie. 'We should go to bed too.'

Ellie nodded. So far they had shared nothing more than kisses, and not particularly passionate ones. But tonight was their wedding night, and all that would have to change. Ellie wished it was more than a sense of duty that drove her up the stairs to the beautifully appointed bedroom. She told herself that people could grow to desire each other, that soon the awkwardness of unfamiliarity would be replaced by the warm comfort of knowing each other's bodies. While Ivan showered, she stripped and slipped between the covers, which was where she was waiting when Ivan emerged, a towel wrapped around his waist.

A sliver of light from the bathroom was the only illumination. He shed the towel and climbed in beside her, pulling her gently against his pale hairy chest.

'Good evening, Mrs Hamblyn,' he said.

'Good evening, your Lordship.'

He smiled. 'Not yet.'

She gazed into his eyes, trying to find a shred of desire inside herself. His skin was cool, his limbs were long and lean. She ran her fingers across his ribs and he shivered. Boldly, she traced across his belly and down between his legs. He was still soft. She stroked him gently. Nothing happened.

He brushed her hand away and turned her onto her back, pinning her firmly. His lips were on hers, his tongue probing her mouth. She took his hands and put them over her breasts, but she could still feel no hardness pressed against her leg. Minutes passed, and still nothing was happening.

'Damn!' Ivan pulled away roughly, putting a foot of distance between them.

'Ivan?' she said uncertainly.

He turned back to her, and stroked her hair from her face. 'Oh, Ellie, I'm sorry. I'm just not good at this business. It's not you. You're very beautiful, dear, and I care about you very much.'

Ellie wasn't sure what to say, so she said nothing.

'Let's just curl up together and sleep. It's been a big day.'

'If that's what you want...'

'Ellie, I know it's what you want too.' He pulled her close and kissed her forehead. 'We'll work this out later.'

After breakfast, Ivan disappeared for an hour to make some business calls, and Ellie took the woodland walk alone. The sun shone brightly, and the border around the fairy grotto was now in full bloom with sweet peas, bluebells and daffodils. She leaned against the trunk of the weeping willow, her fingertips exploring the coarse ridges of the bark. One day she would own this tree. The thought was curiously hollow this morning. The distance between now and when she might take ownership seemed vast, impossible to navigate.

'Ellie?' This was Ivan, calling from far off, his voice travelling on the summer breeze.

She moved out to the path. 'Down here!' she called in return.

He took his time. The sun picked up auburn highlights in his hair, and he smiled as he approached. He really did seem fond of her, which made last night's fiasco all the more puzzling.

'Finished all your business?' she said.

'Yes. In fact, I made quite an important phone call this morning to an old friend, Louis Decaux. I hope you don't mind, we talked about you.'

'About me?'

He nodded, and wouldn't meet her eyes. She grew suspicious. The leaves of the tree stirred in the breeze.

'Yes, Louis is an entertainment agent. He specialises in opera singers. He finds them work all over Europe.'

Ellie knew where this was going now. 'I see.'

'He took very little convincing. He wants to take you on. He thinks he can find you some work straightaway, though not in England. And you'll have to be happy with small roles. Of course, I'll make sure you have somewhere nice to stay wherever you go.'

She didn't demand to know why Ivan had not introduced her to Louis before. She suspected Louis was not an 'old friend' at all, but a passing acquaintance contacted frantically in a time of need. An acquaintance who would perhaps dance to the tune of Ivan's money and power, and she thought about Andre's observation that this business was more about who one knew than how one sang.

'But if I go away...won't it cause problems with your family?'

'They won't know, dear. As long as you're back for Christmas and birthdays, they won't know.'

Ellie reflected on the practicality of Ivan's solution, and admired him all the more. Spontaneously, she threw her arms around him and kissed him full on the mouth. He flinched in surprise, then returned the kiss.

'Thank you, Ivan,' she said. 'You're turning out to be a wonderful husband.'

'I think our guests were right about us, Ellie. We *are* a beautiful couple, just not the kind of couple they think we are.' He took her hand. 'Come on, let's say our goodbyes to Mummy and Daddy. We need to get back to London.'

They retraced their steps up the woodland walk. Ellie's head was full of dreams and hopes, and she didn't regret marrying Ivan. Not one little bit.

TWENTY-NINE
1981

*I*t was a beautiful night for a party.

The September sky was clear and cloudless, and dusk still retained the warmth of the day. The sea breeze made the string of lanterns around the b & b swing rhythmically. Angela was frantically busy as usual, arranging the platters of souvlaki, stuffed calamari, and fava dip, carting bottles of ouzo and *retsina*, taking a phone call, organising fresh towels for a Lebanese man who had already gone through four towels on his two-day stay. But it was a buzzing, happy busy. Tonight was the culmination of a long period of hard work.

She had finished another round of renovations in the low season, and now Mia's Place had a second storey. Jerry had carefully overseen the whole thing, down to hanging the last painted shutter. The b & b had been consistently booked out every week, she now had three full-time staff and a part-time breakfast cook. And in the last two weeks, the final touches on the new, revamped Mia's Place had been completed: a refitted kitchen with enough gas hobs to make twenty-eight breakfasts at a time if need be; and an outdoor extension to the dining room, which looked over the bluff and out to the sparkling blue waters. A perfect location for a celebratory party.

Music and coloured lanterns and laughter and hot food and sea air. It was intoxicating, as was the champagne, brought from the mainland by Jerry on one of his many trips. He and Captain Lianis had almost come to blows over the cartons of expensive alcohol. Jerry had only booked a passenger fare and piled the cartons along the side of the seating rows; but Captain Lianis said that six cartons constituted cargo and he should pay appropriate rates. An agreement had been reached, with Captain Lianis happily taking six bottles of champagne for his trouble. Jerry's ability to charm anyone was becoming legendary on Petaloudos, and she knew that some of the older village women had begun to gossip about a possible wedding for the island's two favourite adoptees. Angela didn't let herself think about those possibilities. She loved Jerry, and he loved her. But she suspected he wasn't the marrying kind so she never mentioned it. Nor did he.

Angela paused a few minutes on the inside of the folding doors to the terrace. It seemed half the island had turned up to her party, and they were busily catching up on gossip, telling jokes, and making quick work of Jerry's champagne. She sipped her own glass and searched the crowd for Mia. She didn't really expect her to show, but she had invited her nonetheless. A celebration for Mia's Place ought necessarily to have Mia in attendance, and she hadn't seen the b & b in…well, it might be years. She never left her house and Angela knew she had deliberately grown a tree to block the view of it from her upper storey windows. Was she not even a little curious?

A pair of warm arms slipped around her waist. Jerry kissed her cheek. 'Enjoying yourself?' he asked.

She leaned into him. 'I am. It's a beautiful night.'

'It is.' He squeezed her hard. 'Can I get you more champagne?'

'I'd better not. What if one of the guests has an emergency?'

Jerry waved away her concern. 'Come on, it's a party. It's *your* party. Let your hair down.' Without waiting for an answer, he moved off to the long table outside to get her a drink. She followed him with her eyes, and realised she could make out a familiar figure in the dark beyond the circle of the party lights.

'Mia?' she said to herself, hurrying through the crowd.

Mia stood uncertainly, eyes round like saucers in her pale, thin face. Angela caught her elbow and tried to draw her towards the party. 'I'm so glad you could make it. Come in. I want to show you what we've done.'

'No,' she replied in a panicked voice. 'I can't go there, I can't...' Mia's eyes were drawn upwards to the new top storey. 'It looks so different. The old house... it's practically gone.'

Angela hesitated. She sounded sad, but Mia's moods were mercurial. Angela didn't want to point out all the parts of the old house that still remained, lest it induce a bout of anxiety. Mia had said too many times that she wanted all those old memories erased. 'Do you like it?'

Mia turned to her, fixing her in a wild gaze. 'I don't like anything. Why would I like this?'

Angela took it in her stride; she was used to Mia's ways. 'Can I get you a glass of champagne? You can stay close by me. I think it would be good for people to see you, you made all this possible through your generosity.'

Mia, in a rare lucid moment, gave Angela a weak smile, and disengaged her arm from Angela's. 'My girl, I did nothing. You did it all yourself.' She patted Angela's hand. 'I'm very proud.'

Angela looked back over her shoulder at the b & b, lit up against the dark sky. 'I'm proud too,' she said. When she turned back, Mia was moving off into the dark. 'Mia! Come back!'

But Mia didn't turn, and now Jerry was calling for Angela and the party beckoned. 'Goodbye, Mia,' she whispered to herself, and returned to her party.

Long after midnight, when everything was cleaned up and packed away and Angela was longing for a shower and a good night's sleep, Jerry took her hand and sat her down at one of the inside dining tables. He looked very serious.

'Well done, Angela,' he said.

'I couldn't have done any of it without you.'

'Ah, you were the brains, I was just the muscle.'

They both laughed, then Jerry's face grew sober. 'Angela, I got a letter from my sister yesterday. She's going to have a baby.'

She was puzzled about where this was going. 'That's lovely news,' she said cautiously.

He didn't even wait for a beat. 'I want to go home. To Australia.'

Cold water. All this time she had expected Jerry to run off backpacking, but still be close enough to use Petaloudos as a base. But Australia? It was the other side of the world. 'But...but, what about the b & b? You've put so much into it.'

'Yeah, and I've loved every second, but it's yours, babe. Not mine. I miss my family, I miss the smell of the gums, the sound of the magpies. I just miss home.'

Angela's heart fell. 'I see.'

'Would you come with me?'

Instantly, she was torn in two directions. Her heart ached, but her mouth moved to deny him. 'I can't. I've just spent the last two years of my life getting the b & b to this stage. I can't leave it now.'

Jerry dropped his eyes. 'I thought you might say that.'

Even as she said it, though, she wondered if it was necessarily true. Maybe she could sell up. But whoever took on the business took on Mia along with it. She couldn't imagine anybody who'd be willing to do that.

'It won't be forever,' he said. 'I'm not ready for roots, yet, you know that. Give me a little time, a year or so. I can come back.'

Angela turned so she was facing him squarely. She took his face in both her hands and kissed him on the brow. 'I love you,' she said. 'And if you think you'll come back, I can wait for you.'

He smiled. 'I'm going to miss you, Angela.'

'I'm going to miss you, too.'

Within a week, he was gone.

Ellie had heard of big breaks, moments for performers when careers turn on their axes and nobodies become somebodies in a single role. She had no such big break. Rather, she rolled up her sleeves and she worked. Europe had no problem with her background as a pop star:

they hadn't ever heard of Penny Bright. So Penelope Bright had no blocks on her path to success. She had the voice, she had the looks and she had her husband's money to get her to auditions, put her up in hotels, and jet first-class between countries for performances at the drop of a hat. Her European debut was a performance of Bach's *St Matthew Passion* for the Bavarian State Opera. They liked her so much, they hired her for a season, playing small roles and understudying main ones. Munich was a city from a dream of her youth: the wide, graceful Marienplatz with its chiming, dancing glockenspiel; the endless galleries of European masters; and the spires of baroque churches piercing the chill grey skies. That season she learned Floria from *Tosca*, Juliet from *Romeo and Juliet*, and Tatyana from *Eugene Onegin*, but sang none of the roles in performance. Her Micaëla in *Carmen* was acclaimed, and led to her being offered a summer concert series at Gran Teatre del Liceu in Barcelona; and then a recital with the Dresden Staatskapelle. Louis, her agent, secured her an audition with Covent Garden but they wouldn't touch her. She was glad. Europe was her spiritual home... England was simply where she lived. Autumn saw her take a soloist role in Verdi's *Requiem* on the stage of the Vienna Staatsoper, and shortly after she was offered the part of Pamina in *The Magic Flute* at the Salzburg Festival. She had to jet back to Germany for the remainder of the season at the Deutsche Oper in Berlin. She stayed in luxury apartments in Charlottenburg, always two steps away from bustling shoppers, and with a view of the ruined Kaiser Wilhelm church from her broad front windows. The grim *Mauer* – the Berlin wall – seemed a long way away from the wealth and gleaming stores of the famous boulevard Kurfurstendamm. While she was in Berlin, the Seattle Opera called, but Ivan wasn't happy for her to go to America.

'Too far,' he said. 'Stay in Europe.'

She obeyed, a dutiful wife. But not from old-fashioned ideas about marriage... No, she was simply a wife who knew the struggle had been taken out of her career by a husband she saw once every month or so. Her repayment was to be available if his family needed proof that he was married. It was a kind of prostitution she supposed, only they still hadn't consummated their union. It would make a wonderful joke, if she had friends who were close enough to tell. But Ellie didn't need the love of individuals. Not at this point in her life. The love of many, of anonymous crowds and generous critics, was enough for her. She was on the verge. She'd had big roles with small companies, small roles with big companies. All she needed was that one role – a Violetta or a Cio-Cio-San – at one of the major opera houses – La Scala, or Opéra de Paris – and she would be on her way. Perhaps she wouldn't even need Ivan's money then . . . What conflicted feelings that thought aroused. It was better not to think of it.

After the season in Berlin, she flew back to London for a break. She was sitting in her first-class seat, sipping a glass of water, when a well-dressed man approached her.

'Excuse me, are you Penelope Bright? The opera singer?'

Ellie braced herself. No doubt some English opera critic, about to tell her precisely what he thought of her. 'Yes,' she said.

'I'm David Wallace.' He extended his hand, Ellie realised it wasn't a British accent at all. At least, not one she'd heard before. 'I'm from the Australian Opera.'

Australia. Where Dieter had run away. As soon as she had this thought, she suppressed it. Dieter had a new life now – a wife, a child. To make contact with him would be wrong. Bringing her mind back to the present, she took David Wallace's hand graciously. 'How do you do?'

'I saw you in Salzburg in summer. Beautiful, beautiful. Would you consider coming to sing for us? We have a wonderful summer concert series that coincides with the northern winter. Actually, I've heard that you interpret the Mahler *Lieder* beautifully, and they would go well on the program. Can I call your agent?'

Ellie didn't know what to say. The Australian Opera were one of the best companies in the world but, like the Met, it would be too far away for Ivan's liking. 'Give me your card,' she said. 'I can't promise anything, but I'll speak with my husband. Perhaps he'd like to spend some time abroad.' Perhaps she could convince him to take a holiday. The lure of sunshine and beaches would surely appeal to him.

She took David Wallace's card and tucked it in her handbag.

Ivan met her, as he always did, at the airport. Usually he just kissed her cheek and took her bag. But this time, he folded her in a warm embrace, picking her up and swinging her around.

'What's all this about?' she said, laughing, as he returned her to the ground.

'Well, Lady Dovercourt,' he said solemnly, 'Daddy's dead.'

15 May 1982
Dear Jerry,

Thank you for the photos. Your niece is beautiful! And as for you, you've gone and cut your hair and I'm not sure if I like it. You were always my long-haired caveman. Is it because of the new job? I can't even imagine you in a shirt and tie, though it must be good to use your degree finally.

Things go the same as ever here. I'm always busy while everyone else is on 'island time', the guests always need fresh sheets at three in the morning, and Silas complains constantly. You know the other day, he was telling me that things were much simpler around here before I came along! This is a man who smokes Cuban cigars now because he's made so much money out of tourists! I reminded him of this, and of course he was trying not to laugh, the old grouch. As for Mia, she's fine, though this week she thinks she has pancreatic cancer. I don't know where she gets these ideas from, but I try to spend as much time with her as I can. One of her cats died last week, and it really upset her. She cried like a little girl, and all I could do was stroke her hair and say, 'There, there.' I felt so useless. I always feel useless around her. I can't stand that she's so unhappy, but I have no way of fixing things for her. Anyway, we dug a little hole in the garden and buried the cat, and I found her out there at the gravesite the next day planting a seedling from somewhere else in the garden, so that's encouraging. Whenever she does something sane, I breathe a little sigh of relief.

So, I've managed to avoid the big question so far, giving you all my small talk instead. I wish wish wish you'd asked me before buying the land from your uncle, because I hate to think you've gone to so much expense on a pipedream. And, yes, I know he sold it to you cheaply, but it's still a big purchase. Where is Coolum Beach anyway? Is it near your parents' place? I had a good look at the photos, and of course it looks like the most amazing location to build a bed and breakfast, but I can't see how I can have anything to do with it. I'm fully committed to my business here, and I thought you were too and would come back one day. Now it seems like you want something else and it makes me feel really unsettled and unsure. I still think of you as my boyfriend (God, such a stupid word, it almost means nothing... like something a teenager would say); but it looks like you're committing to something over there in Australia. I don't know what to think, and all I know is that I should have given up on you a long time ago but I can't. You're 'the One' and that's all there is to it. So, be honest with me: if I don't come there (which I can't) will you ever come back?

I'd better sign off and get this in the post or else it won't get away until next week. Just put me out of my misery, all right?

With lots and lots of love,

Angela xxx

Ellie carefully folded her skirts into a large suitcase, but this time she wasn't off to sing for a season in Europe. This time she was travelling only as far as Sussex, to Dovercourt Manor. Ivan was already there, ostensibly to comfort Lady Dovercourt; though she didn't, to Ellie's mind, appear as though she needed much comfort. She seemed almost cheerful that her husband was dead. Ellie was reluctantly packing up her things from the London townhouse; taking her time. Ivan said they might not be back for months, and the thought of living with Lady Dovercourt for that long was not a pleasant one. She hoped the manor was big enough for her and her mother-in-law to avoid each other. To top it off, Ellie had been compelled to cancel two engagements in Italy, but a summer festival in Paris waited for her at the end of the third month as a reward.

The doorbell rang, and she hoped it wasn't the car already. She checked her watch. No, she still had half an hour. She picked her way over the suitcases on the bedroom floor. The rest of the house was empty and quiet. Ivan had spread the furniture with dustcovers and put his paintings in storage. And, of course, his dog Mimi wasn't scuttling about underfoot and getting in trouble for jumping on the sofas. She opened the door to her cousin Linda.

'Oh,' she said, instantly flustered. 'I hadn't expected you.'

'I hope you don't mind,' Linda replied. 'I was at a conference just around the corner. It seemed a shame not to drop by. I tried to phone...'

'We've just disconnected it. We're moving. Temporarily.' She opened the door. 'Come in.'

'I've brought a cake,' Linda said, plopping the cake box on the coffee table and pushing her silky red hair behind her ears. 'Can we have a cup of tea?'

Ellie could never understand the English fascination with tea, and drank coffee whenever she could. But Ivan had packed away the coffee machine, so tea was what she made.

Ellie had seen Linda only twice since the day she had been up to Wallingham to visit the family. Linda, for her part, had tried very hard to make their meetings more frequent. Ellie had rebuffed her for a number of reasons – she was busy, she was hardly ever in the country – but she knew the real reason was that she was embarrassed. Her mother's family had been devastated not to be invited to the wedding, and she hadn't yet brought Ivan up there to visit them. It was hard enough pretending that they loved each other madly for Lord and Lady Dovercourt. To do it for her family as well, people who really did believe in love and commitment, would make her feel like the worst kind of fraud. The truth was that she liked them, and overcompensated by sending them expensive gifts for birthdays and Christmas. She especially liked Linda, and was glad that she persisted despite the mixed signals Ellie had sent.

They sat on dustcovers in the lounge room and Ellie cut the cake.

'What a lovely house,' Linda said in a perfunctory tone. 'You must be so happy.'

'I am,' Ellie said, guardedly.

Linda seemed agitated, but waited until they were sitting politely in the English fashion, poised with teacups on their laps, before divulging the reason for her visit.

'Ellie, Malcolm is in hospital.'

Ellie froze, a spoonful of cake halfway to her mouth. 'Is it serious?' Malcolm, of all the three cousins, seemed the least likely to fall ill with his booming voice and his sturdy shoulders.

Linda nodded, her lips pressed down to hold back tears. 'He has a tumour in his lung. They're operating tomorrow, and it could go either way. He might sail through it, he might...he might not make it.'

Ellie put down her teacup and plate, and reached across to stroke Linda's hand. 'I'm so sorry. How are your mother and father dealing with the news?'

'Mum's trying to be cheerful, but Dad's devastated.' Linda looked down, blowing out breath so she wouldn't cry.

Ellie felt the urge to put her arm around Linda, but awkwardness held her back. Instead she said, 'You can cry, it's all right.'

Linda fished a crumpled hanky out of her pocket and rubbed her nose. Then she squared up her shoulders and looked Ellie in the eyes. Linda held her gaze for a long time. Ellie felt something shift inside her; nobody had looked at her like that since she split with Dieter. As though they wanted to see all the way inside her to her heart. A feeling of loneliness, regret, a feeling like homesickness washed over her. Uncomfortable, Ellie looked away.

'Ellie,' Linda said at last, 'I have to tell you something, and it may be a shock.'

'What is it?' Her heart had stopped. She braced herself for some dread news, all her old half-forgotten fears of poverty and loss flooding back to her.

Linda bowed her head. 'You have a sister.'

It was the last thing Ellie had expected to hear, and it caught her off guard. She couldn't speak, her mouth opening and shutting like a fish drowning in air.

Linda raised her eyes again, and Ellie could see she already regretted telling her. Her words rushed out. 'You have a sister. I overheard Mum and Dad talking about it six or seven years ago. They would *kill* me for telling you. Whatever happened to her created a huge rift between Dad and your mother. Your father did something… I don't know. But you do have a sister and I thought you should know.'

A million questions jumped onto her tongue all at once. 'Where is she? *Who* is she?' But as Ellie said this, she suddenly knew who this sister was. Of course. It accounted for the extraordinary similarity of their looks and their voices: all at once it seemed ridiculous to believe that she and Penny Bright *weren't* related.

Linda held up her hands in a slow-down gesture. 'I'm sorry, I don't know much. I certainly don't know where she is or what her name is. I doubt Mum and Dad do either. Your father wouldn't tell them a thing, and he wouldn't let your mother speak of it either.'

Ellie sat back in her chair, lost in thought for a long time. A sister, somebody of her own flesh and blood. She wondered if they shared the same parents, or only one. Mama was dark: perhaps she had given birth to Penny before marrying Papa. Perhaps that was why Papa didn't like to speak of it. Yes, that must be it.

Finally, Linda rose. 'I should go,' she said.

'I want to know something,' Ellie said, coming out of her reverie. 'Why are you telling me this? Your parents didn't want me to know…'

Linda sighed. 'Because this moment, on the verge of losing my brother, is one of the saddest of my life. Because siblings matter. Because I just think you should know.' She shrugged hopelessly, tears springing to her eyes. 'Please be praying for Malcolm tonight, Ellie. We need all the prayers we can get.'

Ellie, who had never prayed in her life – Papa had been a cranky atheist with little patience for churches and those who staffed them – grasped Linda's hand and nodded. 'I will.'

Linda, shoulders stooped, left. The tea and cake were unfinished on the table. Ellie closed the door firmly behind her and turned to press her back up against it. How was she to concentrate on packing? Her world had been turned upside down. *She had a sister.*

The doorbell rang again. The car this time. Perfect timing, but not to go to Dovercourt Manor. She had another visit to make first.

It didn't matter that Linda had no idea where this sister was. Because George Fellowes probably did.

THIRTY

When the doorbell rang on Saturday morning, George assumed it was some borderline religious group looking for converts, and relished opening the door to tell them to go away. But instead, he found himself looking at a familiar pretty face. His heart caught on a hook... Penny?

'George, it's Ellie,' she said, reading in his expression that he wasn't sure.

His face fell into a scowl. 'I'm busy,' he said, trying to close the door.

She jammed her foot in the door. 'It's Saturday.'

'You should have called first.'

'You would have refused to see me.'

He couldn't fault her logic, and pushed the door open a little way. 'I'm not going to invite you in.'

'I don't want to come in.' She gestured to the gleaming silver car parked on the kerb. 'I'm on my way somewhere. We can talk out here.' She reached for his wrist and pulled him out of the house, guiding him to sit on the front step next to her. It was a cool, clear morning and the traffic was light. The smell of breakfast cooking at the café on the next block was enticing, and made his tasteless breakfast of bran cereal seem unduly austere.

She took her time. 'How have you been?'

'Well enough, I suppose.'

'I hear you manage Charlie Crowe now. Congratulations. He had the number one single at Christmas.'

'I don't manage Charlie. We parted company six months ago.' *And it's your fault*, he wanted to say. Charlie had been keen to tour the US; George had thought it too early, but started finding his old contacts nonetheless. Half of them had been unsure about Charlie, the other half had told George that after the Penny Bright tour had fallen through, they couldn't trust him. Charlie blamed George, George blamed Charlie. On top of all this, Aila may have been able to put up with George's jealousy, but Charlie had grown tired of it quickly. *I don't need this, guv*, he'd said, right before signing with EMI for a novelty Christmas single. At least with this defection, George felt he had probably got what he deserved.

'Oh. Well, I'm sure you'll find somebody else marvellous to work with.'

'I'm really not much in the mood for pleasantries,' he said. 'Why don't you get to the point?'

She took a deep breath. 'George, I have reason to believe that the real Penny Bright is related to me. That she's my sister.'

George kept a poker face, hiding the confusing feelings that this declaration had aroused. 'Why do you think that?'

'Because my cousin told me that my mother had another child. The similarities between us...it's obvious if you think about it.'

'How certain are you?'

Ellie shook her head, smiling. 'Not at all certain, but one hundred per cent certain at the same time. My cousin only had hearsay to go on, no details. And I can't figure out the timing of it. So far as I know, Penny and I were very close in age. I can't believe for a moment that my father was also hers, because he would never have given her up. So I have to assume that my mother had an affair, or had an illegitimate child before she met Papa, or... Look, it must be her. I want to find her. Do you know where she is?'

A long silence beat out between them as George contemplated what she had told him. It was a reasonable assumption for her to make, he supposed, but he doubted she'd ever find Penny… He had never managed to. 'No. I haven't heard from her since this whole business started.'

'Her real name is Angela Smith. Is that right?'

'That's right.'

Ellie pondered a few moments. 'Smith. It's such a common name.'

'That's right. And she could be anywhere in the world: Africa, India, America… You won't find her.'

'She's never contacted you?'

'Never.'

'If she did… would you tell me? Please?' She cast her eyes downwards. 'I don't really have anyone else.'

'You have Ivan.'

She brightened, but George could tell it was fake. 'Of course. We're very happy.'

George raised a sceptical eyebrow. 'I know you well enough, Ellie. I know why you married him.'

She shrugged, the smile disappearing. 'Think what you like. The world's opinion of my marriage is not my concern.'

There was a brittle tone in her voice that made George momentarily sad, and he was reminded that they'd both suffered from the breakdown of their relationship, and that she probably had as many regrets as he did. But then he hardened his heart again: it had been her choice.

'George?' This was Aila, approaching the doorway. Then she saw Ellie and her mouth turned down. 'Penny?'

'Hello, Aila,' Ellie said, 'I'm just on my way home.' She stood, smoothing her skirt. 'It's been nice to see you, George, and if you get any information for me about that matter, I'd appreciate you sharing it.'

It was on the tip of his tongue to say, 'It will be a cold day in hell when I help you out with anything,' but Aila's presence stopped him. Her criticisms of his cynicism were too common these days, and he didn't want to arouse any suspicions about Penny and Ellie anyway. He watched Ellie go, then turned to Aila.

'What did she want?' Aila asked.

'Business. Nothing important,' he mumbled, pushing past her and into the house.

Aila followed him, questions spilling out of her. 'Why was she here? Does she want you to take her back? Is that what you want? I thought it was all over –'

George turned and growled, 'I told you it was nothing important.'

'There's no need to shout at me.'

'I didn't shout,' he said, but realised he must have. He calmed. 'I'm sorry. You know how I feel about the whole Penny Bright disaster. Seeing her... it made me angry. I'm sorry.' He pulled her close and stroked her hair. 'I'm sorry.'

Aila's voice was muffled against his chest. 'I don't really understand, *lemmikki*. Business is like that. It has ups and downs. Why did losing Penny hurt you so much?'

'It didn't.'

She stood back to look at him. 'You changed after it happened. It's like it poisoned you. The ugly business with Charlie... it all stemmed from losing Penny.'

George's defences rose. All at once he didn't want to hold Aila, he didn't want to be pressed so close to her. He gently, but firmly, pushed her away. 'You're imagining things,' he said. 'I have work to do. I'm going down to the studio.'

'It's Saturday.'

But he didn't answer her. He opened the door to the staircase and left her behind, feeling the cold stone in his heart grow harder.

The sky had been washed clean by a violent summer storm the night before, and now the hot sun was drying the puddles and baking the roofs of the village. Angela left her cook in charge of the morning breakfasts and headed out for the walk to Mia's. She had a sheaf of papers under one arm for Mia to look at. Over the years she had found that Mia was more lucid in the mornings. It was as though the day weighed too much for her, so that by the hot afternoon her mind was confused by it all.

The storm had woken Angela of course. Nobody who cared about the roof over her head could sleep through a storm of that intensity. Shutters had been banging in the kitchen, the gutters overflowed, the terrace was awash. But it had passed without any damage to the property, and she'd eventually gone back to sleep. Now as she made her way further up the hill, she saw that she had got off lightly. Broken branches were strewn about, and tiles were missing from seven or eight roofs on the high end of the slope. She hurried her step, worrying now about Mia's house. As she crested the rise, one glance at the front of the house told her the storm had hit her hard. A width of tiles was missing from the roof, and one of the plane trees was down. Poor Mia. Angela wondered if she'd find her cowering inside, still terrified, or climbing around in the ceiling with a torch looking for leaks. Either was a possibility. Mia had given her a key to the front gate so that she could bring her shopping in, but ordinarily Angela didn't like to use it. It felt like an intrusion and Mia was always there to unlock the gate from the inside. On this occasion, however, she fished in her pocket for the key and let herself in.

'Mia!' she called, her voice echoing around the empty living room. Angela had cleaned up downstairs a few months ago, but it had returned to its dusty, disorganised state. The cats, even the wild outdoor one, had now colonised the downstairs of the house, and they looked at her disdainfully, as though she was an intruder. She made her way up the stairs. 'Mia, are you okay?'

Still no answer. She went straight to Mia's favourite bedroom to find her standing statue-still by the window, gazing out at something.

'Mia?'

She turned. She was very pale and had dark rings under her eyes. She was still in her silk dressing-gown. Angela knew immediately she hadn't slept.

'Oh, Mia,' Angela said, moving towards her and taking her hand. 'You should have called. I would have come up. Were you worried?'

Mia shook her head wordlessly and turned back to the window. Angela craned to see what Mia was looking at. Realisation. The loss of the tree had provided a clear view down over the rocky island to the house on the bluff. Without a word, Angela moved Mia out of the way and closed the shutters. It was as though a spell had been broken, and now Mia was able to turn away and sit on the end of her bed.

Angela crouched in front of her. 'Come on,' she said, 'let's go downstairs. I have something I need you to look at.'

'Can't I look at it up here?' she asked. 'I'm tired. Far too tired to be going up and down stairs.'

Of course. Angela settled next to her on the bed. 'It's very simple,' she said. 'I'm having a sign made for the front of the b & b. I've had an artist on Paros draft me three designs, and I want you to pick which one you like best.'

Mia didn't acknowledge her, but this didn't deter Angela, who was used to her ways.

'Here,' she said, placing the papers in her hands. 'I think I like the second one the best. What do you think?'

Mia leafed listlessly through the papers, her mouth moving silently. Then she handed them back. 'Mia's Place,' she said, then began to mutter, 'Mia's Place, Mia's Place.'

'Did you like any of them particularly?'

'I don't like it being called Mia's Place.'

Angela was taken aback. 'But that's what it's always been called.'

'It's not my place anymore. It's yours. Everything about it that was mine has been erased.' She stood and opened the shutters, staring down at the b & b again. 'You'll have to change the name.'

Angela was weary suddenly. Years and years of this . . . 'Mia, I can't change the name. We're in all the guidebooks as Mia's Place, so we have to keep the name.'

Mia turned, eyes flashing with sudden anger. 'No! It's not my place, I don't want my name on it. My place is gone. You've made sure of that.'

'At your urging,' Angela said. '*You* made me change everything.'

'I never did. You came here and you pushed me around and I had no say. You haven't even paid me in years!'

Angela kept her voice calm. 'I've paid you every week. You don't bank the cheques.'

'Look at it!' she shouted, banging her knuckles on the shutter so hard that Angela feared she might hurt herself. 'Just look at it. That's not Mia's Place. That's Angela's Place. You stole it from me.'

Angela took a deep breath, telling herself to relax. Mia hadn't slept. Later, perhaps tomorrow morning, she'd feel differently. She packed up the designs and rose quietly. 'I'll come back tomorrow. Try to get some sleep.'

'Don't come back,' Mia said in an expressionless voice, but she didn't ask for her key and she didn't turn to check if Angela had gone.

Angela soon forgot the exchange, tied up in the busy tasks of her day. In the deep of night, though, around two o'clock when she should have been sleeping, she woke with a needling worry. Mia hadn't cashed a rent cheque in years, and Angela had come to expect it. She wasn't sure what the law was but, should Mia turn sour and try to bank them all at once, it would be a significant blow to her finances. She knew she wouldn't sleep until she'd gone over the accounts, worked out precisely what she owed Mia and how much she had in the bank to cover it.

By a dim light, she sat in the dining room with her account books, going over rows of figures. She yawned widely. Her eyes were sore and her head was heavy, it was almost impossible to focus. She leaned forward onto the table and rested her forehead on her arms, just to close her eyes for a moment...

Something roused her. What was it? A scuff of footsteps? One of the guests going to the bathroom perhaps? But before she could work it out, she caught an eerie crack and pop, the whiff of smoke.

Fire.

She leapt to her feet and raced into the hallway. The kitchen was filling with smoke, but she couldn't see flames. She ran to the entranceway and opened the door. The glow of firelight, the strong smell of kerosene. The new eastern wing of the b & b was on fire.

'Wake up!' she started screaming, running back into the building and down to the bedrooms. 'Everybody. Wake up! Wake up! Fire!'

Noise and motion. She fumbled for the master key, threw open the doors. Unbearable brightness. She found one of her guests – a young English backpacker – overcome by smoke in her room. The flames were starting to eat their way inside. Angela coughed as though her lungs would split in pieces. Supporting the girl under her arms, she made her way out. Voices shouted to each other in the hallway. Smoke was stinging her eyes, choking her. The glass in the window cracked inwards, sending shards everywhere. She had no idea what to do except to keep moving. A man waited in the hallway, one of Lilika Stathakis's brothers who had come to stay for a week. He shouted something to Angela in Greek, but she was too panicked to understand. She handed the girl to him and hurried to the next room. The door was already open, they had already got out. Hurried footsteps on the stairs, the guests had heard the alarm and were moving. Angela ran to the phone to call the local police officer. The line was dead.

The Greek man was shouting over his shoulder at her again, and this time she understood. 'Get out! Get out! All the rooms are clear.'

A horrible thundering cracking noise alerted her to the fact that the roof of the eastern wing had caved in. She was frozen: all her work, her business, her *life* was in here.

'Go! Get out!' He bumped her roughly with his shoulder to propel her forward, and she ran out of the burning building and into the smoke-filled night.

About three hundred feet away, her guests had gathered in shock to look back on the b & b. Angela counted them with her eyes. Everyone was here, nobody had died. A young American backpacker was giving mouth-to-mouth to the girl. An Italian woman had run off to the village to raise the alarm. But nothing could save the building now. The upper storey, the one so lovingly designed and overseen by Jerry, was being eaten by hot orange flames. The sound of smashing glass, of cracking timber, was overwhelming. Lilika's brother began to run back towards the burning building.

'Wait!' called Angela. 'What are you doing? All the guests are here.'

'There was a woman. I saw her in the laundry. A thin woman in a silk dressing-gown.'

'No, all the guests are here.' But as she said it, a cold chill crept over her. A thin woman in a silk dressing-gown. *Mia!* She remembered the smell of kerosene and knew in her gut what had happened.

'I'm coming with you,' she said, hurrying after him.

'No, stay here.'

'She's my friend!' Angela shouted, and realised that she was sobbing. 'She's my friend.'

Somebody had seized her – one of the other guests – and now held her, while Lilika's brother started back towards the building. He made it only a few feet before there was a deafening crash, and the top storey collapsed. The building caved in on itself, the fire feeding on the new timber of the extensions. The stone walls still stood, but nobody could still be alive in there, under the weight of the burning timber. Angela wriggled free of the arms that held her and fell to her knees, clutching her stomach and sobbing. 'Mia!' she screamed. 'Mia!'

A pair of warm hands grabbed her shoulders, and Silas pulled her up into his embrace. 'There, my girl, there,' he said. The police officer had arrived, and Doctor Moscopolos. Crowds were moving down to the bluff to witness the commotion. Angela burrowed into Silas's tobacco-scented shirt and wept and wept.

Paris in summer was a hot whirlwind of colour. The Moulin Rouge turned its wings languidly in the warm breeze, the prostitutes on the Boulevard de Clichy donned their pretty summer frocks, and the Spanish and Greek painters worked on La Place du Tetre, smoking their cigarettes and arguing politics. Ellie sat on the tiny patio of her rented room in Montmartre, gazing out over the rooftops to the peaks of the Sacré-Coeur gleaming against the soft blue sky. It was the fifth day of the summer concert series, and her first day off. All her energy was concentrated on trying to stay cool. She decided if she just didn't move, she wouldn't perspire.

The phone rang, putting paid to her plan.

'Hello?' she said, scooping it up and stretching the cord as far as she could to get back to the breeze.

'It's Ivan,' he said, and he sounded grim.

'What's wrong?' Ellie asked warily.

He sighed. 'First, let me ask how you are?'

'I'm fine. What's wrong?'

His tone was resigned, tired. 'The solicitors... Daddy's will... Ellie, it's bad.'

'How bad?' The phone line wouldn't quite make it to the patio, so Ellie sat on the edge of her bed. Perspiration trickled down between her breasts. She was always ill-prepared for bad news, as was anyone who had suffered an early life of deprivation.

'Things aren't so clear-cut as we had hoped. It's complicated, it's...'

'Stop hedging. Get it out. Have we lost it all?'

'We might have.' He laughed nervously. 'Oh, Ellie, how far are you prepared to go to be Lady Dovercourt?'

She thought about this, and realised that she was prepared to go a very long way. She had rapidly become accustomed to living in luxury apartments in exotic cities, to imagining herself the lady of the manor. 'We're a team, Ivan,' she said. 'I'll go as far as you will.'

'Getting married wasn't enough. Daddy will only pass on the title – and the manor – if we have a child.' The nervous laugh again. 'I suppose he was sharper than we thought he was. The family line was always on his mind.'

A child. Ellie's head spun.

'We have two years from the date of his death. If there's... nothing, it all passes on to Raymond. Of course, he'd probably let us keep the London townhouse. We wouldn't be destitute, but... the manor, Ellie. The manor.'

Cold feelings shivered through her despite the warm air. A marriage of convenience was one thing when it was between two consenting adults, but to bring a child into it...

'Look, we'll talk about it when you get home. That will give us a week or so to think about what to do.' He sighed. 'I think we should, Ellie. It might be nice.'

'It might,' she said, forcing brightness into her voice. 'We can work this out, I'm sure.' But as she hung up the phone, she wasn't sure at all.

It took two days for the cinders of the b & b to be cool enough to walk on.

Angela stood in what had once been the kitchen, but now had sky for ceiling. She was looking for something, anything, that could be a keepsake of her time here. But there was nothing. Bent, blackened pans, the twisted remains of an egg-beater. Her own bedroom, with all of Jerry's letters and photos, had been completely gutted. Angela glanced up at the blue arch of the sky. The sadness rolled over her again. Why had Mia done this? On reflection, perhaps all of her hypochondria was a sign not that she wanted attention, but that she wanted to die. Angela's heart broke, imagining what profound unhappiness had triggered such drastic action. But she was the only one in the community who felt sorry for Mia. The destruction of the b & b, the near-death of tourists and loved ones... Mia was now hated more in death than she had been in life. Angela could understand their anger, but couldn't share in it. In many ways she was like Mia: she was afraid of the world, she was hiding here on the island, she couldn't deal with her past...

Her eye caught on something in the ashes, and she crouched to pick it up. A spoon, streaked with soot. It was a souvenir spoon, with a little picture of the b & b on its handle. She'd had them made last year, but had only sold three or four. It was suddenly precious to her, and she pressed it against her chest as though it was made of pure gold.

'Angela. Get out of there!' This was Silas's voice.

She picked her way through the rubble and climbed back over the remains of the wall. Silas looked cranky as always.

'You shouldn't be in there, it's dangerous.'

'There's nothing left to fall down,' she remarked, then held out the spoon. 'See? Something to remember it by.'

He leaned both hands on his cane and sighed. 'I'm so sorry, my dear.'

She turned around to look at the ruins again. A sea breeze picked up her hair, whipping it across her face. A flurry of ashes swirled up, then settled again. 'Silas, what do you think happened to Mia here? Why did she hate it so much?'

Silas shook his head.

'You must know something. You've lived here forever.'

'There was a yacht,' he said grudgingly. 'We think she arrived on it. A luxury yacht that moored in the harbour for two nights. I thought I saw two people on a dinghy, rowing back towards it on the third day. They had too much luggage, I feared the dinghy would sink but it didn't. Then the yacht sailed. Forty days later Mia turned up at church to be blessed. There was curiosity, I'll admit. She responded by spitting venomous words at everyone... That was our introduction to her.'

Angela turned all this over in her mind. If she was like Mia, how long would it be before her fear of the past, of what was out there in the wide world, would turn her mind in on itself too?

'It doesn't matter now, anyway,' Silas said. 'She's gone. Now we look to the future, not the past. What are you going to do? Rebuild?'

Angela shook her head. 'Not here. But I am going to rebuild my business.'

Silas turned a puzzled face to her. 'What do you mean?'

'Have you ever heard of a place called Coolum Beach?'

Silas shook his head, his expression sad. 'It's a long way away, isn't it?'

She kissed his leathery cheek. 'I'm going to miss you, Silas.'

'And we're all going to miss you. Don't forget us.'

Angela smiled, thinking of everything she had forgotten already. 'I won't,' she said. 'I promise.'

∞

It was Ellie's last day in Paris and she found herself dreading returning to London. The weather had cooled, the sky was dull grey, and she found herself walking and walking, trying to fill the time between now and her departure to the airport, trying not to think too much.

The concerts had gone brilliantly, and she was finding it difficult to accustom herself to the idea of returning to England for a few months, to the long stretch before rehearsals for a late winter performance of *Hansel and Gretel* in Stockholm. Long breaks made her twitchy; this one potentially even more so for the new problem she had been given to solve. What to do about Ivan, about their future? About a baby?

The Seine, all sluggish and dreaming of the ocean, carried her load of tourists in little boats; the smell of coffee grinding was heavy in the air; the trees were vibrant green; kissing couples lounged on benches. Ellie found herself at Les Quais de la Seine, meandering through the stalls of books and curios.

'Penelope?'

Ellie looked up from the bundle of old black-and-white postcards she had found. It was Chantelle Veron, the French soprano with whom Ellie had shared top billing at the summer series. She had been very friendly to Ellie but Ellie, as always, suspected her motives and kept her at a polite distance. 'Oh, hello.'

Chantelle propped her sunglasses up on the top of her head. 'I'm so glad I've run into you. I had hoped to catch you at the end of the last concert, but you disappeared so quickly. Are you heading home soon?'

'This afternoon.'

'That's a pity. I wanted to invite you to dinner with my family.'

'Your family?'

Chantelle glanced over her shoulder, indicating where a dark-haired man was crouched next to two little girls, about four and six years in age, sunlight in their hair. The man saw them looking and waved.

Ellie stared. 'You manage to have a career with two small children?'

'Oh yes. I often take them with me on engagements. I can't bear to be apart from them too long.' Chantelle turned back to meet Ellie's eyes. 'You don't have children?'

Ellie shook her head. 'No. Not yet.'

'Ah, it's marvellous. They make you human.' Chantelle laughed. 'I suppose that sounds crazy.'

'Not at all.'

'Mama!' This was the older girl, beckoning grandly with both arms.

Chantelle lowered her sunglasses again. 'Goodbye, Penelope. I enjoyed working with you very much.'

'Yes. Likewise,' Ellie replied, realising far too late that she would have liked to be friends with Chantelle, to talk about things like balancing life and performance, or children, or what made a person 'human'. She watched them go, especially the two little girls. *Sisters.* In her mind's eye, she reconfigured the scene. It was Ivan whose arm was lovingly and casually slung around his wife's back. It was Ellie who leaned up to him to whisper conspiratorially in his ear. And each of them held the hand of a little girl: skinny legs wrapped in patterned tights, coloured bobbles holding up uneven ponytails.

Ivan was a good man, and she loved him in her own way. History was full of stories of arranged marriages that had grown into great loves. Though there would never be passion between them, they could make a life together nonetheless. The late Lord Dovercourt's insistence that they have children was perhaps not misplaced; perhaps he knew from his own experience that children cemented unions such as hers and Ivan's. A baby might make love grow.

Ellie closed her eyes. She was being pulled by a tide that she could no longer fight. It would be easier to stop swimming against it, to be carried by it. She made her decision.

Ivan wasn't at the airport gate waiting for her, which was strange. Perhaps he had been confused about dates or times. Ellie caught a cab instead.

Outside their townhouse at Marylebone, she paid the cab driver and stood on the footpath, taking a deep breath. She let herself in, could hear the shower running. It reminded her of their wedding night at the manor, how she had waited in bed. Perhaps this time she wouldn't wait for him, this time she would strip off and jump in the shower with him. She felt a twinge of nerves, but she smiled to herself anyway.

But in the bedroom, she became confused. Ivan was lying in the bed, naked.

He sat up with a start, gathering the sheets around him. 'Ellie! I thought you were back tomorrow.'

The shower was still running, Ivan was pale with fright. It took her five full seconds to figure it out.

'Ivan?' she said, flabbergasted. 'You're seeing somebody else?'

The shower stopped. Ellie heard the door slide open. Ivan turned horrified to the doorway; Ellie didn't know whether to be curious or angry. Who had finally got under his uptight defences? Had made him become interested in 'all that nonsense'? The door to the bathroom opened and standing there, wrapped in a towel, was Ivan's cousin Cornelia.

Ellie closed her eyes with a sigh, cursing herself for a fool.

'Oh!' Cornelia said.

'I can explain,' Ivan was burbling. 'Cornelia and I, we... we have a connection. We always have but Mummy and Daddy wouldn't hear of it...' They were both talking, but Ellie didn't hear a thing. She found a quiet place inside herself and sheltered in it for a few moments. How close she had come to committing an awful moral sin: bringing a child into the world to be raised by parents who didn't really love each other. A child couldn't change anything. And even though he had been so good to her, and she couldn't blame him for trying to find happiness somewhere, she was profoundly hurt that he would have let her fall pregnant, have a baby, knowing all the time that their marriage would remain forever empty.

Finally, she opened her eyes. 'I'm leaving you, Ivan.'

'No, Ellie. The will...'

'You'll be all right. People like you, you're always all right. You don't know what it is to go without. You'll never love me... not the way...' She felt like an idiot. Her fantasies about having children with him dissolved like sugar in the rain. Shock, anger, disappointment

405

in herself: she had made such a mess of things. She had married for money: there, she admitted it. How on earth had she expected things to turn out well? She began to cry.

Cornelia slipped back into the bathroom, Ivan pulled on a dressing-gown and came to comfort her. She shrugged him off and ran, out of the house and down the street. The afternoon shadows were growing long, and she found herself in a green square, fumbling in her handbag for a tissue.

Instead, she found an old business card. David Wallace. The Australian Opera.

She clutched it, determined to put as much distance as she could between herself and the mess she'd made of her life.

ACT IV

...if you must die,
If the dreaded word is written by Fate,
Try again, twenty times,
The pitiless card again: Death!
Again, again! Always death.

En vain pour éviter FROM *Carmen*, GEORGES BIZET

Western Queensland, Australia: 1997

*S*he worked on the dining room table, while the cockatoos clattered home through the dusky sky. Her house was very neat, and very spare. Beautiful, elegant things, but few of them. She spread the letters in a pattern around her, edges parallel to edges. The author had taken far less care. The threats were written in a scrawl, half-on and half-off the lines. Now she had twelve letters. After the eleventh there had been a lull, and she had almost stopped worrying. *Almost.* She had managed to convince herself that Sergeant Osbourne was right, that this person meant only to frighten her, and cause her no harm, that he or she was already tired of the joke. Then, this morning, another had arrived.

You and I both know what you did. But only I know when you'll suffer for it.

It was no more or no less frightening than the others, but its arrival after the long break had caused an awful dread to engulf her. So now she had decided not to sit passively by and hope for it to stop. She had to figure out who was sending the letters, and ask the police to intervene.

With a clean sheet of paper in front of her, Ellie began to write the names of those people who might have something against her, and who knew about the Penny Bright deception.

First suspect: George Fellowes. She hadn't laid eyes on him in years, but last time they'd met he had still been furious. She wrote to him periodically, to tell him her new address in case he heard anything from the real Penny Bright, who she still believed to be her sister. He never wrote back. She had tried to follow his career in the press, but he hadn't had a hit in years. Perhaps if he was washed-up enough, he might turn on her. She had, after all, ruined his big chance in the US.

Second suspect: Ivan Hamblyn. He had been quick to grant her a divorce, perhaps in the hopes that he would find another luckless fiancée who could produce an heir before the two years ran out. She hadn't spoken to him since.

Third suspect: Penny Bright, or rather Angela Smith, herself. Was it possible that after all this time she had decided that Ellie owed her? This one nearly frightened her the most: If she came back what might she demand? Money that Ellie didn't have? The media scrutiny alone would be unbearable.

Fourth suspect: Dieter's wife, Ingrid. Here Ellie put down her pen and pinched the bridge of her nose with a sigh. She must have failed greatly at life to have so many people on this list, and to be sitting here in the vast outback alone. Lonely, if she admitted it.

She cheered herself. If these were the only suspects, then she probably had little to worry about. None of them were killers. But there remained the small possibility it was someone she didn't know, somebody who had the capacity to harm her, even though she was so far away. She had to remain on her guard.

Ellie pushed back the chair and went to the stove to put on the kettle. She glanced down into the wastepaper bin; the envelope from today's letter sat on top. A jerk of fear caught her heart. She bent down and picked the envelope up, hands beginning to shake.

She hadn't noticed before, but now it was obvious. The postmark was not English. The stamp was not English. It was an Australian stamp, and it had been through an Australia postal centre three days ago.

The kettle forgotten, Ellie raced for the phone. At the police station, an answering machine creaked into life. Sergeant Osbourne's nasal voice, impossibly slow: 'You have reached Sergeant Gordon Osbourne...' Ellie waited for the end of the message, then said in a rush, 'Sergeant Osbourne, it's Penelope Bright at Mununja. I have another letter, it's from Australia. Could you call me? Or come by? Please come by, I'm very frightened...' The tape ran out, and Ellie returned the receiver to its cradle, breathless.

She strode to her roll-top desk, threw open the lid and pulled out one of the drawers. Taped to the bottom was a key, which she took to the gun cabinet by the door. Tonight she wouldn't sleep alone, tonight she would sleep with a shotgun in her bed.

THIRTY-ONE
Sunshine Coast, Australia: 1989

'How can I help you?' The receptionist, a kind-eyed woman in her fifties, smiled up at Angela from her desk. Angela wondered if all psychologists' receptionists were kind-eyed. It was probably one of the job specifications.

'Angela Smith here for an appointment with Doctor Hardie.'

The receptionist checked her book. 'Take a seat, he won't be long.'

'Could you tell me,' Angela said, casting a glance over her shoulder to where Jerry was trying to entertain Bo with a Duplo aeroplane, 'how long will the appointment run for? My son...he's only four, he can't sit still for long.'

'An initial consultation will usually take an hour. The doctor has to take a case history.'

Jerry approached, Angela smiled up at him. 'It's going to be an hour. Maybe you should take Bo to the park?'

'Okay, babe.' He kissed her forehead. 'Have fun in there.' He grabbed Bo's hand. 'Come on, buddy. Let's go find some swings.'

Shortly after, the door to the consulting room swung open and a bespectacled man with thick grey hair called her name. She took a deep breath and plunged in.

She settled in the leather armchair offered to her, jiggling her leg with nerves. Doctor Hardie sat opposite, a blue clipboard in his hands. A faded sticker on the back announced 'Mental Health Week 1984'.

'So, Angela,' he said, pen poised, 'what can I help you with?'

Angela took another deep breath. 'Fourteen years ago, I lost my memory.'

He started scribbling. 'For how long?'

'It's still gone. I mean… I don't know what happened. I woke up in a field, I'd fallen I think… and all I knew about myself I got from my passport.'

Here the doctor laid his pen and his clipboard in his lap and gazed at her. 'Fourteen years?' He frowned. 'Traumatic retrograde amnesia is usually transient. Were there other factors involved? Excessive alcohol consumption? Drug abuse? Sedatives?'

'I don't know. But I think I was running from something. I think something bad had happened to me.' Her heart sped, and she said her little mantra: *Forget, forget, forget.* There had been a long period of quiet. She and Jerry had been busy with their lives. Coolum Gardens, the bed and breakfast hotel they had built across the road from the beach, had benefited from an explosion of tourism to the area. When she'd fallen pregnant, it had been a happy surprise but a surprise nonetheless: they hadn't planned it, they weren't even married. Right up until the morning she went into labour she'd been on deck at work, she'd assumed she'd be right back there soon after the birth. Then Bo was born, and everything simply had to change. The idea of leaving Bo in somebody else's care made her want to sob so Jerry hired an assistant to replace Angela. The combined impact of becoming a parent and finally having quiet time not consumed with the business, had worked on her mind, dislodging old unwelcome memories.

Over the last year, they were becoming more frequent, more vivid, and they terrified her. In the most common one, her hands were tied, she sat in a damp cold room, a man with a knife – his face always hidden by shadows – leered over her. The fear was so primal and so intense that it tied her stomach in knots. She was becoming scared of everything. A deep psychological scar was opening inside her; as though a time bomb had been set ticking.

Doctor Hardie picked up his pen again. 'Ah. Psychogenic causes, then. Those I can help you with. Though I must tell you, global amnesia like this is extraordinarily rare. More common in the movies.' He nodded with encouragement. 'So, you want me to help you get your memories back?'

'Doctor Hardie, my memories are coming back, by themselves.' Angela shook her head vehemently. 'No, I'm here so you can help me keep them buried.'

Sydney, Australia: 1989

Expectation was in the air: more so for Dieter than for anyone else in the audience.

At the Domain, an open-air concert performance of *Madama Butterfly* was about to take place. The sky was pastel-wash dusk, the big Moreton Bay fig trees were silhouettes against it, bats black shapes above. Coloured lights shone on the stage, waiting for the performers to take their places. All around him were over-perfumed women, men in musty tweed jackets, murmuring politely, enjoying the soft evening air. But Dieter twitched his toes and wondered what on earth he was doing here.

It had all started one Saturday afternoon, about three months earlier. Alex was only eight weeks old, and Ingrid had handed him over and declared she was going to take a nap. Sarah, their daughter, was playing at a friend's place. Dieter had thought it a wonderful opportunity to introduce his son to the joys of soccer. Baby under his arm, he flicked the dial on the television looking for the right channel. But there was no soccer, there was opera. And it took him less than a moment to recognise her beautiful face.

Ellie. Playing Rosalinda in *Fledermaus*. He stopped, enthralled, to watch her sing her aria. A caption came up beneath her. Penelope Bright, principal artist, Australian Opera. Ellie was in Australia?

He sat back on the couch and watched. Then Ingrid's voice had emerged from the bedroom.

'Turn that awful noise down.'

Guilty, he had switched the television off. But he couldn't get her out of his head. He had thought her in Europe, playing the diva in exotic places, surrounded by rich men. But to know she was just here, breathing the same Sydney spring air as him, sparked old machinery into life. *Ellie.* The one that got away.

Idly, he had started to glance through classical music magazines at the newsagency near their North Shore home. Only once had he found an article about her, but it told him everything he needed to know. She lived in Sydney. She was unmarried. And she was still beautiful. The photograph showed her in a crimson dress, her dark hair unbound and flowing around her shoulders.

The idea of her had rapidly consumed him. At home, between nappy changes and helping Sarah with her maths homework, Ellie was on his mind. At work, as he unfolded dropsheets and painted cornices, fantasies wove themselves in his imagination. In the darkest hours of the night, while he sat up to keep Ingrid company at the two o'clock feed, warm memories of Ellie plagued him. Her smile, her body, the smell of her hair.

Fantasies, he knew, were not harmless. They prepared the way for action. When he'd seen the advertisement in the paper – Opera in the Park; starring Penelope Bright – he was helpless to deny himself. He thought about bringing Ingrid with him, but she was so consumed with the baby and dreaded going out. In the end, he told her he was meeting a friend from work for a drink.

The orchestra began to tune up. The audience quietened. Dieter caught his breath.

Something was about to begin.

Ellie stood at the side of the stage, waiting for her cue. Holding herself very still, focusing in on her throat to see how it felt, a little nervous but not overly so, ready to stride out into the open and raise a grateful hand to the applause. This wait was very familiar to her now. Nobody worked harder than Ellie, she knew this was a certainty. She never took a season off, she accepted every offer of work. She had started as a guest performer with the Australian Opera, singing Giorgetta in *Il tabaro*, then been asked to stay another season. She used the time between seasons to take up minor roles in America, with the San Francisco Opera and finally at the Met. Europe called, but she declined. Perhaps she could have been a bigger star by now if she had gone back to Europe, but the place was too full of bad memories, too full of her own shameful past. It was the place where she had learned her most painful lesson yet: love and affection weren't to be bought and sold; wherever they were to be found, they were to be handled with care.

By the time she had been employed as a salaried principal with the Australian Opera, she had also built up a profile in America and Asia that kept her constantly travelling, constantly working in guest roles, constantly earning money. She often wondered if work was becoming an obsession: she couldn't stop. Life seemed so vast, so in need of filling. It made her anxious to think of taking a break, as though she might lose her footing and simply disappear.

The shapeless music of the orchestra tuning ceased, and was followed by the magnificent figures of Puccini. She took her place centre stage, and began to do what she knew best: sing.

At the first interval, the lights dimmed and she glanced towards the crowd to see if many had come. Faces and more faces, most of them obscured by darkness. One face caught her eye. Was it...? Then somebody moved into the line of her gaze, and she couldn't be sure anymore. But it had looked like Dieter Neumann.

She wandered backstage, distracted. Was it Dieter? Or was it a trick of the light, a figment of a hopeful imagination. Of course she had thought about him from time to time, had even flipped through the phone book looking for him. But there was no D. Neumann in Sydney, and she had presumed he had moved elsewhere, maybe even back to Germany. Besides, he was married, and she was determined not to make any more mistakes of the heart. She didn't pine for him, she got on with life and tried not to measure every man she met by

Dieter's standards. She had even had boyfriends, though none of them lasted beyond a season or two. The constant separations usually finished the romance off. Nobody could fall in love with a woman who was never there.

In the performers' tent, she drank bottled water and made jokes with the woman performing the role of Suzuki. She realised she was on edge, talking too fast, laughing too easily. Act Two went out, Puccini was on much stronger footing here as the tragedy unfolded. The stage lights made it impossible to see beyond the first two rows. Ellie managed, for the most part, to keep her mind on her singing. The crowd roared, there were four curtain calls. She retired to the tent to change into street clothes, hoping to hurry out and look for him again.

'Ms Bright?'

She turned. One of the security guards. 'Yes?' she said.

'There's a small crowd gathering. They want autographs.'

Of course. Autographs. This wouldn't happen at Bennelong Point, where the famous arches of the Opera House kept people awestruck enough to stay away. These community concerts invariably attracted autograph hunters, and she knew that she couldn't turn them away.

'I'm coming right now,' she said, hanging her gown on the rack and picking up her handbag. A sense of disappointment. Then she told herself she was being foolish. It probably wasn't Dieter at all.

She sat at the side of the stage, head down, signing autographs for twenty-five minutes. It was only when she glanced up to talk to an elderly woman who was hard of hearing, that she saw him at the end of the queue. Dieter. Their eyes met, hopeful gaze to hopeful gaze, and that old electricity, that knowingness that had always laid between them, came to life. It made her catch her breath. She smiled, he smiled in return.

She leaned up to the security guard. 'Five more minutes,' she said.

The security guard nodded, and began to discourage other people from joining the line. She signed quickly, haphazardly. Finally, he was there.

'I can't believe it's you,' she said, trying not to smile too broadly, worried about what time had done to her since he'd last seen her. Lines where there had been dewy skin, curves restored to their rightful place. For his part, he was still profoundly attractive. If anything, the extra years had given his face a lived-in charm, his boyishness replaced by an air of self-possession.

'Ellie.' He moved forward, took her hand and squeezed it once before dropping it. 'You sang beautifully. You...are beautiful.'

She had to drop her head to hide her delight. 'Thank you.'

'I... I suppose you're busy now? You have somewhere to go?'

She met his gaze again, frightened by how those deep, deep eyes made her feel. She thought of her bare flat, boxes packed for another move. Not even a cat waited for her, and she had enjoyed that solitary existence. At the moment, though, in Dieter's company, it seemed sad and empty. 'No. Nowhere to go,' she said.

'Would you like to find a place to sit and talk? We could get a coffee.'

'I'd like that,' she said.

It was a short but uncomfortable walk, the dark gardens too romantic a setting for two people avoiding acknowledging their romantic feelings. They exchanged awkward pleasantries, dithered over where to go next. But once they sat down in a back corner of a café on Phillip Street, Ellie told herself to relax.

'Well?' she said, meeting those deep hazel eyes bravely. 'What have you been doing the last decade or so?'

Dieter seemed agitated. He drummed on the table with his fingers. The waitress came. They ordered strong black coffee. Alone again, he began to fill her in. 'There's not much to tell. Ingrid and I had Sarah when we first arrived, she's nearly ten now. Then Alex, our baby boy, was our second surprise package. I started out here working as a painter for a big company, but now I've got my own business. Ingrid does the paperwork, and we're doing really well. Better than I ever expected I would. Look.' He fished in his pocket for a business card, which he pushed across the table to her. *D. and I. Newman,*

House Painters. She immediately saw why he wasn't in the phone book under Neumann; he'd anglicised the spelling.

Ellie picked up the card, heart drooping behind the smile she wore. *Ingrid, Sarah, Alex.* His family. There was no place for her. She was just an old friend he was catching up with.

'I'm so pleased for you,' she said, wondering if it sounded as flat and unconvincing as it felt.

'We've got a house on the North Shore, and we've got an investment flat at Elizabeth Bay. A lovely little art deco place.' He laughed. 'It's empty at the moment, the last tenants set fire to the kitchen by accident. Thank God for insurance.'

'Your English has improved.'

He shook his head ruefully. 'We spoke German at home until Sarah started school. She made us switch over.' He fiddled with the loose catch on his watchband. 'How about you?' he said at last. 'What have you been doing?'

'Singing.'

'Married?'

'I did get married, it didn't work out. There were no children, so I'm on my own.' She filled him in on the terrible mess with Ivan, with the various stages of her career, and how she felt she couldn't stop working and travelling long enough to buy a home, build a nest. The night deepened, as their conversation turned to the past, childhood memories, happier times.

'Have you been back to Kokondorf?' he said.

She shook her head. 'No. You?'

'We went back two years ago for a visit. The village has changed. Ingrid's father bought the farm, then sold it five years later. They subdivided it, built eight little houses.' He grimaced. 'Progress, I suppose. It hurt me, seeing our old front fence but these new places behind it. All the neat roofs, the pebbled driveway. The farmhouse is like something from a dream now, vanished into nothing.'

His words aroused in her a feeling of yearning, of things lost that couldn't be recovered. Melancholy descended. Dieter seemed to feel it too, and long seconds passed before either said anything.

Then, Dieter said, 'There are many things about the past that I regret losing.'

'Dieter...' A tumult of emotions. Sadness, longing, wild hopes.

'Once, a long time ago...' Here he smiled self-consciously. 'Ellie, you made me promise never to hide my feelings from you, no matter what the circumstances. I just wanted to let you know that you've been on my mind.' He reached for her hand then pulled his fingers back at the last moment, as though afraid. 'Do you...ever think of me?'

'Of course I do,' she said, smiling ruefully. 'But we've had our time. You belong to somebody else now.'

He cast his eyes down, his face taking on a boyish softness. Desire flared into life through all her senses, and she realised that this rendezvous, which had seemed so innocent, was actually very dangerous.

She stood. 'I have to get home,' she said.

He nodded quickly. 'Yes, me too. Ingrid will be...' He trailed off, and she was glad. She didn't want to think about Ingrid, what time she expected him, what she might do or say if he was late.

'It's been really nice,' she said.

'Yes, really nice.'

The bland words hung between them, the moment grew magnetic. He leaned forward to kiss her, she turned her head slightly, caught his lips on her cheek.

'Can I get your phone number?' he asked, all on one breath.

'I don't think that would be right,' she said, sadly.

He looked away, chastened.

'Goodbye, Dieter,' she said.

'Goodbye.'

Then she was off into the soft summer night, trying to get the thought of those lips out of her mind.

THIRTY-TWO

At first George stood as he supervised his big mixing desk being dismantled and removed from the basement room. It was too important an occasion to do otherwise. Who sat down while their life's work was erased? Aila had suggested he go out, come back when the room was emptied. No longer a studio, but a space ready for something else: wine racks, perhaps, storage for golf clubs.

But eventually he got tired, pulled up his leather swivel chair in the corner and watched them work. Rolling up leads, taping mic stands together, stacking blank tapes, manhandling the filing cabinet – divested now of all its important papers – up the staircase. It had all been sold to an independent record label in Manchester, that expected the shipment that afternoon.

As he sat and watched, he mused on how casually a business could go from turning a big profit, to a small profit, to no profit and then into the red. Something had happened to him, to his sensibilities, his instincts. His confidence had been shattered by two big failures – Ellie, then Charlie – he couldn't read the market anymore. He signed people desperately, then watched them flounder. He lost thousands in attempted chart-padding; the market had become too big for that to work. When the business had run up so many debts that it was impossible to continue, Aila's family had offered to bail him out so at least he didn't have to close the recording studio. He'd refused. Out of pride, but also out of exhaustion. It was over. He was in his late fifties now, with too many failures behind him. The industry had lost faith in him, he'd lost faith in himself.

Aila came down and approached him, soft and graceful. She brushed his hair from his eyes, a maternal gesture. '*Lemmikki*? Not too sad, I hope?'

George shook his head, unable to speak. He was always unable to speak to her lately, but she hadn't given up on him yet.

'Can I make you tea?'

'I don't think it would help.'

'You did everything you could,' she said. 'Take comfort in that.' She tried a smile, but her sadness for him overwhelmed it and he could have wept for the expression on her face. She still loved him. After all he'd done, *she still loved him*, and wasn't that enough?

'I'll leave you be,' she said, retreating before she cried. 'We'll go out for dinner tonight, perhaps? Do something nice.'

His words were frozen inside him. As she left, he turned over in his mind what she had said and found himself growing irritated with her. *You did everything you could.* Of course he had. None of this was his fault, he didn't blame himself. He blamed Ellie.

If Penny had been his lucky charm, Ellie had been the dark side of that charm. He could identify the moment when the cloud had moved over his life as the moment she had arrived. Her stubbornness had started it all. Penny had been so sweet, so... malleable. Momentarily, he was gripped by deep shame. That had been the real difference between them, hadn't it? Penny lacked certainty about herself, was eager to please, easy to boss around; Ellie was the opposite. They were like the wings of a butterfly, identical in reverse.

Sisters. Ellie had been sure of it. So sure that she wrote to him periodically, every time her address changed, reminding him to let her know if he heard anything from Angela Smith.

I realise we may never find her, she had written in her last letter, making George laugh bitterly at her use of 'we', as though there was any kind of togetherness for them.

422

My Uncle recently died and took to the grave with him my mother's secret. But I refuse to give up altogether. If you hear anything, any little clue, please contact me.

George responded as he always did. With silence. Without telling her that even if he did know where Penny was, he wouldn't share it.

'That's about it, Mr Fellowes.' This was one of the removalists, clipboard in hand, gesturing around the emptied room.

'Thank you,' he replied numbly, wondering why he was thanking anyone.

'The...ah...the chair?'

George glanced down at the chair he was sitting on. 'Is that on the list?'

He turned the clipboard so George could see. *Leather office chair x 1.* George stood, the chair was seized, and they were gone.

George lowered himself to the floor, pressing his palms into the wood. Years of music must have soaked into these floorboards. Now there was only a hollow emptiness surrounding him, creeping into his heart.

For the twelfth time that day, Ellie asked herself what she was doing.

With Dieter's business card and the street directory on the seat beside her, she cruised into the suburbs. She told herself she was just curious about how he lived, but she knew it was more than curiosity driving her. Since their meeting, she had been unable to put him out of her mind. She knew she shouldn't call him, but she felt a strong need to get a better picture of how he lived, what his world was like now.

His house was a red-brick bungalow on a level corner block, scrappy rose bushes struggling in too much shade, a tyre-swing hanging from the lower branches of a sturdy pepper tree, mismatched pot plants in a rusted plant stand on the patio. A sign attached to the front fence advertised his business.

Ellie pulled over, but didn't switch the engine off. She had no intention of knocking on the front door, though she secretly hoped she might see Ingrid. She wondered what this rival looked like. Pretty? No doubt. Dieter could pick and choose.

Her hands gripped the steering wheel uncertainly...maybe she *should* go in. Just as an old friend. Sneaking around avoiding his wife was proof of her romantic feelings for him.

She watched the house for a long time. Time stood still. She shook herself. It was eleven o'clock on a Thursday. Dieter would be at work; Sarah at school. Ingrid was probably busy with the baby. There was no place for Ellie at this address.

Ellie put the car back in gear and pulled out into the street. All at once she felt embarrassed. A grown woman, pining out the front of her ex-boyfriend's house. She switched on the radio and hummed along with a Mozart aria, wondering if it would be possible to put Dieter out of her mind.

Knowing that it wouldn't.

'Mummy, Pop says I can ride Savvy.'

'Good for you, darling.' Angela perched her teacup on the edge of the wrought-iron table and pulled Bo's safety helmet down firmer over his ears. They were at Jerry's parents' acreage in the hinterland above the Sunshine Coast. It was a warm, breezy afternoon, and she drank tea with Jerry's mother, Leila, on the wide patio, surrounded by climbing roses, wind chimes, and crystals catching the sun. 'Make sure you hold those reins really tight.'

'I will.' Bo put his little hand up for Jerry's father to grasp, and they headed down towards the horse paddock.

Angela watched them go, worrying as only a mother can about her little boy on a big horse like Savvy.

'Don't fret,' Leila said. 'Savvy's very calm, and Richard won't let go of him.'

Angela turned to her. 'Can you read my mind?'

'Well, that time I just read your expression.' Leila smiled mischievously. 'But I could read your mind if I wanted to.'

Leila was nothing like an ordinary grandmother. She was seventy going on twenty. Her long red hair was woven through with rainbow threads, she wore a flowing gypsy dress and her fingers were crammed with silver rings. She was an artist, an amateur philosopher, and a part-time tarot-card reader at the local bookshop. Nor was she anything like an ordinary mother-in-law. She had become like a mother to Angela, in equal parts wise and interfering. Angela loved her dearly.

'If we had another one, do you think I'd still worry so much?' Angela asked.

Leila arched her eyebrows. 'You mean if you had a spare?'

Angela hid her smile behind her teacup.

'Yes, you worry no matter how many you have. That's part of being a mother.' Leila feigned nonchalance. 'You two aren't thinking of having another, are you?'

Angela didn't know how to answer that. Yes, *she* often thought of having another, but *he* didn't. Jerry thought their family was complete.

'Three of us, Angela,' he would say. 'It's a manageable number. If we wanted to take off, go round the world. We could do it with three. Bo's getting to a good age now. If we had another one, we'd just be trapped here for longer.'

Trapped here. How long had he believed himself to be trapped?

'Your silence is very telling,' Leila said, reaching for the teapot for a top-up.

'Jerry's taking a long time cleaning that barbecue,' Angela said.

Leila didn't tease her for her awkward subject change. 'You know Jerry. No such thing as cutting corners. Everything has to be done right or...'

'Not at all,' Angela finished for her. 'Yes, I know.'

'He told me about the psychologist.'

Angela shook her head slightly, laughing at herself. 'He couldn't help me. Eight years of practice and he'd never met a patient who wanted help to stay knowingly in denial.'

Leila's eyes went to the line of trees that bordered the creek, but the almost imperceptible downturn of her mouth told Angela that she hadn't changed her mind on this issue.

'Go on, say it,' Angela laughed.

'Well, I just don't understand, Angela. How can you not want to know?'

'Because I know who I am *now*. What if I don't like who I was then? It would do my head in. Like trying to fit two people in one body.'

'But you wouldn't feel that way. You'd just be able to join up the old Angela and the new Angela. One person, lots of different experiences.'

Angela shook her head, and refused to respond.

'I have these feelings about you, Angela... I think you have wonderful memories too. Don't you want them back?'

Wonderful memories? Of being hit with a man's belt, photographed naked, tied up in a basement with a knife held to her throat? Leila didn't understand. Nobody understood. Her life now, all the positive experiences she had filled it with, dear little Bo... She couldn't have that tainted by a grim past.

To her relief, Jerry appeared then, sweaty, wiping his hands on an old rag. 'All done,' he said, scraping a chair across the tiles to join them. He collapsed into it, stretching out his long legs. 'I could use a beer, Mum.'

Leila nodded, pouring her tea into a nearby pot plant. 'Actually, so could I. Angela?'

'No, thanks.'

Leila slipped into the house, the bells on her skirt tinkling softly.

'This heat's a killer,' Jerry said.

'You're just hot because you've been working.'

'Still. Imagine Germany now. It's probably snowing. A white Christmas.'

'I don't want to go to Germany.'

'I didn't ask if you wanted to *go* there, I asked you to imagine it.'

'But you implied it.' Angela mused on how a sore point in a relationship could grow, so that safe ground for casual comments shrank away to nothing. Jerry was desperate to be on the move again. Now that their business was flourishing, he wanted to lease it out to somebody else, and use their money to see some more of the world. He fixated on places. For a while it had been South America, then South-east Asia. Now it was Germany and Eastern Europe, slowly opening up as the Soviet empire crumbled. Six weeks ago they had watched the fall of the Berlin Wall together on television, and Jerry had wept. The only other time she had seen him cry was in the delivery room when Bo was born.

'I wish I could be there,' he'd said, and she slowly realised the tears weren't tears of joy for the triumph of human freedom, but tears of yearning to be part of the excitement in a different hemisphere.

The problem was, Angela wanted to go nowhere. She loved her new home, she felt safe here. And until she had these memories under control, she was determined to stay in a holding pattern.

Leila returned with the beers, and a few minutes later Bo was running up the slope excitedly chattering about horses and Pop's beard. The tense moment between her and Jerry evaporated, but Angela knew that his feelings ran too deep to merely flow away.

The inside of the letting agent's car was chilly. She obviously took the humid summer air very seriously.

Ellie glanced through the photocopied pages of vacant rentals, annoyed with herself to be moving once again. Her problem was she kept signing short leases, imagining she might be ready to buy a place soon: she certainly had the money to do so. But then a season in Beijing or San Francisco or Wellington would come up, and she'd baulk at buying a place when she would be out of the country for the next few months. Her lease would run out, she'd quickly find another place to go, and the cycle would start all over again.

She'd already looked at three places this morning, but found something wrong with all of them. Too large (she didn't like cleaning). Too close to the neighbours (she practised very loudly). No pets allowed (not that she had any, but what if she wanted a cat one day?). The letting agent was masking her impatience: no doubt she thought Ellie overly fussy.

'So do you want to see the one at Glebe?' the woman was asking as they pulled into traffic.

427

'I suppose so. Does it have a garden? I'm not home enough to take care of one.'

'It has a paved courtyard.'

'Let's go and have a look.' She kept flipping pages. Grainy picture after grainy picture of places to live. She was usually much more decisive. Perhaps her problem was that she didn't want another short lease, another interim home. This indecisive malaise had descended on her since she'd met with Dieter. It was as though she was waiting for something...she didn't know what. One of the pictures caught her eye. *Elizabeth Bay. Art deco.*

'What about this one?' she said.

The letting agent glanced away from the road for a moment to see where she was pointing.

'No good,' she replied. 'The kitchen is being replaced. It got burnt out. It'll be a while until it's ready.'

'I can eat out.'

The letting agent pulled up at lights, turned to Ellie and slowly raised her sunglasses. 'Are you serious?' Ellie could almost read her mind. 'No pets' was a problem, but 'no kitchen' wasn't?

'I'd like to see it.' She swallowed down the feeling that she was doing something wrong. Dieter had a flat to let, she needed to let a flat, and Elizabeth Bay was a good, central suburb.

Of course she knew it was much less innocent than that. She was flirting with the edges of danger, just as he had been when he came to see her, talking of the past.

The letting agent indicated to change lanes. 'Sure, we'll go there right now.'

Despite its elegant exterior, nothing about the flat particularly stood out. The kitchen was just a tiny alcove off the lounge room, streaked with carbon. A hole waited where the stove had once been. Under other circumstances, she wouldn't have looked at it twice.

'This will all be fixed by the end of January,' the letting agent told her, with a click of her acrylic fingernails on the blackened benchtop. 'The owners are putting in a nice modern kitchen. Electric stove this time. Safer, don't you think?'

'Hm-mm,' Ellie said as she went ahead, surveying the rest of the flat. Only one bedroom. She wouldn't be wasting time vacuuming space she didn't use. The bathroom was miniature. She stopped once again in the lounge room and assessed the view out the window. The neighbour's garden wall. Good, they wouldn't hear her.

'Lovely view from the kitchen window though,' the letting agent said. 'Beautiful little garden. Communal. You wouldn't have to do anything.'

Ellie nodded, not meeting the agent's eyes. 'I'll take it.'

The agent hesitated a moment, obviously surprised. 'Oh. Sure.'

Her heart thudded, as she considered what she was doing. Tying herself to Dieter. 'How soon can I move in?'

'When the kitchen's finished, I suppose.'

Ellie shook her head. 'I can live without a kitchen a little while, but I need a roof over my head before Christmas. Can I move in Wednesday?'

'I'll check with the owners.'

'I'm sure it will be all right.'

Ellie received an unexpected visit from Dieter the following Wednesday afternoon, as she began to unpack the first box of books onto the narrow bookcase. She was sweaty, her hair pinned up carelessly, trying to stay cool by a cheap pedestal fan when he knocked.

'Dieter,' she said, hand going self-consciously to her hair. 'I wasn't expecting anyone.'

'I'm sorry, I hope you don't mind.'

'No, not at all.' She paused, hand still on the door handle. He was wearing blue. She loved him in blue. She remembered herself. 'Come in. Sit on a packing crate.'

He shook his head. 'I can't stay. I just wanted to talk to you about something.' He cleared his throat. He was uncomfortable.

She met his gaze steadily. 'Go on.'

'You...you knew, didn't you, that this was our place?'

She nodded, her pulse fluttering guiltily in her throat.

'I'm not sure what to make of it, Ellie. I thought...you gave me the impression that we should stay away from each other.'

She hesitated, choosing her words slowly. 'We should,' she said. 'But people don't always do what they should.'

The space between them grew hot. Her gaze went from his eyes, to his lips. She knew she would die if he didn't kiss her.

He didn't kiss her. She didn't die. He broke his gaze and cleared his throat again. 'I need to ask you a favour,' he said. 'With the lease... could you... you have to deal with the letting agent. Don't call me about it and should you ever meet Ingrid, don't mention that you're in here.'

Ellie bit her lip, feeling foolish, a home-wrecker. 'Um... all right.'

'It's just...' He ran a hand through his hair, then all his words came out in a rush. 'You're an ex-girlfriend. Ingrid knows that. It would just cause trouble.'

'I don't want to cause any trouble.' The tide of feeling was pulling away now. Moments ago, they had seemed the only two souls in the world, lost in the stars together. Now it was leases and letting agents and his wife. *His wife.* What was she thinking?

He looked behind him, a guilty gesture, then turned back to her. He took a deep breath. 'Ellie,' he said, 'my wife plays mah-jong. The first Monday of every month.'

Ellie was puzzled. It was the last thing she'd expected him to say.

'She takes Sarah. There are other girls at the club. And Alex of course. She won't let him out of her sight. The thing is, they're busy. They wouldn't miss me... that would be a good night to see you.'

Keep your head, Ellie. 'I'd like that,' she said warily.

'Just as old friends,' he said, quickly, shoving his hands in his pockets. 'I'm not asking for anything more than that. You're right, of course, we should...'

She nodded eagerly, a gesture at odds with how she felt. 'Just friends,' she said.

He seemed about to say something else, but changed his mind. She wanted to know what had been on the tip of his tongue; she was sure it was profound, a sentiment of passion and desire, of memory and love and togetherness. She told herself not to be such a dreamer, to listen only to what he *did* say, not to speculate on what he didn't.

'The first Monday in January, then?' she asked.

He hedged. 'Sorry, no, Ellie. We're going away for the Christmas holidays. We usually head up to Queensland. To the Sunshine Coast. Sarah has a friend there who used to go to her school.'

'Oh. I'm sure you'll have a lovely time.'

'We usually do.'

A family holiday. Ellie felt acutely what a long way outside his life she was. Ingrid was there at the centre, and their children. Twenty-four hours a day he belonged to them. Six weeks at the seaside he belonged to them. *Forever* he belonged to them.

'February, then,' she said. 'Here?'

'I'll come by. Seven o'clock.' He released his hands from his pockets, rubbed his palms together. 'I really have to get going. Sorry I can't help you unpack.'

'It's fine. I'm fussy about where everything goes, anyway.'

She watched him go, then listened to his footsteps receding down the stairs. She wanted to cry. Sitting back on the carpet, she did the maths. A dozen Monday evenings in a year. Take away a few for when she was overseas, or when he was on holiday with his family. Perhaps that would leave her eight meetings, of perhaps three hours' duration. Twenty-four hours. One day a year.

Even though she knew she would meet with him, and enjoy their brief time together, she promised herself she couldn't put her life on hold for Dieter Newman. She had to be careful to remember that he hadn't put his on hold for her.

THIRTY-THREE
1992

$\mathscr{T}$he day before Bo's seventh birthday, Angela received a letter from Greece with a black stripe down the side. It was amongst the rest of the mail, most of it bills and business. With Bo at school, Angela was slowly resuming work, though she did most of her duties from their home, two blocks back from the b & b. She left the rest of the mail on the desk in her cramped study, took the letter to the back patio and sat in the covered garden swing. The morning was grey and still, the famed Queensland sunshine nowhere in evidence. A grey day for sad news, she mused to herself, for she was certain that she knew what lay inside the letter.

Silas was dead. The letter was brief, written by one of his daughters. Angela scanned it sadly. He had been ill for a few weeks beforehand, but had died surrounded by family, just before his ninetieth birthday. Enclosed with it was another envelope, folded down the middle, something he'd wanted her to have. She unpicked it, and found inside two thin sheets of writing paper with Silas's handwriting on them, and a creased photograph of herself in her twenties. An inscription in Cyrillic letters was written on the back.

> *Dear Angela,*
>   *Forgive an old man saying goodbye in a letter. So cowardly. I should have called you on the telephone, but I don't trust myself to*

say the right thing. Some of my happiest memories are of time spent with you, my dear, and I think of you often now my time on earth is running out.

Enclosed is a photograph. When Mia died, somebody had to collect her cats and I was elected. This was beside her bed. You've probably forgotten all your Greek, so I'll tell you that the inscription on the back says, 'Beloved Angela'. I should have sent it on to you immediately, but I'm a stubborn old fool. Now that death draws close, I find I don't mind about Mia's ways so much. I can even feel pity for her. The solicitors are still searching for her next of kin as no will has been found. So far, nobody has come forward. It makes me sad to think of her being alone. You always saw the good in her, and for that you are a better person than me.

So in the spirit of confessing my wrongs, I have to admit to you that I lied to you the first time I met you. I did indeed know who your parents were, although their names weren't Smith and they were never part of our community. I wasn't sure at first, but when I became sure I saw no gain for anybody in telling you this. Less so when I saw how much your old life frightened you, how desperately you clung to the new.

Don't worry, I shall not reveal all here in this letter. It's for you to decide if you want to pursue the truth. But there are a few old-timers left on Petaloudos who would probably reveal everything if you pressed them. Theo Moscopolos certainly knows. Forgive us for not telling you, but we were only trying to protect you; just as you protected Christos, that first day that you arrived.

Goodbye, Angela. Bless you.

Silas

Angela was paralysed. A light rain began to fall, pattering into the little pond where Bo kept his turtles. The wind chimes Leila had given them for Christmas rang softly. She laid the letter and the photograph in her lap and tried to stop herself from crying. But it was no use. Silas's death, Mia's tender inscription, and then the revelation that Silas had known something about her past and never told her…too many emotions to deal with all at once. She wished she wasn't on her own. She wished Jerry was here to hold her and stroke her hair, or Bo to distract her with one of his drawings of a new invention.

She picked up the letter and read the line again.

I did indeed know who your parents were, although their names weren't Smith and they were never part of our community.

What did that mean? Why? And what was their real name?

As these questions tumbled through her mind, she grew terrified that they would burrow under the shadow that lay over her memories, lift it and bring light to times past. She realised she was bunching her shoulders with anxiety. She stood, began to pace up and down the patio as the rain intensified and clattered on the green plastic roof above her. Damn Silas, didn't he realise this would upset her, bring her nothing but sleepless nights? She couldn't let Jerry see the letter. He'd be on the phone to Theo Moscopolos in a flash. Hurriedly, she stuffed the letter back into the envelope and took it to her bedroom. She shoved it into the back of the bookcase, behind a dusty hardcover series of Victorian classics that Jerry would never look at. He was growing exasperated with the way she held back the tide of her memories, he kept nagging her to set them free.

'It's my decision to make,' she always told him.

'It's your moral responsibility to face your past,' he would invariably respond.

Then she would laugh, tease him about his qualifications for being the judge of 'moral responsibility', and the tense moment would blow over into a joke as all their tense moments did. Though the trace of frustration with each other always lingered.

The letter hidden, Angela returned to her study and tried to focus once again on her work. But her thoughts kept skipping and slipping, and she fervently wished that Silas had taken his secret to the grave with him.

∞

Ellie had travelled great distances for her work, but nowhere had ever felt so distant as Mununja.

It had started with the overnight train trip, sleeping on a narrow fold-down bed. Every time the train stopped on its night journey, she would wake with a start and look out the window. The train stations grew smaller and smaller. Finally, by eight in the morning, they arrived at the end of the line. Here, Desmond Overton, the principal of Cunnamulla High School, met her with a firm handshake. Despite the winter cold, sweat patches grew under the arms of his polyester shirt.

'So glad you could come, Penelope,' he said. 'The others arrived on the bus yesterday. They're already out at Mununja. I'll take you there in a little while. I thought you might like some breakfast first.'

He took her to his home, a weatherboard house backing on to an expanse of dust that might have once been a park. His wife had cooked an enormous breakfast of bacon, eggs, sausages and grilled tomatoes. Endless slices of thick white bread popped out of the toaster and landed, dripping with butter, on the plate in front of her. She ate what she could, too polite to tell them she'd had coffee and toast in the dining car at six that morning.

Then the long drive to Mununja, through miniature towns, and past acre after dry acre of farmland. Desmond took her in a rumbling four-wheel drive covered in red dust. They hit four kangaroos on the way. Desmond blessed the bullbar every time. She was almost certain he sped up to hit them.

The landscape outside was like she imagined Mars to be. Red, rocky, scrubby, dotted with strange twisted silvery trees with silvery leaves. From time to time, they'd pass a brown, muddy creek and Desmond would tell her that once it had been a great river, with lush green grass and wildflowers on all sides.

'The drought has affected the area badly then?' she asked.

'Yes and no,' Desmond said. 'This is mulga country. Ugly as hell, but you can always pull the trees over if your stock need something to eat. The leaves make excellent fodder.'

Ellie considered the landscape beyond the heated cabin of the four-wheel drive. She wouldn't call it ugly at all. Unusual, certainly, but almost beautiful in its starkness.

'A good man with his head screwed on can keep a station going out here,' Desmond continued. 'Unfortunately, there wasn't one of them running Mununja.'

He told her the sad history of the station. Once a flourishing wool business, the lack of rain and a series of bad management decisions had meant bankruptcy for the family who had owned it. The husband, father to three small children, had hanged himself in the shearing shed. The livestock and all the assets had been sold, but nobody wanted to buy the property. It had sat empty ever since.

'It'll be nice to have life and laughter out there again,' Desmond concluded. 'We've been trying to organise this music camp for nearly eighteen months. Bloody government are as stingy as hell with their money.'

'So the other musicians?'

'A cellist from Perth and a composer from Sydney University.'

'And the kids, they're from your school?'

'My school, plus other schools in the area. Quilpie, Thargomindah...schools that don't have anything. Kids that don't have anything. Aboriginal kids, white kids with alcoholics for parents, kids whose families have lost everything with the drought. But all kids who have a talent for music.'

Along with the privileges of being a highly paid artist with a busy schedule, came responsibilities as well. Ellie had been involved with company fundraising, with the requisite charming of sponsors and donors. But she had started to want to do more. Her own secure financial position had not made her feel safe and happy; instead, it made her see how few people were safe and happy. Perhaps it was a reaction to the creeping dissatisfaction she felt with her job: she had worked hard, she had done it all, and at the fulfilment of the dream were the long years stretching beyond it. The same thing again and again? No, there had to be something new to enhance it. When the invitation to attend this one-week music camp had arrived, she had accepted. The pay wasn't even a tenth what she could get if she took the summer series in Chicago that she'd been offered. But she knew first-hand how lack of money translated all too often into lack of opportunity. When she imagined how useful it might have been for her to meet a real live opera singer in her youth, she couldn't say no.

Gradually, the sealed road ran out and gravel and dirt took over. Stones popped under the car, and they rattled over cattle grids. Six gates marked the long driveway into Mununja, but all of them had been left open. There was no livestock here to contain. Finally, the house appeared in the distance.

Somebody had built and decorated it with love and care. It stood on a rise: gleaming white weatherboards, a tin roof, painted shutters, a huge deck. As they drew closer, she saw that the remains of a garden – dry flowerbeds and scrappy bushes – surrounded the house. A stone angel had fallen and been forgotten amongst the weeds. Desmond pulled up out front, and switched the car engine off. Ellie slipped off her seatbelt and climbed out of the car, pausing to look around.

Desmond joined her, and began pointing out buildings. 'That's the old shearers' quarters. The kids are all sleeping there. You and the other musicians and Stephen will have bedrooms in the house. That's the shearing shed, the dog shed, and that one's the garden shed. We found a three-metre King Brown in there the other day when we came to clean the place up.'

'A King Brown?'

'A mulga snake,' he said with a wink. 'Deadliest in Australia.'

He went round to the back of the car for her suitcase, and something else he'd said occurred to her. 'Who's Stephen?'

'The music teacher from my school. He's running the show.'

'You won't be here?'

He shook his head. 'Too busy. The sports carnival is on tomorrow. Come on, I'll show you to your room.'

The main bedroom of the house had been set aside for her. There was no furniture but a mattress on the floor. Desmond explained the budget hadn't stretched too far. Ellie hid her surprise, told herself a week roughing it would be character-building, and put her suitcase on the floor next to the mattress. Desmond led her on a tour of the rest of the house, winding up in the kitchen where three men and a woman sat on folding chairs, drinking hot chocolate by the wood stove. They were introduced as the cellist, the composer, the housekeeper, and Stephen the music teacher.

Ellie would later have to admit that her first impression of Stephen was no impression at all. He was much younger than her, perhaps only twenty-three, and she was preoccupied with learning everyone's names. He was good-looking, with thick dark hair and intense blue eyes, only an inch or so taller than her but extremely well-built, with broad shoulders and muscular, tanned arms. She had a chance to observe these things about him over dinner that evening, which they all ate on a rickety second-hand table in the otherwise empty dining room. He had thought to bring a portable tape player, which was plugged in and sitting on the floor, playing Billie Holiday. His conversation, like his gaze, was intense, and they were still debating the relative virtues of teaching children *voix blanche* in choirs, long after their companions had gone to bed. It was only when she had retired to her own bedroom that she realised his intensity, his focus on her, and his reluctance to say goodnight, might signify a romantic interest. She smiled to herself, thinking about how young he was. Then she undressed for bed. The children were arriving tomorrow; she needed to get a good night's sleep.

Ellie had never faced a tougher crowd. Twenty-five children, ranging in age from ten to fourteen, were arranged cross-legged on the floor – looking slightly bored – while she spoke about her career and gave them a demonstration of her singing. One of the smallest children down the front, a little Aboriginal boy named Tyrone, actually winced when she hit a high note. But they clapped politely afterwards, and turned their attention to the cellist. Ellie was sent off to a special one-on-one session with a fourteen-year-old girl named Melissa. She was a plump girl squeezed into jeans too tight for her, she wore too much eyeliner and had too many earrings (including one through her nose). But while many of the children were interested in singing, Melissa had developed a particular passion for opera that had baffled her parents, teachers and friends.

They sat on the front steps of the house, in a band of winter sunshine. They talked about opera, about favourite roles and arias. Ellie told her a little about her background, and felt almost jealous that Melissa had such a mentor. If only she'd had somebody to show her the ropes... Ellie opened up the score of *The Magic Flute* and began to discuss Pamina's opening scene.

'So you see here,' Ellie said, pointing to a bar. 'This is quite a difficult vowel sound on the E flat.'

Melissa bit her lip, didn't say a word.

'Melissa?'

'Sorry, Miss Bright. But I can't read music.'

Ellie stared, first at Melissa, then at the score. She suddenly saw it through Melissa's eyes: lines and dots and symbols that signified nothing. Worse, they signified her inability to understand them. *How can you want to be a musician and not know how to read music?* she wanted to ask. But it wasn't Melissa's fault. Ellie, who had long been of the opinion that she grew up tough, now saw just how privileged she had been.

'Why do you want to be an opera singer?' Ellie asked, curious now.

Melissa shrugged, an habitual gesture of adolescence. 'I just like it, y'know? I saw this lady on the television...Joan Sutherland.'

Ellie nodded encouragingly.

'Anyway, she just opened up her mouth and this sound came out. Like angels. It just got me, y'know? Got me here.' She pushed her palm against her heart, then gave another shrug. 'I got me dad to buy me some tapes. I listen to them all the time. He thinks I'm crazy.'

'Well, I don't.' Ellie tapped the page in front of her. 'So you can't read any of this? You don't even know what the clefs are for?'

Melissa shook her head sadly. 'Does this mean I can't work with you?'

'I...of course not. It means we have to work even harder, that's all.' She flipped the book closed and on the blank back cover drew a stave and a treble clef. 'Let's start with a C major scale.'

They worked through the morning, a little on notation, but mostly on technique. Melissa had a good raw voice, and Ellie enjoyed seeing her improve in the short time they had together. At the end of the week, Melissa would go back to her home town, to her father who didn't understand her; but Ellie hoped that a seed had now been planted that would continue to grow. She was surprised at how satisfying she found that thought, and realised with a little shame that satisfaction up until now had meant a gain only for herself.

Ellie found herself up late with Stephen again, in front of the wood stove, sharing a bottle of wine. He encouraged her to talk about Europe, where he had never been. He had grown up in a country town on the far north coast, studied to be a teacher, and had been working out here ever since. The night grew weary, but Ellie didn't. In fact, she had caught a second wind. Stephen was flirting with her, and she had to admit she liked it.

'So, you've been all over the world,' he said. 'What makes Australia different?'

'The people, mainly,' she said, considering. 'People here are humble, somehow, kind. And the heat. I sometimes long for a freezing German winter.'

'It's cold out here. In winter.'

'Nowhere near as cold.'

'I bet it is.'

'I bet it's not.' She smiled at him, swirling her wine in its glass. 'Once when I was nine, it was minus-twenty degrees. The snow came to the top of our door.'

'Sure, we don't get snow. But it's cold out here. A special kind of cold.' He leapt out of his chair and reached for her hand. 'Come on.'

'Where?'

'Outside.'

She put her glass aside, taking up the challenge. 'All right.'

'No coats. Just as you are.'

She took his hand. 'All right.'

They opened the front door, giggling, and stepped out onto the verandah. Stephen moved ahead, down the stairs.

'Where are you going?' she asked.

'Come on. Away from the house. Just the stars and the ground.'

She scurried after him, feeling like a teenager. A slightly drunk one.

'Cold enough for you yet?' he called to her.

'This is nothing!' she responded, enjoying the game.

He climbed over a fence and into what might once have been a sheep paddock. The ground was stony, and broken trees dotted the landscape. She followed, careful not to catch her skirt on the fencing wire. The buildings of Mununja were a long way behind them now, silent grey shapes in the dark. Ellie started to run to catch up, Stephen ran faster. She was laughing, excited and afraid all at once. Her ears and nose were icy. Finally he stopped, she caught up with him.

He took her hands in his. 'Look up,' he said.

She did. 'Oh, it's beautiful.' Here, away from electric lights, every star was visible. Constellations spun above her, bright scattered dust in a velvet sky.

'Close your eyes,' he said, and she did, catching her breath.

'Now,' he said, 'feel the cold.'

No snow, no sleet, no wind. No tall trees, or buildings, or mountains to give the impression of shelter. Just stillness. Cold, cold stillness. And while the temperature might not have been as low as a January morning in Germany, she realised what he meant. It felt as though they were just one of those distant stars, shivering out at the edge of the universe. The emptiness was cold. Not just on her skin, all the way into her soul. She was suddenly very sober, and opened her eyes, shivering.

'See?' he said, grinning. 'I told you.'

She thought about her travels in the most exotic places in the world, the historic buildings and art that she had feasted her eyes on. And yet none of them felt as old as this place, as ancient and as elemental, gleaming coldly under the grey starlight. The great cities of the world all at once seemed frantic, trivial, chattering with self-importance. Here there was peace, the profound stillness not of death, but of what precedes life. Of all the places she had been, this one alone had the power to transform someone.

Meanwhile, Stephen still held her hands, and she realised he was gazing at her meaningfully.

She smiled. 'Why me, Stephen? I'm fourteen years older than you.'

'I don't care if you're seventy. You're the most beautiful thing I've ever seen.' He leaned in to kiss her, but she flinched away.

'I'm sorry,' he said softly, dropping her hands. 'I thought… Is there somebody else?'

How to answer that question? Of course there was somebody else. There was Dieter. Ellie dared not add up the length of time – was it more than two years? – that they had been meeting. Once a month, at her flat: two old friends catching up. Only it was so much more than that and they both knew it. They drank wine, talked of the past, of their hopes and dreams for the future, divulged all their secrets to each other. The relationship was intimate, but not physical. She saw in his eyes that he wanted her, and she certainly wanted him. But a good mixture of guilt and self-preservation made her keep him at arm's-length. A chaste kiss on the cheek was their only contact. She knew, though, that their intimacy was still a betrayal of Ingrid. Ellie ached for Dieter, Dieter ached for Ellie, but they resisted each other. The evenings always ended with Ellie feeling frustrated, unfulfilled. Like promises had been made to her and not kept. In between dates, they didn't call each other, didn't mention each other to friends, tried not to think of each other. But then they would meet again, the fires would be lit anew. It was an affair, if not of the body, then certainly of the mind.

In that time, Ellie had not dated anyone else, though she didn't know why. Dieter was still married; it made no sense to save herself. Especially when Stephen's warm body was so close, here in the dark.

'No,' she said, 'there's nobody else.' This time she took his hands and drew him towards her. His body was hard, his lips insistent.

They moved inside, and when they finally bid each other goodnight it was already morning.

Ellie lay in her bed long after, chasing sleep. She liked Stephen, so why did she feel so desolate? She turned on her side, pressing her face into her pillow and fighting tears. *Be honest, Ellie.* Stephen's problem was that he wasn't Dieter. With dazzling clarity, Ellie realised that after all these years, she still wasn't over her first love.

Dieter loved what Ellie had done with the flat. She had turned a bland space into something inviting and exotic. It smelled of sandalwood and vanilla. She had beautiful furniture, hand-carved wooden pieces that were polished to gleaming. Gorgeous filigreed lamps cast pools of soft light. Ellie greeted him at the door, her long black hair loose and her feet bare. As always, the sight of her made his breath catch on a hook. All his nerves and veins took a jolt of electricity. He was afraid that, eventually, it would destroy his body, turn his brain to a twitching mess. But he couldn't stay away.

'Hello,' he said.

She offered her cheek for a kiss. 'Come in,' she said. 'I'm just opening a bottle of wine.'

As he watched her, he experienced that familiar mingling of desire and melancholy. Everything about her – the soft curve of her waist, the swing of her long hair – worked on him like the pull of the moon on the tide. But then the sadness would roll over him. He had chosen a different life. He loved his children, his wife had been good to him. And he longed for his youth, when things had been uncomplicated, when Ellie had been his.

She sat opposite him and he forced himself, as always, to open the conversation on safe ground. 'So,' he said, 'how was far western Queensland?'

She surprised him with the eagerness and vigour of her answer. She had loved it. The place, the students, the work. As she related what she had done out west, he noticed her using one name more than most – Stephen – and felt the first stirrings of a misplaced jealousy. He drank his wine a little too fast, in the hopes it might make the feeling go away.

'So, I might not be able to meet you next month,' she said guardedly.

'No? Are you off on tour again?'

'Maybe a holiday. Stephen has invited me back.' She wouldn't meet his eyes. That was for the best. It wouldn't be good for her to see the naked jealousy there.

'Oh. You and Stephen…? Is it serious?'

Her lips pressed together as though she was considering some complex problem. 'I'm not sure what it is, Dieter,' she said plainly. 'He's much younger than me, he lives a long way away.'

'Well. Those things are small problems, don't you think? If you love him.'

Ellie laughed, turning her head away. 'I don't love him. I like him.'

A small relief. He wondered if she had made love with Stephen. The thought made all his teeth ache.

'Do you think I should go?' she said, and he knew she was being provocative.

'It's not my decision to make,' he muttered.

'Let me ask another way. How would you feel if I went?'

He found himself annoyed with her, with the situation, but mostly with Stephen. 'I would feel… I have no right to feel the way I would feel.'

'Jealous?'

He nodded. He thought she might smile, take pleasure in his jealousy. But she looked sad, a little lost.

'What are we going to do, Dieter?'

'I don't know,' he said helplessly. He sat forward, placing his wine glass carefully on the coffee table.

Her bottom lip trembled. 'We can't be together.' It was half-statement, half-question. The closest she had ever come to suggesting he leave his family for her. But he couldn't. He wouldn't. He loved them, he had a duty to take care of them.

'Are you happy with Ingrid?' she ventured, forcing a smile.

'Yes,' he said, hearing the lack of conviction in his voice. Of course he and Ingrid weren't happy. They had married for all the wrong reasons, and discovered too late how little they were suited to each other. His passive nature, which she had once found calming, now irritated her. Perhaps unconsciously, perhaps not, she did things that she knew would annoy him, to try to provoke him to a reaction. Her feistiness, which he had once found sexy, now descended all too often into petulance and egotism. So he learned to tune out her complaints. Perhaps if real love had been underlying these problems, it might have been enough to overcome them. But love born out of duty was not forgiving, and so compromised happiness was all they could manage. How long had he known he couldn't be truly happy with her? From the start, he supposed.

He lifted his gaze, found her looking back at him. They had played out the same moment a hundred times, but on this occasion it had new significance. Something pressed his heart. He stood, she shrank back in her chair, an expression somewhere between fear and desire in her dark eyes. He seized her hands and pulled her to her feet, in one smooth movement pushing her hair back and kissing her throat.

'Ellie, Ellie,' he murmured, the searing reality of her body in his arms making his skin prickle. 'I love you. I have always loved you.'

She didn't fight him, as he'd thought she might. Her hands fluttered across his ribs. His mouth found hers. He tried to kiss her tenderly, but he was too fuelled by adrenaline and jealousy. His passion was brutal. He crushed her against him. She moaned, melting in his arms.

Then suddenly she stiffened, pulled back.

He released her. 'What's wrong?' he said, listening to his pulse hammering in his ears.

'This is wrong,' she said, her hands palms up in front of him, a defensive gesture.

'Ellie, I –'

'Nothing can come of this. I think we need to cool off. I think we need to have a break.' She was talking too fast in her anxiety. He was so used to her being calm, collected Ellie that he almost laughed. 'You should go home. To your family.'

'I...perhaps you're right.' But how was he going to survive if he couldn't see her? He was wise enough not to say this, not to press the issue. 'Next month, then?'

'No. Give me a little time. A few months.'

A few months? The thought of life without Ellie, even if it was only a handful of stolen hours a month, seemed barren and drained of its colour. But he knew she was right: they needed to cool off. He was betraying his family; she was squandering her chances of finding a man who could love her. Yes, they were connected, spirit to spirit. But spirits inhabited people, and people had to make life work: hold down jobs, keep marriages together, raise children...

She was smoothing her hair now, regaining her calm. 'You'll have to go. I'm sorry. I think we both need to get back into our own lives. This is a fantasy, we can't continue with it.'

'When...?'

She looked at him sternly. 'You have my number, I have yours. We'll know the right time.'

Dieter reluctantly said goodbye. She stood back, discouraging even the last touch of his fingers on her wrist. As he descended the stairs, he wondered if 'the right time' would ever come. And if it didn't, how was he to keep living without the other half of his soul?

THIRTY-FOUR
1993

*A*ngela rang the counter bell and waited for Jerry to emerge. He saw her and smiled. 'I thought you were a real customer,' he said.

'I am,' she replied. 'I just dropped Bo off at school and I'm at a bit of a loose end. I wondered if you have a room free.'

At first he looked puzzled, but then a knowing smile took over his face. He grabbed a key off the hook, and opened the counter gate. 'Come on, then, madam,' he said, grabbing her hand. 'I believe the Love Suite is free.'

It was an old joke between them. They had named the six rooms after local plants: Frangipani, Bougainvillea, Hibiscus and so on. But they had nicknamed the upstairs room, with its private balcony overlooking the wide ocean, the Love Suite because so many newlyweds requested it for their honeymoon. Jerry had declared it the sexiest room in Coolum.

All the rooms had been freshly decorated, their bold eighties colours now replaced with muted plums and soft creams. The sea breeze stirred the heavy curtains. They tumbled into bed, and she forgot the anxieties of the morning that had driven her to Jerry's arms in the first place, caught up in the pleasures of the moment.

Afterwards, he lay on his side and stroked her hair while she listened to the sea. He kissed her shoulder. 'So, why did you come to see me this morning?'

The dread returned. 'I had a memory. While I was dropping Bo at school.'

'A bad one?'

'They're all bad, Jerry. I haven't had a good one yet.'

'What was it?'

'It was the same one…the dark room, the man with the knife. Only this time I knew his name.' Her heart raced.

'What was his name?'

She almost didn't want to say it, as though saying it might conjure him up in the flesh. 'Benedict,' she whispered.

'Is that his first name? Or his last name?'

'I don't know. It's just a name. It popped into my head and… it's like it's stuck there. Flying around and around like a vulture.' She closed her eyes, but that brought no relief. The anxiety was constant now, background noise. Every now and again it would peak – a bad dream, a flash of memory. There was no respite from it.

Jerry folded her into his arms, and she breathed in his warm, male scent.

'Why do you put up with me?' she mumbled against his shoulder. 'I wasn't this way when you met me. You must be getting tired of me being so crazy.'

'Ah, you know what they say. For better, for worse.'

She laughed. 'We're not married.'

'I don't think you're crazy, Angela. I hate to see you so anxious, but I'm not going to give up on you,' he said. 'I just wish that you'd see somebody who could help you get your memories back. Then you could deal with them, and it would all be over.'

Now she wanted to cry. He didn't understand, he couldn't. There were memories that she hadn't told him about, too ashamed to. The man with the camera, pleasuring a lorry driver in the front seat, submitting to the caresses of an overweight businessman… Once she had thought she might have had no sexual experience before Jerry, but now her memories had proven the opposite to her. What other awful things about herself might she discover?

She sat up with a sigh. 'I suppose you'd better get back to work.'

'Yes, I suppose so.'

She reached down for her clothes, and passed Jerry's trousers back up to him. As she did so, something fell out of the back pocket. A letter. Curious, she turned it over. Jerry snatched for it, but not before she'd seen a return address in England.

'What's that?' she asked.

'It's nothing.'

'It's not nothing,' she replied. 'If it was nothing, you wouldn't have snatched it from me.'

'It's from a...' He started to lie, then thought better of it. 'You're right, it's not nothing.' He handed the letter over and she tipped it from its envelope. She read it while Jerry dressed. It was from an architecture firm in Hounslow, offering Jerry a job.

'I don't understand,' she said. 'Why would they offer you a job?'

'Because I applied for a job.'

'You...? Why? We live here. Why would you apply for a job over there?' When he didn't answer, she answered for him. 'Because you want to go there. Because you *always* want to be somewhere other than here.'

'Yes,' he admitted.

Angela leaned her head back against the pillow. A gust of sea air caught the curtain, rattling it on the rail and allowing in a shaft of hot light.

'Angela, don't be mad at me. I never expected to get it. I was just mucking around, but the interview over the phone went really well and... God, it's just the most amazing job, travelling all over Europe, working on renovations of historic buildings. The pay's not that great but we'd manage.'

She considered him in the dim room. Desolation washed over her. She couldn't go back to England, didn't he understand that? She didn't want to go anywhere near Europe, where this Benedict person might find her again. She wasn't even sure if she was brave enough to step on a plane again. She had changed, she was weighed down by her shadowy memories. She wanted to stay put. But he needed to move. All at once she saw he was a trapped bird; she and Bo were the cage.

'I'm so sorry,' she said, tears prickling her eyes. 'I'm so, so sorry, Jerry, but I can't. I just can't go there.'

The expression that crossed his face was a spear to her heart. Hope dissolved into acceptance. The corners of his mouth turned up sadly. 'It's okay, babe. We don't have to go anywhere. I'll turn the job down. Don't cry. Just don't cry.' He held her, and at first she was relieved. She had got her way. But then she thought about all the long years Jerry had been hoping to get away, and she knew it wasn't right to win this time.

'Jerry,' she said, straightening up and pushing her dark hair off her face. 'What if it wasn't forever? What if you just went for a year?'

His face lit up. 'Yeah? You'd come for a year?'

She shook her head. 'I wouldn't come.'

Now his expression was more cautious. 'You mean, go without you?'

'Yes.' She took a deep breath. 'If that would help scratch this itch.'

His eyes went to the glimmer of sunlight beside the curtains. She could tell he was considering it, even as he was shaking his head. 'I'd miss you too much. I'd miss Bo. God, what would I do without him?'

'Bo could come to see you in the holidays. Leila could bring him. I'll stay, I'll look after the business. We can afford to hire somebody to help.' Already she felt the wrench of his absence.

He nodded slowly. 'I guess it could work. It would be hard.'

'It wouldn't be as hard as trying to keep you here against your will,' she said with a sigh. 'Oh, Jerry. I just want you to be happy.'

'I won't be happy without you and the little guy.'

'It's only for a year.'

Quiet fell between them, as they each considered how to deal with a separation. The sound of the ocean continued regardless.

'Would you be okay?' he said at length. 'With all this stuff going on in your head?'

'I'll be fine. Maybe I'll go and see a psychologist after all,' she lied.

He smiled, and he looked like a man who had just been given his youth back, and she knew she had made the right decision, no matter how difficult it was going to be. 'All right, then,' he said. 'All right, I'll tell them I can start next month.'

Dieter came home from work on Monday afternoon to a house in chaos.

Ingrid was on the phone. Suitcases had been dragged into the hallway. Sarah was listening to loud pop music in her room, pulling out clothes and flinging them onto her bed. Alex was running about with a little Thomas the Tank Engine suitcase.

'What's going on?' he asked Sarah.

Sarah didn't turn around. 'Opa died.'

Dieter's heart seized on a beat.

'Oh, sorry,' she said with an apologetic smile. 'Mum's father, Dad. Not yours.'

He released a breath, but still adopted a suitably sober expression.

'We're going to Germany for the funeral,' Sarah added.

Dieter was confused. He went to the kitchen and touched Ingrid on the shoulder. She turned and gave him a weak smile. She was speaking in exasperated German to somebody. 'Well, they can't bury him until I get there... No, they'll have to wait... I understand, but it takes a long time to get there from Australia.'

He rubbed her arm gently, reading over her shoulder the scrappy notes she was taking on the back of an envelope. Flight numbers and times. He realised with a shock that she had booked a flight for tonight, in four hours' time. He had clients to call to cancel...

Finally, Ingrid was off the phone. 'Papa died,' she said, and her bottom lip trembled.

He embraced her. 'I'm so sorry, Ingrid.'

She extricated herself, nodding, holding back tears. 'He was old. I didn't expect him to live forever. My cousin has organised the funeral, we'll be racing to get there.'

'It's all right, we'll make it. I just have to phone a few clients –'

She put a hand on his arm. 'I'm sorry, Dieter. You've misunderstood. Only the kids and I are going.'

He paused, looking at her curiously.

'You have a lot of work on. We can't really afford for you to be away and not earning for a week. Besides, he wasn't your father. You never even liked him.'

Dieter fought with his annoyance. He remembered the awful fear he'd felt when Sarah had said Opa was dead. His parents were ageing. When was he going to get a chance to see them? And now that Ingrid had spent money on three airfares to Germany, when would there be enough for all four of them to go back again? 'I wish you'd checked with me first.'

'There wasn't time.' She was bustling down the hallway now. Dieter nearly tripped over a suitcase following her. 'Besides, you know we really can't afford for you to be off work unexpectedly. Now, I need you to be ready to take us to the airport in an hour.'

His annoyance grew. Sometimes she treated him as though she owned him. 'You can be so bossy, Ingrid.'

'We have to get there somehow.'

Sarah emerged from her bedroom. Since her thirteenth birthday she had taken to wearing battered sneakers, old threadbare jeans and a man's shirt that was too big for her. 'Hey, you guys aren't fighting, are you?' She shook her head. 'For God's sake, speak English so at least I know if you're fighting.'

'It's all right, darling,' he said, smoothing her hair.

'Why are you wearing that ridiculous outfit again?' Ingrid asked. 'Put something decent on.'

'It's comfortable! Dad! Tell her!'

The phone started ringing. Dieter threw his hands up in the air. 'I'll get it.'

The intense discussion about Sarah's clothes continued down the hallway. Alex ran after Dieter, grabbing his leg as he answered the phone.

'Hello?'

'Dieter?'

452

It was Ellie. Alex was singing a little song about wanting a drink of water. Dieter didn't hear. It had been months since he'd heard her voice, but he'd know it anywhere. He glanced behind him. Ingrid was nowhere in sight.

'Hello,' he said guardedly.

'Daddy, I said I want a drink of water.'

'Is this a bad time?' she asked.

Dieter reached for a plastic cup and filled it from the tap. Alex took it in one hand and immediately slopped it onto the floor.

'Oops! Daddy, clean it up.'

'Not now, Alex.' He turned his attention back to Ellie. 'Is everything all right?'

'No.' Her voice caught. 'No, it isn't. I've had some bad news and... I need someone to talk to.'

Ingrid and Sarah had stopped fighting. He watched the hallway warily. He had to be quick. 'Later tonight. I've got to take my family to the airport.'

'Daddy! Clean it up!'

'I'll wait for you.' The phone clicked. His head spun. Just when he'd thought he might be able to put her out of his mind, she was back.

Something about being in the car together always led to George and Aila having an argument. Perhaps it was the confined space. At home, the distance between them had grown. It was impossible to argue with somebody who simply wasn't there.

The traffic on the M3 was heavy, and George was stuck behind a lorry. He drummed his fingers on the steering wheel, humming absently. Aila sat next to him, gazing out the window. She was all in white, crisp and immaculate. Her hair was nearly white now, as the ash-blonde faded with age. And yet, even though it was her sixty-second birthday they were celebrating this weekend, she still had a dewy softness about her. Sometimes, at the end of a long day of silence, when he had been consumed with a book and she had been cross-stitching on the couch in the next room, she would appear next to him with a soft smile. 'Would you like anything special for dinner?'

He would shake his head, unable to shed his surly mood. As soon as she left he would soften, thinking about her hopeful blue eyes. She was still there for him. Over a decade of battling with the black dog of depression, and he hadn't driven her away. His sufferings were mild by most standards: the loss of his successful business had not stripped him of his wealth or good health. But a cocktail of guilt and regret and anger over the collapse of his dreams had poisoned his heart. George was trapped inside himself now, and every year it was as though another layer of hard ice formed around him. He retreated further and further away from her, away from light and hope.

'Now, remember,' Aila said, turning from the window. 'Daddy is nearly ninety now, and he doesn't get to see us often. So be nice.'

'I'm always nice to him.'

'Last time you got angry at him, as I recall. You called him a fatuous old sod.'

'Not to his face.'

'No, but he can tell you get impatient with him.'

'He's got no idea about politics. He'd vote for the Nazis if they stood for election.'

'He's *old*. You can't change him now. For heaven's sake, George, be patient with him. You'll be old one day.'

For heaven's sake, George. Once she had only ever called him *Lemmikki. George* was saved for arguments. Now the pet name was lost in a happier past. The lane next to him started moving and he quickly indicated and tried to pull out. Another car swept past at speed, the lorry put its brakes on suddenly. George had to brake too, and stay in the blocked lane.

'Damn!' he shouted, whacking the horn.

'Who are you beeping at?'

'Nobody. Everybody.' He scowled, gripping the steering wheel. 'Sorry, if I'm human and lose my temper.'

She turned back to the window again. 'Yes, well. I know a lot of humans who don't lose it quite so much, George.'

Silence. Rain descended. The traffic started to move. Soon they were taking the turn-off towards Aila's father's home. He sped down a country lane. The road wound down and up, lined with trees.

'Did you remember to pack the camera?' she asked casually.

'Pack it?'

'In your suitcase.'

'Why would I have brought a suitcase?'

His eyes were on the road, but he could see from the corner of his eye her exasperated expression. 'Because we are staying the weekend, George.'

'Are we? Why?'

'Because today is Friday and my birthday is Sunday and we've been invited to see Daddy *on my birthday* which is not today, ergo, we must be staying the weekend.'

'Why didn't you say so?'

'I thought you could work it out yourself. Really!' She shifted in her seat. 'So you've brought nothing. No change of clothes? No toothbrush?'

He didn't confess to the two bottles of whisky he'd packed in the boot. 'No, nothing.'

'I'm sure I saw you take something to the car this morning.'

'It was your suitcase. You left it by the door.'

'And it didn't occur to you then that we must be staying?'

'I don't know.' He felt embarrassed now, and angry. 'Didn't it occur to you to tell me what your plans were?'

On it went, back and forth. George vaguely remembered another time, when the very thought of them speaking so harshly to one another would have appalled him. What a horrific disappointment life was. It started full of promise, but then reality bit hard. Careers failed, marriages turned sour, and age undermined wellbeing. Despite his early hopes, life had proved to him to be pointless, utterly pointless. Not that he was allowed to express such feelings. If he did, Aila would start talking about him needing to 'see someone', that it wasn't 'normal' to feel that way. George believed that any sixty-something-year-old who *didn't* feel that way was a fool or a liar.

George became aware of an expectant silence. Aila had asked him something, he had no idea what...

'Well?' she said. Then when he still didn't answer. 'You weren't listening, were you?'

For some stupid stubborn reason, he couldn't admit that he wasn't. Perhaps because a drifting mind was a sign of old age. So he said, 'Of course I was listening. I just didn't think it was a question worth answering.'

Her shocked silence alerted him to the fact that this was entirely the wrong thing to say.

'Aila?' he said.

'I... How could you say that?' Her voice was terribly hurt. It alarmed him. What the hell had she asked him? He turned to glance at her, to see if she was crying.

'Don't start with the tears,' he said.

'George!' she shrieked, pointing directly ahead.

His eyes went to the road. A car was approaching. The lane was too narrow for both of them, and George had drifted right out into the middle of it. He braked and wrenched the wheel to miss the car, the road slipped. Bushes were thudding up under the car. A tree loomed. He pulled the wheel.

A violent, flat bang. Metal crumpling around him. Glass falling like rain.

Then silence.

'Aila?' He unbuckled his seatbelt and leaned over her, noticed his hands were cut and bleeding. 'Aila?' He shook her and she flopped like a rag doll. 'No, no, no...' He couldn't think of anything else to say. 'Aila? Aila?'

'Are you all right?' This was the driver of the other car, a young man, who had pulled over and raced down to check on them.

'My wife,' he said. 'She's not answering me.'

The young man went to Aila's side of the car, which was mangled out of shape. He leaned through the broken window and felt for Aila's pulse. 'She's alive,' he declared. 'I'll run up to the nearest house and call an ambulance.'

He disappeared. George tried to move, but became suddenly aware of a cruel pain in his right leg. So instead, he grasped Aila's hand and kissed it wildly. 'Hold on, darling, hold on,' he said. Reality was stripped bare; he finally saw what mattered most and despised himself for being careless with it. He remembered his father, a man who had allowed his black feelings to kill his wife. And hoped he wasn't to suffer the same fate.

It was growing late, and still Dieter didn't come.

Ellie felt more embarrassed than concerned. A woman in her late thirties, dolled up in a slinky dress and full make-up, waiting for a married man. She wished she'd pushed him to name a time so she would know if he was late or not coming at all. She finished a glass of wine alone, then lay down on the couch and closed her eyes, fighting tears.

She had thought twice about calling him, of course. But in the end, she didn't know who else to turn to. She had friends now, but nobody knew her so well as Dieter, and she wanted nobody's comfort more than she wanted his. She had been to the doctor today, who had referred her immediately to a throat specialist. A persistent hoarseness was creeping into her voice. She had tried remedies for acid reflux, dehydration, post-nasal drip…none had worked. The throat specialist had put a tiny camera down her throat, frowned and told her devastating news. 'Nodes,' he had said. 'Little calluses on your vocal folds.'

Every singer knew what nodes were, and most were clever enough to avoid them. But Ellie worked harder than most singers. She hadn't had a holiday in over a decade, working instead season after season, all over the world. Now it was catching up with her. There were two remedies for nodes. Surgery she wouldn't contemplate. There were too many horror stories about slips of the scalpel, scarred voices. Rest was the other option. *Rest*. She had just renegotiated with the Australian Opera, and signed contracts for work in San Francisco, Beijing and Wellington. Rest could ruin her career. And yet she must rest, or risk losing her voice forever.

Tonight of all nights she needed Dieter. Waiting for him, not knowing when he'd arrive, reinforced all the more keenly how he wasn't hers, how he had only ever been on loan to her. If she couldn't sing and she couldn't have Dieter, what else was there to do? It startled her that such a full life could feel so empty.

It was a windy night, and the panes in the windows rattled with it. She started to doze, slipped into a dream where she was looking for something vital that she knew was in a golden box, but people kept interrupting her before she could open it. She blinked back to wakefulness with a start. The lights were all on still. The clock read eleven. She was momentarily disoriented, then heard it again. A very soft knock at the door.

She stood, the blood rushing away from her head. A brief second of dizziness. She steadied herself, then hurried to the door.

'Dieter.'

'Hello.' He smiled uncertainly. 'Sorry it's so late. Ingrid's flight was delayed.'

Ellie couldn't think clearly, the shreds of sleep still clinging to her. 'Come in.'

She stood aside and let him in, followed him. By now, her make-up was smudged and her dress was creased. She laughed at herself; he hadn't even noticed.

He sat down, eyeing the empty wine glass. He wore a loose white shirt and black cords that were half an inch too short for his long legs. He explained that Ingrid's father had died and she and the children had flown immediately to Germany. 'I came straight from the airport,' he said. 'I hoped you'd still be awake.'

'I was dozing,' she replied. 'Having a bad dream...can't remember it now.' She met his gaze, those unfathomable hazel eyes, and her heart flipped over. She longed for him. Her bad news returned to her memory and she was overwhelmed by a sense of desolation.

'Ellie? Are you okay?'

'It's been a rotten day,' she said, forcing a smile. She told him about the voice doctor, about the problem and its unbearable solution, and despite her best efforts, she began to cry. He was flustered by

458

her tears. She realised she was making him uncomfortable and tried to stop. 'I'm sorry, Dieter,' she said, taking a deep breath. 'You must think me a fool.'

'No. No.' He rose and came to sit next to her, tentatively putting an arm around her shoulders. 'If it feels good to cry, you should cry. I can't solve your problem, but I can listen well enough.'

Ellie felt the weight of his arm, the heat of his skin, acutely. Physical contact, denied her for so long. She felt giddy and her tears vanished. No rational thoughts were admitted, she leaned into him, slipped her arms around his ribs.

'Ellie,' he breathed, a wary note in his voice.

'Please,' she begged, hating herself for begging. 'Please, just hold me.'

He embraced her, and she breathed in his clean, soapy smell, intoxicated by it. Seconds ticked by, and she knew he would soon release her and this moment of comfort would be over. But he didn't release her. Desire stirred deep inside her; she was almost afraid to look up at him.

'Dieter,' she muttered against his chest, 'don't go home tonight. Your house is empty. Stay with me.'

She turned her face up to his. Their lips met. A spark. Then he was pressing down, soft lips moving against her mouth, his breath hard and reckless. The panes rattled again, as the weather outside grew wilder. She clung to him, wild herself. His tongue was in her mouth, his hands spread around her ribs as though he wanted to crush her, and the feverish heat between their bodies overrode anything else: like commonsense, or duty, or honour. There existed only desire. Clothes were removed, skin met forbidden skin. While the cold wind stalked outside, they lost themselves in each other, submitting to temptation as though it was the only force with any meaning left on earth.

The half-light before dawn crept under the blind in Ellie's bedroom. She shook herself awake, yesterday's surprise still waiting for her.

Dieter, asleep in her bed. She watched him a while and, as though he could sense her gaze, he woke.

'Ellie?' he smiled.

'Don't go. Stay with me.'

'I'm here, aren't I?'

'Stay all week. Until they get home.' She couldn't bring herself to use Ingrid's name, it would poison the dream.

He pulled her down next to him. 'All right. I will.'

THIRTY-FIVE

'Mr Fellowes?'

George looked up. His heart was paralysed. What the doctor said next might change his life forever. The hospital corridor was noisy, busy. But it all seemed to him to be happening a million miles away. In this moment, there was only him and the young doctor.

'She's come through the surgery brilliantly. She hadn't lost as much blood as we feared. I expect her to recover fully.' She smiled broadly. 'You can go in and sit with her if you like. She'll come around soon. Room fourteen.'

Lights, music. His head swam. 'So...she'll be all right?'

'She'll have to take it easy for a while, so we'll keep her here five or six days. But after that, yes. Perfectly all right.'

He couldn't believe it. He'd been so sure that this day would end with the blackest of news. Instead, he was following the doctor to room fourteen, managing poorly with crutches for a sprained knee. Aila lay there, eyes closed and pale. The sheets had been tucked tight over her abdomen. He pulled up a chair beside the bed, and the doctor left him alone with his wife.

George took Aila's limp hand and leaned on the bed, gazing at her. The veins under her eyelids gave them a bluish hue. Her pulse was soft at her white throat. Her vulnerability overwhelmed him, and he began to cry, great heaving sobs. A dam had burst inside him; feelings, too long denied, flowed free. *I nearly lost her.* He realised what she must have asked him before the accident, the question that he'd said was not worth answering. 'Do you still love me?' The answer was yes, yes. He loved her more at this moment, this hinge in his life, than he had ever loved anyone or anything. He loved her desperately, and he knew that he had to change. Whatever had happened to him, whoever had been to blame, it had never been Aila's fault. And yet he had punished her the hardest. He let his tears flow, silently vowing that he would do whatever was necessary to shake the darkness that he'd gathered around him; whatever was necessary to make it up to her.

'Mmm.' She stirred.

His head jerked up. Her eyelids were fluttering. She smacked her lips together.

'Are you thirsty?' he said, looking around for a water jug. 'What do you need?'

Her eyes opened fully. 'George? What happened?'

He smiled at her. 'Everything changed,' he said.

It was a dangerous game and they both knew it.

Every morning, Dieter woke up in Ellie's bed. He showered while she made breakfast, she kissed him goodbye at the door and welcomed him home again in the evening. Apart from one trip to his own house for clothes, he behaved precisely as if he was married to her, and not somebody else. He held her hand while she phoned her agent and cancelled three seasons of work, dried her tears afterwards. They made love like teenagers, in every room of the flat, at any time of the day. He made one phone call to Ingrid in Germany, while Ellie remained perfectly silent in the background, heart thudding guiltily in her throat. They lived a fantasy of togetherness, both of them denying the truth, that he belonged to somebody else, somebody who would return soon.

By the end of the week, though, Ellie was unwilling to relinquish him.

Her heart felt sick with sadness as he dressed for work in the morning. He would be going back to his own house directly afterwards, picking Ingrid up early the following morning, resuming life as it always had been. She tried to read his expression. Did he feel the same sense of dismay and yearning?

'I hate that you have to go,' she blurted, trying to keep tears in check.

He didn't answer, head bent to button his shirt.

'Dieter? What are you feeling?'

He sighed, sat heavily on the bed next to her. 'You really want to know? I feel horribly, horribly guilty.'

She blinked, trying not to be disappointed.

'I don't expect you to understand, Ellie. You haven't betrayed anybody.' He leaned forward, resting his forearms on his knees. He looked tired, defeated. 'I've been so selfish. I've let everybody down.'

'You haven't let me down.'

He turned his head to look at her and smiled sadly. 'I have, Ellie. I've encouraged you to put your life on hold for me, I should never have contacted you or I should have ended it completely long ago. You've wasted years on me. Time you could have been finding somebody else, having children of your own.'

'I didn't want children.' That was a lie. She would have gladly had children with him; but with some other man? It was too awful to think about. Her brief affair with Stephen had tripped on precisely that issue. He was keen for marriage, family. She had shied away, stopped returning his phone calls. She cited distance as the problem, but he probably knew he had frightened her off. 'Besides, plenty of women have children later now. I still have time.'

A sad silence chilled the room. Things unspoken. Time ticked on, he would soon have to leave for work.

'Dieter, do you have to go back to her?' she asked, in a soft voice, dreading the answer, hating herself.

'You know I do.'

'Why?'

'We have children.'

'Sarah's a teenager. She'd understand.'

Dieter laughed bitterly. 'You've obviously never met a real teenager.'

'But it's better for her. To see that it's not right to stay in a loveless relationship.'

'My relationship with Ingrid isn't loveless,' he said vehemently. 'It's just not...not like this.'

'Do you love me?'

'I love you like...' He stretched his hands out, reaching for words that wouldn't come. 'I love you so much that I have to let you go.'

Panic seized her. 'What do you mean?'

'We can't keep seeing each other. It's too hard on both of us; on you especially.'

'I don't mind,' she said frantically. 'We can keep meeting once a month, like we used to.'

'We can't go back to that now,' Dieter said, pulling himself up straight. 'Are you mad? Seeing you and not being able to touch you...'

'Then see me and touch me,' she said. 'Just don't deny me. I don't care if it's only once in a while.'

He shook his head sadly. 'Listen to yourself, Ellie. Listen to what I've done to you.'

The awful realisation: he was right. She sounded desperate. Emptiness engulfed her. Without Dieter, without her singing, what was there?

Dieter took her hands in his, tried to meet her eyes. She glanced away, but he held her firmly. 'I think that we have to say goodbye,' he said. 'I think it would be better for both of us.'

'Better for you, maybe.'

'Ellie...'

'Have you known all week that you were going to do this?' She couldn't keep the edge of anger out of her voice.

'I've known for two days,' he conceded. 'Since I spoke to Ingrid.'

She shook his hands off. 'Then you should have told me. You should have told me before I got in deeper.'

He gave her a dubious look. 'I don't know that it would have made a difference.'

Although he was right, she was angry and hurt enough to want to punish him. She ranted at him, accused him of using her, and he remained his calm self, with his sad liquid eyes and his patient brow. She hated him and loved him all at the same time, but she couldn't keep him.

And so, karma returned to her. Just as she had broken it off with him all those years ago, so he broke it off with her now. She refused to cry. He touched her shoulder at the front door but she shrugged him off.

'I hope you'll forgive me in time,' he said.

'I'll never forgive you,' she replied.

He smiled, seemed about to say something – maybe to repeat some knowledge about her that only he had discerned – but he remained quiet. He turned to go, in paint-splattered overalls, suitcase in his hand. At last she was alone.

The day weighed on her heavily; all those hours to fill until the hollow evening. She wished she could run away, leave all these feelings behind her. She slumped into the couch, the glimmer of an idea circling in her mind.

Perhaps she could run away after all.

It was a strange, sad kind of peace.

Angela returned home from taking Jerry to the airport. Before they'd left, the house had seemed full, noisy, all confusion. Suitcases in the kitchen, the phone ringing, Bo and Jerry playing sword-fights with sticks from the garden. Now it was too quiet, as though something had been lost.

'I might go and play in my room for a while,' Bo muttered, making to slip away.

'Wait, sweetie,' she said, grasping his hand and pulling him towards her. It was his way to retreat into himself when he was upset about something. She enfolded him in her arms. At eight, he was getting so tall, all long skinny legs and arms. He allowed her to cuddle him, reluctant and grateful all at once. She heard a little hiccough, knew he was crying, and squeezed him harder.

'How exciting will it be to see Daddy in the holidays?' she said, standing back, smoothing his mousy hair. 'All the way to England on a plane.'

His eyebrows had gone red from crying, just as they did when he was a baby. She wondered when he would grow out of it. 'It would be better if you came.'

'I can't. Somebody has to run the business. Besides, Nan's more fun than me, isn't she?'

He grinned. 'Yeah, she is.' He wiped his face on the shoulder of his T-shirt. 'I'm going to go and read or something.'

'All right.'

He disappeared, closing his door behind him. She wished she could lie on her own bed and indulge her misery too, but there was too much to be done. Lost in preparations for Jerry's departure, she hadn't looked at the accounts or ordering for a week. She sat down in her study, and felt a strange sense of satisfaction that, at last, she was back to full-time work.

Busy, the days sped by. Leila came down every second weekend to look after Bo, and the assistant they had hired covered the work after school and on the other weekends. Work made sure she couldn't spend too much time feeling sorry for herself; and she worked hard. Even in the low season, she rarely had an empty room. Months had passed before she realised that she hadn't had a single bad dream or memory since Jerry left. She was cautiously hopeful that this was the end of the long dark tunnel. The memories were going to stay buried. Now she really would never know.

Dieter pulled the ute up into the driveway behind Ingrid's little Toyota. Dusk was lowering overhead, and his body ached from a ten-hour day of painting. Demand for his business was growing, and he had to decide whether to put on another employee or start knocking jobs back. Both options had their negatives.

He was turning this question over as he entered the house. Ingrid was in the kitchen, cleaning out a cupboard. Plastic containers surrounded her on the floor. She wore gloves, and the smell of bleach powder was strong.

'Where are the kids?' he asked, aware of the emptiness in the house.

She glanced up, didn't smile. 'At Jessica's.'

No other explanation was forthcoming. Ingrid hated Jessica, their next-door neighbour's sullen daughter who always dressed in black. But Ingrid turned back to the cupboard and he was tired and needed a shower. So he kept moving, up into his own bedroom to find some fresh clothes in the dresser.

But before he found the clothes, he found a letter. Addressed to him, with *Private* written in big letters across the bottom of the envelope. No return address. He picked it open and unfolded the letter.

It was from Ellie. He caught his breath. Why was she writing to him? Didn't she know that writing *Private* on the front meant nothing to Ingrid? It would only arouse her curiosity. But then, why would Ellie know that about Ingrid? He'd told her virtually nothing about his wife, and he'd certainly tried his hardest never to complain about her. He hadn't heard from Ellie or seen her in eight months. The last he knew of her was the phone call from the letting agency that she had moved out of his flat, and left no forwarding address.

'Did she leave a message for me?' he'd asked.

'No, sir. Should she have?'

Of course she shouldn't have. But he'd hoped for something. A goodbye, a good luck, an I'm sorry.

He tucked the letter into his overalls and went to the bathroom. Here, he locked the door, turned on the shower, and sat on the edge of the bath to read it.

Dear Dieter,

Forgive me for writing to you at home. It has been some time now since I last saw you, and I thought you would not mind this short communication, just to let you know where I am and what I am doing.

I have taken a lease on the house where I last stayed in far western Queensland. You'll remember that I told you how much I loved the space and the silence. They suit me very well, and I find myself in no hurry to return to the opera stage just yet. My voice still needs some time to recover, and in the meantime I am enjoying the pace of country life. I am not seeing anybody. My friend Stephen comes to see me from time to time, but I've made it clear that he is only my friend. I tutor one day a week in the local high school, teaching music. I would like to do more, but must take care of my voice. I spend a lot of time in silence, like a nun who has taken a vow.

I've put my address and phone number on the top of this letter if you want to contact me. There are no streets or street numbers out here. I am very hard to find without directions, so make sure to phone me first if you'd like to visit. I regret the last thing I said to you, about forgiveness. However, I regret nothing else.

Best wishes,
Ellie

Dieter tucked the letter carefully back into the envelope, and then into the pocket of his overalls. His heart thudded. He stepped under the shower, turned the heat up so that steam engulfed him. Ellie again, always in his thoughts. Those old feelings returned: longing, love. When would he get over her? When he was one hundred and had no hot blood left?

Ingrid was waiting in the hall when he emerged from the bathroom. 'We need to talk.'

The first stirrings of unease. 'We do?'

'Come on. Kitchen table.'

Dieter dropped his overalls on the end of the bed and followed her. She was going to ask him about the letter, who had written it, why it was private; he had to think of quick lies.

He sat opposite her and realised that she was holding back tears. 'Ingrid?' he said, warm fear flooding him. 'What's wrong?'

She banged the table with her fist. 'I read the stupid letter.'

'You...?'

'I steamed it open, I read it.'

'But it was private.'

'That's why I read it, and don't you *dare* get angry at me. When did you see Ellie? How many times?'

Dieter couldn't concentrate on her questions. He was too busy re-reading the letter in his head, assessing how much it had divulged. 'I saw her...a few times,' he managed.

'Why didn't you tell me?' She shook her head. 'I know why you didn't tell me, why am I even asking? It's all there in her letter, talk of regrets, of who she's seeing. She's tried to hide it but she can't. You had an affair, didn't you?'

Dieter opened his mouth to lie, but it wasn't in his nature to do so. One lie would lead to many, tangled skeins of deception. Besides, he'd made enough of a fool of Ingrid already. He took the path of least resistance. 'Yes,' he said. 'I'm sorry, Ingrid.'

Her eyes rounded with shock. She'd been expecting a denial, he saw now, she'd been *hoping* for one. 'Tell me everything,' she gasped.

'It's over, that's all you need to know.'

'You slept with her?'

'The week you were away.'

'At my father's funeral?' She leapt out of her chair and turned away. 'Get out of my sight,' she said. 'What kind of a person are you?'

He rose, uncertain. 'You want me to go?'

She turned. 'Get the letter.'

Numbly, he did as she bid. She took the letter and methodically tore it into tiny pieces. Dieter watched her. He felt like an actor in a play, who had forgotten what he was supposed to say or do next. The pieces were consigned to the rubbish bin. She was crying again, but he didn't know if it was from anger or sadness. She shrugged off his attempts to comfort her. Finally, she composed herself.

'Do you love her, Dieter?'

He shook his head, afraid that trying to deny it with words would be impossible. 'You're my wife, Ingrid. You and Sarah and Alex are my family. I know I put it all at risk, but I swear to you it's over.' Saying that aloud hurt.

She glanced away, sniffling. 'I don't believe you. I know you, Dieter. I know that you wouldn't have slept with her if you didn't love her.'

He couldn't answer. She drew herself up, squaring off her shoulders. 'I'll need some time.'

'Of course.'

'The flat's empty at the end of the month. I think you should go there.'

'You want me to move out?' He thought of not seeing his children every morning, bleary with sleep, as they ate their breakfast. It twisted him up inside.

'For a while.' Her voice became brittle. 'This is a separation, Dieter, it's temporary. Don't you go after Ellie. I don't want my children having anything to do with her.'

'Don't blame her. It was –'

'Don't you defend her!' Ingrid shouted, thumping the table with her fists. 'If I find out you're seeing her, you won't be able to see the kids. It's that simple. If you care about this marriage –'

'Of course I do.' His children. How had he got himself into this situation? Of course he knew: a great love was not an easy thing to manage, and he'd acted blindly. Now the full realisation was upon him, what he'd risked, what he might yet lose.

He thought of Ellie. He still couldn't regret it.

Saturdays were always busy, but this one more so than others. It was the first weekend of the high season and all the guests arrived at once. Meanwhile the young couple in the Love Suite had forgotten the ten o'clock check-out time; lunchtime had come and gone. Her assistant had gone to the markets for fresh fruit, and Angela was dealing with everyone single-handedly.

'I'm so sorry for the delay,' she told the last woman checking in, as she showed her to her room. 'I'm afraid it's been quite a day.'

'The room's lovely, thank you,' the woman said, parking her suitcase in the corner. She was elderly but in good shape, with a kind face. 'I've been meaning to ask since the moment I laid eyes on you, dear. Are you related to Penelope Bright? You are so very similar to her.'

Angela faltered, taken aback. She remembered a long time ago somebody asking her the same thing. 'Is she a pop singer?'

'Opera. Though I think she once sang pop. Have you heard of her?'

Angela shook her head. 'Not really... I mean...'

'Ah, I expect not many people have. Opera has a pitifully small audience here. There are the big names – Sutherland, Pavarotti – and the others all have to settle for not being well-known. But she's a very successful soprano, based in Sydney.'

Angela realised her stomach was churning. 'I don't think I'm related to her,' she said.

'Ah well. They say everyone has a double, somewhere in the world.' She winked. 'I hope mine has aged better than I have.'

Angela left her and went to buzz the couple in the Love Suite again. Perhaps they'd gone out. She kept herself busy the rest of the afternoon, but all the talk of Penelope Bright had unsettled her. It must have got under her skin, for that night she had a dream.

The man, Benedict, was leering over her. Dark shadows gathered around him. Her heart fluttered madly. 'You killed him,' he declared in a flat voice. 'You killed my father.'

Angela woke, panicked and breathless. She switched on the lamp next to her bed, chasing the dark away. *You killed him. You killed my father.* It had felt real, a memory, not a dream. Dreams were mixed up, full of symbols and things that didn't make sense. This was full of detail, order. So if it was a memory, then could it be true? Had she killed somebody? The thought froze her to her core. Is this what she was trying to forget?

She rose, went to the kitchen to make tea, turned on the television and watched it for hours. She was jittery and twitchy. There was no way she could get back to sleep in this state, and yet she had to be up at six for the breakfasts. Her head was heavy with weariness, and three a.m. was approaching.

In the bathroom, she searched the medicine cupboard. Jerry had been prescribed sleeping tablets about a year ago, though he had only taken one or two. She found the packet, read the back. The medicine sounded relatively harmless. It was only for one night after all.

She returned to the kitchen, poured a glass of water and took two of the tablets. A noise behind her. She turned. Bo stood there, in crumpled cotton pyjamas, rubbing his eyes.

'Mum?'

For some reason, she felt guilty. 'I'm sorry, sweetie. Did I wake you?'

'I heard a noise in the bathroom.'

'That was me. Looking for something in the medicine cabinet.'

'Is everything okay?'

'I'm fine. Don't worry.' She hoped she sounded convincing. 'Come on, let me put you back to bed.'

She tucked him in then went back to her own room, dreading returning to bed and turning off the light. Her muscles were starting to relax, perhaps the sleeping pills were working. She got into bed, decided to leave the light on. She needed all the help she could get, keeping the shadows at bay.

THIRTY-SIX

*I*t was just the same as any other family holiday in so many ways. Arriving at the airport, picking up the hire car, driving up the highway towards the Sunshine Coast while Sarah commandeered the tape deck and Alex dozed in his booster seat. But this one was different because Ingrid wasn't here.

'I hate this song,' Sarah muttered, fast-forwarding.

'Why do you have the tape then?'

'I like all the other songs on it.'

'They all sound the same to me.'

'Da-ad. Do you pretend to be daggy on purpose?'

The holiday had been booked months in advance and Dieter had hoped that it might provide him and Ingrid with a chance to patch things up. The tension between them was unabated. Sometimes, when he came to see the children, it felt as though the air was actually six degrees colder in the house than outside. On good days, Ingrid would talk to him politely but coolly. On bad days, she'd snarl and rant. Dieter couldn't imagine how they could ever get back together, but she still insisted she wanted the separation to be only temporary. Months had passed; he had begun to doubt her motives. It was all made worse by the fact that Sarah had taken his side, happy to find another way to get under her mother's skin. Not that she knew what

Dieter had done; Ingrid was determined, for the sake of her dignity, that nobody would be told.

So, when the time had come to decide what to do about the trip, Ingrid had told him coldly that she wasn't coming, that she needed some time to herself. Dieter, still trying to reconcile the situation, could do nothing but agree to her request.

'Dad, you missed the turn-off.'

Dieter shook himself out of his reverie. 'I did?'

She took the map out of the glove box. 'Away with the fairies,' she muttered. 'Take the next turn-off. I'll direct you back.'

'Thanks, Sarah.' She enjoyed bossing him around, so he let her. They wove down through the sub-tropical landscape, verdant greenery and silvery gums standing shadowless under the brilliant sun. He was enjoying Sarah's music, it made him feel young and carefree. It would be lovely to spend some time alone with her and Alex.

'It feels different without Mum, doesn't it?' she said, reading his mind.

'It does.'

'It's quieter.' She laughed. 'No fighting.'

'I'm sorry, Sarah. I'm sorry I'm not there, I'm sorry about the whole situation.'

'What did you do to her, Dad? Why is she so angry with you?'

'It's complicated,' he said. 'But don't worry, we'll sort it out.'

A soft voice. 'I hope so.'

He glanced at her. For all her teenage bravado, she was still a child really, one who hoped her parents would get back together. He felt a bolt of cold guilt.

'Next left,' she said, back to her bossy tone. 'That's it right there. Coolum Gardens. Do we have to share a bathroom?'

'I'm not sure. Your mother booked it.' He drove in under a wooden arch, overgrown with vines and flowers. The gravel drive ended in a circular parking lot. They moved from the chilly airconditioning of the car into the moist sea air. He and Sarah got out their suitcases and carried them up the four front steps. Alex followed, thumb jammed firmly in his mouth. As they stepped through the double front doors, a little bell chimed overhead. They dropped their suitcases and waited.

'Hello, how can I help you?'

Dieter turned towards the voice; his heart stopped.

An uncomfortable silence must have passed. Sarah nudged him. 'Dad?' she said in a low voice.

'I... We're booked... Newman...' He couldn't make the words come out. This woman, standing in front of him, was the exact likeness of Ellie. He would have believed it to be her, if there had been any glimmer of recognition in her eyes. But there was nothing, just a wary puzzlement about his strange behaviour.

'O-kay,' she said slowly, in a gentle English accent as she flipped open her appointment book. 'I'm Angela Smith, I run the b & b. What name did you say?'

'Newman. Like the film star.'

She consulted her book. 'I've got a reservation for four people.'

'There's only three of us. My wife... couldn't make it.'

'Can we swim at the beach over the road?' Sarah asked chirpily.

'As long as the flags are out,' Angela Smith answered. She pulled out a map and began to explain the locations of the various beaches to Sarah. Alex had found the stand with tourist brochures on it, and was rearranging them with his usual solemn air of supreme concentration.

Dieter watched her avidly. She was a little thinner than Ellie, her skin had seen a little more sun. Apart from that she was identical, and Dieter knew immediately who she must be. But how to ask her in front of Sarah without mentioning Ellie's name and having it get back to Ingrid?

'Can I have your credit card, please?' she asked Dieter.

He handed it over, cleared his throat. Then said, 'I'm sorry, Angela is it?'

'Mm-hm.' She was punching numbers into an EFTPOS machine.

'Did you... in the seventies, did you sing? Pop music?'

She froze, lifted her eyes to his slowly. Shook her head. 'No,' she said, 'you must be thinking of somebody else.' He could see that

475

he'd made her anxious, and remembered that the real Penny Bright had run away from that life. Perhaps she was still running.

Sarah leaned up to whisper in his ear. 'Dad, you're being *so* weird.'

He gave her a kiss on the cheek. 'Sorry,' he mouthed. The EFTPOS machine rattled into life. Dieter stole glances at Angela Smith. He thought of Ellie, how she had spoken so passionately about having a sister somewhere in the world, one that she hadn't been able to find. And here she was, tucked away in a little b & b in Queensland.

Angela gave him the room key, and showed him up the corridor to his door.

'I'm sorry, I'll have to dash off,' she said. 'I have to take my son to cricket practice. If you need anything, my assistant should be around. Help yourself to tea and coffee in the kitchen, and the barbecue on the back deck is for guests as well. Have a great stay.'

'Thanks,' he muttered.

Sarah opened the door and dropped her case, then sat sulkily on the bed. Dieter switched the television on for Alex, and began to unpack his clothes. Then noticed Sarah hadn't moved.

'What's wrong?' he asked.

'You were so weird with that lady.'

'She looked like somebody. Somebody who used to be famous when I was young.'

'You were totally flirting with her.'

'I wasn't.'

'You couldn't stop looking at her. Is this why Mum's so angry with you? Are you seeing other women?'

Dieter was flabbergasted. He sat next to her on the bed and put his arm around her. She leaned against him.

Alex had stopped watching television and now watched them instead. 'Daddy? Sarah?'

Dieter patted the bed next to him, and Alex climbed up and tucked himself under his other arm.

'Seriously, Sarah, she just looks so much like somebody else, I had to ask.'

476

'Did you have to stare? She probably thinks you *like* her.' She turned her face up to him. She had her mother's eyes, big and blue, with long pale lashes. 'Dad, don't fall in love with somebody else, okay? I want you guys to make up. I want all of us to be together.'

He squeezed them both hard. 'I won't, Sarah. I want that too.'

Angela hurried back from the chemist with one eye on the storm clouds brewing overhead. She'd left the windows open in the breakfast room, and it looked like it would start raining at any moment. She dropped her package on one of the dining tables and started lowering the windows. A crack of thunder alerted her that she was just in time. The first fat raindrops fell. She sat at a table under the window, watching the rain, turning the package over and over in her hands.

The lull had been all too brief. Bad dreams and memories plagued her almost every night. So she had to get sedatives. From three different doctors.

'How many nights a week are you finding it difficult to sleep?' the latest doctor asked her.

'Oh, once or twice,' she lied. If she told the truth, that it was every night and it wasn't unusual to need an extra dose at three in the morning, he would be as stern with her as the previous doctor had been. Cut out caffeine and alcohol, go for a walk, meditate, see a psychologist... He couldn't understand. Her problems were not ordinary problems. There were no ordinary solutions. But the Valium tablets relaxed her, and enough of them could help her sleep dreamlessly.

Of course, if Jerry was here, if she had his arms to shelter in, perhaps she wouldn't need help. But he was a long way away, and proving very reluctant about returning.

'Just another six months, babe. There are a couple of great projects coming up, I don't want to miss them. One's in Prague. You know I always wanted to see Eastern Europe.'

She didn't know what to make of how much he loved being somewhere else, being away from his son. Bo had been over twice so far, and Leila was happy to continue taking him twice a year. He had grown used to it, and came back from his visits happy and full of stories about exotic places his father had taken him. She often wondered if Jerry was seeing somebody else, but he rejected the notion with real hurt in his voice. *How could you even suggest it? I'm yours.*

But he wasn't hers. Some relationships ended with noise and bluster, but some went with barely a whisper of protest. She couldn't insist he come back, any more than he could insist she join him. She was desperately lonely, missed him until it hurt. But he didn't miss her, she could tell. And so she pretended everything was all right, and tried to accept that he might never return.

'Excuse me?'

Angela looked up, and immediately her shoulders tensed. It was the man again, the one with the light accent and the dark hazel eyes, the one who said she looked like that seventies pop singer. 'Yes?'

'My little boy ... I'm so sorry, but he's lost one of your towels at the beach.'

She smiled. 'It's all right. Don't be cross with him.'

'I'll pay for it, of course. Only ... now he doesn't have one for the bath.'

She pushed herself up, pocketing the package of sleeping pills. 'Come with me.'

The rain intensified overhead, and thunder rumbled. She led him down the corridor to the linen cupboard, unlocked it and handed him a towel. 'There you are. And don't worry about paying for the other one. I lose a half-dozen or so every year, and most people don't confess. You must have an honest spirit.' She smiled at him, but he didn't smile in return, and she braced herself.

'Angela,' he said in a low voice. 'I know who you are.'

Her blood turned to ice. 'Stop. Don't say another word.'

'But –'

'I said, stop!' She slammed her hands over her ears. 'Please, please. Don't tell me anything.'

His forehead creased with concern. 'It's all right, it's all right,' he said, holding his hands palms out in front of her. 'I'm sorry, I didn't mean to upset you.'

Thunder boomed overhead. She lowered her hands, and he lowered his. They faced each other in the narrow corridor. Her heart thudded hard. 'I don't know anything about myself,' she said breathlessly. 'And I've made the choice to stay that way.'

He frowned. 'You know nothing?'

She shook her head. 'I lost my memories. Bad things happened to me.' He opened his mouth to speak, but she cut him off before he could. 'No, don't say a word. Any little thing could trigger an avalanche.'

He blinked once. 'All right,' he said. 'I'll leave you alone.'

'I'm sorry, I know it's hard in high season. But...could you go? Find somewhere else? I'll pay the difference.'

'I don't want to see you distressed,' he said. 'We'll leave first thing in the morning.'

He left, and Angela locked herself in the bathroom. She popped two of the little pills into her palm and choked them down. Then she sat on the closed toilet lid and cried silently, wondering if she was doomed to this distress forever.

Dieter dropped the children home after the holiday, his mind unable to focus on Ingrid's serious tone. She sent the children to the shop for bread, and had started to talk about divorce. Apparently during her time alone she'd decided that it might be better all round. He hadn't been responsive enough, and she'd grown angry at him. But all he could think about was contacting Ellie, to tell her about Angela Smith.

He returned to his flat, now a bachelor pad of sorts, with a fold-out bed for when the children stayed. It bore no resemblance to the gleaming, tasteful place it had been when he and Ellie had had their affair. Ingrid had destroyed the letter with Ellie's contact details, so he started with phoning the operator. No listing for Ellie Frankel or Penelope Bright. He supposed she had taken a silent number. He tried to remember the names of friends she had mentioned, but couldn't come up with a single one. He racked his brains for the name of Ellie's agent, but couldn't recall it. Their relationship had been so insular, so divorced from the details of reality. So he phoned the Australian Opera office and asked there.

'I'm sorry,' the receptionist said, 'this is rather an odd request. We certainly can't give out artists' phone numbers.'

'I understand,' he told her. 'Could I ask for a message to be passed on? It's very important.'

'I'm not sure... I'd have to check with somebody. Can you hold?'

'Fine,' he conceded.

Tinny music in his ear. He waited. How else could he find her? Phone every school in western Queensland and ask for a music teacher named Stephen? Was that the name of the friend she had made? Or was it Simon?

'Mr Newman?' The voice was in his ear again. 'I'm sorry, it appears I can't help you.'

'But if I could just leave a message for her –'

'It's not that. We don't have any details for Ms Bright. No forwarding address, no phone number. She doesn't want to be contacted.'

'Is there somebody there who might know where she is? Anybody? Her agent? Or...' He realised he sounded desperate. 'I'm an old friend. She'd want to hear from me.'

'I'm very sorry, but we can't help,' the woman said. 'She's disappeared.'

Some days, Ellie felt she lived at the very end of the earth.

Heat shimmered on the red horizon. She sat on the verandah, catching the afternoon breeze. The silence was only broken by the occasional cry of a bird going overhead. She hadn't conversed with anyone in over a week, hadn't uttered a word herself. The silence was slowly making its way inside her. *Deep, still.* It was as though she'd found an extra ten per cent of space in her lungs.

The unbroken peace could help her heal, she knew it. Not just her damaged voice, but her damaged heart. She hadn't heard from Dieter. Months were racing past. She had to accept it was over, he wasn't going to contact her. And so, the sooner she schooled herself to solitude, the better. The bustle and chatter of the city seemed very distant. Perhaps she'd never go back. Perhaps she would continue to tread this soundless space like a ghost, alone. There was a community nearby if she needed company, there was a piano in the lounge room if she wanted music but, just for now, only silence mattered. Silence, stretching ahead of her into an unknowable future.

THIRTY-SEVEN
1996

*A*ngela *is in a dark room. She can't make out shapes and she knows somewhere around here there is a hole in the floor. If she steps through it, she will fall forever and forever. She moves hesitantly, toes stretched ahead of her. But then she hears him behind her. His hot breath. She must move quicker, he mustn't catch her. She must get back up the stairs and out the door. The room swells and grows, she can't find her way. He draws closer, terror crushes her ribs, she begins to run.*

'You killed my father!' he screams, and the words buzz in her head like poisonous wasps. 'You killed my father!'

Angela woke, gasping gratefully on dream-free air. The sun was streaming in her windows, making her hot, uncomfortable. She rolled over, checked the clock.

Her heart started.

How on earth had she not heard the alarm? She threw back covers, raced to the bathroom, nearly tripping over her suitcase, packed so neatly the night before. No time for a shower, she grabbed clothes, her heart still thundering. But another glance at the clock told her it was no use. She was more than an hour from the airport, the flight was going in forty-five minutes. She would miss it. She *had* missed it, really.

Her movements slowed again, she sagged, sitting heavily on the bed and crying into her hands. Bo would be so disappointed, Jerry would never forgive her.

She flopped back down amongst the rumpled covers. Tiny specks of dust swirled up, made visible by the morning sunshine. She knew how she had slept through the alarm: a few too many sleeping pills at two in the morning. There had been no option, ever since Jerry had forced her hand, made her commit to a trip overseas to see him, she had been a nervous wreck. How was she supposed to fly to London, when a trip to the suburban shopping centre exposed all her nerves? Bo had gone over at the start of his Christmas holidays, and she had been meant to join them.

'They're predicting snow up here in St Albans,' Jerry had said. 'A white Christmas.'

It was only fair, after all. Jerry came home for five weeks every year. This time it was her turn, to see this other life he lived without her. He was working on a big project, an eighteenth-century library that his company was rebuilding from within. He was proud of his work. 'It's beautiful, Angela. The ceiling I designed is a work of art, I can't wait to show you.'

But even for Jerry, even for Bo, she was reluctant to do it. Fear had long ago paralysed her. She went through the motions, booking flights, organising somebody to look after the business. And all the while the tension grew and grew, until there was nothing inside her but tangled knots of anxiety. As soon as she was tense, the dreams and memories grew worse. Once, those things forgotten had been held back by a suffocating shadow. Now, they existed on the other side of a fragile rice-paper screen, their dread silhouettes always visible.

On top of them she threw sedatives and then, when she couldn't get going in the morning, she took something else to perk her up. It was a crazy, miserable roller-coaster, and it had never been worse than it was in the time between Jerry's insistence that she come and

483

this morning. Now it was over. She had failed him, she was a slave only to the task of holding back the memories.

She checked the time. It was ten in the evening in England; she supposed she had better phone Jerry and confess.

'Hello?' His warm voice, starting to pick up an English accent.

'Jerry.'

'Angela?' A pause, then, warily, 'Please tell me you're at the airport.'

'I'm sorry, I'm so sorry.' Tears flowed. 'I slept through my alarm, I don't know what's wrong with me... I...'

He listened to her apologies in stony silence, then said, 'There are other planes, Angela. Other flights.'

She caught her breath, realised that deep down she had been relieved to miss the flight. 'I can't, Jerry.'

'Bo is going to be gutted.'

'I just... can't.' Guiltily, 'Is he awake?'

'No, he's asleep. He spent all day making up a list of things we were going to do together when you got here.'

'Don't make me feel guilty.'

'I will make you feel guilty, Angela, you deserve to feel guilty. All we asked was for you to get on a plane and come here to be with us.'

Now she felt anger rising. 'You left us, Jerry. Not the other way around.' Then, quieter, 'It may be easy for you to get on planes and switch countries, but it's not for me, okay?'

His voice was gentler, but still firm. 'Angela, I was talking to a friend's husband at the office Christmas party two nights ago. He's a psychiatrist.'

'Don't, Jerry, you know I want nothing to do with those people.'

'I told him about you,' he continued, as though he hadn't heard. 'Do you know what he said? He said that to go on denying those memories could cause acute psychological damage.'

'I said, don't,' she replied, but the words had already made their way under her skin. It was what she feared most: that there was no way out of this situation except tighter and tighter knots that would eventually strangle her.

'You have to confront your past,' he said. 'Without doing that, I don't know what kind of future you'll have.' His voice became very quiet. 'Without doing that, I don't think *we* have a future.'

Jerry was right. She eyed the empty blister pack on the bedside table. She had failed him, and she had failed her son too. This situation couldn't continue; something had to give. But she was afraid that when it did, everything she knew about herself would be blown to pieces.

As she locked up the shearers' quarters for another year, Ellie felt both sad to see the children go, but relieved to be on her own again. Since she had been living at Mununja, she had worked with the local school to run yearly music camps. She didn't get involved herself, unless there was an aspiring singer among the group. Stephen usually organised it all, she just provided the space and managed the meals for the visiting musicians. It was nice to have the company of professional musicians, to see the students improve their skills and learn something about a life outside their small towns and broken families. It was even nice to see Stephen, who was now married and expecting his first child. But she only really relaxed when they were all gone, when the floors had been swept and the many voices swept out too. Then there was just her, a glass of unwooded chardonnay and the long view from the verandah.

It wasn't that she didn't want to sing anymore. In fact, she sang every day. Loudly, to the birds and to the distance. Her voice was fixed, back in its purest, strongest form. She just didn't want to return to the city. Not yet, at least, though she knew she would have to go back eventually: her savings wouldn't last forever. She had once laughed at those of her generation who talked about 'finding' themselves; but here, in the middle of nowhere, she had done precisely that. She had found herself, her true self. She had confronted her avarice, her ambition, her tendency to judge others – all traits of her father – and didn't wonder anymore at why she had failed in all her personal relationships. It wasn't bad luck that she had lost Dieter twice, but bad management. It wasn't distance that had separated her from her family, but her own reluctance to maintain contact with those who loved her simply for who she was. It wasn't fate that she had failed to have children, but bad choices, one after the other. She was entering her forties, and her voice would never sound better. But she could never have her twenties and thirties back, to work on the things that really mattered.

It was a very still day. Grey clouds hung low, and rain was on its way. She hoped the minibus would get back onto sealed road before the downpour turned the way into slippery sludge. It would be nice to have some rain, always so infrequent out here. Nice to lie there in bed at night and hear it pattering on the tin roof, and nice to see wildflowers dot the paddocks. She liked to go out after rain, picking wildflowers and watching the creek flow again. Once she had slid on the muddy embankment and nearly ended up in the water, clutching a posy of paper daisies like some outback Ophelia. What an operatic way to die, that would have been. Sometimes it seemed like her whole life was like an opera: doomed love, wealth squandered, an unknown sister, a retreat to hermit-like solitude. But the drama of the stage disguised the mundane truth of such a life. There was a lot of waiting and yearning, a lot of regrets and uncomfortable truths to bear.

She sat a long time watching the rain come in. Her wineglass beaded with condensation, the dark grey clouds swept over, bringing a chill to the air and, finally, a deluge. She watched as water gushed from the gutters, weighed down the branches of the saplings in her garden, pooled muddily on the driveway. The difference between night and day was blurred by the clouds. She was just thinking of going inside and turning the lights on when the phone rang.

'Hello?' she said, scooping up the receiver.

'It's Stephen.'

Always, the disappointment. She wondered when she would stop hoping it was Dieter phoning her.

'I just wanted to let you know we got back safely. Before the rain started.'

'I'm glad,' she said. 'I had wondered.'

'And you? Are you all right?'

'I always am.'

'I sometimes worry about you, out there alone.'

She smiled to herself. 'Don't worry about me,' she said, meaning it. 'I can look after myself.'

George had never imagined himself moving to the country. He had always seen himself as a city-dweller, a sophisticate. But now escaping the city made perfect sense. He dreamed of quiet mornings with Aila, hot tea, a tabby cat; he even dreamed of gardening. If he could go back in time, tell his young self – perpetually dressed in black – that he would be cultivating petunias later in life…well, he would have rejected the notion totally. But time changes people, and he understood that now.

So, the Lambeth townhouse had been sold, and a cottage in Oxfordshire had been purchased, and it was time to pack up the vestiges of one life and transform them into another. Aila was tackling the upstairs rooms, George the downstairs rooms. Cardboard boxes and scrunched-up newspapers and packing tape were everywhere. The removalists were due early the next morning, and they had far too much to pack to be ready by then.

Aila came down at nine o'clock, her usually neat hair escaping from under a pale pink scarf, with an armful of art supplies. 'I'm worried we're going to run out of boxes,' she said.

'Me too,' George said, glancing up from where he sat on the coffee table, sorting books. 'This pile is going to have to stay here, I'm afraid.'

She came over, started to look through them. 'I'm starving,' she said. 'I should make us something to eat.'

'I've packed the kitchen. Do you want me to go out and get something? Indian?'

'But it's freezing out there.' Aila's stomach rumbled audibly. She laughed. 'Maybe it's a good idea.'

London was damp and chilly. The sky was overcast, and caught the amber glow of the streetlights. He saw the familiar route to the

Indian takeaway with fresh eyes: the last time he would walk this way. Nostalgia blurred to pleasing softness everything he experienced. The noise of the traffic, the smell of a passer-by's cigarette, the icy sting of the rain as it intensified. London, his beloved London. Now he would only return as a day visitor, his edges smoothed by country life. Happy-sad feelings rolled through him, but he knew he was doing the right thing. He returned half an hour later, to find Aila sitting on the couch sorting through a lapful of papers.

'Sorry it took so long,' he called, hanging up his coat and scarf. 'They were very busy.'

When she didn't reply, he continued. 'Shall we just eat on the floor?' He held up the plastic bag full of takeaway containers.

She looked up. He noticed that her face was stained with tears.

'Aila?' His eyes went to the papers. His heart froze. 'No!' he cried. 'How did you find those?'

She stood, the papers spilled on the floor. 'I found this first,' she said, brandishing a letter. 'In the box marked "Old business records". I thought perhaps you wouldn't need them, we could use the box. But then I found this and it led me to the other...' She was rambling, blubbering on sobs.

He strode across to her and took the letter from her hands. One of Ellie's, listing her new address, reiterating her desire to find her sister, the 'real' Penny Bright. But that was nothing compared to the other documents, carefully hidden all these years. Why on earth would she go through his old records? Why couldn't she leave them alone?

'Is it true, George?' she said, and the sorrow in her voice made him ache. 'What am I saying? Of course it's true. Legal documents don't lie. But we were married then! Married! Till death us do part. You said you loved me.'

'I did love you,' he said. 'I still do. This changes nothing.'

'It changes everything.' She palmed tears off her face, took a gulp of breath. 'The worst part isn't what you did, George. The worst part is that you've covered it up for over forty years. That's most of my life, living a lie. Believing that our marriage vows meant something.

And you let me keep trying over and over to have children…' She descended into sobs again. 'Babies, George, babies!'

George was unable to utter a word. The room was suffocating, nightmarish. *She had found out.* After all these years, she had found out, and it was just as bad as he had thought it would be. She was desolate, she was furious, and he knew that this crime was perhaps the only thing that she couldn't forgive.

'Well?' she demanded. 'What do you have to say for yourself?'

'Don't leave me,' he gasped. 'I'm sorry.'

Her indignant mouth turned upside down as she tried to hold back tears. 'I'm glad your things are packed,' she said. 'It's too late to be sorry.'

It was two days later, in the cheap hotel room, surrounded by suitcases of clothes and boxes of books, when he realised he still had the letter from Ellie that had started it all. He must have shoved it in his pocket that long night while pleading with Aila, their argument turning round and round in circles until they were both exhausted and hysterical. He smoothed it out, read and re-read the address. Ellie. Turning up in his life again like a bad penny. He laughed. A bad Penny, indeed. The start of everything that had gone wrong, and the end of it as well.

She had been so keen to stay in touch. Now it was time to pay her a visit.

THIRTY-EIGHT
1997

*A*ngela scanned the stream of people emerging from the Customs area at Brisbane airport. Traveller after weary traveller then, finally, the beloved face of her little boy. Not so little anymore as he approached twelve. Leila was just behind him, rust-grey hair swept up gracefully on top of her head. Angela waved, Leila waved back. Bo stared at her stonily.

She waited for them to round the barrier then leapt forward to hug him. He stiffened, and she knew that he was still angry at her for not making it to England for Christmas.

'I'm so glad to see you,' she said regardless. 'I missed you so much.'

'You didn't miss me enough,' he said, shrugging her off and stalking ahead.

Leila forced a smile. 'I'm afraid he's taken it to heart,' she said.

'But it wasn't my fault, it was...' She glanced over her shoulder. Bo had stopped and was sitting on his suitcase near the exit doors.

Leila touched her arm. 'I'm sorry, Angela. You know I love you. But it was absolutely your fault.'

Tears pricked her eyes. She nodded, then moved away from Leila to approach Bo. He lifted his gaze reluctantly, and she saw the hurt in his eyes. He looked so much like Jerry that it took her breath away.

'I explained, Bo. It was a stupid mistake. I slept through my alarm clock.'

'There were other planes.'

'I'm terrified of flying.'

'You're terrified of living,' he said, and she was amazed that someone so young could have seen so deeply into her heart. But then, he was her son, he lived with her, he saw her every day. He dropped his voice. 'Mum, I know why you slept through the alarm. I've heard you up late at night, I've seen the pills in the medicine cabinet. Other kids' mums don't take drugs.'

'They're not drugs. It's medicine, legally prescribed by a doctor.' The echo of her own words rattled in her head, and she had the horrible feeling that she had articulated this protest before, just as passionately and just as wrong-headedly.

He bit his lip, thinking very hard about what to say to her. The noise and bustle of the airport continued, oblivious to the tiny drama being played out in its midst.

'Mum,' he said at last, 'if you love me –'

'Of course I love you,' she said, desperate. 'How could you think – ?'

'Listen to me. If you love me, you'll stop taking those pills.'

She was taken aback, though dimly aware she shouldn't be. He knew she took too many sedatives, he blamed them for his Christmas disappointment, it was perfectly reasonable for him to ask. But she was inhabiting a different reality, where the pills were the only thing keeping her together. 'Did your father tell you to say that?' she said, regretting the sharp edge to her voice immediately.

He adopted an expression, somewhere between hurt and disgust, and she was suddenly deeply aware that this was the foretaste of his teenage years. At odds, not knowing each other, losing him.

'No, he didn't tell me to say it,' he responded hotly. 'I've been thinking about it a lot, that's all. You make me sad. I don't want to feel sad all the time.'

His words cut her deeply, and something inside her gave. She turned and beckoned to Leila, who approached warily.

'Leila, will you come down to stay with us for a week or two?' she asked.

'Of course, if you need me,' she replied.

'I do need you. I'm going to get off these pills.' She smiled weakly. 'I can't do it without you.'

Sarah didn't have an appetite for the bag of chips she had bought, and nor was she interested in the movie she had rented. Dieter glanced at her from time to time. Her gaze was stuck in middle distance, her black thumbnail being worried between her teeth. It was unusual for her to turn up on a Saturday afternoon on his non-access weekend. Something was troubling her, but he knew better than to ask outright.

The movie finished. Dieter rose to open the curtains, and let light back in the room. Sarah blinked, as though waking. He wondered if she'd seen any of the movie at all.

'What did you think?'

'Pretty boring.'

'What do you want to do now?'

She shrugged, tucked her feet up under her on the couch. 'Dunno. What do you want to do?' She had lightened her hair to platinum and had adapted to an indoor life so well that all her freckles had faded. But still he recognised the child in her, around her mouth and eyes.

He sat next to her and put his arm around her. 'You don't normally come to see me on my weekend off.'

'No.'

'Is everything all right?'

'Yes.' She glanced away. 'I mean...'

'Do you want me to make us coffee?'

She sighed, then met his gaze fully. 'Dad, Mum told me about your affair.'

Dieter was taken aback. 'She did?'

'Yeah, I'm a big girl now. We were fighting.' She rolled her eyes. 'As usual. I said something about going to live with you. She came out with it.'

He felt a sense of shame so profound that he knew his face was

492

flushing. To be confronted over infidelity by one of his children...
'I'm so, so sorry,' he said.

'Did you love her, Dad?'

'I did,' he said. 'I still do.'

'Then don't be sorry. You and Mum, you weren't that good together anyway. She was always picking on you, you were always giving her the silent treatment.'

Dieter gazed at her, overcome with amazement and pride at the woman she was becoming. 'Thanks. It means a lot to hear that from you.'

'Do you ever see her? The woman?'

Dieter shook his head and explained the whole situation, glad to have a willing listener to unburden his heart. He'd loved her, she'd slipped out of his grasp. Sarah listened, nodding, squeezing his hand.

'Dad,' she said when he'd finished, 'I bet I can find her. We've got access to the Internet at school. You can find all sorts of stuff.'

'I doubt that it would help.' Dieter smiled. 'Are you offering to find the other woman for me? The one that split up your parents?'

Sarah nodded. ''Course I would. If it'd make you happy.'

He pushed her over-bleached hair off her cheek. 'I hope Alex is just as forgiving.'

'He will be. You're his dad.' She wrapped her arms around his neck and hugged him like she hadn't hugged him since she was a little girl. 'We both love you, no matter what.'

George had travelled to many parts of the world, but he had never been to Australia. It seemed a fitting location for the end of things: the other side of the world.

It had taken a few months to organise everything. First, of course, he had to make very sure that Aila wasn't going to forgive him. When she put the Oxfordshire cottage on the market and deposited half of the money in his bank account, he'd accepted that it was over. She was living with her very elderly father now, and would no doubt stay on there after he died. She had friends and family in the village. She would be fine, and he was glad about that. His own burden of pain was so heavy, he couldn't bear hers as well. He imagined her future without him; she would grow old and still be beautiful, full of grace. His heart ached, and then he couldn't imagine anything at all except finding Ellie and giving her what was due to her. Then everything would be put right.

He didn't want to waste a moment. Hesitation would undo him. He picked up a hire car at the airport and started to drive. It was warm here, a different kind of warm from what he was used to. Bright, flat. But it hadn't the power to reach inside him, to ameliorate the cold deep in his core.

George still wasn't sure how he was going to do it, but he knew a gun was out of the question. His foster-father's words came back to him from all those years ago: *There's great shame in having a murderer for a father, and a self-murderer too. Let everything be different, and guard yourself against repeating his mistakes.* He didn't want to be like his father, so he would find another way.

He tried not to think too much on his drive to Ellie's house. A deep well of numbness grew inside him. Numbness was good. If his mind lit for a second on what was positive and bright about the world, he would lose his nerve. The journey didn't take as long as he thought it would. He found the address easily.

George parked the car, walked up to the front door, and knocked.

The phone was ringing when Dieter got home. He kicked off his shoes at the door and scooped it up.

'Hello?'

'Dad. Where have you been?' It was Sarah.

'At work.'

'Until six? I've been ringing for ages.'

'I was fitting in an extra job.' Always an extra job. He was consumed with his work, it filled the long empty hours he would otherwise have spent alone. 'What's up?'

'I found her.'

Electricity. 'Ellie? You found her?'

'Penelope Bright. That's what you said her stage name was.'

'Yes.'

'I found an article about her on an education department website. I printed it, you want me to read it?'

'Go on.'

'Okay, so: "An innovative-practice model of hands-on music education is taking place in far western Queensland. Opera singer Penelope Bright is hosting her third annual music camp for disadvantaged children at her outback property, Mununja, two hundred and forty kilometres southwest of Cunnamulla. The nearest town, Bywong, has only twenty residents, fewer than the number of students that benefit from her generosity." There's a lot more stuff about the camps and what they do, but that's all you need, right?'

Dieter scribbled the details down. 'Yes, that's all I need. I can't believe how easy that was.'

'Modern technology, Dad. Get with it.' She dropped her voice. 'Gotta go, Mum's coming.'

'Thank you, Sarah.'

'No problems. Go get her, Dad.'

Dieter paced afterwards. What to do now? He still had no phone number, and Ellie had written in her letter that the property was very hard to find. But surely if he stopped at the nearest town, somebody could direct him. He had to work the rest of the week, but there was nothing stopping him getting into his ute on Saturday morning and just driving...

But what if she didn't want to see him? It had been years. Maybe she'd found somebody else after all.

A letter, then. He started searching for notepaper, then realised he was still covered in paint dust. He went to have a shower.

As he was drying himself in the tiny bathroom, he heard a knock at the door. That was odd. He wasn't expecting anyone. He half-wondered if it was Sarah, finally kicked out by her mother. He pulled his dressing-gown around him and went to the door.

Nobody there.

A brightly coloured plastic bag on the doormat caught his eye. *For Ellie* was written on it in large black letters. He picked it up, momentarily confused. Why would somebody leave something here for Ellie? But then, of course, she had lived here for years. Whoever they were, they still had this address for her.

He brought the bag inside and sat it on the coffee table. The timing was strange, surreal. Would it be wrong to open it? After all, he had her address now. He could simply forward it on. It would give him a good reason to get in touch.

His hands were moving without his brain's permission. He pulled out of the plastic bag a sheaf of papers. On top was a long, hand-written letter. He flipped to the end. It was signed, *George Fellowes*. Curious, he turned back to the beginning and started to read.

> *Dear Ellie,*
>
> *I owe you an explanation, and it's rather a long one, but I don't want to leave out a single detail. Call it my way of making reparation for a very old sin…*

Dieter was late for work the next day. He had to write two very important letters, make a trip to the newsagent to photocopy the documents in the plastic bag, and then to the post office to post one set to Ellie, and another to Angela Smith on the Sunshine Coast. He doubted Angela would welcome the package; Ellie, too, might find some of the information very hard to take so he would leave her alone until she contacted him. It wasn't for him to be the guardian of their secrets. They had to work it out from here.

George wandered the night like a ghost, and eventually found himself at the water's edge. Water, the symbol of feeling. Yes, finally. He had decided. It was right, and he had regrets but at least he hadn't been like his father, he hadn't taken anyone else with him.

He waded out, the water rose, its chill tickle on his knees, his chest, his throat. Finally closing over his head. It crushed his lungs, and the pain, the suffocation turned his last thoughts not to Aila, but to Euphemia Angelis.

THIRTY-NINE
Vienna, Austria: 1954

*E*uphemia Angelis was, indeed, a star. Although she was only one player in the cast of *Il trovatore*, the audience treated her as a soloist, applauding loudly when she made her entrance. George was immediately fascinated by her beauty. She was petite, but carried about her an aura of immense energy and self-confidence. There was fire and passion in her performance, and at the curtain call the audience even demanded she sing an encore, calling over and over, 'Angelis! Angelis!' She gave a dazzling smile, instructed the conductor, then launched into a scorchingly sexy rendition of the gypsy dance from Carmen. George may not have liked opera, but he knew star-quality when he saw it. He turned to Karl and approved the advance on the spot.

'Do you want to meet her?' Karl asked.

George had to admit he was curious to see her up close. 'All right,' he agreed. 'But I can't stay long.'

There was a closing night party back at her apartments in the Hotel Albertina, a beautifully preserved historic building a short walk from the Staatsoper. George and Karl waited an hour, politely mingling with cast and crew, while Euphemia Angelis changed out of her stage clothes and made her way to the party. Apparently she liked making an entrance under any circumstances. Finally, she arrived, to a roomful of applause. She blew kisses, tossed her black hair, and quickly surveyed every face in the room. Her eyes lit on Karl, and she made her way directly over. Karl introduced her while George assessed her. Her Greek ancestry had blessed her with dramatic colouring, her exotic eyes were lined thickly with kohl, her soft mouth was painted red. But it wasn't her obvious beauty and her ability to highlight it so expertly that made her entrancing. It was the fire in her gaze, the energy buzzing just beneath her skin. At first he thought she must be a Greek goddess incarnate, but there was something too earthy, too sexual about her to be a goddess. She was more like a sorceress.

They exchanged polite conversation, spoke about the details of the contract, the performance. Then she was being pulled away by somebody else.

'I must go,' she said, 'but we'll talk again this evening. Don't you leave.'

'Of course not,' George replied, forgetting his warning to Karl that he couldn't stay out too late. 'It's been a pleasure to meet you, Euphemia.'

'Oh, my friends don't call me that,' she said. 'Call me Mia.'

'All right, Mia, we'll talk again.'

The night wore on. He watched Mia with more interest than he cared to admit he felt, as she did rounds of the room, chatting, laughing, entangling men in her hot gaze. But she didn't settle on any one of them, preferring having all of them love her a little. George mused on how different she was from Aila. Her colouring, her personality... Thoughts of his wife made him vow not to wear that stupefied expression of yearning that every other man in the room wore.

'Karl, I'm going to have to leave.'

'But she told us not to,' Karl replied, obviously under the sorceress's spell.

George smiled. 'You can stay. But I'm tired. I'll see you at the office tomorrow.'

Mia caught him at the door, glass of champagne in one hand. 'But you can't go!' she said, fixing him in her gaze. 'We're still having so much fun.'

He was careful not to meet her eyes too fully. 'I'm sorry. I have to get home. My wife is expecting a call from me.'

At the word 'wife' she almost physically recoiled. 'You're married?'

He could see the game she was playing: every man had to be in love with her. He took pleasure in not playing his part. 'Very happily.'

'But you're so young.'

'I was lucky. I found the right person early.'

She turned up the corners of her mouth in a forced smile. 'Ah, well. I won't keep you. I'll see you in at the TRG office, perhaps?'

'Perhaps.' He nodded politely. 'Goodnight.'

He returned to his apartment, the operator still couldn't get a call through to England. His bed felt very empty that night. He missed Aila, but it was Mia he found himself thinking about as he dropped off to sleep, into half-dreams, half-fantasies of flesh and desire.

The phone calls started soon after. First, to his office, then she somehow got his home phone number. Mia always had an excuse, a question to ask about the contract or the timing of the payments, but he knew it was more than that. She was attracted to him, of that he was sure, and his coolness towards her drove her mad. How could he be anything but cool when he was married, when his wife was back in England nursing her dying mother? But this rationalisation was the smooth surface of a torrent of wayward feelings and guilty fantasies. He thought he would be safe so long as he kept a distant voice on the phone.

Then one day, she turned up at his apartment.

'Happy Saturday,' she said, as he opened the door. She was dressed all in black, in a tight-fitting skirt and wool shirt that hugged her curves. Her shoes were bright red, high heels. Even with them on, he still towered over her.

'Hello, Mia,' he said.

'Can I come in?'

He hesitated, and she noticed and frowned. 'Please?' she said. 'I'm heading off home in a few days. I just want to talk to you.'

The thought of her not being around anymore made him feel a surge of disappointment, and he realised very clearly that he was playing a game with her after all. He *liked* her reaction to his off-hand manner, he *liked* to see such a beautiful woman dance around him. George stood back and showed her in.

'Would you like tea?' he said.

'Oh, you English!' she said, laughing. 'No, I wouldn't like tea. Nobody else in Europe likes tea.'

'Coffee?'

'It's after midday. Do you have any whisky?'

George shrugged. 'I do. How do you like it?'

'Just neat.' She sat on his couch. 'Your apartment is very small. I would have thought a big management wig like you might have a grand place.'

He went to the kitchen and poured two glasses of whisky. 'I'm saving my money,' he said, wondering why he was bristling. 'I want to build my own studio when I get back to London.' He returned and handed her a drink, carefully sitting on the coffee table in front of her.

'Ah, so I finally get a little bit of insight into the mysterious George Fellowes,' she said, glancing around as if taking inventory. 'He's creative, he has ambitions.'

'Why did you come to see me?'

'To say goodbye before I go home. I can't stop thinking about you, George.'

He didn't answer and she laughed. 'I sometimes wonder if you're cruel to me on purpose.'

'I'm not cruel to you.' He shifted, changed the subject. 'So, where is home?'

She bit her lip. 'Actually, I'm between homes at the moment. I had an apartment in Athens, but I sold it and bought a little house on an island in the Cyclades. A tiny island called Petaloudos, so pretty. It's shaped like a butterfly.' Her hands drew a butterfly in the space between them. 'That's why I bought there. I love butterflies.

500

They can change, be something completely different. Something better, more beautiful.'

'They don't live long.'

She sighed. 'George, do you ever think about running away from it all?'

He shook his head. 'I've nothing to run away from.'

'Just from life, from the buzz of it.' She made a gesture with her hand, bees flying around her temple. Then she looked up, guilty. 'I don't mean to make you worry. I can fulfill my recording commitments.'

'I'm not worried.' He studied her, closely for the first time. She looked tired, her eyes were a little wild. 'You're going to the island then?'

'I'm not sure. Probably. I haven't lived there, yet. What if I don't like anyone?'

'I'm sure you can charm them.'

She smiled, and he realised he'd just given her precisely what she wanted. The gleam of self-confidence returned to her eyes, the tiredness evaporated. 'I'm sure I can too.'

There was a silence, and George wondered if he should make an excuse, ask her to go. But he didn't. In that twenty seconds of hesitation, he was lost.

'I could be persuaded to stay in Vienna,' she said.

He shrugged. 'What do you mean?'

She leaned forward, pressing her fingers into his knees. 'You know.'

'Mia, don't,' he said, so half-heartedly that it almost made him laugh. He had fantasised very clearly about a moment like this, always thinking that fantasies were harmless. But they weren't, he saw now. They had rehearsed him too well. His heart thudded, his skin prickled, and a slow vein of electricity began to pulse inside him. Aila had never made him feel like this, *never*. She made him feel protective, vulnerable, even sad sometimes. But never had she aroused in him such a primal response; he didn't just want to make love to Mia, he wanted to crush her.

Mia fed on his desire; it was, after all, what she had been trying to provoke from him for three weeks. She slid forward, he caught her, and the next few minutes were a hot tangle of passion and skin, so intensely physical that George felt for the first time in his life as though he was truly inhabiting every inch of his body. There wasn't even time to get to a bed; he took her on the floor, slamming his passion into her while she gasped and shouted. He didn't care if it was pleasure or pain.

Then, immediately afterwards, the sickening guilt crept in. She was smug, lying next to him on the rug, making no attempt to cover herself.

'You won,' he said, catching his breath. 'You made me give in.'

'I didn't make you do anything,' she said. Her smile said it all: *I got you, I got you.*

'It won't happen again.'

She laughed. 'I know you. I know you better than you know yourself,' she said. 'You'll give in again. And again.'

Mia was right.

Mia started to tire of him within a month. But by this stage he was caught tighter and tighter in her spell. The more he wanted her, the more he begged her to come to see him, the more she pulled away. The affair was heading towards a catastrophic meltdown, when Aila phoned early one morning.

'She's dead, George,' she said. 'Mama's gone.'

It was as though curtains had been wrenched apart, and now he could see the hot, clear light of reality. Aila, his wife. *What had he been thinking?* Choking on remorse and sorrow, he made arrangements to return to England for the funeral, then to return to Vienna as a couple. The affair with Mia was over without even a final phone call. He didn't call her, she didn't call him. Business with her was now conducted through an agent, there was no need for their paths to cross again. He blamed the whole business on the folly of youth, and prayed Aila would never find out. To hurt her, to lose her, would be the worst thing that could happen.

The leaves on the elms in the Volksgarten were beginning to look weary and brown when he heard from Mia again. He and Aila were snuggled together in the narrow double bed, sleeping peacefully, when the phone rang.

George rose. Aila turned on her back and looked up at him in the dark.

'What time is it?' she asked.

'Five,' he answered, frowning. 'I hope it's not bad news.'

He went to the lounge room and picked up the phone. 'George Fellowes,' he said, his voice catching on sleep.

'Hello, George.'

His heart froze. Aila was nearby now, curious. He covered the receiver with his hand and said to her, 'It's business.'

'At five in the morning?'

He smiled and shrugged. She shuffled back to the bedroom.

'What do you want?' he said to Mia.

'I want to see you.'

'No.'

'You have to say yes. I'll keep calling otherwise. Maybe next time Mrs Fellowes will answer.'

George shuddered. 'All right. When?'

'Now.'

'Are you serious? The sun hasn't even come up yet.'

'Outside the Staatsoper.'

'This is ridiculous...'

'You don't have a choice.' The phone clicked.

George ran a hand through his hair, unsure what to do.

'Who was it?' Aila called.

He leaned in the threshold of the bedroom. 'We have an artist, an opera singer. She's very...difficult. Unmanageable. I have to go and meet with her immediately.'

Aila shook her head with resignation. 'This business... I suppose you have to do what you have to do.'

He could have wept. She trusted him, she believed everything he told her.

'Yes, I do. Go back to sleep. I'll be home for breakfast.'

Outside, the first light of dawn was still a few miles distant. Streetlights were still on. He could hear delivery lorries puttering by on the Ringstrasse, the rattle of the trams. The streets were emptied, but ready to begin filling up again. His heavy black coat kept out most of the early autumn chill, but his hands felt smooth and icy. He made his way towards the Staatsoper. She sat on a bench outside, long black hair loose, wrapped up in a too-large overcoat.

George approached. She didn't smile and neither did he.

'What's all this about, Mia?' he asked.

'Sit down.'

'I can't stay.'

'I don't want you to stay. I want you to sit down.'

He sat. She turned to him. 'I'm expecting a baby,' she said. 'It's yours.'

At first, it was as though she was speaking another language. None of what she said made sense.

'Oh, don't sit there gaping,' she said, and he realised that she was angry. Perhaps another woman would be frightened, even sorrowful, when delivering such news. But she was furious with him. 'I don't want it. If I'd realised sooner I wouldn't have got this far. But I'm five months pregnant, the dates match up, it's yours.'

'I don't know what to say, Mia,' he replied, meaning it. Years with Aila, so difficult to conceive a child, impossible to keep one... a few careless weeks with Mia, and she was pregnant.

'It doesn't matter. I don't want cuddles and cups of English tea. I want you to help me get rid of the damned thing.'

'Get rid...?'

'It's too late for a termination. We'll have to adopt it out.'

In that moment, in the grey light before morning, George was faced with a cruel choice. Should he admit to Aila what he had done, and give her the child she desired so much? He knew she was forgiving, and that she was desperate for a baby: but what if he misjudged, what if she left him? So should he keep hiding the affair, and adopt his child out to strangers?

His child? Now he was just being sentimental.

'All right,' he said. 'I'll organise everything.'

And so, part of every day at the office became about managing Mia and the child growing inside her. He rationalised it as being just a part of his work at TRG – she was one of their artists after all – and that way he could leave the whole shameful business at the office and return to Aila as though it didn't matter, as though it wasn't the very thing that could ruin everything between them.

Mia was keen for the pregnancy to go unnoticed by the public, so George arranged her confinement at a business contact's villa in Spain, with a young housekeeper named Estrella for company. He took very few people into his confidence. Estrella, of course. And a solicitor in London: his German wasn't strong enough to deal with Viennese adoption agencies and, besides, with a private adoption he had more control over who would eventually become the parents of his child. Mia said she didn't care who the baby went to, but he did. There had to be music in their home, and so when the solicitor found a German music teacher and his wife living in West Berkshire, George was pleased and relieved. Forms were signed and witnessed, couriered back and forth between London, Vienna and Montoya. Now all he had to do was wait for a call from Estrella, and tell the couple to arrive shortly after the birth to collect their bundle of joy. In the meantime, he maintained a perpetual state of anxious readiness, should matters become complicated.

Matters became complicated.

The first hint was when Karl knocked at his office door one drizzly November morning, with a pained smile on his face. It was about Mia, he said. Her recording schedule had been pushed back because of 'illness', and everyone had so far accepted that she would fulfill her obligations in the following year. But Karl had concerns.

'I ran into her old manager at DG,' he said. 'I made a joke about stealing his prize artist, and he just laughed at me. They were keen to dump her, George. They say she's crazy.'

George shrugged. 'We know she's difficult to work with.'

'No, George. Crazy. Not metaphorically, literally. She had three breakdowns in the two years she was with them. Maybe she's not ill at all, at the moment. Do we even know what's wrong with her? Where she is?' He shook his head. 'I should have known this. I shouldn't have brought such a risky artist into the company.'

George reassured him, but he couldn't reassure himself. He saw things Mia had done and said in a new light. Times when she hadn't made sense, times when that heavy weariness washed over her. He knew she was unpredictable, but if she lost her ability to be rational, what might happen? What might she say or do to upset his carefully organised plans?

In the snowy depths of January, he got the call from Estrella.

'She's gone.'

'What do you mean gone?' Mia's words from their first night together came back to him: *George, do you ever think about running away from it all?*

'I mean gone. Last night she wasn't making sense, rambling, talking to herself. She left early this morning, before I woke. The note says she doesn't want the child to be a Spaniard. She wants it to be Greek, to have a connection to its heritage. I'm leaving this instant to see if I can catch her at the train station.'

'Don't. I know where she's gone.' *A tiny island called Petaloudos, so pretty.* 'Book a flight to Athens. I'll call you back in ten minutes with the name of the hotel where I'll meet you.'

He threw things in his suitcase, making excuses to Aila about an urgent business meeting in Athens. She was calm, trusting, as always, and he cursed himself over and over on the way to the airport.

George and Estrella caught up with Mia at the port of Piraeus, just outside Athens. It was the only port with a service to Petaloudos. She was sitting in a band of winter sunshine, her enormous belly wrapped in a dark blue coat. She looked sad, defeated. He approached her gently.

'Mia?'

She turned, half-smiled. 'You came.'

'What are you doing?'

'I'm going to my little island, my home. The service doesn't run today, so I've chartered a yacht. It sails in an hour.'

George didn't point out that Petaloudos hadn't yet been her home. A tired expression haunted her eyes. 'I think you should come with us. We'll take you to Athens. You'll have the best medical care.'

'No. I'm going to the island. It's quiet there. I'm sick of all this noise. I'm sick of all these arms and legs wriggling inside me.'

Estrella sat next to her, putting an arm around her shoulders. 'We only want what's best for you.'

Mia sneered at Estrella. 'You don't care about me.'

'I do,' George countered, and was surprised to find that he meant it. Seeing her here, looking so vulnerable and overwhelmed, had aroused feelings inside him that he hadn't felt for many months. He loved Aila, and would never leave her, but he recognised that he and Mia shared a similar dark energy, and were connected by it.

'Then if you care, you'll let me go to the island.' She put a hand on her belly. 'Please?'

'All right,' George conceded. 'We'll come over with you, find you a doctor, get you settled.'

She smiled, he detected the gleam of triumph and felt a cold spear of trepidation.

Within two hours of their arrival at the rambling house on the bluff, Mia revealed that she had been having contractions since early that morning. Estrella berated her for not saying earlier, but Mia pointed out they would never have let her come 'home' if they had known. George offered to go to the village to find a doctor.

'No!' Mia shouted. 'Send Estrella. Don't leave me, George, I'm frightened.'

Estrella shrugged. 'I'll be quick.'

George tried to settle Mia on the couch, but she refused to sit. Estrella was taking forever; the labour progressed exponentially. Mia paced, stopping every few minutes to hang onto the wall and groan. George was terrified, confronted with the stark reality that his foolishness was about to result in a live human being entering the world, one with thoughts and feelings, needs and desires. He followed her with his eyes, unsure what to do.

'Is there anything you need?' he asked.

'Just don't go away. Not until after...'

'I won't go. I'll stay with you.'

'They're coming, George. They're coming.'

George turned to the window. 'Yes, I'm sure Estrella will be here soon, with the doctor.'

'No. The babies. The babies are coming.'

'The babies?'

'There are two. I can feel them.'

George froze. Another contraction hit Mia, and she was speechless again, hanging on to the back of a dining chair. He reminded himself that she was not in her right mind, that she was wrong... but what if she was right? He'd arranged for one child to be adopted, but what would he do with a second?

The front door burst open and Estrella hurried back in with a young doctor she introduced as Theo Moscopolos. Everything happened very quickly from this moment. Estrella and the doctor took Mia into one of the bedrooms. She screamed for George to come too, but he was paralysed. He sat on the edge of the couch, his hands clutched against each other, his head resting on his thumbs. Estrella bustled in and out. Towels, blankets, a jug of water. An hour slipped by, another on its tail. Then Mia's screaming stopped and there was a little, coughing cry. He leapt up. Mia started shouting again. Doctor Moscopolos was shouting back, telling her to concentrate and push. Estrella emerged with a tiny red baby wrapped in a blanket.

'There's one more,' she said, eyes saucer-wide. 'Twins.'

There was one quiet moment, a sad parody of a happy family.

Doctor Moscopolos had been back to bind Mia's breasts for her. He signed the forms for the birth certificates, declared the two little girls healthy enough for travel, and left. Estrella had gone to the village for groceries to put in Mia's empty cupboards. George sat on the side of Mia's bed. Two drawers had been removed from the dresser and padded with blankets, and one little girl slept in each. Mia's eyes were haunted, as though she had been through a nightmare and couldn't quite believe she'd come out the other side.

'How long will you stay here on the island?' George asked.

She shrugged. 'Until I feel better. Are you worried about the record?'

'A little. But mostly I'm worried about you. Make sure you take the time to recover properly.'

She glanced over at the babies, and her bottom lip trembled. 'I'd like to keep one.'

George's pulse fluttered. 'You can't, Mia.'

'Why not?'

Because I'm a married man and they are evidence of my infidelity. 'It would be the end of your career. How would you look after her and keep singing? And what about the scandal: a child out of wedlock?'

'You'd stand by me, George. Wouldn't you?'

He made his voice cold. 'I'm married, Mia.'

'But where will she go?'

'I'll put a call through to my solicitor in London as soon as we're on the mainland. He can contact the adopting family, they'll take her. Nobody would split up twin sisters, I'm certain.'

She began to cry. 'I'm so lonely,' she said.

Estrella returned, poked her head in the bedroom door. 'Señor Fellowes? It's time to go.'

They took a baby each. George had never held a baby, was unprepared for how strong their little limbs pushed and wriggled. Mia sobbed, but George turned his heart to stone. He needed the children to disappear.

George was wrong about the adopting family. The solicitor phoned him in a panic, the morning he returned to Montoya with Estrella.

'He's not going to take both,' the solicitor said.

'Why not?'

'He says he can't afford two. The wife's hysterical, she doesn't want to separate them, but he's a stubborn bastard.'

A stubborn bastard. George wanted to tell the solicitor to pull out of the deal, not let either of his children go to a man so stubborn, a man who hinted there were financial problems. But then he scolded himself for thinking of the girls as 'his' children. They were not. They were the unfortunate result of a few mad weeks of weakness. If he didn't make his heart harder, he would be allowing that weakness, that madness, to ruin the rest of his life. With a forced coolness in his voice, he asked the solicitor to find another couple. Relenting a little, he expressed a wish that perhaps the couple would be Greek, so that Mia's hopes for the child to have a connection to her heritage might be honoured. Then he left both babies in Estrella's care until their new parents came for them.

It felt as though months had passed, but in fact it had been only a handful of days since he had left Aila behind in Vienna. He paid the cab on the street and walked up to the apartment. He could smell food cooking, could hear music playing. Wherever she went, she made his house a home. He opened the door. She was sitting on the couch reading a book. She glanced up, her eyes lit with excitement to see him. 'I'm so glad you're home,' she said.

Guilt strangled his greeting. He folded her in his arms and pressed her close, feeling her vulnerability so acutely that it squeezed his stomach. But it was over now, it was behind him and he could leave it there. So he held her and let her innocence, her trust, wash him clean.

FORTY
1997

'*W*elcome home!'

Angela was startled. She had just opened the front door of her house, to find Leila, a few other family friends, and some of the staff from the b & b in her lounge room. A 'Welcome Home' banner was hung from one side of the kitchen arch to the other, and paper bowls of chips and sweets covered the dining table.

Leila approached. 'Surprise party, dear, try to look happy.'

Angela forced a smile. 'Thank you, everyone. Thank you.' How deeply, deeply embarrassing. She'd been in a private hospital for two weeks, coming off her addiction to prescription drugs. Who would think it appropriate for her to have a welcome home party? But she knew, of course. It was Leila. She had been to see her every day, saying the same thing again and again, 'This is nothing to be ashamed of.'

Well, maybe not. But she wasn't proud of it.

Bo was at her side then. She squeezed him hard. 'You don't mind about the party, Mum?' he said.

'Not a bit,' she lied. 'Somebody pour me a champagne.'

She couldn't celebrate, not really. The nightmare of withdrawal was over, but the other nightmare still remained: the terrible dread of her memories. Two psychologists had worked with her at the hospital, but she still steadfastly refused to try to remember anything, no matter that the whole world conspired against her.

On her second last morning in the hospital, she had been listening to the radio when a news report had flashed on. The body of a man found in Sydney Harbour had been identified as once-famous London music producer, George Fellowes. The name had sent an electric jolt to her system, though she didn't know why: Was this person important to her or just a name she had known *before*? It proved to her too clearly that the memories were there, waiting. The shadow had gone, and all she had to do was focus a little harder... But she shrank from it, again and again, a child afraid to pull off a sticking plaster.

The party was over by two, and Bo went next door to play computer games with her neighbour's teenage boys. Leila checked that she was feeling all right then got into her little Toyota for the drive back up the mountain. Weary, Angela decided to go and lie down.

On her bed, there was a package. A sticky-note attached to it, signed by her assistant at the b & b, said, *This came for you on Wednesday*. It was addressed to Angela Smith, care of the b & b, but labelled *Private and Confidential*. She frowned, turned the package over. The return address was in Sydney, the sender was Dieter Newman.

Why did that name sound familiar?

Then she had it. He was the man with the German accent, the one who said he knew who she was.

She dropped the package as though it was on fire. Began to pace. Then left it in her bedroom and went to the garden.

Around and around she walked, growing wearier and wearier. So what was she going to do to keep the memories away tonight? She couldn't take sedatives, she would let Bo down. Again and again, around the garden, like a trapped animal. She had hit a dead end. The only way out of it was to open the package, or to die.

She didn't want to die yet.

With purpose, she marched back into the house and picked the package up. Tore it open. A folder with a note pinned to it. The note was deliberately vague.

Dear Angela,

I know that this communication from me will not necessarily be welcome, but I think you'll agree that it is not for me to decide what's good for you. The information is here, it is up to you to read it or not.

Kind regards,

Dieter Newman

So far she was all right. She took a moment, a few breaths then opened the folder. A long letter, addressed to somebody named Ellie. She put it aside unread, going further among the documents. Found four birth certificates. She leafed through them. Two of them had been marked in handwriting 'amended'. She read through the names, trying to make sense of them. Ellie Frankel: that must be the person to whom the letter was addressed. Angela stared at her birthdate: 21 January 1955, the same as hers. Parents' names were Kasper Frankel and Maria Frankel nee Drummond. The next amended certificate had her own name on it, or at least a version of it. Angela Annette Kyrikos, daughter of Nicholas Kyrikos and Margaret Kyrikos nee Smith. Margaret Smith.

Her mother. A shudder of revulsion, a woman's face leering close in her mind's eye. *Little whore, God will see you burn.*

Angela caught her breath. Rice paper tearing, silhouettes looming closer. It was going to happen. There was no stopping it. She had come this far, she may as well keep going.

Heart speeding, she flicked to the next certificate, this time marked 'original'. The child's name had been left blank, but the birthdate was the same. This time, the parents' names were listed as Euphemia Angelis and George Fellowes.

One shock after another. The first was seeing Mia's name on a birth certificate for a female child born the same day as her, the second was the way that the other name, the name she had heard just two days previously on the radio – George Fellowes – unlocked a tumble of feelings. A face came to mind, dark eyes, dark hair... Was it her father? Or somebody else?

Confusion reigned. Her mind was reeling and she couldn't make sense of the documents, so she went no further. Instead, she turned back to the letter, and started to read.

And so the worst happened and it was awful, unbearable. Long after Angela read the letter, she was still lying on her bed, following her memories from one to the next along shadowy threads. Victim, runaway, nude model, con-woman, prostitute, self-hater, drug addict. Strangely, none of it was a surprise to her, not even the knowledge that she had been a famous pop star. She had known it all along, in her cells and blood if not in her conscious memory, and so it was not a discovery of a new self, but a return to an old one. She felt nauseous with shame, repulsed by the knowledge that this body she inhabited had been so ill-used. But while she had been terrified that the return of her past would split her in two, the opposite happened. She felt as though she had been sutured back together, albeit in a malformed, misshapen way. Leila had been right, the memories made her whole. But it was not a whole that Angela yet felt comfortable with.

The memories of Benedict were the worst, of the night she was abducted. It had taken a lot to push through that barrier, and remember it all. But in the end all the memories were connected. The return of one inevitably meant the return of them all. Her heart pounded, her hands shook, and his words – those words that had been echoing in her dreams – had come back to her with dread clarity. *You killed him. You killed my father.* What blessed relief that now, at least, she could remember that it wasn't true.

The saddest part of the whole process was the recognition of so few warm moments. She hadn't had many friends or allies, it seemed. The excitement of performance was bright, but hollow. And the memories of George, with his gruff affection, were tinged by the sadness that he was dead. There would be no opportunity for her to see him again, listen to his fatherly advice.

She could have laughed. *His fatherly advice.* He *was* her father. The letter explained it all, how he had asked his solicitor to keep him informed about the two girls, how he had lost touch with Ellie when her family took her to Germany, but how he had always known about Angela, and had fought with his conscience for weeks before signing her up as his music project.

And along with a father, she had discovered her real mother. Mia, or Euphemia Angelis as she was on the dozens of uncashed rental cheques for the house on the bluff. All the explanations, the rationalisations, were in George's letter; but there were no words for the profound sadness she felt again at Mia's loss, the anger at Silas who knew and didn't tell her, or the happy relief that at least she had known Mia, just for a little while.

The fact that she had a sister, something that might have once been a huge revelation, was almost incidental. She figured out from George's letter that this twin sister had stepped into Penny Bright's shoes when Angela had stepped out, and that this was the woman who people kept telling her she looked like. But she was too emotionally drained from the return of her memories, the truth about Mia, to feel anything but numb about Ellie Frankel. She could deal with that another time.

'Mum?' This was Bo, slamming the screen door behind him, despite her repeated entreaties that he close it gently. 'Where are you?'

'In here,' she replied, realising that the sky had grown dim and she was sitting in darkness. She switched on a lamp and Bo entered cautiously.

'Are you okay? You look like you've been crying.'

One look at his face, and a profound realisation washed over her. No matter how she felt about what she had done in her past, it had brought her here to the present, to this moment with Bo – the love of her life – and she couldn't regret anything. She'd do it all over exactly the same way to make sure she still had him in her life.

'I have been, darling,' she said. 'But I'm going to be all right from now on.'

⌒∞⌒

She phoned Jerry later that night, while Bo was watching television, and told him everything. He listened patiently, murmuring words of encouragement and, importantly for her, forgiveness.

'There's something else,' she said, when it was all over and she had brought her tears under control again.

'What is it?'

'I need to know about the man who abducted me. I lost my memory before his trial. Can you find out if he's still in prison?'

'I'll do what I can. We have one or two solicitors who we consult with. I can ask one of them. What was his name?'

'Benedict Marten.' Saying his name aloud made her feel sick and shaky. She spelled the name and he spelled it back to her.

'All right,' he said, 'got it.' There was a pause. 'I'm proud of you, babe.'

'You are?'

'You walked into the fire. It was really brave.'

She smiled, feeling vulnerable, lonely. 'I miss you, Jerry.'

'I miss you too.'

After the phone call, she had a warm shower and then made herself a cup of hot Milo. Bo's movie was ending and as the credits rolled, Angela sat at the kitchen bench simply remembering... allowing her life to be stitched back together, and finding that the new Angela and the old Angela weren't so different at all. Bo came up to give her a kiss goodnight. The phone rang and he answered it.

'It's Dad,' he said, handing it over.

Angela frowned. Why was he calling back so soon? 'Hello?' she said.

'Angela. I've found out about the Marten fellow.'

'Already?'

'This library we're working on is in the process of compiling a news database. I hopped on it just after I spoke to you. He was paroled in January, then was immediately involved in a fake identification scam. He's skipped the country.'

Angela's heart stopped. *He's coming to get me.*

'Angela? Are you there?'

'You don't think…?'

'What? Oh, no, Angela, of course not. He could be anywhere. Peru, Bali… Who knows?'

'He thinks I killed his father.'

'It was more than twenty years ago.' His voice grew concerned. 'This is probably just more of that paranoia, Angela. It leads you into bad places. You have to shake it.'

'What if I'm not being paranoid?'

'Babe, if you're really worried, take Bo and head up to Mum's for a few nights.'

She considered this. Their assistant was on duty for the rest of the week, and it would be good to be in company while she recovered from the shock of her memories returning. 'All right, I think I will,' she said.

Bo looked at her expectantly when she got off the phone. 'Mum?'

'Pack your bag, sweetie. We're heading up to Nan and Pop's for a few days.'

Angela sat at Leila's kitchen table, drinking hot chocolate and trying to fight her fear. Bo and his grandfather were playing cards in the rumpus room, undisturbed by the long conversation his mother and grandmother were having. Angela told her everything, the second time in the space of two hours that she had repeated the story, and it still didn't feel quite real.

'So that's how we've ended up here,' she finished.

Leila frowned, and the lines around her lips deepened to crevices. 'But Angela, this Benedict fellow probably has no idea that you aren't Penny Bright anymore.'

This statement of truth dazzled her. *Of course.* How had she not figured this herself? She supposed there had been too much else to think about. But the relief was followed immediately by a new concern. 'Ellie Frankel,' she said.

'That's right, dear. If he is determined to find you, it's her he's going to find first.'

With a sudden rush, the knowledge that she had a sister – a twin, with whom she had shared a womb – finally sank in. And she knew she couldn't let Ellie be hurt by Benedict. Not for Angela's sins.

Angela stood and began to pace. 'I have to warn her, don't I?'

'I suppose, but you don't want to frighten her. After all, we're not sure where this Benedict character really is.'

'He hated me, Leila. He probably still does.'

'He's just spent more than twenty years in prison, he won't want to go back. He's probably on a beach somewhere, soaking up the sun.' Leila smiled brightly. 'Isn't that what you'd do?'

Angela stopped, chewing the skin around her thumbnail. 'He's not normal, though. He's…weird. I'd never forgive myself if something happened to Ellie, to my sister, because I hadn't warned her.' She snapped her fingers. 'Dieter Newman. I bet he has her phone number. Do you mind?' She gestured to the phone.

'Go right ahead.'

A quick call to directory assistance and then the phone was ringing at Dieter Newman's flat.

The phone rang twice before he answered. 'Hello?'

'Dieter?'

'Speaking.' His voice grew hopeful. 'Ellie?'

'No, it's Angela. Angela Smith. You sent me a package.'

There was a pause. 'I wondered if I'd hear from you.'

'Where is Ellie?'

'So you read it?'

'Where is she?' Angela repeated. 'I think she could be in danger.'

Dieter became alarmed, so she explained as quickly as she could. 'All I know is the property is called Mununja,' he told her. 'It's near a town called Bywong. I haven't got a phone number. She said it's hard to find but… I mean, my daughter found the name of the place on the Internet. He could get it too.'

His voice was tense, and Angela felt guilty for worrying him. She found herself playing the situation down, reassuring him that she didn't know for sure, she just wanted to let Ellie know.

'I'll move a few jobs, see if I can go up there sometime this week,' Dieter said. 'I haven't seen her in a long time, it will give me a good reason to see her.'

'I'm sorry to disturb you,' Angela said.

'No, no. I'm glad you called.' A pause. 'Do you think you'll contact her yourself? Eventually?'

'Do you think she'd want me to?'

'I know she would.'

After the phone call, Angela still couldn't settle. It might be days before Dieter got there. She drummed her fingers on the kitchen bench. 'I think I should call the police in Bywong,' she said to Leila.

'Do what you have to, dear.' Leila kissed her forehead. 'I'm going to bed. You should too. It's been a big day.'

At the police station, an answering machine picked up. 'You have reached Sergeant Gordon Osbourne...'

'Damn,' she muttered, then hung up without leaving a message. Maybe Leila was right. A good night's sleep might make her feel better. She brushed her teeth, slipped into the stiff, laundry-scented sheets of the spare bed. She lay there a long time, listening to the house. Bo and his grandfather finished their card match. The sound of showers, footsteps, teeth being cleaned, an owl in the macadamia grove beyond her window. Lights were switched off, sleep settled on everyone but her. She could have laughed: her first night out of hospital, and already she was craving sleeping pills. She did what her therapist had told her to do: get up, find something else to think about for half an hour or so.

She found herself quietly poking around in Leila's bookshelves in her pyjamas. Within minutes she had located what she was looking for: a road atlas of Queensland. By the narrow pool of light from a floor lamp, she examined the pages in front of her.

Bywong. There it was, a tiny speck on the map, in the middle of nowhere. The nearest towns lay hundreds of kilometres on either side. But it was almost directly west of where Angela was now. She imagined it would take most of the night to get there.

What was she thinking? It was the middle of the night. She should wait until morning, see how she felt then. But her mind fidgeted and her body wouldn't relax. Ellie Frankel was her sister: flesh and blood.

Without a second thought, she dressed, left a note for Bo, and climbed into her car.

FORTY-ONE

*I*t had been nearly thirty years since she had seen her mother's face.

Ellie felt light, lifted out of herself, aware that she was dreaming but not willing yet to wake up.

Mama, she said in her thoughts. She wanted to reach her arms out and draw the woman close to her, but found she couldn't move at all.

We have something to show you. Papa was there too, the dream vision opened up. They were in a field. A damp, earthy smell curled around her. *Your inheritance.*

Ellie bristled. *Inheritance? You left me nothing. I struggled. Nothing has been easy for me.*

But we left you this. A mountain of dirt, peaked on top. Black, clinging together moistly.

You left me a pile of dirt?

It's fertile soil, said Papa, *and you have grown so many things in it.*

Ellie woke. She became aware that something was poking her in the side. She sat up, and felt around in the dark. The shotgun, its metal warm from spending the night against her body. She smiled at her dream, warmed by memories of her parents, by pride at her achievements. She moved the gun aside, put a pillow over it, and closed her eyes again, hoping to catch the last shreds of the happy dream.

Angela stopped once along the way, but only briefly. She bought petrol, and a sandwich and strong coffee at Mitchell, phoned the Bywong police again and still only got the machine. The road unfolded endlessly and endlessly underneath her into dark grey distance. Her Jeep had led a privileged life of wide, sealed roads and suburban traffic: it was no match for the roos and emus that crisscrossed the road, so she swerved to miss them, taking her over and over again onto the soft shoulder or the wrong side of the road. It was death-defying driving, but it kept her awake. Her eyes felt as though sand had been thrown into them, and her head throbbed. But she knew rest wouldn't come until she'd seen Ellie Frankel, and told her about Benedict.

An hour after dawn, she drove into the little town of Bywong. One street of houses and a pub. She spotted the 'Queensland Police' sign outside a neatly painted weatherboard house next to the pub and pulled over on the grass verge. She rattled up the front stairs and banged on the door.

No answer.

She banged again, and this time realised that the door was not locked. She glanced around. No movement on the street.

'Hello?' she called, gently pushing the door open. 'Police?'

She found herself standing in the front room of somebody's home. Mismatched furniture and empty silence. 'Hello?' She looked around, spotted a filing cabinet in a room at the end of the hallway. The chatter of birds outside was muffled by the closed windows. Her heart thudded, but she didn't know if it was apprehension or simply exhaustion. She made her way down the hallway to where a light was glowing, poked her head around the corner.

Then recoiled with a shriek. A man's body in a police uniform, face down in a pool of blood.

Morning crept under the blinds in Ellie's bedroom. The happy feeling of her dream still warmed her, and she rose, singing softly, to put the kettle on the hob. Her answering machine light was still dark: Sergeant Osbourne hadn't returned her call. She decided that she'd drive into town this morning, go to see him, stress how anxious she was. If he couldn't help her, then maybe she would find out who his superior was and contact them.

Then she heard the crunch of tyres on the gravel driveway outside and presumed he'd decided to come and visit in person. She quickly returned to her bedroom to dress, leaving the gun in her bed. She felt mildly embarrassed at the thought of Sergeant Osbourne catching her returning it to the cabinet. So far, all she'd shot at were a few snakes and a wild pig that got into the house paddock. With no success.

By the time she got to the door, Sergeant Osbourne's footsteps were already on the stairs. She opened the door.

It wasn't Sergeant Osbourne. It was a stranger, dark, time-scarred, tattooed from one arm to the other.

The kick of adrenaline almost knocked her over. Her senses were suddenly heightened, her vision overly bright, her skin prickling with hot ice. The scream that came out of her was instinctive, startling her. She turned to run. The big man roared, started after her. She only made it as far as the kitchen, where the kettle was whistling cheerfully and endlessly. He tackled her to the floor. Her breath was pulled from her lungs.

'I got you, you bitch!' he spat. 'It took me twenty years, but I got you.'

Ellie didn't waste her energy with more screams: she knew nobody would hear. Instead, she concentrated all her strength into her legs and kicked against his grasp. He tightened his arms, moved to pin her with his upper body. His breath smelled strongly of toothpaste and it registered that he had bothered to brush his teeth before coming out to kill her. It was a surreal moment, almost as though she were dreaming. But as his elbow dug in under her ribs and winded her, she realised it was very real. He was fumbling with his spare hand at his waistband, and at first she thought he intended to rape her. With all her strength, she wriggled her knee free and brought

523

it up hard between his legs. He shouted in pain, went limp, she rolled him off her and scrambled to her feet, making for the door.

Immediately she realised what he'd actually been looking for at his waistband. A gunshot went off, but he was still on the floor doubled over so it glanced off the top of the door jamb and then she was running madly across the house paddock, her heart thudding wildly in her ears. But where to? There was little shelter for miles, so she had to find somewhere to hide. The shearers' quarters were locked, the garden shed was too close. She remembered the shearing shed, and redoubled her speed, making her knees ache and her heart pound as though it would split her ribcage open. She just needed to get out of sight before he got up.

Another gunshot, echoing loud and flat across the red landscape. She skidded at the bottom of the stairs, ran up and threw the door open. It smelled of cold dirt and old sheep dung. She pounded across the deck, then found the hatch that opened in the floor, where the shearers dropped the shorn sheep to wait in the pen under the deck. She pulled the hatch, jumped into the pen, then pushed the hatch back up until it clicked into place.

Panting, she waited for her eyes to adjust to the dark. Six empty ten-gallon drums were lined up nearby. She began to roll one over to the bolted pen door, stood it upright and crouched behind it to catch her breath and think.

Perhaps he hadn't seen her go in here. Perhaps he was forcing his way into the shearers' quarters. Then what? If he didn't find her there, he would look here next. There were so few places to hide, but she couldn't run out in the open, not if he had a gun. Her skin shivered just thinking about her back, vulnerable to his bullets.

She remembered the shotgun, hidden in her bed. If she could just get back to the house...

A crunch on the dirt nearby. Footsteps. She curled herself into a ball and fought back sobs. She didn't want to die; life suddenly seemed impossibly precious.

'Angie? I know you're there. Come out and get what you deserve.'

Was it worth trying to reason with him, tell him that she wasn't who he thought she was? But she knew he wouldn't believe her, so she remained silent in her corner, praying and praying that he wouldn't find her.

The door to the shed creaked open, and a shaft of light was visible through the cracks in the walls of the pen.

'Where are you, bitch?' he shouted. 'I can smell your fear, you know. I've got four bullets left and they've all got your name on them.'

She cowered, wanting to scream, to sob, to disappear. His feet creaked on the boards above, and she wondered if he'd spot the hatch, figure out where she'd gone.

The hatch boomed open. She crushed herself against the door, paralysed with terror.

'Come out, Angie. I don't feel like playing this game anymore.'

Ellie's fingers closed on the rusty bolt of the door. She worked it slowly, as calmly as she could. To wrench it would create a noise, and she had to get out quietly.

It was almost free. She grew too anxious, the bolt squeaked. His footsteps hastened towards her.

Then she was out of the pen and into the sunlight again. She slammed the door, looking around for something to pin it closed. There were more drums. She shouldered one up against the door, jumping back in terror when a bullet splintered out of the door and whizzed past her ear. She ran again, knowing the drum wouldn't hold the door closed for long. Even if it did, there were other doors. She pounded towards the house, but it didn't seem to get any closer. Meanwhile, a curve of the creek veered close on her right, trees clustered around it. He would expect her to go back to the house; he wouldn't expect her to hide near the creek.

She changed direction, ran for the creek, skidded in the mud and crouched down between the roots of two box trees. She waited, her heart banging. He appeared and headed, as she had thought, directly for the house. She gasped, sagging against the tree roots with relief. But it was short-lived. He would see she wasn't there, he would come back to look for her. The closer she was to the house, the easier she was to find. The further she was from the house, the harder it was for her to survive. The creek was nothing but a series of muddy puddles, undrinkable; her nearest neighbour was sixty kilometres away. If it was sunset, she might make it; but in the full heat of the morning sun she would collapse from heat exhaustion before she'd even passed Mununja's outer fence.

Frozen with indecision, Ellie crouched in the mud and cried.

Covering her mouth with her hand, Angela tried to still her heart. Her head pounded and her eyes ached from lack of sleep. The sight of the body was surreal. She kneeled down next to him, felt for a pulse. Nothing.

Benedict had already been here, she knew it and it horrified her, but she refused to be a slave to the fear. The policeman's gun was still in its holster at his waist. She unclipped it and took it. Its weight in her hands brought the reality of the situation into sharp focus. Her veins iced with fear. She had to get to Ellie. Benedict was on his way.

On the wall above the desk, a faded map of the area hung. She scanned it for the name Mununja, found it and quickly scribbled down the route, knowing that Benedict had probably already done the same thing. Adrenaline surged. She didn't allow herself to think any further. She ran back to the Jeep, put it into gear and roared out onto the road.

Ellie knew there was only one way out of this situation, and that was to get back to the house and get that gun. She tried not to think beyond that, about the horror and mess of death. But if somebody had to die today, she was going to make sure it wasn't her. She knew if she followed the creek around she would come out near the fourth gate of her driveway. From there she could make her way back to the house. Yes, she would be out in the open, but she was counting on the stranger looking for her behind the house paddock, not at the front. She climbed to her feet and started to pick her way along the slippery creek bed, more frightened than she'd ever been in her life.

The sun grew warm behind her, burning her neck and arms. She was desperately thirsty. Eventually, she had to leave behind the shelter of the trees around the creek. It made her feel sickeningly vulnerable, dazed by the hot light. She made her way around, kept to the shallow dip of the table-drain, so that if she did see her assailant, she could at least drop to the ground before he saw her.

Or to dodge his bullets.

Finally, she could see the gatepost that housed the large mailbox. That meant the house was about a kilometre away now. Had he gone out looking for her, or was he lying in wait inside? She doubted her plan a thousand times, cursed herself for not going for help. But more than a half-hour in the morning sun had already made her dehydrated and dizzy: a few more hours might very well be the death of her.

A noise behind her had her dashing for cover behind the gatepost. A car. But it couldn't be his; it was coming from the other direction. Sergeant Osbourne at last, she knew it! She peered around, was puzzled to see a blue four-wheel drive racing towards her. Spooked, she hid again, not sure what to do. She didn't recognise the vehicle; what if it was one of the stranger's friends? What if he'd called in reinforcements?

The car slowed for a cattle grid, then accelerated again. Ellie took a deep breath and chanced a peek. She caught a glimpse of the driver.

And froze.

She was hallucinating surely. The woman in the car looked exactly like her.

But it was no hallucination; she had seen it, and realised immediately who it was. Her sister. It had to be. The woman that the stranger really wanted.

And she was driving directly towards him.

Ellie leapt to her feet, waving her arms madly, but the car was going too fast. Despite the heat, the exhaustion, Ellie started to run. Now there was more at stake than ever.

∞

Angela pulled up outside a neat homestead with well-kept gardens, a little oasis in the flat red landscape. She put the car in neutral and pulled on the handbrake, but couldn't make herself move. The adrenaline had burned off, leaving only fear behind. Her hands were frozen on the steering wheel. To get out of the car, to walk the short distance to the front door, seemed impossible. *Benedict might be here.* A white sedan was parked in front of the house. Was it his?

The radio kept playing, some inane country music. Life went on, somewhere else. One song finished, another started, and still she couldn't make herself move. She just stared up at the verandah, wishing she could send a psychic message to Ellie, rather than go up and risk that Ellie was already dead, that Benedict was waiting for her.

She picked up the gun. She had no idea how to use it. Just point and shoot? Or did she have to do something first? She turned it over to study it, the engine hummed softly.

A sudden loud bang, and her windscreen shattered around her. At first she couldn't figure out what had happened, but instantaneously the fiery knowledge of it was inside her head. *Somebody is shooting at me.* She screamed, fumbled with the gun. Panic made her blind. She aimed nowhere and pulled the trigger. Nothing happened.

Another bullet, this time its oily heat grazed her shoulder. Suddenly there was a lot of blood and she knew she had to get out of the car, she was an easy target here. She ducked, opening the door and crouching behind it. Then she heard his voice, and terror seized her by the throat.

'Hold still so I can kill you, bitch!' he screamed. His footsteps were growing closer. Her blood was soaking the left arm of her shirt, and the wound stung hotly. She checked the gun again, trying to figure out how to get it working. A shadow fell over her, she looked up into Benedict Marten's eyes. He aimed the gun, she pulled hers up to aim at him. In that second, he flinched, she slid over to the side, vainly pulling at a trigger that wouldn't give. There was a bang. It wasn't her gun, so she must be dead.

But she wasn't dead. Their tiny movements had misaligned them enough to save her life. The bullet had smacked into the dirt, leaving a crater. She slid onto her stomach, crawled under the car. She could hear the little animal noises she was making, and a small detached part of her wondered at how desperately humans hang on to life. There was no way she could get away from him, now. The car was hot underneath, and she tried not to scald herself on the exhaust pipe. Her mouth was full of dirt, her shoulder was throbbing cruelly, and she could see his feet at the front of the car. The engine cut. The keys were tossed as far as he could throw them. He crouched, smiled at her, pointed the gun, pulled the trigger...

Nothing happened.

He swore, threw the gun on the ground. She breathed again. She pulled her revolver in front of her face. A catch on the side read 'safe'. She flicked the metal snib.

Ellie could see the two figures as though they were actors in a movie. The stranger was on the verandah, Angela was in her car. Shots were fired. Then he was stalking towards the car. Ellie's heart pounded. She slowed. If she drew closer he'd see her, but if she hung back here, Angela would be killed. Then they were both on the ground, half-under the car. There would be no better time to make her run across to the house. She sprinted, tried to keep behind the garden, though its low bushes were little cover. She pelted down the side and found herself at the back of the house. A ladder leaned against the water tank, and she lifted it and walked it to her bedroom window, rusted flakes of paint falling into her hands.

Her window was closed but not locked. She prised it open, snapping a fingernail off halfway down the nail bed. Blood oozed. Her own breathing was very heavy, she felt dizzy. She crawled over the painted windowsill, tumbling to the floor next to her bed. The smell of roses from the pot-pourri dish on her dresser clashed with the oily smell of the gun. Her hands closed over it. With a deep breath, she cocked it, and hurried out to the front verandah.

Hands grabbed Angela's ankles. She shrieked, trying to bring the gun around. Her wounded shoulder bumped on the underside of the car and she cried out in pain. Benedict dragged her out in the open, she had the gun ready, but he wormed his heavy torso on top of hers and began to wrestle her for the weapon. A desperate surge of energy infused her limbs. She kicked, she struggled, but the gun was being pulled away from her. So she bent her arm back, threw it under the car, heard it skid along the dirt.

Now he had rolled off her and was wriggling under the car. She leapt to her feet, and raced around to the other side. It became a complex mathematical problem: Who would get to the revolver first? Angela, light on her feet, but taking the long route around the car? Or Benedict, heavy-set, on his belly, but much closer?

Their fingers closed on the gun at the same time. Then he had it. He fired, but he couldn't aim, and she danced out of the way. Now he had to wriggle back, or through. She tried to run, but he had grabbed her ankle with his free hand, had to drop the gun to grab the other. She went down. He emerged from under the car, pinned her with his body, felt around for the gun.

Angela turned her eyes to the sky, noticed how beautiful it was. If she had to die, she refused to look into the face of her killer.

Her sister was struggling on the ground, her attacker was flailing for the handgun. Ellie strode up, her stomach was weak but she forced her movements to be strong. He didn't hear her, but he saw her shadow fall over him. He looked up, his eyes widened. 'Who...?'

Angela turned her head, saw Ellie and closed her eyes in relief.

Mouth set hard, she pulled the trigger. Somebody yelped, an animal noise: it may have been her, or it may have been Angela. But it wasn't the stranger. He was limp, silent. Ellie dropped the gun, her heart thundering. 'Oh, God, oh, God,' she said, hands on her knees. The urge to vomit was strong, but she bit it back, put out a hand to help Angela to her feet. Her sister was covered in blood and dirt, sobbing uncontrollably. Instinct drew them into each other's arms, in shock and relief.

'You saved my life,' Angela gasped.

Ellie began to cry now. She had saved her sister's life, and there could be no doubt that the stranger would have taken both their lives if she hadn't acted. She steeled herself. Yes, she had killed a man, and she didn't regret it. An odd calm washed over her.

Ellie stood back. She brushed the hair out of Angela's eyes, gazing at her pale, dirt-streaked face, wondering at the similarity. Feeling for the first time in her life that she owned something precious and lasting. She smiled gently. 'Pleased to meet you, sister.'

FORTY-TWO

*H*er sister sang at her wedding.

Angela stroked Jerry's hand while Ellie, in a loose-fitting red dress, unfolded the most sublime *Ave Maria* that Angela had ever heard. Leila's garden had been colonised by the nuptials: a marquee, chairs decorated in white and gold, tables heaving under the weight of canapés and champagne glasses. Afternoon sunshine lay quietly on the scene, long shadows trailing behind it. The weather had been perfect for a garden wedding: clear, warm. While Ellie sang, even the birds in their roosts stopped to listen.

Angela glanced at Jerry, caught him looking at her. His slow smile was still able to make her heart flip over. She bit her lip to stop the silly, happy tears she'd been fighting with all day. She had known him for so long and had always allowed herself to believe that marriage wouldn't change anything. It did. It was profound, life-affirming. Bo, long teenage limbs marshalled into a suit at the next table, looked so full of pride that he might burst.

The last *Amen* rang out, and the assembled guests couldn't help but applaud, to shout, to tear up with the beauty of the music and the happiness of the event.

Angela clapped, leaned back into Jerry's warm arms. He kissed her cheek, his hands closing over hers.

'I'm so glad you came back,' she said.

'I'm so glad you came to get me.'

She smiled to herself, remembering the courage it took to get on the plane to London, to surprise him in his little apartment in St Albans. But after what she'd been through with Benedict, with the inquest over his death, and managing the media attention over the sisters' incredible story, flying had lost its power to make her anxious. Jerry had since agreed to come home to Queensland until Bo had finished high school. After that, they were going to spend some time travelling. Together.

Now the DJ had started playing an old swing classic, and people began to move around, swapping tables, getting drinks from the bar, laughing and conversing in loud voices. Angela turned slightly, so she could look up into Jerry's face. 'I guess we were meant to be together.'

'Yeah,' he said, chuckling softly. 'I guess so.'

Ellie was making a path through the tables, stopping to receive compliments along the way. Angela watched as Dieter stood and embraced her. It cheered her to see them together. She knew they'd been through a lot since their reunion: hostility from his ex-wife, a cool welcome from one of his children, and then Ellie's health had become an issue. Forty-two wasn't the best age to fall pregnant. Ellie whispered something to Dieter, then continued on her way, stopping in front of Angela.

'It was beautiful,' Angela said. 'Thank you so much.'

'Perhaps you can return the favour one day?'

'I don't even know if I can still sing.'

'Of course you can, you're my sister.' She spread her hands theatrically. 'You're Euphemia Angelis's daughter.'

Jerry leaned forward. 'Thanks, Ellie. It's not every day a famous soprano sings at your wedding.'

'A nice re-entry into professional performance,' she said. Then she stroked her rounded belly. 'Though I'm thinking of taking a little more time off. I don't know how being a mother at this age is going to go. I'm so tired already.'

Jerry laughed. 'Leila had me when she was forty-two.' He gestured towards the dance floor, where Leila was dancing with a much younger man, her hair swinging across her back, her tie-dyed dress swirling above high-heeled sandals. 'I think it kept her young.'

Ellie watched Leila for a moment, and Angela watched Ellie, struck by the gorgeous disbelief of it again. A sister, a twin. She gently pulled herself free of Jerry's embrace, and took Ellie's hand. 'I need to talk to you.'

Ellie nodded, and they left the chattering voices under the marquee behind, and found themselves under a shady mango tree a hundred feet from the wedding party.

'Jerry's had a solicitor-friend in England working on the inheritance.' Among the papers that George Fellowes had sent to Ellie, was Mia's will. It named her two biological daughters as her heirs. 'We should see the first of the money by the end of the year.'

'Is there a lot of it?'

'It's nearly a million pounds.'

Ellie raised her eyebrows. 'We can make good use of that.'

'We certainly can.'

Ellie met her gaze squarely. Angela was growing used to this serious expression. 'Now be honest with me, Angela, are you really happy to spend it the way I suggested?'

'Absolutely. I have a nice life, I don't need much else. But there are plenty of people who have nothing.' She and Ellie were setting up a fund in memory of George and Mia, to help underprivileged children study music. Angela sometimes wondered why Ellie was so keen to have their biological parents honoured in such a way: she'd never known Mia, and she and George had had a mistrustful relationship. Certainly the grieving process, the sorrow over opportunities lost and things unsaid, had not affected Ellie the way it had Angela. But beneath her smooth, practical exterior, Ellie had a strong compassion for those who had less than her.

'Good,' Ellie said, then paused thoughtfully. Finally, she said, 'There was a time when I thought money was everything, you know. I was ambitious, greedy.'

'I can't imagine it.' As Angela spoke, a gust of wind rattled through the treetops, sending down a swirl of jacaranda petals.

Ellie turned up her face to watch them fall, an expression of delight on her lips. Then she returned her gaze to Angela, reached out to squeeze her hand. 'We still have a lot to learn about each other.'

Angela smiled. 'I look forward to the journey.'

The sisters returned to the wedding party, fingers intertwined, Angela's head leaning on Ellie's shoulder. Low beams of sunshine illuminated the petals as they fell, silent and soft in the golden afternoon.

Acknowledgements

*S*elwa Anthony, who never gave up on me, and whose wisdom and friendship I count among my many blessings.

Kate Morton, who read and commented on early drafts and who understands like nobody else how panic and productivity operate together.

Mary-Rose MacColl, who knew when I needed space to work in and made sure I got some.

Louise Cusack, whose critique of an early draft helped me to strengthen it in all the important ways.

Ron Serduik for the encouragement (and the goss!)

Leida Bele, whose support and assistance went well beyond the regular duties of neighbours.

Rebecca Sparrow, who kept saying the book would be wonderful even when she had little evidence to go on.

Vanessa Radnidge, who believed in it and, more importantly, believed in me. Nicola O'Shea and Barbara Pepworth for their thoughtful and intelligent editorial advice.

The 2006 Year of the Novel cohort, whose insightful questions helped me understand more about storytelling than I thought possible.

Nicole Ruckels, Harry Ruckels, Anna Judd, Frances Steer, and especially Megan Jennaway, who delved into their own memories for wonderful details.

Janine Haig, who didn't seem to mind that her home became Mununja, and edited me with love.

My father, who encouraged in me a lifetime commitment to creativity; and my mother, who read and read and read.

My husband and children, of course.